**She couldn't believe it. Of all the times for the killers to come back, this had to be the worst...**

*Oh, God help us!* Her heart froze in her chest. She saw square sails coming steadily onward toward the foaming waters breaking over the coral reef. She ran back to Mick, the bucket forgotten in her hands.

"Mick—t—they're coming—it's the junk. They're really coming. There's no saving storm for us this time, and they're nearly to the reef."

"I'll take a look. Wait here." He ran toward the beach and looked, careful not to be visible. The square-rigged ship stood just outside the reef, keeping a good distance from the jagged coral. He also noticed, with a grateful heart, the receding tide. "Thank you, God, for that, anyway," he breathed. The devils couldn't get a boat over the reef for hours, not until high tide came again.

As it was already late in the day, he guessed they'd wait until daylight. This gave his group several hours to secure themselves in their hiding place and erase all evidence of the camp. It was fatal for Jim, but so were the deadly drug-trading pirates. The choices had narrowed to certain death for Jim.

There could be no heat treatments while the men from the junk searched the island to destroy witnesses. They'd mercilessly wipe out anyone who could testify in a court of law. A sick man like Jim would be lucky to warrant a merciful bullet.

Mick walked back. The women looked at him. They read the truth in his pale, drawn face and knew what they faced. It had been discussed, but Jim hadn't been in deadly peril then. There could be no treatment to save his life while hiding in a cave.

At a "fat" convention in Tahiti, an attack by pirates, during a storm at sea, leaves Jamie Moran stranded on a deserted island with Mick, a craven, yet devilishly handsome drug smuggler she'd pulled from the raging water. Fearful of being alone in a terrifying place, she tends his injuries, while he teaches her far more than mere survival. Joined by two others, they work to stay alive, while Jamie fights a hopeless sexual attraction to this secretive man of mystery. As they wait for a rescue that never comes, she becomes slender and healthy. Facing a devastating typhoon, death-dealing smugglers, and dangerous wild animals, Jamie and Mick are drawn into love with dire consequences. But he promises her that it will all work out, and he will be with her in the end. Finally rescued by a US Navy cruiser, Jamie dreads the trial in Tahiti that will have Mick hauled away in chains to spend long years in a tropical prison. Has he made a promise he can't keep?

# KUDOS for *Survivors*

In *Survivors* by Ramona Forrest, Jamie Moran is attending a "fat" convention in Tahiti after divorcing her mentally abusive husband. Now single again, she wants to lose the weight she gained during the marriage when eating was her only comfort. At the convention, several attendees, including Jamie and her new friends Felicia and Jim, take a scenic schooner ride out on the ocean. A terrible storm comes up, but that's not the worst of the problems for the little schooner. A band of pirates/drug dealers attack the ship, sinking it. Jamie and her friends manage to get into life rafts, and, while at sea, Jamie picks up a sailor from the schooner who she knows was in cahoots with the pirates. But he's a human being and she can't let him drown. So she pulls him into her raft, and they make it to an island, soon after to be joined by Felicia and Jim. Jamie operates on the sailor, Mick, with his Swiss Army Knife, and takes a bullet out of his shoulder, saving his life a second time. Stranded on the island, it's clear to everyone that Mick is not what he appeared to be on the schooner, and Jamie is soon head over heels for him. But what kind of future can she have with a criminal, even if he is too well educated and well spoken to be the illiterate sailor/drug dealer he pretended to be on the ship? As usual, Forrest's story is heart-warming and romantic, with vivid scenes and wonderful characters. If you've ever wondered what it would be like to be stranded on a tropical island, this story will give you an idea—both the good and the bad. A really good read. ~ *Taylor Jones, The Review Team of Taylor Jones & Regan Murphy*

*Survivors* by Ramona Forrest is the story of a young woman, recently freed from an abusive marriage, who longs to be her old self and find real love. Jamie Moran has just divorced her mentally cruel husband and received a generous settlement. Free at last, but obese due to the overeating she did while trying to cope with her marriage, she wants to have her figure and self-esteem restored. So she attends a fat convention in Tahiti, and on a whim, goes for a jaunt on the ocean in a schooner. And that's when the trouble starts. As a severe storm arrives, some members of the crew won't let the captain head for port because they are waiting for another ship to arrive. When a Chinese junk appears, they tie up the captain and put him the brig, then board the junk, which shoots a cannon at the schooner, sinking it. Jamie manages to get into a small six-man life raft that is barely big enough for her expanded size. She makes it off the ship, and into the middle of the storm. Then an arm appears over the side of her raft, and Jamie recognizes a member of the crew, one of the ones waiting for the junk. She knows he's a criminal, but it isn't in her nature to let him die, so she pulls him into the raft, and they eventually make it to a small deserted island. But Mick is an enigma, and nothing like what he pretended to be on the ship. They fall in love, but Jamie knows they have no future. Mick is a criminal, after all, isn't he? With a well-thought-out plot, some surprising twists and turns, and enchanting characters, Forrest has crafted a tale that will make you laugh and cry. *Survivors* is a fascinating, charming, and thoroughly enjoyable story. ~ *Regan Murphy, The Review Team of Taylor Jones & Regan Murphy*

# SURVIVORS

## RAMONA FORREST

*A Black Opal Books Publication*

GENRE: ROMANTIC SUSPENSE/ROMANTIC THRILLER

SURVIVORS
Copyright © 2010 by Ramona Forrest
Cover Design by Jackson Cover Designs
All cover art copyright © 2017
All Rights Reserved
Print ISBN: 978-1-626947-37-5

Originally published as No Way to Lose

Published by Black Opal Books http://www.blackopalbooks.com

# SURVIVORS

# CHAPTER 1

Jamie Moran clung tightly to the lines looped around her small raft and turned her face away from the pelting rain. Water-blinded, she wiped her eyes and searched frantically across the turbulent waves for a glimpse of her friends. She'd only known Big Jim and Felicia for a day, but right now, alone on a stormy sea, they were the only friends she had in the world.

Before yesterday, she'd never even seen the Pacific Ocean. Quiet Colorado lakes and streams were her idea of water. Now she'd been shoved off a sinking boat during an unbelievably violent and noisy storm. She found herself alone in the midst of this huge body of water, away from the comforting presence of new friends, and fighting to stay afloat.

Pounded by gigantic waves, Jamie longed for a solid deck beneath her feet. Her heart pounded at each wave that swirled about her craft and broke over her, one upon another. Drenched to the skin by the wind-driven rain, she could no longer see their sinking schooner. By the time she'd gotten off, the boat had been far gone, sinking so low into the ocean, their part of the deck was already awash by the time Jim had her raft ready.

There hadn't been enough time for many souls aboard to locate a raft. She knew their sad fate. That lovely schooner had foundered and sank beneath the angry waves. With that loss, Jamie Moran's once secure world no longer existed.

Battered by stormy seas, sickened and horrified by the evil, murderous acts she had just witnessed, a weakening sense of terror overwhelmed her. Alone in this madly heaving ocean, she imagined herself sinking deep into those strange, mysterious, and unbelievably dark depths. She mourned, knowing her friends had been swept away in the wild sea and were gone.

With no one to help, she faced her situation. Angry at her helplessness, a hitherto unknown inner fortitude rose within her traumatized mind. Jamie squared her shoulders and decided to do what she could. She'd witnessed the violent destruction of their graceful schooner and certain death of her captain and many innocents aboard by the fiendish actions of scoundrels.

Determination built within her and she fought for survival against the wild sea that threatened to consume her.

Steadiness and purpose of action lightened her spirits. Jamie searched frantically in a pocket and found a collapsible plastic bucket. Instinctively knowing its purpose, she began bailing madly, tossing buckets of seawater into the sea.

Huge waves sloshed against her, and her arms ached from constant bailing.

"I'm scared," she cried into the flailing wind, "but I'll not die out here, not after all the hell I've been through!" Voicing determination increased her needed strength to fight against the fearful odds she faced.

The driving rain felt cold against her body, yet the heaving waters of the gigantic waves felt warm. The strangeness of the ocean rollers and the spray off the top of them sopped her already sodden clothes as they washed over her tiny craft. She bailed madly, facing impossible odds to stay afloat. The work of it tended to calm her desperation and panic. It was something she could do.

Weary of the stinging lash of the driven rain, she faced away, letting the maelstrom beat against her back. Scooping water over the edge, she stopped, frozen in surprise. A hand came over the side, clutching desperately onto her raft for a hold.

Jamie saw a man's strong hand, sinewy and bronzed, though washed pale in the raging green waters. Realizing that another human soul was lost in the tormented seas, and with no thoughts of caution, Jamie reached out for him.

As she pulled the man toward her, his face appeared above the rim of the wildly pitching raft. Horror struck, she recognized the tall, sinister sailor whose very appearance had turned her into icy panic earlier. Her breath nearly left her body. Fear, as well as anger, gripped her to the point where she forgot her own desperate situation. She knew this man to be the most evil of men.

But his face, blue and pale, bespoke his desperate situation. Her feelings softened toward him and her fear and anger diminished rapidly. He barely clung to the sides of the little fabric raft. He'd soon lose his feeble grip and sink down into the turbulent waters. She hesitated. *I ought to let this evil soul go to his maker.*

"Please—please, help me!," he gasped, "I've been shot and nearly drowned. I've hung on for so long. I'm done in—please—oh God—I can't hold on any longer!"

His weakened voice cried out to her better instincts. But this man, this murderous devil, had caused the loss of their ship, with that tragic loss of life. She ought to beat his hand away. She had ' witnessed his crimes and knew him for what he was—a murdering, drug-selling devil.

Yet, Jamie couldn't let that pale hand go. In spite of her fear and disgust of the man, she could not deny him her aid, little though it may be. Her heart racing madly, she tightened her grip on that cold, slippery hand. Bracing her feet against the side, she pulled the fearful soul into her water-logged raft.

The man's long body slithered over the edge and flopped into the bottom. He lay helpless in the water. A large amount of seawater washed into the wildly pitching raft along with him. Blood seeped into the water, verifying his claim he'd been shot escaping that chunky appearing Chinese junk that had approached them in the midst of a terrific storm.

Ignoring him for the moment, she bailed madly to keep them afloat. He lay inert, as sea water washed over his face. Believing him unconscious, Jamie stuck her foot beneath his head to keep his head out of the water and kept bailing.

She watched him as much as possible but, along with the effort of constant bailing, she realized the storm was nearly forgotten, as well as her fear of the man. She'd found the strength she needed.

With the lessening of the waves, Jamie noted the storm had abated. With enough sea water cleared from the tiny raft, she rested her aching arms and legs. Turning her attention to the man she found so fearful, she noted his eyes were closed. His hair was midnight black, and long dark lashes lay against tanned cheeks. He had a fine, strong chin with an indentation. His straight, rather narrow nose seemed to match his long length somehow. The wispy moustache, straggly with seawater, revealed wide, firm lips, pale and blue.

No longer sinister in his helplessness, she felt no fear of him. Wondering what would cause a man with such good features to involve himself in a life of crime, she shook her head. Her hair, soaked and sticky with saltwater, stung her face as the sodden salty clumps hit against her cheeks.

Rummaging again in the side pockets, she found a tightly bound pack of canvas fabric and put it under his head. Her mind spun in a fearful whirl. The raft seemed more stable, and she'd stopped her worry of the ocean waters. Now she worried, having this evil soul in her raft. *He's not frightening now, thank God. But when he awakens, what then? It'd be best to shove him back over the side. If he ever comes to, he'll throw me overboard and take this raft. After all, I could be, and certainly will be, a witness against him, and gladly, if we ever come to land.*

Yet, surrounded by heaving seas, and no safe harbor in

sight, she realized she was no longer alone. This man was another human being, and her thoughts ran rampant. *He's a sailor and might know how to find land.* Jamie reached the only possible conclusion, *I cannot rid myself of this devil, not after saving his life. He might take mine, but no, I cannot.*

Occasional jolts of fear crept through her when she looked at the sailor. He'd shown himself to be a criminal of the worst kind, but that knowledge was tempered by the fact he might help her. This knowledge brought an uneasy comfort to her. She was no longer all alone in a place so totally foreign.

She felt, rather than saw, that the waves had lessened further. Daylight had faded, patches of stars stood out in the darkening sky. She breathed a small prayer of relief. The respite gave her time to think. "We should be in Papeete at our *fat* convention," she murmured under her breath, "talking about the wonderful day we had, sailing on the beautiful Pacific. Instead, I'm lost out here in a water-logged raft with a criminal who'd surely see me dead if he were able."

She'd bailed most of the water out since the waves had lessened, yet she felt a pounding at the flimsy raft from beneath. She considered fearfully. *Are those sharks below—waiting, nudging this raft, looking for a meal?*

Jamie's throat was parched and her generous stomach rumbled with hunger. She foraged in the side pockets and found a container of water. Tasting of plastic and warm, it was potable and soothed her throat. The sailor moaned, stirring weakly in the growing darkness, his legs moved.

She bent closer to him. "Are you awake?"

He moaned softly. "You've helped me—you won't be sorry—is there any water? I'm horribly thirsty, though I've swallowed half the Pacific."

Jamie placed the plastic container to his lips and he drank several gulps. She took it away. "We have to save some. We don't know what we'll have for tomorrow." He remained silent and she believed him unconscious again.

Unable to see what his wounds were, she noticed there wasn't as much blood seeping from him. She saw that much in the growing darkness.

Cold, wet, and sticky from seawater, she found a bundle of canvas fabric in another pocket. Her numbed and trembling fingers fumbled with the straps and opened it. Unable to decide what it was, she gave up, putting part of it around herself and part over the wounded sailor. She heard a soft moan, but nothing more during the darkest part of the night.

"Oh God, I'm so miserable," she cried aloud. Her blouse felt sticky, dirty, and soggy. It chafed against her skin. Her skirt, torn and twisted around her legs, was sopped with seawater. Everything was wet, and her entire body felt bruised. Her hands trembled. Her arms ached from bailing and she wanted to dissolve into tears, but couldn't let go. *Oh, Jamie girl, what's going to happen to you now?* She hugged her knees for warmth, and waited out the night.

It grew into daylight. Her stomach rumbled constantly with the gnawing sensation of increasing hunger. She sipped more of the water and touched the sailor on the shoulder. He moaned. A wave of relief passed through her. He had not died during the night.

"Do you want more water?"

"Yes," came the whispered reply.

Jamie drew off the canvas and he looked up at her. She thought his very dark brown, almost black eyes looked feverish, or were they burning from the salt water like hers?

She gave him a few sips. "Where are you wounded?"

He grunted softly. "It's on the back, up rather high, I think. I'll try to turn if I can. I need to move, and I'd like to get off my back. It hurts like hell after lying here all night."

Jamie heard moaning, tight-lipped sounds of pain accompanying the effort while he worked to realign himself in the small confines of their raft.

"Can I help you turn?"

"No thanks, I can manage."

He slowly moved to his right side, facing away from her.

His shirt was crumpled and blood stained. She knelt beside him and gently pulled it away from the wound, seeing a swollen area with a rounded bluish hole in the center. It was up high on his left shoulder.

Touching this devil's body made no immediate impact. She only knew she was not alone and took comfort from it.

He hadn't complained of loss of breath, so she guessed it hadn't touched his lungs. She'd read somewhere, there'd be bloody froth on the lips if the lungs sustained traumatic damage.

There were no signs of bleeding about his face. She wondered about his heart. But a man in his line of work had none. The wound bled a slight seeping of pinkish fluid down his long, smoothly muscled back.

Jamie rummaged in the pockets and found a basic first aid kit. She showed him the contents and he told her what to use. No doubt the wound was clean after the amount of salt water that had washed over it. That was probably a good thing, but she didn't know for sure. She dressed his shoulder as he directed and heard his soft, "Thanks."

Hunger drove her to search further in the side pockets. She found a few hard biscuits. They each ate one. She was thinking of her daypack with all the goodies she'd packed. *Maybe some fish is enjoying my Snickers by now.* She imagined the mushy chocolate of a Ding Dong in her mouth. At the thought, her mouth watered and her stomach rumbled again, aching with emptiness.

Later, the sailor struggled to sit upright. The effort hurt him, bringing beads of sweat to his forehead. He looked intently at her, perhaps better able to see her for the first time. Jamie felt his searching eyes on her and her heart rate increased. On the schooner, he'd kept his distance from passengers, but things were different now. She had saved his life and dressed his wound. They had a bond together, whatever the circumstances. She feared him. Why wouldn't she?

He broke the silence, looking at her intently. "I want to

thank you for saving my life. I was at the end of my rope when your raft came my way."

Fear shot through her body at his appraisal of her, with eyes so dark, piercing, and shadowed by pain. Yet, she was surprised at the quality of his speech, no longer sounding like an ignorant sailor. The poor broken English they'd heard on the dock did not belong to him now. Puzzled, unable to think clearly, she kept those thoughts to herself as she stared back at him. "That's okay, and whatever happens, I'm glad not to be alone. Maybe you know where we are, I don't, and I don't know what to do."

He said nothing more, but scrutinized her at times. His intent gaze made her feel hunted. Maybe it was his elongated facial features, so reminiscent of a wolf. But despite the tremors she felt under his gaze, she was comforted that he was with her. She feared him, knowing what he was, but being alone in this unfamiliar, trackless, wilderness of water, held a far greater terror for her.

With little conversation, they continued drifting along over gentle swells. The storm had gone, the cloudless sky, blue to the far horizons, allowed the sun to beat down, mercilessly. The two lost souls suffered under a burning sun, scorching their eyes and salt-drenched skin.

Jamie became increasingly hot and thirsty. The reflection off the ocean inflamed her eyes, already burning from the salt water. Hungry, hair and clothes crusted with salt, she felt bruised and painful all over. Wondering what had happened to Jim, Felicia, or any of the others, tears came. They soothed her salt-ravaged eyes and that alone felt good.

Thirst became everything. Jamie knew not to drink ocean water, though it looked cool, inviting, and wonderfully wet. She drifted off to sleep thinking about lakes, rivers, and cool mountain spring water.

Raising a glass of cool water to her lips, she was jolted awake by a hand dashing the plastic bailing bucket of seawater from her lips. It fell, splashing into the raft.

"Don't drink that. You'll go mad if you drink salt water," the sailor explained gently, as if to a child.

Abashed, Jamie sat quietly, looking down at her feet. Suffering,, they continued drifting in drowsy, miserable silence under the searing glare of the sun until she heard him exclaim.

"Look over there, miss." He pointed across the shimmering waves to the far horizon. "I believe there's land. We can try to row this thing toward it. I can't do much, but I'll try to help."

She squinted in her effort to see it, holding a hand over her eyes to shade them against the glare off the slick, oily appearing ocean surface. Looking in the direction he indicated, she saw a low greenish shadow on the horizon and cried out, "Oh, thank you, God! We might make it. It looks quite green. Please, pray it has water when we get there."

Searching for oars, she found oarlocks but only one oar. The other one must have been lost in the storm. Using the single oar, she paddled on one side and then the other, trying for a straight line toward the land. Her arms tired quickly, not being used to the exhausting physical exercise of rowing against the constantly undulating ocean waves. Sweating profusely, she worked desperately, moving the little raft toward the green haze on the horizon.

Painful blisters formed on her hands and broke open. Salt water burned the open raw flesh of her hands and blood seeped onto the salt-soaked oar handle. Only desperate thirst drove her on.

# CHAPTER 2

The sailor watched Jamie working the paddle. The raft went in many directions while she toiled against huge swells, though the waves had quieted. A compelling respect for this young woman had already formed within him. *She's a big woman, well put together, but most of all, a damned brave one.* He saw dark shadows of pain in her salt-ravaged eyes. *She's not had an easy time of it somewhere in her life.* Despite the ravages of the sea, he saw vestiges of her crisp curling hair, the fine straight nose, and the extra pounds. Yet, beat up by the raging storm, her former beauty, remained evident. *No whining, no complaining, and doing all she can to help me, though she sees me as the foulest creature on earth. I want her to fear me.* He felt an aching sense of loss. *It's better that way.*

He saw the bloody mess her hands had become, but she never stopped. His admiration for her grew, impressed by her willingness to try so hard, and the valiant spirit that kept her going. He wanted to know her name, more about her, and he would. But it was not a good idea to become intimate with strangers. His lifestyle precluded such intimacies.

Many tiring hours later, he heard the surf pounding the outer ring of coral that surrounded the scattered atolls in this part of the Pacific. The island appeared very small, yet the bright green growth indicated trees, and, hopefully, drinkable water. The sight aroused desperate hope within them both.

"We're getting close," he affirmed, considering the new worry of getting over the coral ring and safely into the lagoon.

As they neared the swirling waters over the reef, he warned, "We must not get caught against that jagged coral you see just below us. We'll need a good amount of water to get over this reef safely." He decided not to mention how the waves would dash them to pieces, if their raft became hung up on the jagged, yet beautiful, coral formations just beneath the surface.

Jamie gripped the oar. "I'll paddle along until there is a spot where we can get across. Those waves look awfully rough where they catch on the reef."

He nodded approval at her quick grasp of the situation.

He searched over the waves, praying there was such a place, and that the incoming tide wouldn't sweep them onto the coral. She wasn't aware of that possibility and he didn't enlighten her.

They'd been lucky so far and her navigation skills had improved considerably.

After what seemed an eternity, with desperate thirst and fatigue, they spotted a band of smooth water that looked wider than their raft. He said, "We can make it through if we both work at it." They approached the opening with fear and determination, waiting until a large swell formed behind them.

"Let's do it!" he yelled.

Jamie paddled desperately to catch the height of it, and the sailor added the use of his right arm. Rising high on the wave, with jagged coral only inches below, they successfully passed over.

He sighed and blew out his breath. "The tide must be in or we'd never have made it into this lagoon. There was very little room to pass over the coral there and no passable area any other place along this reef."

Safe from the coral, deadly thirst forced her to continue. Her efforts had become weakened. When they hit the first bit of pale pinkish sand, she fell over the side, crawled up onto the beach, and flopped down.

The sailor struggled to get out of the raft. He soon gave up and called to her. "Please, could you give me a hand? I can't make it on my own."

Struggling to get herself moving, Jamie finally stood up and tested the firm feel of sand beneath her feet. After some moments, she staggered to the side of the raft. Her voice was firm. "You'll have to stand up so I can help you over the side. I can't possibly lift you. There are trees up higher and there's shade," she told him, hoping to tempt him with the mention of coolness on the beach.

With her steadying his right arm, he rose slowly to his feet. He was weak, but with her help, stood up and stepped over the side of the raft into the shallows and onto the sand. He murmured what sounded like a prayer to Jamie, "Oh, God, I can't believe how good it feels to stand on solid earth at last."

She found it unbelievable an evil man like that could whisper a prayer. She helped him walk toward the graceful palm trees where his long body sagged from her grasp onto the soft, shady sand. She sat down a short distance away.

After a while, she got to her feet. Standing had cost a good part of her waning strength. "I must find water. We can't go much longer without it."

"Yes, yes, take both the bottle and bucket," he whispered in a weak croak, "and if you find some—please!"

Jamie took both the plastic container and bailing bucket. She moved slowly down the beach until she spotted a green streak of plant growth running to the beach. It contained a tiny stream running into the lagoon. Tasting it, she found it good, and drank frantically, filling the plastic bottle over, and over again and thinking about the worth of water. *God in heaven, I never knew what it meant to be thirsty, so horribly, desperately, thirsty. Nothing is worth more than a drink of sweet water when you need it to survive—what a terrible lesson.*

Her strength returning, Jamie rinsed the salt from her face, neck, and arms. She filled both containers and took them back to the sailor. Walking up the beach, the sand was soft on her bare feet, firm, and pleasant to walk upon.

She wondered where her Teva sandals had gone. *Probably down with the Snickers bars, and, oh—I'm so hungry! We had breakfast on board, the day this happened, but never that nice lunch they'd promised.* She felt surprised she could smile about it.

Jamie approached the sailor, thinking him asleep, but as she came near, he moaned softly. He managed to raise himself up on his good arm. "I heard you coming. Did you find it?"

Jamie sank down beside him and offered the water container. "I found a small stream and it's good."

He raised his head to drink frantically for several gulps then lay back, groaning. "Oh my God, that's good!" he gasped as he lay on the sand. "Thanks for bringing it." He rested for a short while then raised himself to a sitting position and drank again, deeply. "I believe this is the best water I've ever had in my life."

A faint smile crossed his face, and, when the skin around his eyes crinkled, a pang of fear created sensations deep inside her. She flushed. It puzzled her.

Jamie shook the strange feeling away. "Those were my sentiments, too. I thought I would never get enough to drink. I had hoped it was good water, but I didn't care, I was too thirsty."

She made two more trips to the stream before he was satisfied.

They sat together a while in silence. He finally turned to her. "What is your name? You've saved my life, and I don't know who you are."

"My name is Jamie Moran, and you are Mick, if I heard right." She didn't like giving him much information about herself, and wondered if she should mention overhearing his conversation on the docks. She could tell that in a court of law. She tried to worry about it and realized she couldn't, not here, in this place.

Remembering the snarling conversation heard on the dock before they sailed, Jamie tried to see him that way now, and found he didn't seem to be the same person at all. Puzzled about the man, she remembered, *He's injured and might be dying.*

"They call me Mick. My name is Michael Sands. I spent time in Australia, and their pet name for Michael seems to be Mick, so I go by that. I've been working around the South Seas for two years, mostly going from job to job."

He sat there telling her this, though he must realize she'd witnessed the entire botched up deal with the Chinese junk. *I wonder what planet he thinks I'm from if I believe what he's telling me*, she mused. *It's good he's wounded, or I'd be scared out of my wits marooned here with a man like him.*

She didn't respond to his proffered information, considering it bogus. She merely shrugged. "Let's have a look at your back. I couldn't attend to it so well out there." She moved near his back and gently pulled the messy shirt off over his head. The small dressing had fallen, or been washed, off. The wound edges were bluish with a slight drainage of blood-tinged fluid that ran down his back. It didn't look infected to her. She got up and made her way to the raft she'd pulled onto the sand. "I need to see what we have to work with. We need more medical supplies as well as food."

She saw her Tevas wedged in the sides. "Wow! Both of them! No good in the sand, but who knows what else we might find in this place?" She found the canvas material they'd covered with during the night. It was some sort of tent or could be used that way. She came upon the small first aid kit and took it back to him.

Jamie dressed his wound as best she could with the last of the meager supplies. She couldn't help noticing his smooth, deeply tanned back. Nicely broad at the shoulders, it narrowed into slim hips encased in faded blue dungarees. The legs were wide at the bottoms. *Must be the kind sailors wear,* she mused, wondering where his red neck scarf had gone. His skin was olive tinted, good in this tropical climate. She checked his chest to see if the bullet had gone through. It hadn't, but he had a lump just under his skin, below the left collarbone.

"The bullet is still in there, right there." She touched it gently. He winced, his teeth clenched tight, beads of sweat broke out across his forehead, and his face turned gray. "I'm sorry if I hurt you," she cried. "If we don't get that out, I think it'll get infected. I'm pretty sure it will. I've read that bullets cause some kind of poisoning."

"You're right about that." He nodded, seemingly in thought, with a faint smile playing about his lips. "I believe it's called lead poisoning. We'll have to figure out some way to remove it. Are you game?"

Jamie drew away from him. "Not me!" Her face felt cold. "I'm no surgeon, not even a nurse. We haven't a knife. How could I do it? There's no way."

Mick stuck his right hand into a salt-encrusted pocket, withdrawing a red Swiss Army Knife. "Thank God I still have this. It has over twenty different tools on it. It may be a godsend to us on this island." Sweat poured from his brow with that small effort.

Jamie realized she'd have to perform the surgery unless she wanted a dead man on her hands. The thought of being left alone on this strange, lost island frightened her, even more than the criminal who sat before her.

The bullet lay just under the skin, not deep at all. Had she ever seen this done on television, a medical show or something?

She tried to think of one, but couldn't remember ever seeing a half hour on bullet removal.

She looked at the red knife. "How can we sterilize this? If we don't, you could die from infection anyway." When she looked up, he gazed into her eyes, a beginning smile across his lips. "What ? Surely, you don't think this is funny?" she protested.

Mick chuckled. "I believe you are the bravest, gutsiest woman I've ever met." His voice was soft and deep, and it struck a cord way down deep inside her.

Jamie smiled. It felt good being appreciated, even by a man of his foul character. It was a new thing for her.

"Just cut the bullet out and pour seawater into the wound," Mick explained. "Salt water's all we have."

Resigned to the task ahead, she dragged the soggy tent up to him. He lay down on it and showed her which blade to pull out of the red knife case, a slim, razor-sharp little blade. He pointed out another device to aid in digging the bullet out. She thought she'd be sick, but with a completely empty stomach, it was not an issue.

Kneeling in the soft pinkish sand, poised over his chest, she felt for the hard nodule. He nodded for her to go ahead. "Do it quickly and don't stop no matter what I say. I couldn't stand another try at it and, if I pass out, so much the better." He shut his eyes and waited for her to begin.

She noted his clenched jaw. "You need a piece of wood or something to bite on." She remembered a scene from an old Western. They always bit on wood or a leather strap during something painful. She saw a trace of a smile cross his lips.

She gave him a small branch to hold between his teeth and then grasped the knife to begin. His dark eyes were on hers as she gingerly placed a finger on either side of the nodule and began. She drew the knife across his skin. Fresh blood welled up and she had nothing to mop it with. He groaned and clenched his teeth, but she kept on. It was now or never, and she knew it.

He panted. "Keep going, there's a brave girl."

He lay still, his body drenched with sweat. His tough, thick skin reminded her of wet, slippery, buckskin. A flitting memory of past days hunting with her father in the wilds of Colorado slipped into her mind as her raw, blistered fingers grew slippery with the smuggler's blood. She dared not stop. She kept on and, at last, the knife grated against the hard surface of the bullet. She heard no moaning or cursing from the inert form beside her and decided he must have passed out.

Pulling the flat shaped tool out of the knife, she dug gently under the bullet. The opening could have been a bit bigger, but at last it came free. As she lifted it from the wound, bright red blood oozed freely. Their medical supplies were gone so Jamie tore a strip off her skirt for a dressing. She had no tape. Holding it tightly to his shoulder for several minutes staunched the flow. If he'd passed out before, his eyes were open now.

Watching intently while she worked, he complimented her. "You did a great job getting that out. I wonder how many times you're going to save my life."

His dark eyes held a warm glow as he looked into hers. The intensity of them startled her. *Oh God, he must have a fever starting. I may end up all alone out here, after all.* She placed her hand across his forehead, felt cool skin, and frowned in wonder. There was no fever, at present.

When his wound stopped bleeding, she decided to get the cloth wet with seawater for a dressing and went to the water's edge. The tide had receded far out. She rinsed the strip of cloth in a pool and took it back to the sailor.

She placed it over his wound and bound it with another strip of skirt.

"I feel better already now the bullet's out," he said. "I'm greatly indebted to you. I'll find some way to make it up to you. Thank you."

He nodded to her. The softness and deep tone of his voice had a way of soothing her fear of him. She found this sensation unreal, but in this situation everything was unreal, including the man's educated speech.

Jamie couldn't stop her thoughts, *Maybe he'll let me live if we ever get off this island.* "I'm just glad you didn't die," she said instead. "I hope you'll get well now." She smiled to herself. *Who would have thought I could do something like that, remove a bullet?*

She removed his soggy deck shoes. With that, he groaned in relief. Seeing his severely wrinkled feet from being wet so long gave her a moment of regret that she'd overlooked them. *I can't think of everything,* she reminded herself as she looked at his long, narrow, highly arched feet. The sight of them surprised her and the idle thought crossed her mind that his were more the feet of a nobleman than those of a common criminal.

It was growing dark again and her hunger, now ravenous, ached within her. Knowing he must feel the same, she went to the raft and looked for more of the hard little biscuits, but there were none.

She gave Mick another drink of water and took some for herself. He slept off and on. Jamie put part of the tent over him and settled herself into the sand. It had retained its warmth, and her skirt had dried. She covered herself with it as well as she could. If they didn't find anything to eat on the island, she could use her skirt for a tent after a while. It had loosened about her waist considerably, in only two days, or was it three? She wasn't sure about anything anymore, certainly not time. "Is this the diet I never wanted?" she murmured.

A scrap of moon became visible in the night sky and a myriad scattering of stars appeared overhead. These constellations were in the Southern Hemisphere and unfamiliar to her. Jamie remembered times spent with her father when he'd pointed out some of the familiar sky markers of the Northern Hemisphere. She was very familiar with Orion, The Milky Way, and others, but the Southern Hemisphere included The Southern Cross. She couldn't remember what it looked like.

Her father—by now he must know about the loss of their schooner, The *Queen Ilikii*. He would turn the world upside down searching for her. "Oh my poor father. I'm all right for now, dad," she murmured softly.

Mick lay softly snoring on his bit of canvas, exhausted too. Tomorrow she would go to the little stream and wash the salt off both skin and clothes. Would she have to help him wash? At this moment, she felt too exhausted to care.

Her mind wandered back to the fanciful day sailing trip she'd taken, unaware of the tragic events that lay ahead. She tried to put things together, to sort out what to do, but felt too exhausted to think. "Maybe tomorrow," she murmured. Too tired to worry and in total misery, with hair sticky from the salt water and clothes stiff and torn, she fell asleep, dreaming of standing under a gushing warm shower. It was so real—the cleansing stream pouring over her tortured body as she drifted off, dreaming of the morning it all started...

# CHAPTER 3

*Two days earlier*:

In the early dawn, a hotel conveyance wheeled up to the docks. Jamie Moran and Felicia Benton, along with a number of bulky-figured occupants, climbed out. Participants of the Annual Convention for Obesity held in Tahiti, they edged toward the dock where a sleek, seventy-foot sailing schooner lay at anchor.

Jamie twisted her hands together. "That boat moves, even tied up."

Held steady by large tan ropes, the vessel heaved and yawed gently on the restless waters beneath.

She referred to the *Queen Ilikii*, a seventy foot sailing schooner, docked there, readying for the twice weekly sailing jaunt out of Papeete beneath canvas. This tour provided a short sailing experience like in days past for those filled with romantic ideas about the South Pacific.

Jamie, moderately overweight and tall, felt the coolness of the morning breeze. It fitted her full print skirt and thin, white, gauzy blouse against her tensed body. Her Teva sandals crunched on the gravel as she approached the schooner.

"I'm beyond nervous, Felicia," Jamie confided to her new friend. "I've barely flown across an ocean, let alone sailed on one. I know I'll be seasick."

"It's nothing." Felicia laughed. "I'm from Santa Monica. We live on the ocean. Give it a chance, it's wonderful.

You'll love it." Felicia tossed her hair in the soft tropical breeze, a habit that attracted immediate attention from any male within sight. Jamie decided that Felicia's hair—a thing of rare beauty, tawny, wavy, and thick—had to be one of her best assets. She wore loose green walking shorts and a thin white top for this jaunt.

They stopped on the dock to watch the bustling activity in preparation for this excursion. Shining metal covered supplies being loaded into the hold kept a number of men busy. Jamie couldn't imagine what the stuff might be and didn't care. Watching the dock workers and sailors held far greater interest.

The flowery brochure boasted that the Ilikii's crewmen, well-seasoned sailors, could set the canvas sails to utilize every zephyr off the undulating ocean.

While satisfying the fancies of romantic landlubbers, the attraction offered a good living for a number of Tahitians. This one-day sailing excursion held Jamie in utter fascination and not a little fear. Hesitant about this much ocean, Felicia's laissez-faire company gave Jamie much needed reassurance.

The dock lay inside a snug harbor. Many crafts lay at anchor, bobbing and pulling against their restraints. Jamie flung out a hand. "Look, everything's moving." The restless scene was all new to her.

Dockworkers and sailors, alike, bore wet stains on their clothing, streaking down into wide-legged dungarees. Sweat dripped from their brows, and salty curses in French flew out in the sodden, warm tropical air, as the men shouldered supplies and carried them into the depths of the schooner. This tropical paradise, hot and muggy to a woman from mile high Denver, had Jamie sweating. She hoped it was cooler out at sea.

Others boarded, slow and lumbering in their movements, and Jamie nudged Felicia. "We aren't the only jumbos on this tour."

The over-sized conventioneers had met to sort out civil

rights omissions and create an accepting milieu for others who bore the same burdens. Jamie's own thoughts about being heavy were different, but she did not voice them. *I hate being fat, and disagree with the convention's premise that being fat is normal, healthy, and should be acceptable to anyone.*

She hated the snide comments, insults, and discrimination the obese crowd endured. Yet, in a sense of fairness, she noticed many of them cared little if they were overweight, but only attended, wanting a change of scene. Maybe they looked for adventure or something different. She understood that too.

Puffing and panting up the gangway, clutching the lines, pulling their bulk along, some moved easily, despite their bulky size.

"Sailing under real canvas seems like a great idea," Felicia commented. "It's very quiet and relaxing. We can sit and enjoy it. I didn't want to hike up into those tropical valleys. I couldn't do it anyway."

Jamie laughed at the idea as she led the way up the gangway, cautiously testing the strange sensation of movement between gangplank and vessel. She'd read the brochure and looked forward to something she'd only read about.

Felicia believed her friend hid an inner sorrow. Those gray-green eyes bore dark shadows of pain. This troubled young woman revealed nothing personal, no clue about herself. Felicia wondered about her as she took in Jamie's hair, curly and glossy brown, framing an oval face. A few freckles dotted her fine patrician nose.

Felicia came aboard. Beads of sweat trickled from her upper lip as she toiled up the walkway. Streaks of dampness appeared in the rolls and creases of her thin cotton top. Of medium height, Felicia had extra rolls of flesh around her arms, thighs, and abdomen, and her breasts jutted out to form a shelf over a generous belly. A wide, well-formed mouth, firm now with determination, gave evidence of a pleasant mien. She carried a daypack over one arm.

Jamie admired this free-spirited woman, and her ready laugh. "Felicia, you've always been a beauty, haven't you?" Felicia's lovely, lavender-hued eyes, encircled by long, thick lashes, twinkled at her, "and that hair," Jamie continued. "Just look at it—shiny, tawny, and curling. It draws attention wherever you go."

Jamie bumped into Felicia and reached for her elbow to steady her. "Got your feet under you? This deck seems unsteady. Will we be okay? I've never been out on an ocean, never seen one before yesterday." She stood with eyes wide, watching in fascination the bustling activity as the sailors prepared for this voyage.

Felicia laughed. "This deck isn't moving at all. I was raised playing in the ocean. This is merely a short sail around a few local islands, isn't that what the brochure said?" She waved her manicured hand, outward. "We'll be moving a lot more out there—more if a wild storm comes up. They have some violent storms in the Pacific." She'd unwittingly tossed a scare into her friend as she nodded toward the open waters. "Wait till we get out there."

"Oh thanks," Jamie retorted, grabbing onto the railing. "Let's find a seat by this edge. I need to catch my breath." They moved to a bench section—each broad beam covering a generous area along the starboard, or dock side of the vessel—and sat down.

Jamie, excited and apprehensive, turned her attention to the unfamiliar details aboard a sailing vessel. The bustling activity of the sweating sailors caught her attention. She noticed several mixed native crewmen getting the last things done in order to cast off. She had long fantasized about sailing on a ship and meeting a handsome captain.

She'd read books about sailing the South Pacific, imagining herself lounging about on the deck of a sleek craft with handsome sailors working on the pitching decks, and casting bold glances her way.

Felicia was a different sort, happy in her life and within

herself. Jamie felt drawn to her casual, free-spirited way, or was it her untroubled outlook on life that had attracted her? She longed to feel that way, after long suppressing a deep sadness. She prayed her carefully hidden past didn't show. Perhaps her fine carriage, dress and efforts at gaiety would mask her reticence about her personal life.

Felicia easily discussed her background. "I hold a degree in Fine Arts. I'm an art critic and manager for a really great gallery. I've never married. Sometimes it's my weight, but not always. Some guys like a lot of woman. Been asked, but never cared enough to go for it." She laughed and tossed her head. "I'm still looking for Mr. Right."

Jamie envied Felicia's satisfaction with herself, her career, and her size. A real beauty, she didn't care about size. Jamie found this amazing. She turned her attention to the others boarding. They idly checked out the group coming aboard, making sly comments as to weight, character, and possibilities, while nudging each other.

Some were familiar, announced last evening at the get-acquainted dinner. Others they'd not met came up, puffing, panting, and sweating. Jamie wondered if they escaped sorrows too painful to mention. Overweight people knew many. She giggled softly. "Looks like they're climbing a mountain, Felicia."

Felicia nodded. "Maybe that big blond guy we saw last night will be on this cruise. I'd love to get acquainted with that dude."

Two women worked slowly up the ramp. At the dinner, they stayed close, holding hands and whispering together. Their names, given during introductions were, Jane Ashford and Corrine...somebody. Corrine, the larger of the two, had dark hair and blue eyes, hair worn very short, and a deep voice. She wore tailored slacks, a shirt, and oxford type shoes, and appeared to be in charge of things. She made all the suggestions and ushered her companion about. Jane Ashford appeared sheepish, smaller in stature, and several years younger.

Wondering about them, Jamie cocked her head sideways. "How about those two?"

"Don't know, don't really care." Felicia flipped her luscious hair. "I'm waiting to see if the blond guy shows."

Jamie giggled, returning to passenger assessment. "I'd say Corrine weighs about two-twenty."

It'd become a game, assessing weights of the other conventioneers. Jane's mousy brown hair hung limp in the moist sea air. She wore thin cotton clothing—a softly printed skirt, a loose cotton top—sneakers, and deferred all decisions to Corrine. They settled on the other side near the railing.

Felicia chuckled. "About two hundred for Jane? A wimp too."

Padded benches lined most of the way along both sides of the schooner with snug compartments beneath, shut, and thickly painted over latches. "Wonder what's under here, what these hold." Jamie whispered, eyeing a native-looking crewman.

Angry sounds of cursing on the dock drew her attention. She turned to see two men involved in a violently heated argument. Snarling at each other in deeply muted tones, they were too far away for comprehension, unless the men spoke in a foreign tongue. She wasn't sure.

She couldn't stop looking at one of them. A sailor, tall and slender with broad shoulders, stood toe to toe in a heated exchange with another man. Strong and loose limbed, he wore a scraggly wisp of mustache and kept his black, greasy hair tied back in a leather thong. Nondescript tropical and western mix clothes, jeans, and deck shoes with no socks. A red print cloth about his neck completed his garb. A slick sheen of sweat lay across his brow, and streaks of moisture trailed long, dark smudges down his shirt. Looking at him affected Jamie in a way she didn't understand. Her blood raced wildly and tremors streaked icy trails through her body. *Why can't I stop looking at that man?*

The tall sailor faced a man near middle age, short and

blond, wearing tan, well-appointed tropical wear. Despite their angry words, the older man edged closer to the tall sailor and turned a shoulder toward the schooner to shield his activity. He furtively passed an envelope to the sailor.

Checking the contents, the sailor snarled and moved closer to the shorter man. "You lousy bastard, you know thees ain't enough! We need two times more. Why pull shit like thees, in last minute? You try'n get us killed, eh?" He held one hand knotted tightly into a fist while the other clutched the soiled envelope. His angry face had twisted into a black, slit-eyed scowl.

"Make it work, Mick. You can if anyone can. Hell, man, that's all I could get." The older man shrugged and, with an arrogant sneer across his lips, turned, and stalked stiff-backed off the dock. The tall sailor shook a balled fist in his wake and muttered curses in a language she didn't under-stand.

"I think that was French," she muttered to Felicia.

Shoving the crumpled envelope into the front of his sweat-soaked, wrinkled shirt, the tall man shouldered the last of the supplies and headed down into the depths of the schooner. Jamie saw his dark face had paled. He wiped beads of sweat from his brow, shook his head, clenched his teeth, and aimed a vicious kick at a box in his path before disappearing into the darker depths of the schooner.

Jamie turned to Felicia, her face feeling like ice. "What was that all about? Isn't that guy one of our crew? What do you think went on there?"

"Probably a drug deal." Felicia laughed and tossed her head, indicating how little she cared about what they'd just witnessed.

Jamie's racing heart slowed. A drug deal wouldn't hap-pen on a cruise like this. Why worry about total strangers cussing in French, when she was about to embark on her long-awaited grand adventure at sea?

For the first time in ages, Jamie felt really alive. Living a life of escapism for the past three years, she'd read about every book available on the South Pacific. Now, shivers of excitement coursed through her. Short and usual this excursion might be to some, it was much more than that to her. She'd waited all her life for something like this.

The scene on the dock between the two men stayed in her mind. Something about the tall dark sailor had taken hold of her. Fear from wondering about what she'd just witnessed lingered in her thoughts. She fought against the idiotic feelings and waves of apprehension. Those things dampened her excitement of this cruise. Upset, she shook her head to clear away her ridiculous thoughts.

This short excursion took precedence over the *fat convention.* Jamie didn't see herself as fat. Heavy at present, she'd never allow herself to remain this way. Overeating had been a consequence of the hell she'd been living, and a refuge. Needing to get away from everything, she hoped coming to Tahiti would heal her wounded spirit.

Shaking off her dismal thoughts, she offered her daypack to Felicia. "Want a Snickers bar—Ding Dongs—Little Debbie Cakes? I've lots of stuff."

Felicia giggled in reply. "Not yet, I've a ton of goodies in my pack too." She carried a daypack well supplied as well with candy bars, chips, peanuts, and more. At this point in their overweight lives, such things were necessities.

As more day cruisers come aboard, they nodded and waved at the ones they knew. Then Felicia nudged Jamie. "The big blond guy's coming, too."

Jamie smiled at Felicia's excitement. Felicia hadn't even met him yet.

Jamie nodded. "He's a big guy all right. Didn't he say he was a prosecutor or something, You'd better watch out, you might be arrested!"

Felicia laughed and flipped her hair. "Ooh, I'm sure I'm guilty!"

It was cast-off time. The sailors pulled the big tan ropes off the thick posts along the wharf and scrambled aboard. The passengers felt increased movement beneath their feet as the schooner moved away from the oily, fish-smelling dock.

An old, but well maintained craft, the thrumming diesel motors moved the schooner steadily out of the harbor.

Jamie grabbed tightly onto the railing and felt the vibration of the engines through the weathered deck. "Felicia, I'm beyond excited," she exclaimed, "and I'm scared to death. I've always been able to see the bottom of the water!"

"Get a grip, girl, you won't be seeing the bottom of anything for several hours." Felicia laughed at her friend's fear of ocean depths. The wind caught her luscious hair in a whirl and sent it fanning out in the gleaming morning sun.

The *Queen Ilikii* backed from her slip and moved slowly down an inlet. Jamie saw hotels on the Papeete side and headlands on the other as the schooner slowly turned to work her way out toward a break in the reef.

Nauseating fumes swept over the craft for the first few minutes as diesel power moved the craft from the confining harbor. "Yuck, I can live without that," Jamie cried.

Then, the brine-filled ocean air swept over the craft, quickly clearing the oily stench. The sweet clean air of the ocean breezes came softly to play against her face. Jamie reveled in it.

The undulation of waves beneath the vessel had her heart pounding with excitement and fear as she clung tightly to the railing. But soon, mesmerized by the easy smoothness of the schooner as it sliced through the blue-green waters of the lagoon, she turned her attention to other things. The schooner made its way toward the darker blue of the deep waters that lay beyond the coral reef. Jamie shivered, wondering how deep it was out there.

# CHAPTER 4

The captain appeared on deck—a stout, stocky man of about forty-five, but with a commanding air of authority. His face appeared darkly tanned and his hair was peppered with streaks of gray. A white cap embroidered with yellow braid and navy anchors sat firmly on his head. Jamie laughed at her ideas. *No going below decks with that one.*

The captain, however, knew his work. Jamie watched in utter fascination as men ran up the two masts to unfurl huge, white canvas sails from the yardarms. The sailors clung to yardarms in the rigging, laughing and shouting to one another as they let out the wide canvas sheets. The billowing sails took on the rosy tint of early morning as they filled and whipped full in the increasingly brisk trade winds.

The lanky sailor she'd seen before, with his greasy hair tied in a thong, was among them. Jamie's eyes drew irresistibly toward that tall, dark form. Afraid to catch his eye, she turned away. Something about him sent strange tremors coursing throughout her body, surprising in their intensity.

The schooner listed, and Jamie grabbed the railing. The tugging wind pulled the schooner farther from the protection of the harbor. The captain shouted again. The engines ceased and wind power took over, pulling the sleek craft over the wide, smooth, undulating waves. Silently, the schooner moved from the protective arms of the lagoon.

Passing over the turbulent reef, Jamie watched the ocean

swells catch against the coral formations and burst into thrashing, foaming swirls. It created a constant, dull, booming sound as they passed them, reaching the darker, cerulean shaded waters of the Pacific.

Splashing waves and creaking timbers, sounds completely foreign to Jamie, made a kind of music of its own. The quiet of it lulled her into an enchantment that eased her troubled mind and heart. The ocean air, wafting cool and clean, carried a salty tang. Far behind them lay the fishy, diesel-smelling docks.

The schooner plowed through the ocean swells, making a gentle heaving movement. The pealing cries of seabirds filled the air. They followed after the schooner, circulating about, catching a ride on swirling updrafts.

Soothed by the rolling movements as the silent schooner slid through the waves, she gave thought to her recent past—staring, grave and unseeing, out over the ocean depth. *Those things shouldn't have happened to me*, she cried silently inside. As the excitement of this adventure worked its magic within her, slowly removing those sorrows, she vowed would have it that way.

Jamie returned to the present. "I should learn the terms for sails, ropes, masts, and other things so unfamiliar. It's so quiet, smooth—incredible. It's good to be alive when it's like this." *Today, for the first time, I feel like I'm going to make it.*

Jamie always dressed neatly. Her clothes bore the labels of Jones of New York's fine quality. Tall, Jamie never worried about her stature either. At five feet, eight inches tall with short dark hair, thick and curly, and a few freckles scattered over her narrow nose, she'd held her own in the beauty department. But now, pale from being indoors too long, she believed she looked like a mere ghost of herself.

Jamie had won a local beauty contest during high school years and had gone on, studying to become a teacher. She'd married before completing her courses. Her new husband quickly discouraged her efforts at completing her education.

"I make more than enough money for both of us," he commanded. "You don't need to work."

Soon after the honeymoon, Jack Moran began his complete takeover of her life, until she realized she was not happy.

Marriage, supposedly a happy joyous union, hadn't been that. Jamie had carefully kept those thoughts to herself. Miserable, she pondered. *What went wrong? How did I fail?* She'd doubted herself and her sense of worth had plummeted.

A master at cutting remarks, Moran destroyed her confidence at every turn. Is she was proud of saving money on an item, he'd counter, "Let me see the money."

He made derogatory remarks about her dress, her speech, and called her ignorant and sloppy. In the company of others, her husband appeared the essence of charm. She had no close friends—he'd driven them away. He was never *physically* abusive, but his words alone cut deep, wounding her tender soul.

Quietly, realizing the tremendous error her marriage had been, Jamie took refuge in food. His associates frequently remarked what a great guy he was, and how lucky she was to have married him. Jamie could only smile.

Before long, the results of her eating became evident, providing further ammunition for abuse. Weight became a primary vehicle in his siege against her sense of self-worth. He tormented her insidiously—"slob, blimp, fat ass."

His assaults turned her inside out. What had gone wrong with her marriage?

As the years wore on, life became increasingly impossible. Thoughts of suicide were almost daily. Was that his goal? Thinking of death, she dreamed of the peace of nothingness, of oblivion, and quiet blackness.

Finally, she confided her unhappiness to her father. He told her he'd suspected something was wrong. He'd seen her sorrows. There were no children and she hadn't laughed for months. Her increasingly fragile mental state had wor-

ried him terribly. "Honey, I'm glad you came to me. I've
known something was wrong for a long while."

He folded her in his warm, strong, arms to comfort her.
She was all he had in the world. Jamie's pain was his.

He'd avoided interference, but when she sought his aid,
he was ready. Only twelve when her mother had died, Jamie
had only her father at a crucial time in her life. He'd been
both parents, and they'd always been close.

Clinging to her father, she poured out the sadistic mental
tortures Moran had inflicted on her. "You know, Dad, no
one will ever believe what I'm telling you." She uttered a
bitter laugh. "Most people think he's the best thing that ever
happened to me. They think he walks on water. The people
at his office worship the man. They see another person en-
tirely."

Thanks to her father, and a good attorney, she'd found
the courage to get out. "What can I say? He doesn't beat
me, provides an adequate living, and yet he plays cruel
mental games." She detailed these things to her attorney. "I
can't stand it anymore." And that day she vowed that no
man would ever put her through such misery ever again.
Death was preferable.

The lawyer nodded. "This is more common than you
might believe. In fact, I frequently hear similar complaints.
We'll take care of you. You'll have the best." And he did.
The settlement was very, very generous. Her husband, a
successful real estate broker, wanted no publicity concern-
ing the divorce.

Newly freed of her marriage, and at loose ends, Jamie
eagerly decided to attend the convention as soon as she'd
heard of it.

A heavy lurch of the schooner, slicing and lurching
through an especially large swell, brought her back to the
present. *It's over now and I don't care anymore what anyone thinks.* She laid her dark curls on the railing. Tears of
release slid from her eyes and dropped into the deep blue
depths of the ocean gliding silently past. "Go to hell, Mo-

ran," she uttered aloud. She looked up to see Felicia's look of surprise.

"May I help? I've been through a few things too." Felicia put a hand on her shoulder, her voice soft and consoling. "I've been watching the big blond guy. I'm completely mesmerized by him, but also by the way we're slipping through the water, the clouds, even the seabirds crying out. But I see your tears, Jamie."

Startled from her reverie, Jamie shook her head. "I'm fine. It's just so beautiful out here. It sort of got to me—silly me, huh? Hey, aren't they setting up breakfast? So far, I think I'm handling the wave action. Look, no problem." She stood up and walked unevenly across the deck, weaving unsteadily.

She was relieved to have deferred questions regarding her emotional state. She had avoided discussing her divorce with anyone but her father. No one here knew she'd been married, nor was she eager to talk about herself. Now was not the time to get into past miseries, and today's adventure would dispel painful memories. She felt elated believing the peacefulness on the ocean was doing just that.

Though the waters were relatively quiet, the sleek, narrow schooner moved considerably up and down, and yawing sideways when least expected. Jamie had heard about getting sea legs, wondered what they were, and knew she hadn't found hers as she weaved her way over to see what there was for an ocean-going lunch.

The sailors had set up a large table near the center of the deck. It had a retaining edge around the outside. They put out several kinds of tropical fruits. She recognized papayas, mangos, kiwis and pineapple, but there were star shaped fruits, melons, and a citrus-like fruit, too. With several breads, juices, and meat varieties, the sailors had provided quite a sumptuous layout, under the circumstances.

The tall sailor passed near her, carrying a tray of meat. His sweaty male scent went through Jamie like a hot knife. She gasped, her heart beating like a trip hammer. She shook her head to clear her senses. *My, God, that man scares me half to death.*

Feeling faint, she concentrated on the table and its contents. The cruise had provided metal trays with compartments, cutlery, and cups. A large native man, Niko, acting as the local guide for the day, worked to bring the passengers to the table, calling out in an accented voice, "Hey—breakfast—ready!"

Everyone gathered around. Steadying themselves, they filled their trays and cups, spilling bits of the contents. Jamie heard frequent outbursts of laughter, amid the clanking of metal trays and cups.

The tall blond man, James Healy, piled his tray high with great enthusiasm. "Hey now, this is great!" With his loaded tray, and his drink, he looked about for a seat. "Whoops, that wave almost did me in!" He laughed as he weaved his way toward the bench along the railing. A warm twinkle in his pale blue eyes, he cast a glance at Jamie and Felicia. "Mind if I sit right here with you ladies?"

His shoulders were broad and solid, and like the rest of the passengers, he was a really big guy. He stood six-four, likely more than that, and was nicely proportioned. He'd mentioned during introductions that he was an attorney from the Midwest. He wanted to be of service to the organization, but mainly wanted to see this part of the world. Jamie recalled that much about him.

He hadn't given out much personal information, or mentioned a wife. Felicia had happily noted that omission.

He nodded to them. "I'm Jim Healy. You can call me Jim, or Big Jim. Some people call me that, either way is fine with me." Jim chatted on. "I wrestled in my college years, and played football. Now I'm a lawyer, dealing with the legal side of law enforcement. I keep up with my physical training. I like the way it makes me feel."

Frequently eyeing the generously sized, violet-eyed, blonde goddess sitting next to him, Jim laid into his lunch. He enjoyed the food and the salt-filled air. Delighting in the warm, scented, and strangely different tropical air, whether real or imagined, he totally enjoyed the relaxed feeling of it all. The food was tasty, the coffee strong, and the company looked better by the moment.

He prosecuted the criminal element. In keeping with his lifestyle, he'd become proficient in the martial arts. He hadn't married. There wasn't much time for the ladies. He never seemed to find anyone who touched his heart enough for that. Life was lonesome at times, but he didn't think about it that much. He figured there was plenty of time for settling down, and he was in no hurry.

Before attending this convention, Jim had spent considerable time studying the Islands of the South Pacific. There'd been more than one reason for coming, the least of these, his size. His interest lay in the heavy drug trafficking from the South Pacific. Kansas City ran heavily infested with the drug trade, and some of the stuff came from this area. He wanted to look around, maybe find out where it came from.

Jamie guessed there were about ten or so from the convention on board, and bending over their trays, no one seemed to encounter motion sickness. If so, it didn't stop the munching, sipping, and delighted comments regarding the outlay of food.

The woman called Jane made several trips to the table for her companion, Corrine. Conversation died away as everyone ate. Food dropped onto the deck, but no one seemed to care. A Filipino sailor moved among them picking up food and mopping up spilled drinks. The continually undulating deck caused numerous accidents. There were shrieks of delight and frequent laughter, as the passengers sailed their way through a generous layout of food on the heaving decks of the *Queen Ilikii*.

Finished with the sea-going meal, Jim walked with Jamie and Felicia for a short stroll on the crowded deck. Jamie related to him the heated exchange they'd heard between the two men. Frowning, his thoughts turned automatically toward the nefarious scum met daily in his narcotics work. It could be something important or nothing at all. He didn't want to cause undue alarm, but asked Jamie to point out the tall, black haired man as soon as she saw him.

"He went up the front mast to let out the sails," Jamie confided. "He's very agile, climbing around like that, a sleazy dresser, sinister looking, wiry and sun-browned. I hope he's okay, but when he argued with the shorter man on the loading dock, he sounded like a man who could be very violent. He was so furious right then, I believed he could kill without turning a hair." She shivered, remembering the ugly scene overheard earlier.

The deck, being rather small, gave them scant room to move about. The waves had become noticeably stronger and higher. Feeling the loss of stability, Jim ushered the ladies to their seats. They hung on to avoid falling on the increasingly slanted deck. Other reeling sightseers sought their seats as well. Jamie forgot the dark man as the quickening wind made them cling to their railings. Shrieks of laughter were heard as others settled on benches.

The guide kept busy, going from one group to the other with stories about islands seen to the right or left. Pride in his island home reflected in his voice and facial expressions as he went about imparting information to the passengers. His face, sun-browned to a mahogany hue with laugh wrinkles lining his cheeks and eyes, gave the impression of a handsome man with pitted skin. He had a soft, melodious voice and winked at several of the *larger* ladies as he went about his duties. Jamie had read that island men liked fat on their women. She discussed this with Felicia and murmured, "He's sure in luck on this cruise."

Niko said Moorea was in view to the south, but it sank below the horizon as they sailed northward between others of the numerous Society Islands. He spent extra time with two exceptionally heavy women sitting farther to the stern, flirting outrageously with them, smiling and winking. They loved it by the way they giggled up at him. One of them looked up at Niko, shining eyes and blushing cheeks aglow. Her hands bunched in her voluminous print skirt as she twisted about. Rolls of fat bounced under her loose-fitting clothes while she tittered at Niko's attentions.

Felicia nudged Jamie. "Look at those two—bet they haven't had that much attention for a while. He's a kick, huh?"

Jamie nodded, barely listening. She managed an "Uh-huh," trying to sort out what Niko was saying. She couldn't tell what direction they were heading, and would never remember the names of passing islands. She wasn't interested in the love life of the big ladies either.

Unable to stop watching the tall sailor as he handled a bundle of rope, she noted his shirt was off, and the long muscles of his back glistened with sweat as he bent over large twists of rope he worked into a huge round coil. He was sun-browned, but for a wedge of pale skin visible over his belt as he bent to his work. She noticed his dark hair curling with strands escaping the thong binding. His face, long and wolf-like, sent chills coursing through her. *What is it? Just looking at him has a crazy effect on me.*

Looking up, the sailor had an ugly scowl on his face when he caught her watching him.

As she quickly looked away, a sick, cold sensation rose in her belly. *My God, if looks could kill, I'd be dead. His eyes are black and cold as ice.*

# CHAPTER 5

Felicia, completely caught up in Jim's pale blue eyes, hadn't seen the dark-eyed sailor at all. "When we get back tonight, maybe I'll get better acquainted with Jim," she whispered to Jamie in dreamy tones. "I love his confidant manner—among other things." She waggled her eyebrows. "He's solid and strong, masculine, yet gentle, too. I just know he'll be a good dancer. His movements are so sure and easy. I'm rarely attracted to any particular man, but maybe tonight? What do you think?" That exotic thoughts rioted madly in her mind was a given.

Jamie shook her head, amazed at the ease with which her friend could contemplate a relationship with a total stranger. "I think he's great. Go for it."

"These are the Society Islands Archipelago. There are thousands of them in this chain. Most of them, they inhabited, but many too small, too far away for people to live there. The locals like TV and modern life too much now," Niko said with a touch of sadness in his voice.

He left two very large ladies and went on to the next group. The women still giggled from his flirting eyes.

Jamie remembered that, when the sinister-looking sailor had scowled at her, she'd forgotten to point him out to Jim Healy. Her heart racing with apprehension, she shivered. *What is it about that man?* Tall and handsome in some dark, evil way, his greasy hair only added to her fearful appraisal.

*Am I the only one to see the ugly gleam in those black devil eyes?*

Felicia turned to Jamie, a comment unuttered on her lips. "Why that frozen look on your face, Jamie, you're pale, what's happened? Seasick?"

Jamie hesitated. "Ah. I'm not, but that sailor gave me a devilishly evil look. It chilled me to the bone. I've a gut feeling. There's something terribly wrong about that man. The evil look in his eyes froze me clean through. He looks so...criminal."

Felicia put an arm around her. "We're only out here for one day. Don't worry about it. There're too many people on this cruise for anything illegal to happen. Forget about him, he's just an ignorant sailor."

Jamie didn't see the frown on Jim's face, or the dark shades of concern shadowing his pale eyes.

Jim sat quietly, deciding it wouldn't hurt to keep an eye out for trouble. This tub went out here pretty much every other day, maybe they *did* have something working. The Chinese and Filipino drug lords had a big trade in this area, according to the information his office received. Sighing, he admitted to himself, there was a large drug trade everywhere.

He wondered how the local authorities regarded the local drug trade, or were they part of it? That wouldn't surprise Jim either. He couldn't stop remembering things he'd heard about.

He sat with the women, watching the waves smash against the sides of the schooner, enjoying the undulating action as the deck heaved and waned. The breeze cooled, while the sun burned. It rose higher and hotter, in a clear sky, while the graceful vessel cut through the waves. There was little sound except for the murmur of voices, the creaking of ropes through the pulleys, the snap of sails, and the occasional call of a sailor.

The seabirds had left off and gone back to the shore. No islands lay nearby, in fact, none were visible on the far horizon. They were a tiny chip on a vast deep ocean.

The passengers had no problems, except for using the head. It was small and cramped for most of the *big folk*. Jim saw Jamie's head nodding as they passed through the waves. She no longer worried about the sailor, and Jim felt a sense of relief. In fact, the man hadn't been on deck for a while.

Roused by an errant wave, Jamie took notice of a couple that had joined the cruise. She'd seen them at the airport in Los Angeles. "Felicia, check out those two. In LA, the woman bought a large bag of Dunkin' Donuts. It was empty by the time they were pre-boarded, and all during the flight, you could hear them crackling candy wrappers and snack packets. They boarded early, I suppose because of their sizes, but they ended up with only one seat each because the plane was fully booked. It couldn't have been a good flight for them or the poor soul who shared their row of three seats. What a squeeze." She shook her head, remembering.

As a pair, the two were over six feet tall, and extremely obese. He was heavy to the point that the huge mass of his body and thick neck rolls of fat made his head look small at the top with a scattered thatch of sandy-colored hair. His face was continually expressionless, and he seemed uninterested in the sights and activities aboard. He had little reaction to anything else. Perhaps it utilized too much energy. The woman, slightly smaller, had much the same hair coloring. She had said they were from Arkansas, but little else, preferring to keep to themselves.

Jamie wondered what adversities those two endured because of their size.

Their names were Brad and Sandy. Sandy did the most for the pair, bringing his breakfast tray and keeping him supplied. Their movements were slow and labored, but his more so. She frequently reached up to touch his cheek or smooth his hair. Were they brother and sister? They looked so much alike.

Felicia, completely comfortable with herself, never

seemed to worry about her size. Jamie wondered if perhaps Felicia's extraordinary beauty eased the way.

The schooner cut through the waves at a rapid clip. The sails billowed and snapped in the wind, which had increased considerably. Pennants whipped smartly from the tops of the masts. Off the port side, on the horizon, appeared a long dark blue build-up of a heavy cloudbank.

Though the sun shone brightly overhead, the power of the increasing wind alarmed some of the passengers. With increasing fear, Jamie saw the waves becoming higher, stronger, and deeper. White foam flew off the crests from the gusting wind and the schooner now pitched and yawed wildly, forcing the passengers to cling tightly to the railings.

Felicia laughed, her face to the wind, hair blowing and whipping in the stiffening gale. Jamie, increasingly frightened at how the waves had deepened, forming monstrous, towering masses of greenish water, clung to the railing, her knuckles white. Warding off thoughts of dark ocean depths was impossible. *How far to the bottom?* she wondered helplessly. She turned her anxious face toward Jim. "Isn't it getting awfully rough out here? Those waves are huge!"

He patted her hand. "I've been watching it for the past hour. I'm no sailor, but I don't think it's too bad, not yet at any rate. Actually, we should be heading back soon. This is a one day excursion. Hey! The sailors aren't alarmed, so nothing for us to get excited about."

Jim tried to sound chipper, but he was worried. *Better not get these ladies in a panic. These guys sail out here every day. Surely they'd know if the weather was getting out of hand.* He sat back on the bench. The wind ruffled the legs of his tan walking shorts, and whipped the white cotton shirt about his rugged body.

A Filipino sailor climbed to the top of the foremast taking a long look with binoculars, not to port toward the cloudbank as he expected, but to starboard. Jim looked too, but didn't see anything. Frowning, he wondered what in hell the man was looking for. The dark, threatening storm was on the *other* side. The sailor skimmed down fast and hurried across the deck to the tall sailor.

The two were soon engaged in animated talk with waving arms and scowling facial expressions. Jim heard the dark skinned Filipino sailor explode. "They way late! Too damn late! Look, those clouds over there. We stay out here, we in hell of a lot of trouble. We don't leave now, we really in it!"

The sailor shushed his outburst with frantic gestures. "Knock it off, stupid ass, you blow thees whole damn thing. Shut the hell up, will ya?"

The Filipino sailor humped his shoulders and stalked away down the deck muttering aloud. He shook his head and shot a wad of spittle over the leeward side.

Jim, fully alert, didn't like the sound of what he'd just heard. *Something's going down out here—but what? There's no one out there.* He looked to starboard, the direction he'd seen the sailor up the mast looking. Jim was not obvious about it so as not to make the sailors suspicious. To the casual observer he merely looked at the waves.

Something emerged on the horizon, but too far away to identify. *That must be what they're looking for. They're having a rendezvous out here. I'm damned sure what that means. I hope I'm wrong as hell! My God, they couldn't pull off a deal like that before all these tourists!*

The women looked at him with anxiety in their eyes. "Jim, is something happening?" Felicia had the look of excitement mixed with a bit of fear in her dark lavender-hued eyes. He caught the scent of her perfume, and it lingered pleasantly in his senses. Momentarily he forgot everything. He liked what he saw in her—a happy free-spirited woman. She tugged at his senses. Drawn to her, he felt himself pulled deeply into those mesmerizing eyes.

He noticed Jamie's frozen expression. Her eyes had grown large and dark with fear, her face had paled. The women clung to each other and turned to Jim. Fear shadowed their eyes, and he hated it.

*Something's going on. This shouldn't be happening. No way do these women deserve fearful circumstances like this.* It angered him. "I don't like the look of things," he warned them. "The clouds over there are getting bigger and the wind's picking up by the minute." He indicated the long angry, dark blue cloudbank with a wave of his hand. "We're in for one hell of a storm by the looks of that mass of clouds. I hear they get some bad ones out here."

"That's not what she means, Jim," Jamie exclaimed. "What about the sailors? They're fighting among themselves, and they're looking for something. So what's going on? Shouldn't we be turning about and making a run for the homeport before that storm overtakes this ship? My God, this isn't a very big boat to be out here in one of those terrible Pacific storms I've heard about!"

She cast nervous glances at the madly cresting waves, and noted how the foam blew off the tops. It had become a wild, stormy scene in a place terribly unfamiliar. She couldn't imagine how far it must be to the bottom, a constant worry. Clinging to the railing, she longed desperately for the feel of firm earth beneath her feet.

The alarm of the other passengers lay forgotten for the moment. Brad, of the huge couple, had gone to the head down through the hatchway and gotten stuck. Forced to call for help, and looking sheepish, he came back with two sailors assisting. Jamie had the idle thought that he must weigh in excess of three hundred fifty pounds. With the heaving of the increased waves, the sailors struggled to keep him on his feet as they weaved their way across the deck. His pudgy face flushed ruddy with embarrassment as he flopped heavily onto his bench. Sounds of giggling were heard from someone across the deck. Jamie and Felicia suppressed escaping smiles of their own, and Jamie noticed a grin on Jim's features as well.

The guide went from group to group with words of encouragement, reassuring the passengers in the face of their rising panic. "The winds, they come up, sometimes. We all good sailors here, you be fine, no worries. We all be okay. Have big adventure." Going to the captain, he railed at the man. "Why we no go back—big storm coming? Look." Niko pointed frantically toward the enlarging line of dark blue clouds boiling ominously across the horizon.

"Soon, soon, it's not bad yet," the captain replied, his words muffled by the stiff winds. "They wanted excitement didn't they?" He scowled, his voice deepening. "Have these passengers been instructed in emergency procedures? That's your job. If not, you'd better get to it."

A strong premonition that something wasn't setting right with the captain, and the worried look over his tightened features, sent a chill chasing through Jim. In surprise, he saw the captain gazing intently out to sea, not toward the oncoming storm, but in the direction his crewmen had looked. *What are they looking for?* Jim glanced to the starboard side to see if what he thought he'd seen earlier was actually there. A stubby little ship with faint outlines of square sails loomed nearer. It carried three masts, holding square-appearing sails of differing sizes.

Standing together, straining their eyes to see what it was, he and the girls clung tightly onto the ship's railing. Walking about had become increasingly perilous, due to the wild pitching of the schooner and severity of the roiling sea.

"It looks like a Chinese junk to me," Jamie said. "See, it has those square sails. I happened to see them once in a book about ships."

Felicia peered intently out over the water with her hand shading her lavender- hued eyes. "My, you must have wonderful eyesight. I can't make out a thing."

Jim came close, inhaling her perfume, as he pointed for her to follow his line of sight. "Look there, you can just make her out. She'll be on us in a little while. This must be what they're looking for. I wonder what the hell they want with us out here in the middle of the damned ocean," he said, trying to sound casual while his heart froze in his chest. *This is the deal, the dirty bastards, out here away from any prying eyes, except for ours, and with a sizable storm brewing on top of it.* He kept his thoughts to himself as his jaw clenched tight. "Damn it all to Hell," he muttered into the stiffening wind.

Jim realized the smugglers' plans must have changed. With frequent sailing tours, drug deals wouldn't normally take place under the noses of so many passengers. He tried to sort it out. *For this one job, they don't give a damn if anyone knows what's taking place out here at sea. It's got to be one hell of a big haul they've planned. It's not usual for them to pull it off in such a reckless way—too many witnesses. If this is for real, a drug exchange at sea, then we're expendable—all of us. My God, these poor souls, I've got to get a grip. I must be imagining this.* His face felt tight and he set his jaw, ready for whatever was about to happen. He didn't have his *Beretta,* damn it all to hell.

# CHAPTER 6

Within the hour, a chunky square-rigged vessel approached the schooner. The center mast was the larger. The other two were varying sizes smaller. All three masts held sails with the lined look of the oriental craft.

"It's a Chinese junk. I saw them once in a book about boats," Jamie repeated. "The stern sits higher than the bow, and it has a long, sharp-looking pole protruding from the prow."

Indeed it did, and Jim's heart sank to see it. The sharp pole was covered in some kind of dull, grayish metal. Sturdy enough to plow through the worst of storms, the junk looked strong enough to punch through another craft if it came too close, or if they wanted to ram it.

The Oriental-appearing craft had a sinister feel about it as Jim made out red Chinese-type lettering on the hull. On her deck stood a mix of Oriental, Filipino, and native sailors, laughing, shouting, and leering at the people aboard the schooner. Most wore bedraggled, mismatched clothes. An occasional eye patch, added to their sinister appearance. The reputation of Oriental sailors was legendary, according to stories about seafarers. Fine sailors these men might be, but alarmed, Jim saw them as evil and sinister in appearance. Seasoned sailors, they were at ease on their wildly pitching deck.

The *Queen Ilikii's* passengers stared at the blocky ship

approaching, more from curiosity, than apprehension. For the tourists, being landlubbers with little or no experience with ships or sailing, this exotic little craft added excitement to their innocent little sailing excursion. At present, their main concern lay in hanging tightly to the railing, to keep from being washed overboard in the approaching storm.

Hand over his mouth and lips compressed, Jim watched the chunky Chinese craft loom closer. The *Ilikii* sailors gathered to watch the junk's approach. As it neared, one of them began waving pennants in a signaling pattern.

The captain stalked hurriedly over to the sailor doing the signaling. Grabbing the man by the scruff of the neck, he snarled, "What the hell are you at here?" His face had reddened. "We don't want any truck with those bastards. Don't you know *who* they are, *what they are*?"

The sailor turned on the snarling captain. "Sorry, Cap, we *know* who they are. We had to arrange it this way. No one will be the wiser when all's said 'n done. We're takin' this ship now and you ain't in no position to have a say, not no more you ain't!"

Hearing that, Jim knew the score. They were in big trouble.

The passengers, along with Jamie, Jim, and Felicia, watched in horror as two sailors crept up behind the captain, and threw a heavy cargo net over him. Cursing and struggling, they dragged him away, hauling him below decks. They heard his cries. "You mutinous bastards, you can't get away with this. You'll hang for it, I'll see to it!"

His muffled voice died away and Jim signaled for the ladies to say nothing. They had no weapons.

Two other sailors turned to face the passengers. One of them called out in a loud voice. "Don't be alarmed folks, nothin' to worry yerselfs about, nothing a'tall! We got 'er under control." He turned to the other sailor and laughed. "Not much this load of fat asses could do about anythin' anyway, devil take the lot of 'em."

They stalked around the deck looking at the passengers

to see if there might be resistance fomenting among them. Menacing, they threatened bodily harm to anyone who would contest their control of the schooner. One of them carried a large wooden stake.

Jim lowered his eyes as they passed, not wanting to start a mix-up he couldn't finish. "Remain calm, we're in big trouble," he told the women. "This shouldn't be happening."

Felicia laughed, her lavender eyes glowing with excitement and her hair flowing in the stiffening winds. Enjoying the action, she believed the entire occurrence had been put on to entertain the tourists. "How colorful they are!"

Jamie looked at him, white lipped. "Something's going on here, isn't it? I'm scared to death, Jim."

"Just sit tight, and don't draw attention to yourself," he cautioned. "We need to see what's happening, but I believe it's a drug deal—right here, right now. Our office receives information on smuggling in the South Seas. It's not pretty, ladies."

Hearing him, Felicia suddenly grew quiet, realization dawning. Her eyes wide with anxiety, she clutched onto him with one hand, and Jamie with the other. "What's happening?"

Jim told them what he knew. "These people hold life cheaply and will kill anyone who gets in the way. If this is what's happening, we won't live another day. These sinister men will not, cannot, leave witnesses alive to report this deal." A deep sickness settled in his gut as he went on, his voice very low, "I'm surprised they'd try a drug deal at sea with a boatload of telltale tourists on board. Their plans must have gone wrong or this would not be happening."

At the sputtering of an engine, Jim pointed to a small, motorized boat moving slowly out from the *Queen Ilikii*. It held two men. The tall black-eyed sailor, wearing a loose print shirt that flapped madly in the increasing wind, sat holding to the gunwales. His hair and thin mustache whipped in the turbulence. The other, one of the men who had taken the captain down with the net, a Filipino sailor, short, dark, and sloe-eyed, ran the small boat.

"Jim, look at those waves," Jamie said. "The storm has gotten worse. They're waves are twenty feet or higher."

They watched the waves foam at the crests and blow away on the howling wind. The little motor boat chugged mightily through the churning seas to reach the junk. It heaved up and down in the raging waters, until close against the side of the sturdy vessel. A rope ladder dropped onto the small boat. Both men climbed up to board the junk.

They heard welcoming shouts from the Oriental-mixed seamen when the two men reached the deck. One of them, who appeared to be Chinese, reached up to slap the tall sailor on the back as he came aboard. The men disappeared into the depths of the chunky little craft as it tossed about, heaving and yawing, in the huge waves.

Sailors of many mixes stood unevenly on the moving deck, looking toward the passengers and crew of the schooner. Jim saw them shaking their heads sadly at the tourists. Some appeared to be laughing and joking, but they were too far away to hear their words. Ugly leering scowls and obscene gestures of others said enough to send chills through him. He wondered how many of the passengers on the pitching deck of the *Queen Ilikii* understood the danger they faced.

They soon heard muffled sounds of gunfire erupting below deck on the junk. The sailors from the *Queen Ilikii* came roaring up from the depths of the vessel and rushed toward the railing, trying desperately to reach their small boat. From the railing, they dove headlong into the heaving seas and scrambled to board the little craft, their whitened hands grasping for the gunwales.

The Filipino made it onto the little tender and, after several frantic pulls, got the engine started. The tall sailor grabbed onto the gunwales as the small boat, now pitching wildly in the storm, moved sluggishly toward the schooner.

Jamie gasped in horror, and Jim held her hand, as two of

the junk's crew fired rifles into the little boat as the small craft moved away. It made slow headway against the heaving seas, trying desperately to distance itself from the junk and reach the schooner.

They watched in horror as a shot struck the sailor running the tender. They saw him lurch forward with a splash of blood spreading over his back. Jamie grabbed Jim's arm as the man fell into the ocean and sank from sight. The little boat drifted aimlessly away on the rolling waves, settling ever deeper into the water. The bullets had punctured the hull. They saw no more of the dark-haired man.

They heard screaming among the other passengers. Her face ashen, Sandy held Brad's head to her generous bosom, as if she sought to protect him from the horror they had just witnessed.

The storm, fully upon them, sent heavy splashing gouts of water across the rain-slick deck of the slim little schooner. They clung tightly to the rails. Niko scurried hurriedly about, showing the frantic passengers where they kept the rafts. He dragged life vests out and opened them. His action added to their confusion and terror. They saw no reason for life rafts or vests. The storm-driven rain added to the discomfort and fear of the soaked, miserable day cruisers.

The captain was a prisoner, was anyone in charge? The remaining crew cared not a whit about the hapless tourists. Jim dragged out a raft as Jamie and Felicia clung to each other, watching in horror as shocked, pale, and frantic tourists rushed aimlessly about the slippery deck. Some were injured as they slid headlong into objects clamped to the rain-slicked deck.

Felicia, fully realizing this had not been done for her entertainment, reached out a hand to comfort Jamie. She placed a hand on Jamie's shoulder, telling her not to worry, while Jim reached under their seats to pull out more supplies.

Jamie opened a life vest and looked at Jim. "These won't go around us if we need them. They weren't made for queen sizes." She let out all the straps and her trembling fingers suddenly seemed very clumsy.

Jim laid the life rafts across the rain-slicked deck and opened one. "We'd best get these ready. We don't know what will happen next."

The schooner pitched wildly in the storm with no one in control. Jamie and Felicia clung to the railing, their clothes sopped with the lashing rainwater. Fear and misery rapidly settled over them.

Three large port-like windows along the broad side of the chunky looking junk faced the schooner. In disbelief, Jim saw one of them open. The sailors shoved the rounded end of some sort of cannon through the open port, and aimed its round metal snout menacingly at the *Queen Ilikii*. Her starboard side faced the junk, but the schooner's broad side tilted and dipped with the increasing ferocity of storm-whipped ocean swells. Like a weird and deadly dance, one ship lifted up, while the other sank into the deepening troughs between the waves.

The passengers screamed in terror as black puffs of smoke preceded the first shot leveled at the schooner. The shot missed when the wave action raised the junk higher and the *Queen Ilikii* fell into a deep wave trough. With wide-eyed fear, Jamie and Felicia both screamed as the next shot shrieked low, hitting the schooner below the waterline about mid-ship. Jim felt the hard jolt and the stricken schooner shuddered beneath their feet. A tangle of rope and canvas, fell crashing down onto the rain-slick deck, creating added chaos among the terrified passengers.

"We're in for it now," he said.

Facing deadly peril, they heard the two exceptionally heavy ladies screaming for Niko.

"Help us here for God's sake. What're we supposed to do?"

Jim saw the huge bulk of one of them, her clothes plastered to her by the rain, rolling about on her bench, clutching the railing. She tried to pull the life-saving items out from beneath, but due to her size, she wasn't able to extract a raft or a vest.

Jane clutched onto her companion, Corrine, as they tried to keep their footing on the wet deck. "Are they trying to sink us?" Jane's voice was shrill with terror. She sobbed and wrung her hands, looking to Corrine for answers.

Jim watched Niko rush to each passenger, telling them to pull out the life rafts and the life vests from the cabinets beneath their seats. He said they were normal size and wasn't sure if they would fit, but hang onto them anyway. "You must try," he cried above the increasing howl of the wind. He shoved life vests at Corrine and Jane.

He hurried to the two very obese and terrified women. There was no giggling now as he approached. Niko talked calmly to them, but their terror increased into panic, in spite of his efforts to return them to reality.

"Oh, please my ladies, you must get into this life vests," he pleaded with them, while he loosened the straps. He pulled a raft out from beneath the benches and inflated it.

The ladies held out their vests, knowing they'd never fit. Their clothing was plastered to their huge, rounded bodies from the lashing rain, outlining every bulge and curve with clinging fabric. Their hair, soaked and torn awry, blew wildly in the storm. "Are we going to sink?" one of them screamed. "They are trying to sink us! Oh my God, Clara." she cried to her companion. "Oh what's happening? Are we going to drown?"

The *Queen Ilikii* shuddered again as another shot struck her. They didn't know where. Screams of fear rose again. The rigging cracked with a hard snap and fell, crashing onto the deck. The foremast took a hit and fell, splintering off to the starboard side. This caused the wounded schooner to list even more, taking on water at an increasingly rapid rate. Jim and the two women heard the big ladies screaming and pleading in terror as Niko tried to help them. He gave them more time and consideration than any of the others. The passing scene froze in Jim's mind.

Struggling mightily to get the rafts inflated, he looked up to see the junk moving away with the smoke of diesel fuel, obviously in use as well as wind power. He realized she had to be out-running the violent storm, fully upon them now. "At least those dirty bastards won't do us any more damage or stay around to eliminate any survivors. God willing, there'll be some." His words were lost in the ferocity of the wind as he fought for footage on the slanting deck. "I'd like to free the captain," he told the ladies. "He's somewhere below decks, but I can't leave you two or the other passengers."

If he left, they'd have no one, but the native guide, who was doing his best, helping where he could. Jim tried to get Jamie and Felicia into their vests and ready the life rafts.

"These rafts are inadequate, at least for us big folk," Jamie said. She didn't say any more. No one needed to hear her thoughts about the usefulness of the rafts and Jim agreed as he laid them out. Made for six normal-sized men, they were none too big.

The back mast canted toward the center of the deck with large splinters sticking out like menacing spears. Under that mast, Jamie saw Brad. He appeared to be unconscious, and his huge bulk lay sprawled out at an awkward angle. Blood seeped from his massive body. The waves washed up to engulf him, as the doomed schooner settled lower in the water.

Sandy clung to his side, crying hysterically and pulling at his arm. "Brad. Oh Brad!"

The blood from his wounds made the deck a slippery mess. One of the splinters had pierced him somewhere, and his pale face appeared lifeless as his blood drained away into the roiling sea.

Jim told Sandy to get into a life raft when he got it ready. She did not heed him, but kept pulling on Brad's arm, crying hysterically. Neither Corrine or Jane were visible on the increasingly tilted deck. Niko tried to get the two big ladies into a raft he had readied. They were screaming hysterically, which made his assistance nearly useless. One of them got into a raft, and it nearly swamped beneath her weight as it got off into the swirling waters. Her terrified screams faded away on the flailing wind.

Jamie and Felicia tried to get both life rafts open while the waves washed up onto the deck. They slipped and worked with fear-numbed hands. Jim pulled the tab that inflated them. He told Jamie and Felicia to get in as soon as he readied them. He urged them to step in as the waves washed up close on the slanting deck. The waves came higher, sloshing against them. The schooner, sinking fast, made them hasten. They had to get themselves away very soon or be pulled down with her.

Two sailors yanked a raft away from a passenger, climbed in, and pushed away from the sinking ship with an oar.

"Hey, you selfish bastards," Jim yelled into the teeth of the wind. He dared not leave his two friends to go to their aid. He had them ready to shove off.

He helped Jamie into a raft, as a wave came up to them, and pushed her raft off the deck. She screamed in terror as she swirled away on the turbulent seas.

Felicia and Jim got off in the next raft and tried to reach Jamie. "Two of us are enough for this raft," he yelled to Felicia. But the rising wind and water took the words away.

The waves buffeted them from every side. They found it nearly impossible to make headway against the wind and waves. Jim tried to get the oars in the locks, but the waves knocked them from his hands. He shouted to Felicia and she caught one oar. "Hang on to that, we'll need it," he ordered

She never heard his voice but clutched frantically onto the sides of the raft and put the oar under her feet as they washed away from the schooner in the heaving waters. Her daypack was a sodden mess, but she'd clung tightly to it when Jim helped her aboard the raft.

The wind and waves washed Jim and Felicia many yards out from the schooner. They turned and watched with great sadness as the lovely, trim *Queen Ilikii* sank silently to her grave. They caught a glimpse of Brad sliding off into the waves and Sandy throwing herself after him. Of Corrine, Jane, or the others, they saw nothing.

They tried to control the raft, but the waves beat against the small craft. Water washed over the sides, filling the flimsy vessel. Tossing madly about on the heaving seas, they tried to bail with their hands then looked in the side compartments for something to use. The storm was fully upon them. They fought the sea, their minds racked with terror and their bodies torn and battered by the huge, beating waves.

They saw nothing but walls of ocean water as they bailed frantically to keep from sinking. They could not see any other rafts, nor could they see Jamie. Felicia called frantically for her, but the wind stole her words away.

# CHAPTER 7

Jamie awakened to the sound of seabirds' pealing cries as they wheeled about in the early morning sky. Her eyes still burned from exposure to sun and seawater, her face felt dirty, and her body burned from traces of crusted salt. The rising sun turned everything a luscious rosy pink, but the agony of her body and an aching, gnawing hunger invaded her senses to the exclusion of all other thought. Her utter misery brought back the incredible events of the past two days.

Shaking her head, she sat up and looked about, trying to bring things into focus. Stranded on a lonely island with the very criminal whose evil acts had created this living nightmare, she nevertheless looked for him, hoping he'd lived through the night. Her searching gaze found him sitting up, watching her. Against all sensible reason, she was glad for his presence. She was not alone.

"Good morning," he said. His voice, soft and masculine, went deep into her in some strange way, but she liked the sound of it. He managed a smile for her, and she surmised he felt well enough after his ordeal of yesterday.

"Good morning, yourself," Jamie replied. She looked about, taking in the beauty of her surroundings. "Are you better, now?" she asked, already knowing he'd improved. His pallor had almost disappeared, and his voice sounded stronger.

Mick nodded toward his wounds. "Come take a look if

you would. My shoulder is stiff as hell, and sore, but it's not infected by the feel of it." He gazed down the beach. "If you'll help me, we'll go to your little stream. We're out of water, and we could both do with a wash-up."

"You *are* better if you feel like walking. It's not far, just down the beach." Jamie indicated to the right with a wave of her hand. Seeing more clearly the lush beauty of their island haven, she almost cried aloud at how different it was. With no wild storm raging, it was peaceful. Trees swayed gently and continually from the warm trade winds, and the sandy beach looked clean and slightly pink. It formed a wide expanse that curved about the gentle waters of the lagoon. The azure-hued waters, quiet within the coral ring, differed from the white foaming breakers encircling it. Mere tiny waves lapped at the sandy shore.

The island surrounded the lagoon on both sides, forming a bay-like area near the size of a city block. A truly beautiful place held in the wildly tangled arms of dense tropical growth, a sanctuary from the fearful ocean depths—and, to a less stressed person—a tropical paradise.

She rose unsteadily to her feet and approached the man to check his wounds. Kneeling on the sand beside him, she pulled the soiled dressing away and found both wounds clean enough, oozing a bit, but no signs of purulence. She offered her opinion. "Your wounds look clean enough to me, but I don't know anything about gunshot wounds." She tore off two more bits of skirt to make new dressings, soaked them in seawater, and tore another strip off to hold them in place. "I hope you heal fast, or my poor ragged skirt will never make it," she murmured.

Jamie wondered if the makers of Jones of New York ever thought of their clothing in a situation like this. She left his shirt off. Soiled with blood, it was not fit to wear. The old dressings—stained, but washed in seawater—were laid in the sun. Jamie believed the sun would sterilize them.

She helped him to his feet. Taking a few unsteady steps with her holding onto his arm, she noticed he hadn't broken into a sweat as he had yesterday. She saw that as a sign of his returning strength. An icy knot clutched deep in her abdomen at his returning independence. *What if he doesn't need me anymore? What then?*

Frightening thoughts crossed her mind as she walked beside him, holding his right arm to steady him. He made his halting way down the beach close against her side. Becoming aware of his male scent, despite her fears, she found it comforting and a warm glow suffused through her body. Her feeling of security in his presence fought against her knowledge of the evil soul she knew him to be.

Unwillingly, she remembered the smooth skin of his back, and how it felt under her hands. *What's wrong with me? Am I so screwed up I have feelings like this about this son of evil? How could I? Is it a man-woman thing because we're alone here? He'll never know he causes these unbelievable sensations in me. The man is a devil. How many people have been killed or lives destroyed by his work?*

They came to the stream, and Jamie dipped water into the plastic bucket. When they drank what they wanted, she faced him. "Is there any possibility of finding something to eat? I am totally famished. I know it wouldn't hurt me to miss a few meals, but we'll both need something soon."

He pointed to several coconuts lying about. "Do you like these? There're lots of them around here. We might find other things when we can explore this island. We might find people on here, but I doubt it, since it's very small and isolated." He pointed out several coconuts lying on the ground near the water. "The storm must have knocked them down, we can start with these. I'm starving too."

He told her to tear the outer husk off on a sharpened stick. With his left arm essentially useless due to his wound, he was unable. She found a small tree which had been broken off, and with his instruction, struggled mightily to get the tough bristly husk off. She then used the Swiss Army Knife to puncture holes in the dark spots. Jamie raised the coconut to her lips and tasted green coconut milk, found it unbelievably delicious, and shared it with the sailor. She cracked it open with a rock and they ate their first food in three days. The coconut meat was soft and they scooped it out with fingers—a spoon would have done nicely. She compared it with the hard, dry coconuts in the grocery stores at home.

*Home!* Jamie realized she no longer felt sad or defeated. She'd survived a shipwreck, and just now, her life was full and exciting. Without a doubt, she was in mortal danger from a drug smuggler, but at this moment it didn't matter. She felt useful, appreciated, and, if she survived, was living the adventure of a lifetime. She couldn't stop the smile spreading across her lips.

"I like your smile." Mick looked at her through half-closed eyes. "Was the coconut that good?"

Jamie laughed. "Well, it was good, and it's nice not to feel so hungry. I didn't know they could taste like that." Never being one to share personal feelings, she assuredly didn't want to share her latest thoughts.

The tiny stream had formed a small pond on its way to the lagoon. Looking at the tiny pool of water, Jamie asked if she could have enough privacy to wash the salt from herself and her clothes.

He nodded and set off slowly up the beach. "My turn next," he said.

She noticed he walked well enough on his own.

Jamie used the bucket, pouring water over herself repeatedly, washing hair, body, and clothes. There was no soap, but getting the stinging salt off her body felt wonderful. How wise of someone to put a plastic bucket in the raft. It had so many uses. She had several bruises over her legs and arms, but no broken skin, except for the bleeding blisters on her hands. They burned terribly from the water and were painfully sore, but improving. She'd been very lucky in this wild adventure, at least this far. She went to find Mick and helped him to the water.

Being careful of his wounds, she poured water over him

repeatedly, rinsing the salt from his hair and jeans. She washed his soiled shirt. He needed to take off all his clothes, but that was not remotely possible. The heavy, soaked dungarees would have to remain on.

Mick felt things were good between them—for the moment. He didn't want to damage their fragile relationship. He needed her help, but he wanted her good opinion even more. It came as a shock and, in disbelief, he realized he'd begun to have feelings for this disheveled, storm-ravaged woman.

He'd never felt deeply for any special woman in his life. There'd always been a woman, if he felt the inclination. But he'd never met anyone like this courageous, frightened woman who'd worked so hard to save them both. He'd never found anyone to tie to, nor would he in the future. His lifestyle precluded ties to another person. Looking at Jamie, that fact gave him a pang of regret. He did not see her queen size or torn and beaten body. He saw a brave and caring soul.

He wanted to tell her about himself. The sense of closeness he felt toward her had created an inescapable aura of intimacy. But rescue would come eventually, and he dared not risk having his activities in the Southern Seas known. The dangers he faced daily forced him to live a life of lies and shadows. Usually, he faded into the background, a memory of an itinerant sailor, casually worked with a time or two.

He would remain a shadowy, scarcely remembered person somewhere in the hazy background, but he found it painful hiding his life from Jamie. Bound to her in some new way, not yet understood, he carefully hid his feelings, allowing no look of pain or bewilderment to cross his sun-darkened features.

The tide surged inward, rising on the beach as they made their way back to the tiny camp. "We must move closer to the stream," Mick declared.

His thoughts were interrupted by Jamie, her hand held

over her eyes, gazing out over the quiet waters of the lagoon as they moved along the beach. She pointed. "Is that something floating out there?"

"It looks like a raft of sorts, like the one we were in, but looks to be empty. It's moving in with the tide. When it gets closer, do you think you could bring it in? Might have something more we could use."

Jamie thought of Felicia and Jim. *Oh, could it possibly be them?* She saw no signs of life on the raft, though it sat rather low in the water. She tried to hurry back to the little campsite, but Mick moved slowly and she wouldn't leave him.

After settling him on the tent cloth under the trees, she put on her Tevas and waded out into the azure lagoon. Coming close enough to see it was indeed a raft, she heard low moaning sounds emanating from it. She hurriedly slogged through the warm waters to reach it.

Coming closer, she saw a sunburned, salt-encrusted head rise above the edge. It was Jim, sunburned, dehydrated, and done in. He must have sensed her closeness. She heard his croaking whisper. "Can you help us?"

Jamie heard him say, *us,* and knew Felicia was with him. "Jim, it's me, Jamie she cried, nearly in tears. "You're safe, you'll be all right now."

She pulled the raft to the shore. When the water became shallow, she looked into it and barely recognized Felicia. Her hair was salt-drenched and matted, her face and arms terribly burned by the sun. She made no response to Jamie's cries of delight.

"I worried I'd never see you again—or Felicia," Jamie told Jim. "You've made it. We have water here. I'll bring you close to the beach, but you'll have to make it the rest of the way. I can't carry you."

The raft scraped on the sandy bottom, and she left them to go get the water container. Remembering her own dreadful thirst, she knew they'd revive much faster with the taste of fresh water on their parched lips, and get themselves up on the sand. No one could drag them. They were far too heavy.

Ten feet from shore, Jamie ran and grasped the bucket of water. She ran back and put the container to Jim's lips.

He drank frantically, clutching the plastic pail. "Oh, God, that's good." he gasped, "Jamie—thank you."

Jamie took it from him and put fresh, cool water on Felicia's parched lips. The sun-burned, sea-ravaged woman responded desperately, drinking the last of the water, clutching at the container. "Where are we? Oh God, Jamie, is that you?"

Trying to talk, trying to cry out, Felicia's throat closed. Her words became croaking sounds. Jamie told them to get out of the raft and walk or crawl up into the shade. She commanded them. They needed that firmness.

Jim crawled out, fell into the water, and pulled himself painfully to his feet. He watched Jamie shake Felicia to get her moving.

"Come on, Felicia," she urged. "You're safe now. We have water and shade. Come on."

Felicia rolled out of the raft into shallow water and felt solid ground beneath her. It revived her enough to crawl up onto the shore while Jamie urged her on. Felicia's clothes were wrinkled, twisted, and crusted with salt just as hers had been.

Jamie finally got Felicia up under the palm trees where she sank onto the soft sand, closed her eyes, and croaked. "I can't believe we've found you, Jamie. Thank you, God, for this miracle. The solid earth beneath me feels like heaven, it's so good, so solid—so real. We're safe at last."

"I can't believe you made it to this same little island either. I didn't know where you were or what'd happened to you," Jamie said. She settled them to rest and made several trips down the beach, bringing water to them until they were satisfied. She observed Jim, now more awake, assessing the situation.

Jim sat in the shade of swaying palm trees, exhausted,

eyes burning from sea and sun. He was bruised, blistered, and beaten from the waves, but he' noticed the tall dark sailor sitting in the shady area. He lapsed into unconsciousness, but not before seeing that Jamie indicated no fear of the man. Jim let his exhausted body fall into a deep, restoring slumber.

Jamie looked over at Mick, sitting quietly in the shade of the softly moving palm trees. His dark eyes gleamed. He'd watched her help her two friends safely ashore. She could not decipher the man's thoughts and realized with futility that she most likely never would.

Mick observed Jamie. *She's light on her feet, and, for her size, has a fine figure, even with the extra weight.* Her newly rinsed hair had dried into a halo of curls about her head, making a wonderful improvement in her appearance. He tried to imagine how things had been for her. He'd seen the haunting shadows of pain in her green-speckled eyes.

Mick watched Jamie with her friends. Now that they had joined them on this small island refuge, he'd caught a tiny twinge of regret at the loss of privacy between them on her face. Happy as she was to see them and know they were safe, Jamie' could never acknowledge something like that to herself, but he'd seen it and smiled.

Mick hadn't moved or spoken since Felicia and Jim had joined them, but he'd watched Jamie's every move down the beach or sitting on the sand. He didn't know how she felt about his constant appraisal of her, but watching her made him happy in some strange way. He thought it made her feel hunted and uneasy, regretted it, but had no plans to stop. She had caught his imagination.

While the others rested, she pulled the newer raft up onto the sand and looked in it for further supplies, hoping there might be a few more of those hard little biscuits. She found nothing in the way of food, but they now had one more oar and another plastic bucket.

Without looking further, she turned to Mick. "I'm going to the pond for more water and a few coconuts. They'll be

hungry. It has to be three days at least since they've eaten."
She picked up the two bailing buckets, walking down the
pearly pink sand beach.

Mick nodded, thinking how her appearance had improved with a bit of personal care. Her skin had taken on a
tanned appearance and her greenish eyes, lined with long,
dark lashes, had cleared from the irritation of salt water. Her
finely arched brows added to her look as well. With the recovery of her friends, he knew she'd forgotten her own dire
situation in the immediacy of their need.

Thinking about their loss of privacy, he'd seen the moment of hesitancy cross her face. She was drawn to him,
even while she believed him the lowest of criminals.

Watching her walk gracefully down the beach, head held
high, skirt swaying, and the once-white blouse flapping
softly in the warm breeze, she looked smaller than he remembered. She carried the buckets to bring back food. He
was hungry again as well. He watched as long as she was
visible.

Jamie returned and awakened Jim and Felicia. "Here's
something to eat. It's not the breakfast you had on the *Ilikii*,
but it's the best in the house."

She kneeled down to them with her knees pressing into
the pink sand. She found a flat rock and cracked open a coconut, offering them soft coconut meat with a clamshell to
use as a spoon. "I found these *spoons* on the beach."

Felicia sat up and tasted the coconut, her hunger ravenous now that she'd eaten a little. "It's not bad. Is this all
you've found so far?" Her voice still croaked. Her face and
arms were severely sun burned. Three days on the open seas
had exhausted and devastated her.

"That's it for now," Jamie replied. "But maybe tomorrow we can do some exploring. We might find something
more."

Jim had suffered severe sunburn as well, his fair skin un-
suited to the glaring tropical sun. Blisters had formed over
his arms, parts of his face, and the exposed areas of his legs.

He was quiet as they ate the last of the coconut meat. Jamie wondered if mashed coconut meat would soothe their inflamed skin—it was certainly oily enough. Was not coconut oil an ingredient in so many lotions and ointments?

Jim noticed Mick sitting beneath the palms. Jamie related how she'd found him clinging to her raft in the midst of the storm. And that he'd been wounded from the smugglers who shot him in the back, when he and the Filipino tried to escape from the junk.

Jamie introduced them to Mick, as if attending a garden party, so civilized they were, as they took stock of each other amid the strangeness of their situation. Mick acknowledged them with a nod.

Jim and Felicia were incredibly hungry. They both drank large quantities of water until they felt replenished. Jamie suggested they go to the little stream and wash up. They set out for the water, leaving Mick to rest in the shade. Walking was a chore in their weakened condition, and Jim hovered close to aid Felicia, carefully avoiding contact with her blistered arms.

As they moved slowly down the beach, Jim asked about the sailor. Jamie explained the best she could. "All I know is that he was wounded, and I had to take care of him. I even took the bullet out of him. If I hadn't, he might have died and left me all alone here. Right or wrong, I couldn't have done differently. I was terrified of him, but even more afraid of being alone on that huge ocean, in that terrible storm, and on this island, too. He does seem to know about these atolls, as he refers to them. He told me how to fix the coconuts."

"You're kidding, you operated on him?" Felicia exclaimed.

Jamie pulled the red knife out of her skirt pocket. "Yep—with this."

Felicia shook her head. "That's the wildest thing I've ever heard of. You are so brave. I don't know if I could have done that."

Jamie laughed a little. "I didn't think he would kill me until he got stronger. Thank God, you're here now. That changes the odds." She felt tears filling her eyes. "I still cannot believe you found this same little island. How'd you ever get over that reef?"

"God only knows, Jamie," Jim said. "I barely remember anything about it at all. It seems like we're waking up from a nightmarish dream, to find ourselves in a veritable Eden. And we find you here with one of them who brought this about. No wonder you were terrified with him in your raft. You're the bravest soul I know." He sighed. "I remember our own days on the open sea, but Felicia wasn't nearly so frightening." He laughed as Felicia gave him a look.

Jamie realized she'd lost much of her fear of Mick. He didn't seem to be the same sort of man they'd seen on the *Ilikii*. What was he then? She'd formed this question in her mind a few times already.

# CHAPTER 8

As they made their way toward the tiny stream, Jamie confided her thoughts about Mick. "His speech doesn't fit with his drug dealer, itinerate, sailor lifestyle. It's certainly not what we heard on the dock before we sailed. Who knows? Out here in the South Pacific, any number of people might come to get lost, wanting to forget where they came from or whatever they may be running from. I can certainly understand that," she finished sadly.

"I guess we'll wait and see," Jim commented. "For now, we're here together. Survival has to be the first priority. Does Mick have any idea where we are?"

"We never got around to talking about that. We haven't really said much, except about his wounds and finding food and water." Jamie told them about taking a makeshift shower and finding coconuts. She didn't mention how Mick made her feel. How could she? She couldn't handle those thoughts herself.

They came to the small trickling stream and Felicia went to the water with delight. "Oh, Jamie, what a find. I can't wait to get this sticky salt off me. My poor face is all sunburned, and my arms too. We didn't have any sun screen."

Jamie brought Felicia to where the water pooled enough to dip into. She helped her wash her clothes and hair. "I don't know how clean you can get without soap but it felt good to me."

She watched the bedraggled woman, worn and burned as

she was, grow stronger with the cool water flowing over her tender, burned skin.

"It feels like heaven, Jamie," Felicia cooed, "washing all this sticky salt off, especially, my poor gummy hair. Do we have a comb?"

Jamie only laughed. "Afraid not."

When they finished, Jamie helped Jim wash. He took off his shirt. Jamie rinsed the salt out of it, and put it back on. His burnt arms and front parts of his legs, had blistered even more. The cool water refreshed him and soothed his burning skin. Jamie rinsed herself again. They all suffered from exposure, but the burning tropical sun had been much worse, reflected off the waves at sea.

"You better believe this feels good." Jim, happy to be alive himself, watched Felicia take on new life, even with their few scanty amenities.

Jamie noticed Jim's tenderness toward Felicia as he told her, "I was afraid she'd never make it to this island, or any place of safety. I don't remember crossing that reef. Look at it, booming and thrashing out there when those huge ocean swells strike against it. How fortunate we were." He shook his head in disbelief.

Jamie chuckled. "Wearing wet clothes isn't too bad in the tropics, is it?"

Jim laughed at that. "You're certainly very cheerful for all the hell you've gone through, my dear."

Jamie, having no answer to his comment, said nothing.

Felicia joined into the spirit of it all, even managing to laugh a little. Jim, elated to see her spirits rise, broke into a big smile. She was not used to hardship, he'd seen that. They had only met a few days ago, though it seemed a lifetime. In reality, they remained strangers, bound together in a bizarre situation.

They watched as Jamie found a few coconuts and set about tearing the husk off on the sharp stick.

"Hey, girl, you've got talent!" Jim exclaimed.

She fed them and did several to take back to Mick. "I

wonder if we could put some of this coconut stuff on your sunburns," she said. "It's oily—might help." She cracked one open on the rocks and scooped the soft meat out with a shell. She patted it gently over their blistered and weeping sunburned skin.

"Oh, Jamie, it feels better with this gooey coconut spread over the burns." Felicia said. "It is soothing, isn't it, Jim?"

"You bet it is," he replied. "Jamie, you're turning into quite a nurse." Seeing the rising blisters on the outer areas of his arms, he gave her a nod of appreciation.

They set out for the little camp. On returning, Jamie went to Mick, checked his wounds, gave him water, and more of the coconut meat.

Felicia, noting how tenderly Jamie cared for Mick's wounds, looked at Jim. "Hum, she certainly takes her nursing duties seriously."

Jamie asked Mick how he felt. He gave her a half-smile. "I need to get up.. I'm stiff and sore— would you help me?"

She bent down, took his right arm, and assisted him. He walked a few steps with her and then, haltingly, on his own.

Mick moved slowly over to Jim. "Mind stepping out with me?" he asked. "We need to have a chat."

Jim nodded. They turned to walk slowly down the beach. Neither man looked strong or steady. As they moved, their figures grew smaller.

Jamie watched them. "Look at them, Felicia. They're from different worlds, thrown together in this place—one, an officer of the court, the other, a criminal of the worst sort."

They watched the men walking shoulder to shoulder down the beach, each barefoot on the sand. Jim was taller and certainly broader. Mick was slender and shorter by an inch or two, his body exuding power like seasoned whipcord, even in his injured condition. Jamie caught that feeling when she tended his wounds.

Watching him in detached fascination, she noted he supported his left arm with his right to relieve pulling on the wounded left shoulder. "He needs a sling for that arm, but I can't afford much more off the bottom of my skirt." She pulled it out with two fingers, looking at the shortened garment with a frown over her face. "Look, my skirt is nearly a mini already."

"It'll be cooler that way," Felicia observed with a smile. She nodded at Jamie. "I see what you mean about Mick. He doesn't fit the image we had of him on the *Ilikii.*" She shook her hair out to dry. It began taking on its original sheen.

"You have wonderful hair," Jamie said again.

Felicia tried combing it out by running her fingers through it. "It feels good, just getting that salt out!"

Then Jamie confided, "I don't know what to think about Mick, I just know I'm glad he didn't die." This admission made her chuckle. "Wouldn't one less drug dealer make the world a better place?"

ᑯᔑᑯᔑ

The men drew away from the camp a good distance. Mick stopped and faced Jim. "I know what you people think of me. I understand that—but know this. This young woman, Jamie, has saved my life at least twice. She's in no danger from me, and never will be. I swear that to you on my life." He told Jim about the events on the raft and the surgery Jamie had performed. "I don't believe I've ever met anyone so brave, and all the while she was terrified of me." Jim nodded and Mick went on. "While we're here on this island, let's not get into anything except our survival. That set okay with you?"

"Suits me. We're damned lucky to be here at all."

They shook hands and Jim noted a sure, firm grip from Mick. Jim liked the look he saw in the black-haired gentleman's eyes, but all the while, thoughts raced through his mind while he hid the frown that wanted to cross his forehead. *This guy is far and away too well spoken for the role he's playing. Jamie's right, there's more here than appears on the surface. What the hell's going on?*

Out of sight of the women, Mick stepped into the under-brush and relieved himself. Jim followed suit. They shared a laugh.

"God, I needed that," Mick declared,

They found a log partially buried in the sand and sat down on it, side by side. Mick offered what advice he had. "We'll need to find us some sort of food. Coconuts are okay in a pinch, but not for long. We have no idea how long we'll be here. We don't even know if anyone will search for us."

Jim shook his head. "Damn, I hope they will. Makes you wonder if they know the *Queen Ilikii* went down. Do you know if there was a radio message sent? Of course, they'll notice when she doesn't return to port."

"It's possible a message was sent, but under the circum-stances, maybe not." Mick moved his head negatively, his lips tight, remembering the ship's captain trussed up in ropes and down in the hold before he and the Filipino went over to the junk. The entire operation had gotten hopelessly screwed up, resulting in the loss of many innocent lives. Not all of the crew was blameless, but the passengers and the captain were.

It was turning dark when they returned to the camp. Ja-mie felt the growing camaraderie between the men and heard them talking as they returned. Maybe somehow to-morrow they'd find something more than coconuts to eat. "I'm so hungry I could eat a horse and I mean it!" she said to Felicia. I'm glad for what we've found so far, but oh what I wouldn't give for a box of Snickers or a dozen Ding Dongs!"

Felicia laughed softly. "I'm starving, too, but I'm very thankful to be here on land and with you and Jim—Mick, too." She squeezed Jamie's hand. "Now, that it's after din-ner, what about our beds?"

They both laughed.

They had two tents now. It was warm on the beach, and growing dark. They spread the tents over the sand and lay down for the night. Jim and Mick tried to share the space on one of the tents, which left them lying on a lot of soft sand. The women had the same situation, careful to keep their sunburned limbs off the coarse sand. It was hard to find comfort, but exhausted from their ordeals and safe from the ocean depths, they rested and no one complained. Lying quietly, looking up at the stars, Jamie imagined each person thought of their perilous situation and how unbelievably lucky they'd been to find this haven.

Jim and Felicia fell into an exhausted sleep. Soft snoring sounds emanating from them. After a little while Jamie rose up and looked in Mick's direction. He was sitting up, resting his arms on his knees, watching her. She whispered. "Are you all right? I didn't dress your wounds again tonight."

Mick nodded and whispered back. "I'll be fine. We can do that in the morning. Good night, Jamie."

She thrilled at the soft timber of his voice, knowing she shouldn't respond to anything about him. *I must be mad! He turns me inside out with a look, and yet I know exactly what he is. What's wrong with me?* He reminded her of a crouching, black-eyed panther, sitting quietly—biding his time—waiting for his chance.

"Good night," she murmured. She lay down with a soft smile playing about her lips. It felt so good just to lie there with nothing to do. She sighed deeply, aware of her rapidly beating heart. *You crazy fool! One rotten devil of a man wasn't enough for you?*

Deeply exhausted from helping her friends during the day, and beyond hungry for something normal to eat, she felt the beginnings of real peace settle over her. Her recent past had been one of disappointment and turmoil. She hadn't felt anywhere near peaceful for so long, she couldn't remember the feeling. She decided her troubled life in Colorado was far away in another world. Wondering, she drifted into a deep and peaceful sleep. Her hips snuggled into the sand, her head pillowed on her arm, and her voluminous skirt, shortened though it was, acted as a covering. It was enough.

Mick sat quietly, arms over his knees. That position felt the easiest for the wounded shoulder. The bulky figures lay near him on the sand, exhausted and sleeping, trying to regain enough strength to face what adversity awaited them when daylight came again. His attention fixed on Jamie's smaller figure, curled up under her skirt, asleep. Flames of heat stole through his body, as his mind struggled with the strange feelings she aroused in him. Heated, yes, but it was more than that. A feeling of tenderness was there as well.

He liked Jim, and felt comfortable with the arrangement they'd made. He was a man's man, one you could deal with. Felicia, he'd wait and see. He admired what he'd seen in Jamie, desired to know her completely, and treasured every moment she tended his wounds or brought him food and water. Her soft, gentle touch made things right somehow. Feelings of this nature toward a woman were new to him, and he was puzzled as he settled himself, trying for sleep. The shoulder hurt like hell. It was sore, but didn't have the hot, fiery feeling of infection. He knew all about those things. He fell into a fitful sleep, thinking of Jamie's soft touch on his body as she cared for his wounds.

# CHAPTER 9

Morning came and Jim rose up on one elbow. Ignoring his growling stomach and sunburned skin, he took stock of their surroundings. The lagoon waters were calm and crystal clear with azure-blue dappling over the lighter areas. He guessed it reflected the sky against the pale clean sand beneath the shallow waters. Along the beach each way, graceful palms bent outward, arching gracefully over the water's edge. The colors were astounding. The scene was wonderfully exotic. He decided this was the way these graceful tropical atolls must have looked when Captain Cook discovered them many years ago, fabulous in their natural beauty.

He edged over to Felicia and nudged her. "Good morning, welcome to the lovely sight of paradise." He kept his voice low, for her ears only, not wanting to disturb the others if they slept.

"Huh? Ooh, I'm stiff as a board. Oh, Lord, I remember it all," Felicia moaned. Her reddened, purple-hued eyes opened to see Jim, smiling down at her. "Hi, Jim, are we all right? My face and arms burn, but they're a little better."

He swept his arm in an arc. "Take a look. This place is an absolute paradise. I couldn't take it in yesterday. I was too miserable, burned, hungry, and I'm still thirsty as hell." He uttered a softly satisfied chuckle as he pointed out the gentle waters of the lagoon and the green of the trees arching over the water.

Felicia whispered, "It is, Jim. It really is. I hope we can catch some fish. I could make sushi out of one, I'm so incredibly hungry."

Jim laughed, his pale blue eyes upon her. "You're a practical one, aren't you?"

Her beauty was incredible even under these conditions. Continually amazed, and unable to help himself, he watched her at every opportunity.

They looked about to see Jamie attending to Mick's wounds. She went to rinse the soiled dressings in the lagoon, and replace them wet over the front and back areas of his chest. They heard her ask if she could use his shirt for a binder to hold them on. He agreed and she bound them gently with it by putting it over his head and under one arm, twisting it to fit over the wounds. Having dried overnight, it was reasonably clean, though terribly stained.

Knowing Mick watched Jamie constantly, and seeing the look of utter bliss on his face, Jim had the idea he relished her ministrations to a greater degree than might be expected. Felicia and Jim looked at each other and shrugged.

Felicia shook her head slightly, and said under her breath, "I think something's happening there. Good Lord, Jim, I hope she doesn't get in too deep with that one."

Jim patted her shoulder. "I saw that yesterday. I don't think either one realizes how great a bond they've forged between them. Once we're rescued, that'll put an end to it. I'd sure hate to see that girl get hurt. He could be a bad one. Intelligence only makes a guy like that worse," he said in soft whispers, pretending to speak of their surroundings.

Mick sat in the sand while Jamie cleaned and re-dressed his wounds. He felt the familiar warm glow suffuse through his lanky body, along with a prickling sensation across his scalp.

He wished she never had to stop. *I must be losing my mind, or maybe it's this situation. I can't believe any woman could do this to me after all these years. Oh God, her hands are warm and gentle.*

Jamie felt him shiver slightly. "Are you cold without your shirt?" she asked.

"No, it's nothing. Will you help me get up now?"

She bent to assist him. Jim and Felicia watched as she gently helped Mick to his feet.

After a few steps, he walked alone. "Thanks, Jamie," he said as he walked a ways down the beach and tucked into the brush for a moment.

With everyone awake, they decided to move everything nearer to the small stream. After loading what little they had into the two rafts, Jamie towed one and Jim the other. "I love the feel of the sand and warm salt water on my feet," she told him. "During that storm, those ocean depths scared me to death, and walking on solid ground is still a wonder to me."

She towed the raft along in the lagoon's gentle lapping waves. There were few rocks in the water on this part of the beach. The tide was going out and the lagoon waters were calm.

For Jamie, the ropes attached to the raft were rough against her sore hands. The salt in them burned against the torn flesh, causing tears of pain.

Felicia walked beside Mick, noticing he moved faster today and except for use of his left arm, he'd regained some strength. She wanted to ask him questions, but was unsure about what to ask a drug smuggler and probable killer. She finally said, "How's your shoulder? Are you having much pain with it? I guess we haven't any antibiotics." She looked up at him, her eyes betraying her curiosity.

He smiled down to her. "It isn't so bad now the bullet's out. I believe it'll heal well enough. Thanks for asking."

Felicia, amazed at the change a smile wrought in Mick's longish features, nearly gasped. *My God, he's one handsome guy—if he manages a smile.*

When they reached the water source, they decided to take stock of their meager assets. They searched both rafts, and all the pockets, laying the items on the beach. Felicia's water-soaked daypack was found and she held it up. "Look, guys!"

Jamie pounced on it. "I wonder why I didn't see it before when I looked in your raft, Felicia. Let's see what we have here." They found a few soggy sweets, flattened in their wrappers, two small jars of peanuts, a comb with large teeth, a melting lipstick, a wet flashlight, a small pack of the hard little biscuits, and a soggy pack of gum. "Looks like a super market to me," Jamie exclaimed as they laid it out in the sun.

Felicia managed a giggle. "Well, except the lipstick."

They now had two tents and two small nets. They found no matches and would need a fire if they ran across something to cook. The flashlight proved useless when they tried it. Felicia looked at the melting lipstick, and tossed it into the lagoon. "We don't need make-up in our lives, now, do we?"

"If we set up the tents," Mick suggested, "we'd best put them out of sight of the ocean. We want rescue, but by the right people. When the men on the junk find our there are survivors, they'll hunt them down and leave no one alive. Believe me, they'll not hesitate to wipe out any possible witnesses. If we are alive, there may be other survivors of the *Ilikii*. Word gets around the Pacific, and those devils have eyes and ears everywhere."

Mick's disturbing speech put a damper on their rising spirits, but Jamie knew, by the tone of his voice, that what he said was true. She took comfort in knowing that Mick was wary of the smugglers. After all, they'd shot him. She got practical. "Let's fix a couple coconuts for breakfast and find us a good hiding place after we eat."

Jim set out to find more coconuts. Felicia found a shady spot and spread out the tents to sit on, moving sluggishly with the effort. "We can have soggy hard tack with the coconuts." She laughed, tossing her hair as she settled on one of the tents. She had difficulty, even now, staying worried about anything.

Jamie saw her gazing in the direction taken by Jim. "You like Jim a lot, don't you?" she asked.

"Yes, even on the boat I thought he was great. There's a lot to like about him, you know. He gives me the feeling of caring. He makes me feel good." Felicia smiled and shrugged. "I'd hoped we could see each other when we got back from the cruise, but now it's like this. Not the same as a casual date, is it?"

Jamie flung out her hands. "Nothing's the same, how could it be?" She went to Mick. "We'll need to get these rafts hidden. I never thought about those devils hunting for us. Glad you did. Now we have to worry about them too." She sighed. "Will this situation ever end, and we'll be rescued?"

Mick regretted the fatigue and worry he saw in her eyes. "Don't worry too much about the drug people. We'll keep watch for rescue craft, but make sure they're the right ones." He wanted to ease her fears, and let his voice exude confidence. He saw her relax a little. She'd been on duty since the beginning and it wore on her.

They finished their breakfast, enjoying the little bit of biscuit.

"This is a waffle with butter and syrup piled on," Felicia exclaimed, holding it aloft.

They laughed at that. For all their misery, they had a survivor's spirit. They shared out a jar of peanuts, savoring the taste of something so familiar.

Jamie felt a smile of delight cross her face. "Has anything ever tasted this good?"

Searching farther up from the beach, but keeping near the stream, they found a partially protected area, beneath a huge, wide-spreading monkey pod tree. It was nearly one hundred yards from the beach.

"How about right here?" Jim said.

Felicia, her head thrown back, tried to encompass the entire mass of the tree, but was too close. "Oh, what a wonderful tree. Look, Jim, have you ever seen anything like it?"

Jim stood beside her, nodding in agreement.

Once they agreed to make the camp under the huge spreading branches, Jim collected stones to build a fire ring. The tops of the tree's branches, sprinkled over all with delicate pinkish flowers, seemed like a huge protecting umbrella, holding long, thick, green arms of security over them beneath the lacy, fern-like leaves.

Mike was pale and sweating profusely from merely walking. Jamie suggested he sit on one of the tents against the massive trunk of the tree. "You'd better rest now or you could have a relapse." Fresh blood stained his dressings and she removed them to examine the wounds.

The women went to clean the dressings in the lagoon while Jim did what he could to set the camp in order. "He's still pretty weak, isn't he?" Felicia said, seeing Mick sitting there, pale and sweating.

Jamie nodded as she washed the bloody dressings. "I guess he'll need to rest a few more days, but he's healing well enough if he doesn't get infected." She noticed the salt water set the stains into the fabric, and the dressings, though rinsed, seemed filthy to her. But her skirt was not generous enough for more.

"You'd better hope Mick hasn't got AIDS with all the blood on your hands," Felicia warned. "Didn't you say your hands were all torn up with blisters when you took the bullet out? In fact, they're still pretty ragged looking."

Jamie shrugged. "Too late to worry about that now, isn't it? I guess I'll ask him about it when we're alone sometime." She took a deep breath. "I'm glad he knew about the smugglers. They shot him, so I guess he isn't one of them."

As they walked back, Jamie pulled the waistband of her skirt out. "Have you noticed how loose everything is getting? My skirt almost fell off my hips when I got up this morning. My bra's in a tighter notch too. What'll we wear when this stuff wears out?"

"I didn't notice that until you mentioned it," Felicia replied. "This could be the diet you never wanted." She laughed and skipped a bit. "If this keeps up, I may become the slender, tan, California girl walking on the beach." She tossed her rippling hair in the morning sun. The big-toothed comb had done its work. "But I don't know what we'll wear if we have to stay here for weeks, or months. Jamie, can you even imagine—months?"

Jamie redid Mick's wounds and settled him back on one of the tents to rest.

He looked at her and smiled. "Thanks again, my dear."

She caught her breath at the flash of his smile and hurried away to Jim and Felicia. Jamie was determined not to get any closer to Mick than his wounds required.

Mick watched her all the time, his black eyes shining. It made her feel restless and tense. She couldn't understand why he did that.

The area was thick with leaves from the wide spreading tree, and Jamie suggested they gather enough to sleep on. "We don't have the sand up here, and we'll need something soft."

They worked at making a primitive camp, having little to work with other than imagination, a bit of canvas, and a lot of leaves.

Later, Jim sat by Mick. "What sort of food could we find in a place like this?" He frequently observed the dark-eyed sailor, wondered about him and what sort he really was—tight-lipped for sure.

"Might be breadfruit trees here," Mick answered. "If so, the fruit is much like bread or potatoes. Below the equator, I believe they produce quite often. Taro roots are good too. I don't know how any of it's cooked, but natives value it highly. There should be fruit here, guava, maybe papaya, star fruit, mangos, or mountain apples. It depends on whether native people come here at times. They often use an island like this as a garden and come to harvest crops at certain times of the year, even if they don't want to live on a remote island like this with no modern amenities."

"When we gain enough strength," Jim replied, "we need

to do some exploring. We can split up and compare notes when we get back."

Mick agreed. "I hope I can do better than today. Walking to this little camp was about all I was good for. I'm damned glad to lie on this pile of leaves."

He saw the women settling into rustic beds to slip into another exhausted sleep. The huge tree spread large, wide branches over them as a sheltering canopy.

When night came, a sliver of new moon appeared low in the sky. Jamie lay awake, trying again to sort things out. The others never noticed it had grown dark as they lay exhausted, sleeping in the soft matting hastily scraped together.

As they had made their primitive home under the spreading arms of a monkey pod tree, Jamie wondered what lay before her. *Am I drawn toward Mick? Please, God, I hope not!*

# CHAPTER 10

With growling stomachs, they repeated the meager fare in the morning—a bit of squashed Ding Dongs and a Ho Ho. They totally relished the bit of sweetness the mangled goodies provided. That taste of chocolate lent them the tiniest touch of home.

"I'm thinking about my beautiful California home," Felicia said, her eyes brimming with tears, "with its big soft beds, showers, and food—lots of food!"

Jamie understood Felicia's longing for the comforts of home. She thought of her father, but had no longing to revisit her life in Denver. Strangely, since being marooned, she felt renewed, in spite of her bizarre situation.

They agreed to rest their traumatized bodies for another day or two before exploring further. Weakness took them with minimal exertion. While they healed their sun-and-sea-ravaged bodies, they ate coconuts, drank water, and slept. Jamie tended Mick's wounds and slathered oily coconut on everyone's healing burns.

❦❦❦

Anxiety about the drug smugglers, as well as the need for additional nutrition, finally urged them into taking a survey of their new surroundings.

"We need food. We can't wait any longer," Jamie declared, desperate to tap their island's bounty.

They divided into pairs for the first exploration. Jim and Felicia went to the right and Jamie went to the left with Mick. He walked well enough, but slowly, as they made their way through the heavy green, tangled bushes. She didn't believe Mick had gained enough strength for this much effort and watched him for signs of tiring.

After seeing her glance into and under bushes as they passed, he said to her, his voice softer than the tropical breeze that wafted over the island. "There are rarely any snakes found on these islands."

She caught the sly smile across his long lips, but hHis information relieved one of her major worries. Bushes in Colorado often hide Rattlesnakes, and she'd learned to be wary of them.

With Mick winded, they sat on a grassy hill to rest. Jamie handed him the water bucket she'd carried, and he took a drink. She watched him swallow, and found her eyes drawn to the motion of his throat as the water went down his bronzed, muscular throat. Rivulets of water coursed down the sides of his face and dripped onto his shirt. How different were men's necks—strong, thick, and solid.

Mick wiped his mouth with the back of his good hand and turned to her. "What is your real name? Jamie's a nickname isn't it?"

She nodded in reply. "Yes, actually, it is, I've gone by it for a long time now. I am Jamilla Shipley Moran. It's from the Arabic. My mom had a friend who worked over there and she said I was *jamilla* when I was born. My mother named me that, it means beautiful." She laughed, uncertain, not wanting to sound vain.

Mick's voice came to her ears, smoothly coated with velvet. "You're well named, Jamie. I think you're one of the most beautiful women I've ever met."

Jamie flushed. "I was thought to be beautiful once, but it all changed." She bit her lip, but kept her counsel. Her sorrows were her own. "I haven't felt like that for a long time, Mick."

"Tell me about your life. I want to know you. I owe you my life many times over, yet I know nothing about you."

His eyes, dark and soft, burned into hers. She felt mesmerized by them and didn't understand it. Held by his look and his speech, icy shivers coursed through her. Despite her fear of him and her natural reticence, she found it easy to speak of her marriage and her escape from it. It came as a release to confide personal things only her father and attorney knew. Somehow, unbelievably, it seemed safe talking to Mick. *I don't believe I'm telling him these things. He's a criminal, and certainly a killer.* Yet, she felt so good in his presence, it was difficult to give those thoughts credence. She enjoyed being near him—like a mouse fascinated by a snake. Did he draw her into intimacy, only to destroy her?

Mick leaned close, put his good arm over her shoulder, and pulled her against his body. He kissed her forehead and nuzzled his lips into her hair. "I knew you'd been hurt sometime in your life. I saw it your eyes that first day on the raft."

At his touch, Jamie pulled away, causing him a flash of pain.

"I'm sorry if I hurt you," she cried. He tried to pull her close again and winced. "Don't do that, Mick. I'll care for your wounds, but that's it," she protested. Her voice wavered and she felt nervous at his closeness, especially after disclosing so much of herself. His masculine scent made her weak in some crazy way. Trembling, she tried to get a grip on her feelings. "Please, I can't do this. I've seen too much—I know what you are."

She moved away from him. *Yet I know nothing about you, not really.*

"Please don't fear me, Jamie. You don't need to—not ever. I'd lose my life before I'd ever hurt you. I doubt you trust what I say, but it's the God's honest truth, and I'll find a way to prove that to you."

She wanted so much to believe him, but found the idea beyond her imagination. "I believe you, Mick, at least, I want to." She looked him in the eyes and did her best to have faith in him. "But aren't you just being grateful?"

"It's more than that, Jamie." They sat there for a while longer. He picked up her hands and looked at them. "There're still pretty sore aren't they?"

She nodded, but couldn't bring herself to mention a word about AIDS.

Despising herself for doing it, she told him even more about herself and uttered a helpless laugh. "My ex-husband said such terrible things about my weight. I have a tough time trying to think any man could find me beautiful."

He smiled at her. "You really don't know yourself, Jamie—*Jamilla*. I see the person you are, and that's the person I care about."

Jamie shook her head in disbelief and helped him up. "We should be looking for something to eat. That's what we're out here for." As she walked beside him, she couldn't help the way she felt—she totally enjoyed his company.

Mick knew the plants and trees and soon spied a small guava tree. The pungent fruity odor permeated the air around it, and birds busily picked at fruit in all stages of ripening. Jamie picked as much as she could carry in her skirt.

She and Mick had eaten several and the juice of the sweet, ripe fruit gleamed on their lips. "It was wonderful to have something so tasty to eat. I'm tired of the steady diet of coconut and glad to have something worth taking back to camp."

They started back. It had been a long day for Mick. She could not take his arm now. He made his own way and she could tell she hadn't needed to hold his arm. Did he merely want to be close, maybe to brush up against her unexpectedly?

*He thinks I'm beautiful! But don't be taken in by a man's sweet words, especially from a man headed straight to prison,* She warned herself. The trouble was she liked the way she felt when near him. Not like the way it was with Moran.

*I never felt excited and trembling inside before, but this tall, black-eyed devil makes me weak all over. I cannot be gullible that way again— no more. I must be on my guard against a man I know full well is evil. Moran was cruel— but Mick—no way in hell..* She frowned. She felt so tired, and now this.

Tears filled her eyes and she kept ahead of Mick so he wouldn't see them. Hadn't she been a fool once? Mick had to be the worst possible candidate for male companionship a woman could find. His involvement in criminal acts made Moran look like a plaster saint.

The four met again, and compared their findings. Jim and Felicia set five large round fruits on the ground and told of a tree with large green globe-like growths suspended from ragged looking branches.

"The tree was wide, tall, and dark green," Jim said, "with large, split, leather-like, prehistoric looking leaves. Never saw anything like it before."

Mick identified their find as breadfruit. "These are fairly common in the islands and are a favorite food among the native people. I don't know how they're prepared, I've never had them. How'd you get them down?"

"I climbed pretty high. Jamie, you could've had another patient." Jim laughed as he nodded to her, pleased they'd found something edible—another food source.

"I carried two of them," Felicia proudly exclaimed. "The skin was rough against my poor burnt arms and they have a sticky white sap." She laughed. "I hope the taste will be worth the effort, and it's good to know they're food."

They ate several guavas immediately, assuaging their constant hunger for a short time. "Well, it looks like we need a fire if we're to bake these green things. At least, I think we bake them from what I read. How do we manage that?" Jamie looked at the others. "Any Boy Scouts good at rubbing sticks?"

Mick stepped up beside her. "Jamie, if you'll reach in my left front pocket, I had a lighter in there before all hell broke loose. I think it's still there. I don't know if it'll work, it had a good soaking." He smiled and a devilish light shone in his eyes. She didn't want anything to do with his front pocket, and he knew it. "I can't get it with the right hand and my left arm isn't up to par." He held his weakened arm out of the way with his right one.

Jamie shrugged and, flushing scarlet, approached him. She wanted to kill him, while absently remembering he still needed a sling.

"I don't think he wants me reaching in there, and maybe not you," Jim whispered to Felicia, a wide grin across his face. "It looks like Jamie's elected."

Felicia hid her grin from Jamie. "I hope there's a lighter in there for his sake," she whispered.

They watched as Jamie, acutely uncomfortable, face reddened, neared Mick from behind. Her discomfort was enjoyed by everyone with tightly constrained humor.

Cautiously, she slipped her hand into Mick's pocket and felt it glide past hard, solid muscle until she touched a metal object. She brought it out very carefully, but not before feeling the burning heat of his firmly muscled thigh. The flush over her cheeks, and the pursed set to her lips, testified to her embarrassment.

It was a lighter, and, if it worked, they'd have a fire. Mick, very quiet about the whole episode, wore a wicked smile, suppressed with tight lips. His black eyes glowed with deviltry and Jim saw it, too.

They gathered firewood, set it up, and flicked the lighter. It worked! As the fire slowly took off, it seemed to content something inside them, and they waited anxiously with the prospect of hot food.

Mick agreed with Jamie about roasting the breadfruit in hot coals. He thought that would work.

The women went out for more coconuts and something to eat from—plates? "I think Mick has a thing for you, Jamie," Felicia said, walking on the beach. "He watches your every move."

They walked along the firm sand looking for anything useable.

Jamie sighed. "I don't know. It's just the situation we're in. He's just grateful I saved his life, but in a nightclub in Papeete, would he see me at all? You are forgetting what he is, aren't you? And don't forget how big I am. It may not make a lot of difference here, but I'll bet it would in another setting."

"It's easy to forget everything, where we are now," Felicia replied. "I suppose you lose your perspective in a situation like this. I like Mick. The way he seems now, it's hard to see him as a criminal. We haven't seen any sign of a deviant sort of personality, not that I've ever been on speaking terms with any. He's very knowledgeable, seems well educated, certainly well spoken, and very good looking in his dark, mysterious way, in case you haven't noticed."

Jamie sighed "Just my luck to find a great guy and he ends up in prison." She believed him a criminal. There'd been no evidence to change her mind on that.

They didn't find any dinner plates lying on the beach, but they took several more coconuts back to the camp. Felicia laughed. "Guess what, guys? We found more coconuts." They were able to laugh about it and the fire cheered them with a hospitable light in the growing darkness.

Jim wrapped three breadfruits in large leaves, raked out a pit, laid them into the coals, and heaped more over the top. They waited for at least an hour for them to bake. It was all so primitive, but no one voiced thoughts on that.

They put the breadfruit onto a large flat rock and opened them with Mick's red knife. It was strange tasting, starchy, and a bit sweet, but edible and nourishing.

"It needs butter and salt and pepper. Sour cream, too," Felicia said. "Here we are eating with clam shells like some lost tribe."

They all felt better. Their spirits were lightened by the infusion of actual food. Their hunger pangs had gone away, if only for the present.

"Tomorrow we need to catch some fish or crabs," Jim said to Mick. "We need protein, and soon. We have these two small nets from the rafts. Do you suppose we could rig up a way to net a few fish? There're plenty out there. In fact, I've never seen so many beautiful tropical fish, not even in an aquarium."

Mick laughed. "How're you are at spearing fish? It's a good way if you can get the hang of it. We can make a few spears in the morning. Jamie's got the knife." He gazed at her sitting near Felicia.

It was drawing into night, and a few stars appeared through the huge canopy of leaves. The moon wasn't fully up, but would be, as the night progressed. They decided not to put up the tents. It was warm and balmy, with no signs of rain. The women settled on one side of the fire ring and the men on the other.

"I really want a shower and my hair feels grubby again," Jamie whispered to Felicia.

"Me too," Felicia murmured, half asleep, "but I'll wash first thing in the morning. I'm so tired. This physical stuff is wearing me out. I'm still sunburned and I wonder what's happening to my complexion." She nestled into the soft leaves. "This isn't too bad, is it? I can't stop thinking of my king-sized mattress at home." A few tired tears escaped into the leaves below as she sank into restful slumber.

Jamie tried to sleep, but rethinking the things Mick had said to her made her ever more confused and determined to keep her distance. It could only lead to heartbreak, and who needed more of that? She closed her eyes, trying to sleep, but her troubled thoughts would not allow the rest she sought.

Later, hearing soft sounds of snoring and deep restful breathing, she raised her head and looked about. In the quiet darkness, with a sliver of new moon showing, she slipped out of the camp and went toward the beach.

She stopped to wash in the tiny stream, taking off her skirt and top. After rinsing her hair and body, she felt re-

freshed and whispered to herself. "I wish I had some shampoo and body wash, but it still feels wonderful."

After enjoying the few moments of privacy, she dressed
and headed toward the lagoon. Walking out on the beach in
the faint moon-glow, she moved slowly along the soft sand
for a while, then selected a patch and sat down, hugging her
knees to her chest. She gazed dreamily out over the quiet
waters of the lagoon. Small waves lapped gently at the
sandy beach, while huge rollers crashed out on the reef,
causing the dull roaring sounds that never ceased. "Here I
am, becoming accustomed to the sounds of the surf," she
mused. "Imagine a girl from Denver feeling a kinship with
an ocean."

She wondered how this adventure would ultimately end.
*Where will we be a month from now?* Though deeply tired,
it felt good to relax and think through all that had happened.
It was bizarre and unbelievable. She shook her head, her
drying hair bouncing into curls. Relaxed, Jamie drifted
deeper into her reverie.

"Jamie—*Jamilla*? Are you all right?"

Hearing Mick's voice, Jamie's heart raced madly. He
moved toward her, softly calling her name. She saw his tall
frame outlined in the faint moonlight as he drew close.

"Just having a little down time, Mick. It's peaceful, sitting here watching the moon on the water."

Tremors of fear shot icicles through her. He'd sensed her
absence and followed her like a predator tracking prey. His
lean face looked wolf-like in the dim light. His hair was
loose, several days' growth of curling beard graced his jaw,
and white teeth gleamed in the soft moonlight against his
dark, features.

"Couldn't sleep?" she queried, trying to calm her racing
heart.

Had he seen her with her clothes off, bathing by the little
stream? She easily imagined him standing in the shadows
watching her.

She wondered, but hoped the darkness had shielded her

naked body from his prying eyes. Just now, she was too tired to care.

Mick settled himself on the sand beside her, his right arm slightly touching. She caught the nearness of him, his masculine scent, and felt the familiar tug on her senses. A sudden heat coursed through her body and, catching her breath, she sighed. *I should be on my feet, running for all I'm worth,* she warned herself, yet made no move.

# CHAPTER 11

You left camp," Mick said. "I had to be sure you were all right. You've had so much put on you these past few days, you're bone tired." He leaned into her side a little. "I worry about you."

She felt the warmth of him, wanted to move away, knew she should, but she didn't—she couldn't.

Chills raced through her momentarily. He'd watched her bathing. Did he stand quietly in the darkness, watching her bend to dip water and, arms high, poured it over herself. The light was dim. She shrugged. *I may be getting smaller each day, but there is still quite a lot of me, maybe there were only shadows for him to see.*

Jamie felt good sitting against him. Tears filled her eyes. She put her head on her knees and let go. Mick pulled her head against his chest, holding her with his good arm. "Go ahead, Jamie, don't mind me. It's okay." His voice, soft and crooning, comforted her.

"Thanks, Mick, I'm sorry to be such a cry baby. I can't imagine what came over me." She dried her eyes on her skirt and laughed. A long forgotten glow of happiness came stealing over her. His soft voice, his closeness, brought feelings that were new to her—she'd never felt this way. Jamie looked at him. "You asked about me, and I've told you more than I should, but what about you? How did you come to be involved with the drug trade, and the terrible people we saw? It doesn't fit with the way you are now." She gazed into his darkly gleaming eyes. "I swear I'll never tell anyone what you say."

"There are things I can never tell you, Jamie, or I would, but I can tell you some of my life." He smiled at her. "Of all people, you've the right to know about me. The Chinese have a saying. *If you save a life, that life is yours forever.* You've saved my life, Jamie, more than once.

"My boyhood was in Quebec, Canada. I'm French Canadian. Strange, a guy from the frozen north bumming around the South Seas, isn't it? I'm thirty-four, never married. My lifestyle makes that impossible. Lately, I've had thoughts that way," he finished with a whisper and tightened his arm about her. She tried to move away, but he held her close. "Don't move yet. Stay here with me. I need this feeling of closeness, and I believe you need it too. If I could, I'd keep you here with me all night long. It feels right, being together like this."

Her thoughts swam in turmoil. *Oh, yes, I do know how good it is, Mick. It's wonderful, but has to stop. I must move away from this warm, strong body that makes me weak, before things get out of hand. Get a grip, Jamie, you fool. We haven't been marooned that long.*

"Mick, I'm glad you can't use your other arm."

She'd loosened her resolve too far already. She hated her weakness, but smiled into the darkness, hoping he didn't see it. Jamie realized, he really hadn't told her who he really was. *What's the man hiding? Who is he?* Would she ever know?

They sat together in the dim moon-glow a long time. Being close and touching, a comfort she couldn't bring herself to give up so soon. Listening to the roar of waves breaking out on the ragged coral reefs brought back the memory of the day they came safely over it. Jamie fought the warm lethargy creeping over her, while sitting against his hard, strong body. She shouldn't stay close. It was a mistake and one she'd vowed not to repeat. "I think it's time we went back now,"

Mick ignored her comment. "Remember the day we came over the reef?"

"How could I forget? Jamie replied. "I'll always see that jagged coral inches below our raft. We were lucky that day."

He tightened his arm about her shoulders. "You worked so hard to save us. I'd like to say more, but not now, maybe never. You're really something, Jamie girl."

Starting for the camp, Mick suddenly pulled her close and found her lips with his. Jamie struggled, but his arm was a band of steel holding her. His lips closed over hers with a narcotic-like effect. A burning weakness swept through her, drugging her senses, sapping her will.

She struggled free of his kisses, her heart pounding wildly. "Stop it, Mick, please. I can't do this. It's no use."

"I couldn't help it, girl, and I can't help how I feel about you." He spoke low, his face close, his dark head bent down to her. He held his long body pressed closely against hers while she cried silently.

"We don't even know each other. How can you say these things? If we continue with this, I'll be hurt, and I can't bear that again. Please." She pulled away from him and started down the beach. Tears she tried to hide slid down her cheeks.

"I told you I'd never hurt you and I meant it," Mick crooned, close behind her.

Jamie tried to hurry, but he stayed close until she finally let him take her hand in his. They walked together back to camp and settled to rest, believing the other two never knew they'd left the little campsite.

Jamie's heart, full of confusion and wonder, slowly returned to normal as she lay beside Felicia, listening to the soft sounds of sleep from her and Jim. Yet sleep evaded her. She lay awake thinking of Mick's burning kisses. *We've only been here a few days—how could I let that happen?* She couldn't think about it anymore, or about being hungry, or lost on a deserted island.

She finally fell into a restless sleep.

Mick lay in the soft leaves, remembering how soft and full Jamie's lips had felt beneath his. *Just a little more and she would have opened them for me.* His thoughts were of her wide, thick-lashed, gray-green eyes, and her warm soft lips. *What the hell is happening to me?* His mind was in turmoil, his body tight with arousal. It was hours before he slept.

€∙∂€∙∂

Ravenous hunger turned their thoughts to catching fish. They were aware of the weakness creeping into their bodies from lack of protein, and fishing took priority. While Jim hunted for slender, straight branches to make spears, the women made breakfast of guavas, coconuts, and left over breadfruit.

Felicia's eyes darkened with worry as she looked at Jamie. "We need something more than this to eat, don't we?"

"That and so much more, Felicia."

Felicia shrugged. "I'm going to wash up and help Jim make spears. He might need help."

"I'll join you."

They headed for the stream. Seeing the sagging fabric of Felicia's green shorts, Jamie offered. "Felicia, let me cut some new buttonholes for you before those shorts fall off. I believe you're growing smaller by the hour."

"Take a look at your own clothes, my dear," Felicia replied. "Your skirt is hanging below your emerging hip bones, and I see a prominent cheek bone showing, too." She pointed at Jamie's sagging skirt. "You need buttonholes yourself." Felicia laughed and flipped her hair in the breeze. "I never cared about being thin, but I do believe I'm going to like it. Wonder what I'll look like."

Jamie looked at her. "Really, am I looking thinner? I was always slim in high school and college, but it got out of hand after I got married." She hadn't said anything about that to Felicia, but now bound together in a way never imagined, she knew they'd always have ties to each other. She decided it would be easy to talk to Felicia about personal issues—if the need arose.

Jamie watched Felicia joyously caper around the little water pool, her sunburn nearly healed into a glowing golden tan. The pain of her fiery, sunburned arms and face forgotten, the young woman's buoyant spirit emerged.

"Jamie, you grow slimmer and more beautiful each day, and don't think Mick hasn't noticed." Felicia busied herself, washing her person with her clothes on, while tossing out teasing comments. "He has his eyes on you every minute. What are you going to do about him?"

"I discourage him at every turn. When we're rescued, they'll arrest him, won't they?" Jamie answered, half-heartedly washing herself as her mind lingered on the searing kiss from Mick's firm, sensuous lips, and the mind-numbing effect it'd had on her. She frequently imagined him being led away in handcuffs and knew it'd cause unbearable pain to see him that way.

Allowing such feelings toward a known criminal, she believed her perception of decency had changed drastically in only a few days of being cast away on a lonely island. But Jamie couldn't shake away the feelings aroused by Mick's kisses. She must keep enough distance between herself and Mick and avoid being alone with him. If not, she feared losing the control she had worked so hard to attain.

She and Felicia started back to the camp, dripping wet, and refreshed. They found Jim working straight, thin branches, stripped of bark. He did his best to fashion sharp points on them.

Mick sat against the bole of the huge sheltering tree. He offered a suggestion. "Put them in the coals for a bit to harden. They'll be stronger and work better." He wanted to help, but could do little.

Jamie noticed he used his left arm more. Some strength

had returned. It increased daily. It made her remember how his good arm felt around her, holding her like a steel band. She flushed, thinking of it.

She went to Mick. "Let me see your wounds." Carefully removing his shirt, she noticed again his long, smooth, back, nearly hairless, unlike his chest, which had a mat of dark curly hair.

The wound, noticeably smaller, with only a slight drainage, looked to be clean and healing. She knelt in front of him to check out the knife wound she'd made while taking out the bullet. It had closed.

"This one is closed now and won't need a dressing," Jamie told him. "We'll have to watch that the back one stays open until it's healed down deep." Aware of his dark eyes gazing into hers, she heard his slow, deep, breathing as she worked. Even that small amount of closeness made her feel giddy and self-conscious. She felt the heat rise over her face in a full blown flush. "Mick, stop it, will you?" she warned, her voice low. "How can I take care of your wounds if you keep staring at me?"

She couldn't stop the flaming heat creeping over her features, and knew the man enjoyed his effect on her.

"You're doing beautifully. I won't look if it bothers you." Mick closed his eyes, his long dark lashes rested against darkly tanned cheeks. "But I do enjoy looking at you. In fact, I never tire of it," he added softly.

Jamie had no answer to that. She rose and went to the lagoon to clean his dressings in the salt water. She'd never asked him about AIDS and decided she wouldn't. It was not a subject easily brought up and, somehow, he did not seem like someone who'd get a transmittable disease like that.

She returned to redress the back wound, worried that keeping it wet so much wasn't a good idea, though it seemed to be working. He'd healed quite well, and she was proud of the care she'd given him.

"Let's try these babies out," Jim announced. He hefted the spears, and they all set out for the lagoon.

When Mick took a spear, Jamie wondered if he'd be able to use it. A pang of guilt swept over her, knowing she watched Mick almost as much as he watched her. She found it difficult not to watch him.

"Look at Jim's walking shorts," Felicia whispered to her. "They're hanging off his hips. My, aren't they narrow, compared to the breadth of his shoulders? I love the solid way he's put together, powerful, but so gentile. He's a man a girl could trust with her life." She caught up with Jim. "Hey, Big Jim, it looks like you'll be Slim Jim soon. If you get any thinner, Jamie can make you new buttonholes. We had to, our clothes were falling off."

Jim laughed. "Well, I'd love to see that!"

He gazed warmly into her lavender eyes and Jamie saw they'd grown much closer—like she was to Mick? Was being lost together the catalyst? Felicia had the most beautiful eyes Jamie had ever seen. Was that what drew Jim? He watched Felicia constantly, too.

They spent the next few hours wading in the lagoon, trying to spear fish from among the many brightly-hued creatures flashing through the clear waters. They stared in amazement at first, ashamed to kill something so beautiful. But hunger prevailed, and they got busy.

Jamie laughed joyously. "If this lagoon was a municipal marine tank, people would eagerly pay to see such fantastic fish. They are glorious!"

Spectacular the fish might be, but they represented food and, after many misses, Jim finally speared a large flat, brightly striped fish. Elated with his catch, he waded ashore. His ruddy face bore remnants of his sunburn and his light blue eyes shone with pride as he held out his catch. He laid the fish up high and went back for more. "Hey check it out. It's a good one."

Mick got a couple more to add to the catch. Jamie had no luck, nor Felicia, but they enjoyed the clear warm water. Watching the men, Jamie thought Mick handled himself rather well for a one armed man. She enjoyed the sight of wet jeans clinging to his wiry frame. His were loose too.

When they had several good sized fish, Jim cleaned them and they all went back to camp, an even more cohesive group. Unable to conceal their jubilance, they'd lost some of their fear, knowing they would not starve.

They hastily made a fire, baked the last two breadfruits, and all the fish, wrapped in large leaves. Eating as much as they wanted, and with appetites sated, the tired four sought their beds of leaves. Jamie had no thoughts of her father or even Mick as she succumbed to contentment. She fell asleep as did the others. They slept deeply, like exhausted children in their own beautiful Garden of Eden.

# CHAPTER 12

Dawn flushed everything rosy, turning the island into a fairyland of color. They quieted their ever present hunger with fruit and bits of breadfruit. The fish were finished last evening. Jamie wondering what else they'd find. She sensed the men had something on their minds. The infusion of protein last evening had renewed their strength, and, with their faces set in concentration, they decided on a plan.

The men sat down with them. Jim spoke first. "We need to decide on a plan if the smugglers come here looking for survivors, for one thing. We need a signal fire to attract a friendly ship or aircraft." He frowned. "For some reason, we haven't seen any sign of searchers. It appears no one's looking for us. We haven't seen as much as one search plane or a passing ship since we came here. It may be too soon or they may not know what happened to the *Ilikii*." He rose to his feet. "We need to see what else is available to eat on this island. Enough food for four mature adults definitely requires more than we've had so far."

"Let's finish exploring as much of the island as we can," Mick put in. "We must survive here until rescued. We might find fruit trees or maybe taro patches. If this island is or has been used as a garden area, we might find goats or pigs. They're common on these islands and survive on their own. Let's climb the highest outcropping and have a good look around. We might find a cave. They're often found on these atolls if there's a decent rocky formation." He looked them in the face, his eyes narrowed. "We may also need a place to hide one of these days. We have no arms for protection."

Jim lightened the mood. "You girls can catch us a couple of pigs for dinner in your spare time." He chuckled, hoping to ease the seriousness of Mick's words.

"Jim, you're having us on," Felicia cried out. incensed. "You can't expect us to tangle with pigs."

Her lovely eyes went wide and Jamie stifled a hearty giggle.

Jim laughed, but he was serious. "I'd say a pork chop would go good about now, but we can hold off on that." He sat beside Felicia, giving her shoulder a friendly little nudge. The warmth and regard between them had increased, which cast Jamie into Mick's company that much more.

She waited with an edge of anxiety to see who went with whom on this excursion, fearful of being alone with Mick again.

Jim settled the question. "We'll go together and see the same things. If we pass the breadfruit tree, I'll get a few more down." He helped Felicia to her feet. She leaned against him and smiled her thanks for the assist.

Mick, observing the look of relief crossing Jamie's face, smiled. His knowing look brought on a few vicious thoughts on her part. He watched constantly for an opportunity to be alone with her. She spent as much effort avoiding just that.

He stalked her with his eyes, but it no longer frightened her as in their first days on the island. Though she was drawn to him, he reminded her of a wolf on the prowl. The dangerous attraction between them kept her thoughts in constant turmoil. Before they set out, she went to the little stream and filled the two buckets with clear, sweet water.

As they left camp, Jamie had one, and Jim carried the other. She noticed his big hand dwarfed the wire handle attached to the plastic bucket.

Occasional clouds floated across the sun, and they walked leisurely in a delightfully dappled landscape of shrubs and trees. It was warm, but the continual flowing trade winds kept it from being hot. Tropical birds called and scolded as they flitted through the trees, their names unknown to the four walking by. Their brightly colored plumage added to the magical charm of the lush island and lifted the spirits of the stranded survivors.

The wonderful scent of flowers pervaded the air about them. They neared a small spreading shrub-like tree covered with waxy scented blossoms. The heavily scented blooms had yellow tinged centers. The air was especially heavy with their odor.

They breathed in the heady perfume. Felicia plucked off a blossom and held it to her nose. "They smell so wonderful. Aren't these the same flowers they put around our necks when we landed at the airport, you know, the flower leis?"

"They are Plumeria, or Frangipani, the natives say," Mick offered. "They grow like weeds in the tropics. You can't eat them, but they do have a great smell." He picked a few sprigs of the fragrant blossoms and handed them to the women with a sly wink at Jamie. He was rewarded with a flush across her cheeks.

The women breathed in the incredibly sweet scent as they walked rather briskly along. The intake of protein had restored some of their flagging strength, and they moved with ease among the Frangipani, some a deep pink, some yellow, or waxy white. It added to the gaiety of their mood.

Except for constant hunger, they'd recovered from their recent experiences on the rafts. Memories of the poor souls on the *Queen Ilikii* lurked in their minds. No one mentioned it. Those thoughts, far too painful, were left unspoken.

They came to the breadfruit tree with its prehistoric look. Though interesting, their interest in food sources made botanical species less important.

Jim climbed again for the large green fruit. "I made it up

before without falling, so here goes again!" He took one of the nets for a bag.

Mick, tired, pale and sweaty, rested as Jim moved about the huge tree. The occasional branch cracking made Felicia gasp in alarm.

For a big man, he made his way about the tree handily, though the branches bent and cracked under his weight. Jamie saw Felicia unconsciously beam with pride at Jim's agility, while she frequently wrung her hands at his danger.

"He's a regular Tarzan up there, Felicia," Jamie remarked.

"Be careful, Jim," Felicia warned as she stood under the huge tree and held out her arms out, as if to catch him, should he fall.

A short while later he lowered himself to the ground, branches cracking and giving beneath him. He carried several of the large green globes in the netting. He set them down and heaved a sigh. "I wish I was sure how to tell if they're ripe or not. I picked the biggest I could find. There's plenty more up there. I hope we aren't eating some native's food supply." He laughed, slightly out of breath. "We can get these later. I don't want to carry them all over the island."

They continued on. Jim and Felicia kept together. Being close to Jim caught most of Felicia's attention. Jamie accompanied Mick. She avoided intimacy and did not initiate conversation.

He knew what she attempted and Jamie, seeing the devilish smile playing about the corners of his mouth, understood his thoughts. Troubled, she walked with him through the dappled, shady undergrowth.

When Mick slowed his pace, she wondered if he'd tired or was trying to put more distance from Jim and Felicia so he could talk to her. *He'll start saying things I dare not hear.* Worrying about that, she noticed they'd started upward. The climb would tire him, but he needed to get the lay of the land from the highest point on the island. It wasn't just a man thing. Jamie wanted that, too.

Mick gasping, tired and breathless, leaned against a handy tree, his face pale and sweating. "Jamie, hold on a bit. I have to catch my breath."

She'd wondered if today's search of the island would be too much for him. She faced him, keeping her distance. "Are you all right? Can you make it to the top? Do I need to help you, or would you want to wait here and rest?" She stepped around to his back, checking his wound. It was seeping a little, and she rebound it. That was all she could do for now. "Your wound is okay for now." She felt him shiver at her touch.

"I'd like to make it to the top if you'll help me. It might be a good idea if I could take a look around from up there." He shot a look at her from beneath his brows. "You're not afraid of me after the other night, are you? Not the bravest woman I've ever met." He chuckled softly. "That meeting on the beach was wonderful, it sort of squared things for me—maybe for you."

Jamie stood her ground, feeling the heat rise on her neck. "Certain things scare me to death if I don't know how to handle them." She couldn't give herself away and hid the way he set her soul on fire. Even now, being close to him made her feel weak and confused. Hopeless heartache was all he could offer. She was no stranger to that kind of pain. She'd only met him a few days ago. —He was a total stranger. The few facts he'd given about himself told her less than nothing.

Jamie sighed. "Come on, you've had a little rest, let's make it up there."

She took his right arm and they slowly made their way to the top. Traces of a faint trail, long unused, lay before them, and they followed it. It was not terribly steep. Mick walked steadily with her close by his side.

The warmth of him, and the male scent of him, filled her mind once more. He needed help with a round of bathing. That was part of him too. Everything about the man affected her deeply. The spell of him overshadowed her senses every time she came near him. She believed he cared for her. It was in his eyes. *Damn,* her heart cried. It made keeping an emotional distance more difficult. They plodded on, following the faint outline of an ancient trail. Jamie prayed they'd reach the top soon, as his breathing became increasingly ragged.

She finally heard Jim say, "Hey, there you are. Good show. Worn out, are you?" He reached out a hand to a pale, sweaty Mick. Beads of sweat dripped from Mick's brow.

She indicated a large rock to rest on. Mick sat down and panted for breath. "Thanks, Jamie, I couldn't have made it up here without you."

She nodded to him and went to stand by Felicia, heaving a sigh and shaking her head, trying to clear away her confusion over Mick. "So, what are we seeing up here?" she asked. The flowing breeze ruffled her dark curls, cooling her brow.

The updraft of balmy air carried the briny scent of the ocean, flowers, and greenery as it wafted up the side of the outcropping where they stood. Birds cried out, scolding them as they flitted and wheeled about on the updrafts. Their cries warned away the human intruders of their island home.

"There is water in every direction," Felicia murmured. "This island is very beautiful. The colors are so vibrant. We are standing on a tiny bit of lost earth in this huge ocean. There's nothing out there. How will anyone ever find us here, Jamie?" Her troubled question spoke for all of them.

Jamie looked about. The entire island lay below her—green, tiny, and lonely, lost in the vastness of an endless blue-shadowed ocean. The scent of Frangipani drifted upward on the blessed cooling trade winds. "You can smell those flowers way up here, Felicia. They must be everywhere on this island and we never noticed. We looked for food and nothing else." She sighed. "Felicia, someone will come and find us. We cannot disappear without a trace and no one searches for us. These are modern times and such things don't happen. My father must be out of his mind by now with worry—your family and Jim's too." *Does anyone miss Mick*, she wondered. *Does anyone wait for him—a mother or sister waiting somewhere perhaps, if not a wife?*

"Well, let's hope you're right. My mother—Oh, Jamie, I can't even think of what she must be going through. I'm not cut out to be an island girl and who knows how long our clothes will hold together? My heavens, we could be running around naked if we're here much longer!" Felicia couldn't help an escaping giggle at the vision of the four of them in the buff, going about their daily tasks. "Can you envision a scene like that?"

"You and your ideas!" Jamie joined her in a helpless giggle at the suggestions. Her spirits, ever uplifted by Felicia's vision of things, soothed her desperate worries. She had a way of lightening a situation. Jamie felt an increasing tenderness toward her. "If I had a sister, I'd want her to be like you, Felicia."

How would their adventure end? Would they be searched for? Would anyone come to find them—ever?

Jim and Mick sat together, looking at their surroundings. They sat atop a high outcropping of rocks, possibly a remnant of some ancient volcanic event of eons past. Mick nudged Jim, pointing to a small mass of yellow-green trees. "Down about there, looks like a banana grove. If so, that'll feed us a little better. We might find some animals, but no sign of any so far."

Jim followed Mick's line of sight, squinting against the sun. "I hope we do find something more. See anything else, anything familiar, any landmarks?"

Mick laughed. "I see a helluva lot of water—that's familiar, but nothing to tell where we might be. These low islands are all similar, mostly coral atolls, and there' are thousands of them scattered about. This one is likely northeast of Tahiti, but we can't be sure because the storm blew us about. I've wondered about that old trail on the way up here. If people lived here once, I wonder why they left?"

"I saw that too," Jim said. Then he voiced an idea. "We'd best build a signal fire and have it ready." He looked about for anything that might burn. "Not a lot of wood here. We'll have to carry it up and cover it against rain. We can manage that."

Mick agreed. "We'll have a trial run, and find a faster way up." He pointed downward. "The breadfruit tree is right there. This island is less than a mile in length and narrower in width. It's small and not all that high if a typhoon blows in." He indicated the backside of the island. "Take a look over there. No landing in that surf. On this side, we have a lagoon and a break in the reef. This other side makes a good barrier. Smugglers can't land there where we'd never see them. It'd make for a hell of a landing. Those waves will smash a small boat, or a big one."

Jim looked at Mick then at the women, laughing and talking together, and felt sick inside. "And if they do come? We have no weapons for defense."

Mick frowned deeply, considering the consequences of meeting the smugglers again. "God help us, right now, I don't know. I was hoping for a cave of sorts. If we find one, we could erase all trace of our presence and hide until they gave up searching." He knew those people well, had met them face to face, and been shot escaping. The bloodthirsty thugs held little value on human life. He wasn't worried for himself. They'd quickly kill a male witness, but he knew those lovely women would face a long, devastating, and terrible end.

# CHAPTER 13

L ooks like you've rested some." Jim stood and gave Mick a hand to his feet. "I'm not Jamie. How'd I do?"

Mick punched him gently and laughed silently, a devilish gleam in his eye. He pointed toward the green grove. "Look down there, ladies, bananas."

Their eyes followed his waving hand.

Felicia's hands fluttered as she looked downward. "I hope so. They're good and no cooking. I could eat a dozen right now, especially the small ones." Her hair tangled about her face, and the silken strands floated up on the breeze. Jim, watching in rapt fascination, stumbled over a rock.

Jamie walked with Mick, descending the same faint trail but on the other side of the outcropping. She wondered about it. "This trail means people lived here in the past, or they come here at times. But what people?"

"I wondered about that, myself," Mick replied, carefully picking his way. "Shrubs have grown into this trail so it hasn't seen use for quite some time."

They descended without incident and entered the yellow-green grove. They found more than thirty graceful, serrated, fan-leaved trees. Excited, the women rushed from one to the other finding the most edible fruit. They had a picnic in the shady, park-like grove.

"No one's been here or harvested these in years," Jamie

said with sadness, realizing again how isolated their island haven had to be.

They found fruit in all stages, from green to having dissolved into moldy refuse. The air was heavy with the odor of it. The trees wore tan raggedy skirts of dried leaves. Old growth had died, leaving their lonely skeletal remains to molder away and eventually feed the eager growth of the new shoots, loaded with bananas in many stages of ripeness.

Tiny cloven tracks were present, mostly covered with refuse and leaves. Jim pointed at them. "Looks like our meat supply just got a whole lot better."

"Sure does. Ever done any pig hunting, Jim?" Mick returned.

Jim shrugged and laughed. "Not lately, but we will, and damned soon.

"It's a great find," Mick replied. "We can mention pork a bit later to the ladies. Time enough for that when we hunt them. Wild pigs can be damned nasty."

The woman collected bananas, and Jamie's skirt became the carrier. Her bottom, nicely outlined by the skirt pulled up in front, did not go unnoticed by Mick. He couldn't take his eyes off her undulating hips, moving enticingly in front of him. She walked ahead, blissfully unaware.

Mick's wide grin, unseen by Jamie, made Jim smile and shake his head. He understood. He had eyes for feminine beauty wherever he found it as well.

Heading toward the camp, they heard snuffling sounds in the scrubby brush ahead and froze in their tracks. They broke into smiles seeing a black baby pig run squealing out of the underbrush followed by a large black and white spotted boar.

Its ugly yellow tusks gleamed in the sunlight. It halted, glaring at them with narrow little eyes before charging into the underbrush.

They heard other pigs scuffling away.

"Well, Jim, there's pork chops on the hoof." Mick

laughed. "Those babies are wild as hell—you'll work hard for them. Look at them go!"

Several pigs ran through an open area some distance away.

"It's good to know they're here," Jim said. "We'll see how desperate we get for something besides fish. Man, living here is one hell of a challenge."

The day had grown warmer and he wiped sweat from his ruddy brow.

"Would you really kill one, Jim?" Felicia looked up at him with troubled eyes. "That baby one was so cute."

Mick suppressed a grin. Felicia was a city girl with no exposure to farm animals. Jamie had hunted with her father in the Colorado Mountains.

"We'll see, the big ones aren't so cute. They can be downright mean if you get between them and their young. You girls remember that if you meet one on the trail. Stay away from the babies," Jim warned. "I know some about them. My uncle Ed raised hogs for market and butchered for their own use. I was a kid, but I still remember the butchering process. It was a long while before I could eat pork again."

"Here's the guava tree we found yesterday, or was it the day before." Jamie inhaled the fruity aroma near the tree and picked some of the nicer guavas to add to the bananas. "We need to record the days. It's hard to keep track of time."

"I don't think it matters much what day it is," Felicia said, "but you have the knife, Jamie. You could notch a tree or something when you aren't cutting new buttonholes for us. It's hard to remember how long we've been here. I didn't know much for a day or two at first, remember?"

"I believe I could use a new buttonhole in my jeans, Jamie," Mick said.

They howled with laughter, unable to help themselves. Jamie joined them.

Embarrassed, she knew Jim and Felicia were well aware

of the attraction between herself and Mick. His black eyes were on her as he laughed. Reading Mick's thoughts were nigh to impossible, but she liked the way his face looked when he smiled. He was very handsome when his eyes crinkled at the corners that way. It changed everything she believed about him.

They headed back to camp with all tensions eased. They'd found another food source, two, if they counted the pigs. Jamie's spirits soared for the moment. They enjoyed a considerable level of respect for one another. Each had something of value to offer as individuals. They worked well together, an unusual occurrence for total strangers thrown together in a bizarre, survival situation.

They were tired when they reached camp, but Jim stood. "I'm going back for the breadfruit. If you have a fire started, we'll have dinner when I get back."

Felicia sighed, looking after him as he walked away. Jamie wondered if they were in love as she went about collecting sticks and dry twigs. Felicia joined her.

Mick lay on one of the tents. Tired and sweating, he watched the women laughing and chatting as they put a campfire together. How many days had it been since the *Ilikii* sank to her watery grave? Lost in thought, he mused. *The best part of my life began that day.*

He observed them. *They're unaware of the striking physical changes in themselves, but their beauty grows by the day. Felicia is a knockout with the weight or without it, but the more she loses, the more stunning she becomes. The biggest plus of all, she's a great person. Jim is one lucky bastard. She's totally gone on him and she's right for him. Jamie, bless her heart, she's right for me. She has no idea how she looks these days, beautiful, tanned, and strong with a new reserve of determination she never knew she possessed. It's not her looks so much. She's just one hell of a woman! I'd hate to lose sight of her now that I've found her. I couldn't handle that—not anymore.*

The women had the fire flaming up nicely, waiting for

coals to form, when Jim returned. He brought up larger chunks of wood and placed them on the fire. They lay down on the tents to rest, tired from their exploring.

Later, Jamie went to Mick. "I need to see how your wound is before it gets any darker." Kneeling down at his back, she carefully pulled his shirt off and began to unwind the strip of cloth. She noted with dismay how terribly stained, frayed and worn the material had become. "How is it?" she asked.

"It's a little sore. Today was hard on me, but it was a good day though, wasn't it, Jamie?" He knew his voice affected her, but she made no answer. Her comforting hands on his back spoke for her.

She removed the soiled dressing with gentle hands and left to wash them in seawater. She returned later to place the freshened, though filthy appearing dressings, over the wound. She tied it with the old strip of her skirt. "Your shirt is a disgrace. I'm going to wash it now before we have dinner. Tomorrow you'll need help with some sort of bath." She said it low in his ear, not wanting to call attention to it. She'd be the one helping him and nervously regarded what that might entail.

She left, and a gnawing sense of loss settled over him as she walked away. He shook his head in wonder. *You poor old sod, you can't bear to have her out of your sight.* He didn't follow her. *If she gets up and goes out on the beach, then I'll sure as hell follow her. A bath—hmm? I'll be waiting for that.* Riotous feelings took over, as he gave thought to Jamie assisting him with the cleansing of his person.

She returned and hung his shirt to dry away from the smoke. He watched, his dark eyes hungering constantly for the sight of her. He muttered a soft, "thanks, Jamie," and saw the warm flush creep over her face.

Later, waiting for enough coals to cook the breadfruit, a heavy, drenching, rainsquall swept rapidly over the island. They grabbed the tents for cover as water literally poured down on them.

Suffering from a lack of preparedness, they'd not had time to plan for everything.

"There goes the fire," Mick called out, "pile some leaves over it before it gets too soaked. Maybe we can save some coals. My lighter won't last much longer." He struggled to attempt it, but, one-handed, accomplished little.

Jamie and Jim rushed to comply. Felicia huddled under the tent cloth trying to keep the rain off. It wasn't big enough and her feet stuck outside the shelter. The rain was warm—everything in the tropics was warm.

Daylight faded, and their fire was out. In the darkness, they tried to set up the tents but, having no poles, gave up. For the remainder of the deluge, the women huddled under one tent draped over their shoulders. The guys sat out against the huge tree. When it was over, everything was soaked. The leaves were wet and uninviting for use as beds. Big drops splattered down on them, a lingering remainder of the drenching downpour.

Felicia whispered to Jamie about the comforts of her home in California. "I don't mind so much being here, because of Jim. As much as I would like being home right now, I love it that I'm here with a guy like him. Jamie, I think I'm in love. He's a wonderful man. The first time I saw Jim, I wanted to go out with him. I hoped we could have a date in Papeete, now here we are." She shivered as she sat close to Jamie, hugged her soaked knees, and brushed off wet leaves, her hair, a sodden, dripping, mass. "What'll happen to us, lost out here on this little island?"

"Felicia, I know how you feel, believe me, I do. I wonder about my feelings toward Mick. He tells me how much he cares for me. He lies in wait like a dark, slinking wolf. I'm falling in love with him, but he's just grateful I pulled him out of the ocean. How can I know what he really feels? And look what he is. We saw him in action. I must not care for him. How crazy would that be? What idiot would fall for a guy with his record?" Jamie glanced over her shoulder, her voice low. "At least with Jim, you have a chance for a good life. He's solid as a rock. Mick, when rescue comes, will be taken straight to prison and me? ' Headed straight for heartbreak. I don't know how to handle what's happening."

Felicia put an arm around Jamie. "Well, let's just take one day at a time. I will say this. Mick is one handsome dude, even with the scraggly mustache, and several days' growth of beard. I'd say a woman could risk getting hurt with a man like that. Besides, we don't know the whole story on him. Remember, my dear, we only get one lifetime for living. You can't run and hide forever."

"Maybe so, but falling in love with Mick would be a lot like jumping into shark-infested waters. You want to take bets on my chances for survival?" Jamie shivered involuntarily, thinking of her body being torn to bits by sharks. How often they saw them cruising in the lagoon and were careful to avoid contact. Mick had warned Jamie to take care while washing his dressings, because sharks easily caught scent of the tiniest amount of blood in the water.

The rain stopped, though the occasional stray drop splattered down from the huge tree above. They spread out the tents and lay down on them. Jamie felt a new closeness to Felicia since they'd shared some of their feelings. Settling side by side into deep and dreamless sleep, the hoped for dinner of breadfruit lay uncooked. Hunger, no longer a stranger to them, was the new norm in their lives.

Mick sat with Jim under the big tree, watching the women huddling together on the tent fabric. Low whispers, and occasional giggles, escaped them. Little was said. Each man had his own thoughts. Increasingly hungry as hell, a banana or two had been their pathetic dinner. Of the small variety, two or three wasn't enough.

Mick lay awake for a long time, waiting to see if Jamie would go out on the beach again. When he was sure she was sleeping, he positioned himself the best he could.

Jim lay snoring softly beside him. They needed to plan against the possibility of smugglers searching for them and, in the morning, he and Jim had decisions to make on that. Mick worried most about the women. He knew the unspeakable things that would happen to them. Long hours passed, mulling over their potentially deadly situation, interspersed with riotous thoughts of Jamie. It was long into the night before sleep came to him.

# CHAPTER 14

Mick came awake in the early dawn at Jamie's soft touch on his shoulder.

"Let me see your wound." Kneeling at his back, she unwrapped the dressing. He felt her brush against him, and her soft breath on his skin. It made his hair prickle and shivers course through his body. But he caught from her attitude that she was all business this morning and made no move to catch her intimate attention. "Humm…looks better each day," she said. "I'll just redress it." She left his side to go to the lagoon and rinse the dressings.

Mick watched her walk away, enjoying the sight of her. He wondered when he was going to have the bath she'd mentioned. He couldn't help his wide grin or stop imagining just how she'd go about it.

Jim took the leaves off the fireplace, looking for any signs of warm coals. "Any Boy Scouts in the bunch? If this fire is out, we'll be having sushi from here on." He poked about hopefully, but the rain had drowned the fire and all the coals, leaving a soggy mess of half-charred leaves, burnt sticks, and ashes.

Mick remained sitting, awaiting Jamie's return from the beach. "Don't worry about a fire. There isn't anything to cook for breakfast. We can fire it up later when we bake the breadfruit. My lighter should be good for a while yet, but when it's gone, there's no corner store to buy another." He beckoned for Jim to come closer. "Today, let's map out a plan in case the smugglers come looking on this island. We owe it to the girls to keep them hidden away if the smugglers come here." He shuddered. "The things they'd do to these women—God! They'd off us fast enough, but not them. We have no defense."

Jim's features grew ashen, his lips tight. "You got any ideas? I'll try anything you'd like to suggest, any damned thing at all!"

"Let's follow this stream to its origin and look for a cave. We need a place to hide if we're threatened, or at the very least, a place to hide the women."

Jim assented with a nod and took up a water bucket.

Jamie returned to dress Mick's shoulder with the soaked fabric. "Your shirt got even wetter in the rain last night, so you'll have to go shirtless a while longer." She re-used the stained and fraying strip of her skirt to tie it in place.

Fruit and coconut made their breakfast. They were used to eating lightly. Felicia laughed, pointing out that coconuts contained saturated fats. "When we get back, we'll need our cholesterol levels checked."

Jamie thought her face had tanned nicely, the sunburned face and arms already a distant memory.

Jim told them to try fishing while he and Mick checked around. "We'll look upstream today and maybe find something more for eats."

Mick handed Jamie his lighter before they set out.

Jamie and Felicia laid the tents out in the sun to dry and took up two of the spears. "The guys looked rather serious this morning," Jamie said. "What are they worried about?"

"They probably didn't sleep so well, with the rain getting everything wet and soggy." Felicia laughed. "Maybe they're just grumpy. My father got like that if he didn't get enough sleep." Her mind on other things, she pulled the waistband of her green shorts out. "Look at this! Got the knife? I need another hole cut in this waistband. I haven't had a waist this small since the eighth grade." She giggled and skipped toward the beach.

"Here, let me do it and I'll cut a new one for me." Jamie enjoyed her friend's high spirits. "It's not the small waist that's got you going, is it? It's Jim."

Felicia laughed, tossing her hair in the sunlight. "I believe it is."

The tide was in, and they waded about in the crystal-clear waters, trying to spear fish. The waters of the lagoon were shallow and warm, and the fish plentiful. Jamie finally speared one and was jubilant over it. "They aren't where you think they are. The water changes the way things look." She showed Felicia where to aim. "There's one—take a stab at him."

The rainbow-hued fish flashed away leaving Felicia's spear empty.

Jamie scored another fish and kept it on the spear until she laid it on the sand. She caught several more and Felicia speared a scarlet striped, flat fish which sent her into a tizzy as it struggled on her spear.

"I've never done anything so grand, Jamie."

They cleaned their catch and tossed the refuse into the shallow water. Horrified at how eagerly the smaller sharks flashed after the fish entrails. Jamie exclaimed, "I wonder if throwing the refuse in the water is a good idea. Won't it bring the sharks closer?" She really didn't know. After taking a long look out to sea, they returned to camp with their catch.

"What were you looking for out there, the smugglers?" Felicia asked.

"Yes, and thank God, I didn't see any square sails heading this way. I'll never forget how they looked." Jamie shivered, thinking of capture by the wicked-looking sailors they'd seen on the deck of the junk, before they'd shot their graceful little schooner out from under them. "Those smugglers would see us dead, if they knew we still lived." She saw Felicia grow pale, but couldn't help adding, "That would be after they were done with the two of us."

Felicia laughed such thoughts away as they reached

camp. "Oh, Jamie, you're just trying to scare me."

They gathered dry wood to set up a new fire and placed the breadfruit in leaves ready to put them in the coals. Taking the dry tent cloths in from the hot sun, they enjoyed bananas and a guava or two while they waited for the men.

*ം ം ം*

Mick and Jim worked their way upstream, noting a large increase in water flow after the heavy rain of last night. As they reached its source, the flow had slowed into the usual small trickling stream. "Must be a spring coming out of those rocks," Mick observed.

"It comes right out of that big jumble of broken rock." Jim halted near it. "This rock wall looks steep as hell, and I don't see any sign of a cave."

Mick pointed off to the right. "There are a few papaya trees over there. It'll be food, if you like the taste. I can't stand them, personally."

They walked over to see a small grove. By the evenly planted rows, it was obviously planted by man rather than the scattered whim of nature. The bare trunks of the small trees bore a circular crown of leaves with green globular fruit clustered tightly together just beneath. Looking up, they saw numerous ripening golden ripe fruits around the lower edges of the clusters.

Jim contemplated the look in Felicia's big, purple-hued eyes at the sight of something more to eat. "The girls will like these."

Mick touched Jim's arm. "Isn't that a small hole, off to the side of those rocks? Maybe it'll lead to something."

They edged around several large rocks to find a smallish, jagged opening, barely large enough for a man to crawl through.

Jim elected to go in for a look. "If I can get in there, then anyone can make it." He laughed, knelt down, and edged his way through the narrow opening into a cave. Sharp edges of rock scraped against his arms and back. Reaching the inside, he called out, his voice echoing from the dimness of the interior. "The floor slants downward for about twenty five feet. It's strewn with sand and rocks and I can't stand up, but it could be a hiding place. Come have a look."

Mick neared the opening and leaned down to peer into the dimness of the cave. "I can't crawl for shit with this shoulder, but it looks like something we can use in a pinch. In fact, it's great!"

A sense of relief flooded over him, seeing a spot that offered a safe hiding place. Actually, they could all fit into it, and he imagined himself squeezed in there with Jamie some moonless night. The sand was good, too. It'd make a half way decent floor after they threw out the rocks.

"How'd you suppose sand got in this cave so far from the lagoon?" Jim wondered aloud. "Who in the hell would carry sand up this far?"

"My guess is it was thrown up here in past years by a typhoon, or at least a storm of tremendous proportions. Those monster waves carry sand and debris everywhere, and since this is a very small island, they'd easily reach up here. Maybe that happened some time ago and destroyed this low island. That'd explain why people haven't come here for so long. It's possible they believe it's uninhabitable and have no idea how well it has recovered."

Returning, they carried what papayas they could. Mick handled two, using the left arm some. It hurt the shoulder wound when he did, but it was healing well enough, a round of thanks to Jamie.

When they rejoined the women, Mick saw the fire going, and the breadfruit nearly done. God, but he was hungry. "Nice fire, ladies, good going."

Jamie had made good use of the lighter and he was glad it'd been good for another flicker.

Jim told them about the cave. "We need to have an idea what to do if the wrong people come here looking for us.

We'll go up and take a look whenever you want. You need to know how to find it. It's a place of safety. If we are in danger, we'll go inside and pull a screen of brush over the opening." He laughed and held out the papayas. "And look here. We found a small grove up there by the cave. We can hide and eat at the same time."

Felicia said she loved papayas. Jamie looked askance at them. "I'll give them a try." She was happy to see the oval, ripening papayas lying on the leaves before them, green turning to gold. It meant starvation lay a bit farther off.

Jamie told them about their catch of fish and set about putting them into the fire wrapped in leaves. The breadfruit was nearly done and they waited impatiently for the forthcoming feast. Fish didn't take that long to cook.

Felicia beamed with pride when Jim complimented her and Jamie on their catch. Soon enough, the food was cooked, ready to eat, and they were very hungry. Banana leaves were the plates and no storm clouds threatened to drown them.

They rarely felt the comfort of satiety, as they'd had in their normal lives. Finding enough food to adequately sustain them took constant searching. Their bodies had responded to the struggle with increased vigor, a new slenderness, and the consciousness of feeling fit and confident. The daily fight to survive and the constant threat of danger kept them on the keen edge of awareness.

It was late in the day when they'd completed the meal of fish, breadfruit, and several kinds of fruit. Satisfied for once, they felt undeniably good and lay down to rest. For the moment, they felt no worries and sleep came easily to the men.

Felicia and Jamie lay awake whispering to each other.

"I'll bet Mick is hoping I'll walk out on the beach," Jamie murmured. "He'll follow me and say those crooning things again. He makes love to me whenever he gets the chance. It's mostly words so far with his damnable black eyes burning into me like a blazing fire. He always watches me. He follows my every move. I still say he looks like a wolf."

Felicia snickered. "Mostly? Jim and I knew he followed you the other night, but we didn't hear any screaming, Jamie, no cries for help. We knew you were in good hands, even a wolf's." She giggled ever so softly and settled herself for sleep.

Jamie sighed. "I was in more danger than you knew, Felicia. It's good he only has the one arm." She laughed softly. "Now I've told him he needs a bath, and he does, but can't you imagine what he'll make out of that?" She heard the sounds of soft snoring and realized Felicia had joined the others in sleep.

"I'm tired too, and tomorrow will be time enough to worry about Mick," Jamie murmured to herself, turned to her side, and nestled close to Felicia. "I wish I had a pillow."

# CHAPTER 15

They discussed constructing a shelter to keep the rain off the campfire. No one was sure how to proceed. The four spent most of the morning discussing possibilities. They needed rope to put the tents over a branch and tie them down.

"You can make ropes from coconut fibers. I saw it on the Discovery Channel," Jamie informed them. "You beat it with sticks until it comes apart, twist it into little ropes, and then into a bigger one. They do it in India."

"Jamie, you never stop surprising me." Felicia had washed her hair and worked on it with the big toothed comb.

Jim's eyes were transfixed, watching her tawny hair shining in the sun. Jamie, noting the deepening closeness between the two, felt only happiness for them.

But, for herself, disaster lay ahead. Irresistibly drawn into a relationship that spelled heartbreak, she warned herself. *I'm a helpless fool being charmed by a deadly snake.* Her thoughts should have aroused anger, but they didn't. They'd wasted half the day, and Jamie didn't care. Instead, she worried about Mick's bath.

She knew, by the occasional sly looks he shot at her, that he waited for the bath she had mentioned. Her thoughts became increasingly malicious while she busied herself, putting it off. She decided he deserved a shove into the lagoon.

Finally, she came to him. "Mick, I'll help you get

washed up now, if you're ready. Your shirt is clean and dry after the rain."

"Sure thing, I'm ready." He meant that in so many ways.

Jamie felt a burning flush creep over her face. He rose from his matting and came to her. His face expressionless, his dark eyes held that devilish glowing look so familiar it turned her inside out. Mick had a male power that made her feel uncertain and off guard. His very presence could shake her to her knees.

"What about I take these jeans off? I've had them on for so long, they feel damned raunchy." He was serious about it. "I do have something on underneath."

"Well, I suppose." She wondered at seeing him nearly naked. "The main thing is not to get any dirt into the wound, or I wouldn't need to help you with bathing. I'm not taking them off for you," she said firmly. "What about sloshing around in the lagoon first? It would be good for the wound and get a few layers off. You and your jeans are both a mess and need a good wash up."

"I'm not that crusty, but the lagoon sounds great. I'm in favor of that. The water looks clean and clear. It's wonderful. I'll dive in. It'd be good for the wound, and my crusty jeans, too." He tossed his head back, laughed, and Jamie thrilled deeply at the flash of white teeth in his deeply tanned face.

They went out to the beach. Both looked out to sea, searching past the waves breaking out on the reef for signs of passing ships, and the dreaded square sails. Jamie kept an eye out for sharks, worried Mick's wound might draw them.

"I see you're keeping a lookout. Good idea. You're a wonder, Jamie. How many women would think to keep watch like that?"

Jamie walked with him to the water's edge. "Probably quite a few women, if they'd seen how threatening those guys looked. I'll never forget the way they stared at us when they were close to our ship that terrible day. Our lives meant nothing to that malicious lot."

They went out into the warm waters. The tide had come part way in and the waves were gentle. "I'll never get these jeans off now they're wet." Mick laughed and moved closer. "Jamie, you make me forget what I'm doing."

She edged away, keeping a safe distance from him. She had no idea how she looked. Her own wet clothes clung to her body, outlining every luscious, though rapidly shrinking curve. Mick caught every move she made as he watched this lush, tanned goddess walking in the water. Her once-white blouse was of thin stuff and tattered to near transparency. The sight mesmerized him.

"Don't run away from me, Jamie. Could you do something with my hair? It's greasy as hell and itches. I can't do much one handed." Mick moved closer, his hair hanging loose from the usual buckskin thong.

Jamie came to him. "Put your head down in the water and I'll try, but we have no shampoo. I wonder, if we used dry sand, it might take up some of the oils. I've been thinking it could be worth a try on my own hair. It wouldn't be so different from a dry oatmeal shampoo."

Mick bent his head into the water, and Jamie tried to scrub his head with her nails. All the while, he tingled madly at her touch, but resisted grabbing her. It was heavily on his mind. He used all the restraint he could muster as the blood raced through his veins. He fought his wild, rapidly heating urges.

Smiling, she took his right arm. "Let's try the sand, I'm not getting anywhere with this. It might take a while to comb all the sand out." She led him to the beach. "Of course your hair's wet, so I don't know if it'll work."

Mick knelt down and bent his head low as Jamie poured warm dry sand over his head and worked it in. "I think this will clean your hair, and if it does, I'm trying it too." After working the sand through his hair, she instructed, "Let's rinse your head. Keep your eyes shut so no sand gets in." She led him into the water and, ducking his head down, washed the sand away. It took a lot of washing, his hair being long and thick. In a paradise of flaming desire, he endured her ministrations, fighting madly for control.

Jim and Felicia stood in the shade of the swaying palms watching the entire scene. "Jim, what do you think of that?" she murmured. "He's having the time of his life with her washing his hair, and with sand. What an idea! Think it'll work?"

"I've no idea, but Mick's enjoying the hell out her trying, I know that for damn sure. I must say she comes up with some ingenious ideas, the coconut fiber-rope business, and now this." Jim chuckled and slid his arms around Felicia's lush body. "I believe my hair could use some attention too, Felicia, how about it?" He put his lips against her cheek, nuzzled her gently, looked down at her, and grinned.

"Anytime Jim, anytime at all," She put her arms around his big frame and gave him a warm hug. Looking up, so he could see the deepening shades of purple in the depths of her eyes, she mused, *He likes me, I know it, and I more than like him. It may be the spell of being lost together on this island, but I don't think it is.*

Mick and Jamie came ashore, heading for the small stream. They were silent as they walked together, their wet clothing clinging. Jamie's dripping skirt and blouse revealed the still generous outlines of her form, and Mick's wet jeans clung to his spare muscular body as he moved beside her. In a state of total contentment, he urged, "come out on the beach tonight, Jamie—please?" He looked intently into her eyes, his black ones boring into hers.

"I'm afraid of the things you'll say to me, Mick," she protested. "There's no future for me with a man like you. I told you about my marriage. I won't be hurt like that again." But he saw her resolve wavering and knew she'd come out with him.

Jamie pulled away. "Come on then, let's get the salt water rinsed off."

Mick continued trying to convince her. "We can talk about our childhood, places we've liked, anything you want. I won't touch you. I need to know you better. Please, come out, *Jamilla.*" It was a command the way he said it, low and intently.

"You shouldn't call me that!" They came to the stream. "Let's get rinsed off. I'll think about it. You confuse me, Mick. It's hard to think rationally around you." She dipped a bucket of clear water and dumped it unceremoniously over his head. "Let's rinse your hair and the rest of you, then I'll fix your wound."

"Hey, are you trying to drown me?" Mick sputtered. He wiped his eyes, laughing as water streamed down his lean frame into the sand

She feared her action had inflamed him, and the look in his eyes confirmed it.

He clearly wanted to tackle her, take her to the ground, drive her mad with his passionate, burning kisses and more. She knew it, seeing his swelling masculine response.

Sudden fear of Mick's blatant sexuality coursed through her. She quickly turned away, cheeks flaming. *He'd better do his own bathing after this. No matter what I do, things only get more intense between us.* She considered, wavering in her resolve not to meet him. *Maybe we should talk and sort out this thing between us.* Jamie shook her head, knowing she was drawn ever deeper into his web.

She finished the matter by redoing his wound and helping him into the clean shirt. She handed him the big-toothed comb. "Here you go, Mick. Comb out your hair. We'll see if the sand shampoo worked." She looked about for the comfort of Felicia's presence, but she and Jim had gone off together.

"I can't get these snarls out. Jamie, would you try?"

She heard his wheedling tone and didn't believe him for a minute. But she went to him and took the comb. It was what she wanted, too. She hungered to be near him, to catch that mysterious male scent, and revel in his mysterious and wondrous masculinity. Even that much satisfied some longing within her lonely soul.

Her experience with Jack Moran had never made her feel so vibrantly alive. He was the only man she'd ever known intimately. She'd wondered what all the fuss was about. But now, she had riotous feelings, fearful and astounding in their intensity. She craved more of them, despite her fear of the disaster that awaited her with a man like Mick. He drew her to him with every move, look, and gesture. She'd become increasingly powerless to combat her feelings. Fear, her only ally, was fading from her consciousness at a rapid clip.

She knelt behind him, gently detangling his dark and slightly curling hair. It took on a clean, shining effect. "I believe the sand shampoo has done a good job. At least something is going right today." She gave a slight yank. "Your hair is clean."

"I feel clean all over Jamie. If I had two hands, I'd wash your hair. Would you like that? I'd enjoy doing it, oh God—I would, Jamie."

His voice, low and crooning, made her prickle all over. Of the effect her touch had on him, she wasn't sure, but his feelings for her were intense, and growing. She knew that much.

His long back stretched before her, and she remembered how it looked in the water, slick, smooth, and tanned. His wound healed rapidly and his physical strength increased. Would he revert to what she knew him to be a criminal and smuggler?

Strongly drawn to him, yet repelled by what she knew of him, tears formed in her eyes from the intense confusion. It was all so hopeless.

Jim and Felicia came into camp, making enough noise in their approach to warn Mick and Jamie of their return. They brought several more breadfruit and laid them on the leaves.

"Well, how'd the bath go?" Jim boomed out with a twinkle in his pale blue eyes and a wide smile across his tanning features.

"Jamie, his hair looks great," Felicia said. "How'd you

ever manage it?" She finished the comment with a suppressed giggle.

Jamie stood up, looked at the two, and seeing their faces, knew they'd watched her bathing Mick. She flushed at their questions, but grinned, knowing how bizarre the entire scene must have appeared.

"I have my ways, and they work pretty well." She bent down and tied Mick's hair up with the thong. "There, that's you, all set."

"Thanks again, Jamie." Mick returned as he got up. "I see you two have brought supper. I think we could use some protein. I'm going for fish." He nodded to Jim. "Care to join me?"

Taking up the spears, the men headed for the lagoon. Jamie and Felicia sat down together. The day was only half over and they were tired.

They took a couple of bananas to eat as Jamie groaned. "I'm hungry again. You were watching us weren't you?" she accused, but she couldn't suppress a giggle. "Actually, it was fun, but where is this leading? I'm attracted to him, and it gets worse every day. Being with him turns me to water. I like touching him, and I'm glad to tend his wound. In fact, Felicia, I can barely keep my hands off him." She finished her words with a shrug and hopeless sigh. "What am I to do?"

"I know how you feel. I'm going through the same with Jim, or should I say Big Jim? He's not quite so big these days. It's hard to believe a person could lose so much size in such a short time." Felicia smiled, her eyes warm with understanding. "Think of yourself as a very old woman, Jamie, when you look back on this time, how do you want to remember it? That you were afraid of a handsome devil named Mick and never found out what might have happened between you?" Felicia grew serious. "I don't want you to get hurt either, Jamie. I suppose I shouldn't say these things, but there's something very strong between you two.

Jim and I see it every time you're near each other. And frankly, I think he's rather a decent sort."

"Felicia, I feel that way, too and I'm more mixed up than ever." Jamie laughed but felt sadness with her mixed feelings. She sat there, picking up leaves and laying them out in a fan shaped pattern. Her head was down and the sun gleamed off the dark curls as she shook her head in confusion.

"Let's eat more bananas, or a papaya. I'm hungry again too, and it's so long before dinner. That is, if it doesn't rain, and the smugglers don't come." Felicia laughed. "I'm getting used to not eating much, but I feel wonderfully well. This could get to be a habit."

"We know what it is, Felicia, and it is not the lack of food. You're the lucky one. Everything is right for you and Jim. For me, nothing is right, it can't be. But I'm really happy for you. So tell me, how *is* it with you two, anything happening?" Jamie had a wide grin on her lips. "I could use some good news about now."

"He makes me feel like a million. When we're alone, he holds me and says wonderful, loving things. We've only just met and I already want him in the worst or maybe it's the best way. We haven't reached that point. I think he's worried about our being marooned here for a very long time, who knows? It could be years. Maybe he saw *Blue Lagoon,* and worries we'll have a two-year-old child before anyone rescues us." She broke into a helpless laugh. "We don't know when we'll get off this island. If things keep on, I guess he won't care. Then it'll be, look out, lady."

"You're no help, Felicia." Jamie joined her in laughter, tossing banana peels into the fire pit. "Let's get some firewood anyway."

Moving together in their quest for dried sticks to burn, they walked farther each day. Nearby wood had been used up. It required more energy for fuel gathering, as well as the constant hunt for food.

❦❧❦

Mick and Jim worked at spearing fish. The sun rode high and hot, clouds gathered on the horizon. The tide was full, but waning. A good breeze ruffled the lagoon's surface into little waves. Palm trees swayed languidly in the steady flow of the trades, and no ship was visible out beyond the booming breakers. Looking had become their unconscious habit since Mick had made them aware of the threat square sails meant.

"We're in for another downpour by the looks of those clouds," Mick offered. "Let's rig up a shelter. My shirt is clean and dry and I'd like to keep it that way."

"Let's rig up those tent cloths into a lean-to under the tree. For sure, we need to protect the fire since I'm not up on rubbing sticks," Jim said as he left the water. "We've got a few fish—I'll clean them to bake before the downpour."

"Maybe Jamie will make us some of that rope she was talking about," Mick said with a grin. "She comes up with some fascinating ideas."

"I wish we had some rope. It'd make everything easier. Actually, there are those lines around the rafts. Why not use those until she makes us some," Jim said with a laugh. "She's quite a girl, Mick."

The dark-eyed man nodded in agreement.

The men returned to the camp and saw the generous pile of firewood.

"All right you two," Jim said. "We'll get some food on as soon as this fire gets going. It looks like another storm coming. Maybe we'll get it cooked before we get rained out."

Jim stirred the coals into a fiery bed and placed new fuel on them. Then he checked the amount of rope-lines strung along the outside of the rafts. He pulled them out of the loops and laid them out for inspection.

"It looks like enough to tie up some sort of shelter,"

Mick confirmed. "I'll go see if I can find a few poles." Before starting out to find something to use, he nodded to Jamie. "Maybe you could help me?" He looked at her, his eyebrows raised. "I only have the one arm."

His voice had that wheedling tone again. Jamie found it amusing since Mick wasn't a man who needed to plead for anything. She sighed and followed him out into the underbrush. "Okay, Mick."

Jim and Felicia looked at each other. "That man uses every imaginable excuse to get Jamie off alone, can you believe it? Jim, will she be all right with him?"

"He's so gone on her, it's all he thinks about," Jim replied. "If he truly loves her, I don't think he'll hurt her. He gave me his word on that in the beginning. And, for whatever kind of man he is, I believe he meant it. Let's not worry about her just yet. She's a grown woman. Let's hope she can handle the situation." He looked into Felicia's eyes to see the worry she felt for her friend and nudged her shoulder. "Hey, I know just how Mick feels, Felicia, God help me, I do. Come on then, let's get this rope together."

They worked, making a shelter from the two small tents as storm clouds thickened over the lagoon.

Felicia felt her heart soaring at Jim's words, and wondered. *Is he saying he cares for me?* So enthralled at the thought, she was of little use to Jim as he worked with the rope lines. Her heart rate had elevated several points, and she fluttered about trying to be helpful. Jim grinned at her in appreciation, and Felicia flushed pink in response. He finally conceded they needed the poles.

# CHAPTER 16

Jamie followed Mick, searching for small trees that would make tent poles. "These look usable. Maybe we could knock off some of the branches," Mick said, turning one over with his foot. "What about this one?" He smiled at her. "My hair feels great, Jamie, you're ingenious."

She grinned, staying out of reach. "Talking about your hair isn't getting any poles, Mick, but I'm glad it's clean."

They sorted out several. The poles needed trimming, but they had no way to accomplish it. Mick tucked three under his right arm, and Jamie gathered as many as she could drag. They headed toward camp with their find.

"Will you come out to the beach, Jamie? The moon's getting bigger every night. It'll be beautiful out there." Mick halted, looking into her eyes. "We need a place to talk. It seems like we never get the chance anymore."

"Anymore? We haven't been marooned here that long. How many days has it been? Or weeks? I lost track of time, days and days ago." She gave him a direct look. "And yes, I will come out. We need to sort things out. Something's happening that I don't understand. We do need to talk." She kept her distance and backed away when he advanced toward her.

Her face had the determined look Mick had become familiar with. She was strong-minded about most things, but he'd rapidly figured his way around it. "I'll watch for you."

He smiled at her, but she turned away to drag the poles toward camp.

Jamie's shoulders slumped forward and her head bent as she walked. Mick thought she was depressed. The air was heavy with the scent of Frangipani, but she didn't seem to notice as they returned to camp.

Mick and Jamie brought in their poles and laid them down. Using his big foot to break off as many branches as possible, Jim fashioned a teepee-like structure, tying the poles together at the top with a bit of rope. They laid the tent cloth over it and tied it on using the grommet holes. Jamie used vines to add to the rope supply.

The approaching storm increased in intensity. They huddled inside the flimsy shelter, hoping the flap over the fire pit would salvage the glowing coals. The breadfruit and fish were baking. The group hoped to have hot food this time, in spite of the heavy deluge pouring down on them. The tent leaked, yet kept them partially dry. They laughed at themselves in their puny efforts to thwart the tropical elements, but the flap over the fire successfully kept much of the rain off their cooking food.

Snug under the flimsy shelter, Jamie felt Mick edge nearer.

He longed to touch and hold Jamie, but was forced to wait until she met him on the beach. He had to be content with moving as close as he could without her noticing. Jim and Felicia sat close together, with no one getting bent out of shape. *Jim is a lucky bastard. He can be in the open about his feelings.*

The storm was turbulent, but short-lived. They left their leaky makeshift shelter and crawled out onto the soggy leaves. From the huge tree above, thick drops splattered down on them while Jamie and Jim dug into the baking food. She put Mick's fare on a wet leaf plate and brought it to him. They ate well for once, using their clamshells for spoons, and had a merry, if soggy, dinner party, lit by burning dry leaves from beneath the makeshift tent.

Jamie noticed that Felicia stayed near Jim so much more lately. This placed Jamie more in Mick's company. She understood, wanting the best for them, but the hopelessness and fear of her relationship with Mick tortured her. Terribly drawn to him, she longed to feel his arms around her and revel in the comfort she found there. Yet, within that steely embrace, she faced unbelievably risky consequences.

Later, as they lay down to sleep, Jamie's heart raced in anticipation of meeting Mick. She waited until she heard the deep, heavy sounds of restful sleep. The sky had cleared and the others slept on what dried leaves remained.

After long moments, she cautiously raised her head and looked at the sleeping figures lying near. Was he one of them? She wasn't sure.

Quietly she made her way out onto the soft sandy beach. The tide was far out, and the remaining tide pools gleamed in the moon's soft glow. Waves crashed out over the reef, but now she saw them as a protection against the smugglers.

"Jamie."

The low whispered word told her Mick approached. Her heart began pounding as he approached.

"Don't run away, girl, come with me. Let's walk a little ways down the beach."

He took her arm and they walked together. It was warm and peaceful with only the crashing surf thundering out over the reef. She didn't hear it anymore in her excitement at Mick's closeness.

They neared the half buried log and Mick led her to it. "Let's sit here a while." He nudged her to sit and sat close against her.

Jamie felt herself coming under his spell and had no defense against it. His scent filled her with mind-numbing weakness. *If he only knew what he does to me, I'd be totally lost. Oh God, it feels so good! I long to be totally immersed in the glowing heat of him, I crave it. I only hope I can hide my feelings.*

"Jamie, are you well enough? You seem so down at

times. I'd like to make things easier—make things right for you." He spoke softly, carefully putting his arm around her.

Holding her, he realized she'd grown even more slender. A tall woman, her head fit just below his chin. Inhaling the scent of her hair, he reveled in the glossy strands, but refrained from laying his head against hers.

"Mick, how could you ever make things right for me? You know what I mean, your lifestyle and everything." She put her head down and leaned forward, elbows on her knees, her chin in her hands.

He reached for her, lifting her face to his. "No matter what happens, you can believe this. I swear to you, I'll never hurt you. I couldn't. Things might happen that will make you hate me, but remember what I'm saying, right here, tonight. I care very greatly for you, and it will come right in the end. I swear it, Jamie girl, you are my dearest, most wonderful woman." Mick drew her close, kissed her cheek, and tasted her tears.

"How can I possibly believe you, Mick? I so want to, I do." Jamie cried, her resolve crumbling, as she turned to him. "You're a drug smuggler and a criminal.. We saw what you did. How can you ask me to believe what you say?"

The moon's glow fell on her tear-stained face. He kissed her gently on the lips and held her snug against the long length of his body. She let her tears flow and, with them, her fatigue and fear. Laying her head in the curve of his shoulder, she let her thoughts run riotous. Her heart raced and her body glowed. *Oh God, if only all this were true and he was an honorable man. I'd be the happiest woman in the world. I care for him, but I'd be out of my mind to let him know it.*

"Mick, I have to tell you. I fear completely what's happening between us. Yet, I can't help enjoying the time we spend together. I want to be with you, caring for your wound, even washing your shirt—all of it. I wish we could be together, but how could that happen?" Jamie raised her eyes to his. "You give me the feeling of hope, where there is no hope. What are we to do, live for the here and now? For a woman, that's a dangerous thing. You know my past. I will not suffer the pain of another unfortunate alliance again, not ever!"

"You care for me, Jamie, I know you do. We'll get out of this. Remember, no matter what happens, please do not lose faith in me. This will work out for us—you'll see when it's over."

He pulled her close against his body, lowered his lips to hers, and kissed her long and deeply. Urging her lips open with his seeking tongue, he kissed her fully, working against her fear until finally Jamie responded with frantic whimpering, clinging desperately against him.

Only a will she never knew she possessed kept her from going on into utter madness with him. "Please, oh please, Mick. Stop!" she cried, struggling to break his embrace. "I don't know how to fight against you." She wiped away her tears and straightened up. "I'm sorry, I really am."

"I'm sorry, Jamie. I couldn't help that. My God, you make me happy, and I haven't known much happiness in my life." His voice, hoarse with passion, reached to the depths of her soul. "You don't know what you do to me, girl."

"Mick, we must stop meeting out here. You have some crazy power over me. It must be some sort of madness that overtakes people thrown together this way. I've tried to hide it from you for so long. I feel happy when I'm with you, even with the clouds of hell and damnation hanging over us. If we don't stop what's happening between us, they'll engulf what's left of me." Jamie drew back and looked at him. "I've tried so hard to keep my distance, but I could sit here with you all night." She shook her head in disbelief. "What am I saying?"

"It's more than madness, Jamie. There is something, a deep bond that has formed between us. Remember what I said about the old Chinese proverb, 'You saved my life and

I belong to you now'? We're bound together, girl, one way or another." He held her close, his head on hers, breathing in the scent of her hair. "I don't want to risk hurting you or to take advantage of you. I am trying, but for whatever it's worth, I'm all yours, Jamie girl."

With that, Jamie knew he cared for her, and her heart soared. She stirred in his arms, causing a wince of pain to his left shoulder. "Oh, I'm sorry, Mick. You're getting more use of your left arm and I forget it's still tender." She looked up at him. "We should go back, don't you think?"

"Yes we should, but I need another kiss from you first." He pulled her closer against him and kissed her mouth, her cheeks, her eyes, her hair, and started downward. His seeking lips moved lower into her half-open shirt until he came to the soft fullness of her breast.

"Mick, please stop while we can. We can't go so far. I'm afraid of what will happen. I'm not sure I can trust myself around you anymore. Please—please, Mick." Jamie pleaded with him, struggling in his arms, until she felt his grip relax. Getting to her feet, she couldn't help the mischievous grin spreading over her face. "Come on, Mick. Let's try to get some sleep."

Against all reason, she was happy. Her heart soared with a glorious sensation, new and wonderful to her.

He got to his feet and held out his hand to her. Together, they made their way along the beach. As they walked, he caught her in his embrace again and again, and when they came into camp, he kissed her again before he let her go.

Jamie moved away, trying to shake off the intense feelings Mick aroused in her. She couldn't stop her riotous thoughts. They were almost constant. *If this keeps up, I know what'll become of me. Oh God, I know it! I constantly crave his attentions to me, and knowing what he is doesn't seem to matter. I've sunk so low. I can't stop what's happening and throwing coconut husks at him doesn't help. I've got to stop playing the fool.*

Jamie lay on her bed of leaves, dry enough despite the

earlier shower. The tent idea had kept off most of the rain. Her mind raced in turmoil over her relationship with Mick. She'd never imagined possible the torrent of emotions he'd aroused in her. She knew without a doubt it would lead to more and more until they went all the way. She also knew she'd never regret making love with him. In fact, she'd die unfulfilled if she never knew that kind of passion.

Her marriage to Moran had been empty of love from the beginning, and she realized it all the more now. She curled up close to Felicia hopefully to sleep, her mind full of visions of herself in Mick's passionate embrace, trying to blot them out. It was late before she finally slept.

Mick sat against the giant spreading tree, his mind racing with passionate thoughts, remembering Jamie's soft lips burning against his. He watched her lying so still, trying to sleep, and knew she wrestled with their new relationship. Could he keep his distance when they were together constantly? He'd try for her sake, but a man could only hold back so long. His eyes took in the shape of her, barely visible in the darkness. He imagined holding her beneath him, and kissing her into submission. *God help me, I can't stop thinking about it.*

# CHAPTER 17

Jim bustled about the camp and had a fire going, though there was nothing to cook. "Let's check out the cave and see about setting up a signal fire. We've been lazing about too long and need to get it done. These girls need to know where the cave is and how to find it. How's that with you, Mick?"

Jamie was eager to check out the cave and each of them hoped they'd find another food source as well. They fished daily for the protein they required and ate their catch almost immediately. Spoilage prevention was important. They'd learned that rapidly enough. Nothing lasted long in the tropics.

They ate a banana or two and more coconuts.

"We'll do that, and bring back some food while we're at it." Mick looked sleepy-eyed. "We're running short by the look of it." He got up slowly, looking at Jamie. An infectious grin crossed on his lips. "My shoulder feels a tad sore this morning."

Jamie, husking a coconut, threw a bit of the husk at Mick, which he dodged with a joyous laugh. "I see you move pretty fast. Your shoulder's doing well enough, looks like to me." She chuckled softly as she came close enough to have a look at the wound. "I'll re-do this dried up dressing. Your wound looks good though. What have you been up to anyway?"

Jim glanced at Felicia, eyebrows raised. He couldn't

voice the thoughts running through his mind, but Felicia knew them. Feelings ran high between Mick and Jamie, a new intensity. Felicia saw it and so did Jim. They knew Jamie met Mick out on the beach late at night. He'd discussed it with Felicia. They worried she was getting in too deep with a deadly criminal, but they also knew something incredibly strong had happened between them. Jamie, as a grown woman, should be able to manage a relationship. But with a man of Mick's past—

"God help her," Jim breathed. He went on with the plans for the day. "You girls need to know about the cave. It might be a hiding place for us if the wrong people come looking here. We can worry about food after that, maybe catch a couple of pigs for supper. How about it, Felicia?" He raised his eyebrows at her, his lips spread in a wide grin. "I'm sick as hell of fish. We have it every day. I could do with a pork chop or two."

Felicia laughed. "I'd like to watch you catch a pig, Jim. How will you go about it? Jamie hasn't made us any rope." She gave a squinty-eyed smile to her friend. "You might use some of that coconut husk you were throwing about."

"I haven't had time," Jamie retorted, her features flushing rosy.

"Been busy, huh?" Jim put in. He ducked when Jamie threw a husk at him. "Hey, save that energy for pig wrestling." He laughed and dodged another husk.

"Give it a rest, you two, and I'm not messing with pigs. And neither would anyone else with a lick of sense."

Mick enjoyed the exchanges between Jamie and her friends. He couldn't defend her without adding to her discomfort. She'd faced their growing intimacy, and could hide it no longer from Jim and Felicia. She continually avoided him, yet was irresistibly drawn to their meetings on the beach. He hoped they'd walk out on the beach again tonight.

He'd never felt such an intense need to be near a woman, to see her, watch her move, or hear her voice. It was a deep longing, new for him, instinctive and compelling. He wanted her.

Jamie returned, silently knelt at his side, and redressed his wound. "You heal fast Mick. Soon you won't need a dressing." She tied the dressing on with the old, stained rag she'd torn from her skirt so long ago.

"I'll be sorry to have this end. I've enjoyed your care of me. It could get to be a habit I'd like a lot."

He spoke low, his soft tones caressing her with every word, and she didn't mistake it. In spite of her knowing his part dealing with the Oriental smugglers, and the sinking of the *Queen Ilikii*, he hoped to gain her trust. He hadn't expected the drug exchange at sea. Not their usual routine. Someone else had pulled those strings, with unforeseen and devastating results, to Mick's bitter regret.

They headed for the cave, with the men in front. Felicia laughed, swinging along, tossing her hair in the sun. She grinned at Jamie as they deliberately lagged behind to talk. "Look at my waistline, check this." She pulled her green shorts out. "I can take up at least four more inches—any looser and they'll fall off. I think I've read somewhere that starvation changes your metabolism. Do you think that's possible?" Felicia grew serious. "I've never ever been thin, even as a child or in Junior High. I never really cared. How long have we been here, anyway?"

"I don't know. I've lost track of all the days or weeks," Jamie replied. "You look good, Felicia. You've always been a beauty, but with the weight loss, you could win any beauty contest going. You know they stress emaciation these days," She was glad to have her mind off Mick "My clothes are looser too," she said. "I'll soon be back to my old self." *Older and wiser. But where am I headed?*

"Say, did you cut a buttonhole for Mick's jeans?" Felicia queried with a penetrating look at Jamie. Far from the men, they discussed personal things freely.

"No, but if I don't soon, we'll be in for a show. Mick, and Jim too, their pants are hanging on them." Jamie laughed and grew thoughtful. "Will we starve here? I worry about it. We're continually hungry. The food we find seems nutritious enough, but there's so little of it," she finished quietly.

"You're stressed, but it isn't the lack of food," Felicia said. "It's that mysterious dark-eyed devil, Mick. Don't worry about never being rescued yet. We'll be searched for. Others may have been picked up by now, that is, if there *were* others." Her face paled. "What if there weren't? We could be stranded here for years, Jamie. Oh, God. As much as I like being here with Jim, I'm no cave woman," she cried, upset at her own thoughts.

Jamie threw an arm across her shoulders. "You're right Felicia, let's not worry about it yet. So far those junk sailors haven't come here, so it could be worse. Hey, how about being stranded here with big, fat Niko or the Filipino guy, how about that—can't you just picture it?"

Felicia couldn't worry for long, and burst into a laugh, envisioning them on the island with those two. "I wonder what food we'd have. Who knows what they eat? You'd have the Filipino and I'd get Niko. You know they like the bigger women. It wouldn't be the same, would it? I doubt you'd be out on the beach at night with the Filipino guy."

Jamie flushed, aware that Felicia knew about her beach outings with Mick. "I guess things could be worse. I'm not doing so well, keeping my distance. He's different from any man I've ever known. He knows what he wants and never holds back. My resistance melts like snow in a flaming bonfire, the way he is with me. He makes me feel drugged or something. Thank God, one of his arms is weak, it's my only defense." Her woebegone tone of voice betrayed her weakening resolve. "Oh why doesn't someone come for us? I don't know how long I can hold out against him."

"Jamie, he's all man, and they have their ways. If they want you, it's almost impossible to say no, especially when they look like Mick—Jim, too," Felicia warned, grinning from ear to ear.

The guys were out of sight, but the women could hear their deep voices and the occasional cracking of a branch up ahead.

Jamie frowned. "I don't know why no one is looking for us. We've not heard so much as a plane in the sky. Why wouldn't we see an airliner—or a sign someone is searching for us?" she added with a sigh.

They worked upward along their faithful little stream toward the high outcropping of rocks. The low murmur of the men's deeper voices became more audible as they got closer to them. "We're getting there," Jamie said as they came into an open area to see the papaya trees. "Look how many there are. We'll have plenty of these, if you like them. I don't, but I'll eat them because they're food." She wrinkled her nose, her feet crunching on dead leaves beneath the small trees.

She saw Mick lounging with his long frame against a large rock. His hair gleamed in the sunlight. It looked clean enough, but she guessed he'd want her to clean it again. The sand shampoos worked so well they all used her method these days.

"Come up here and have a look at this cave," Jim said as the women joined the men. He indicated a wall of rock with jumbled, broken boulders piled above it. It looked like it could come crashing down with the slightest jarring of the earth. He took Felicia's arm and guided her toward the cave opening. "It's just up here behind these shrubs. We can hide in here if the need arises. It only needs a bit of disguising, maybe a screen of vines or shrubs."

Mick stepped up to assist Jamie, but she walked ahead, ignoring his offer. "You'll have to crawl in. I couldn't, my arm still hurt like hell the last time I tried it." He came close, and his nearness sent a searing heat flickering through her. She heard him breathing just behind her.

"Maybe you could do it now, Mick, your arm is so much stronger." Jamie faced him and looked into his eyes, trying to be firm. "Want to try it?"

"You bet I want to." He grinned, his black eyes burning deep into hers.

A few loose strands of hair played about his face, his firm lips widened, and the indentations along his jowls deepened. Were those dimples? She wasn't sure, but it added to his devilish look. Wild alarm bells clanged inside her. She knew what he wanted to try.

"Oh! Do you never quit with your innuendos?" She felt like kicking him in the shins, but it'd only add fuel to the flames that burned behind his gleaming eyes. Shaking her head, she turned to look into the darkness of the small cave. Mick kept close behind. Acutely aware of him, she could change nothing.

Jim and Felicia sat near the opening, and Jamie knew they'd watched yet another intimate interchange between herself and Mick.

"It isn't very big," Felicia said. She looked at Jim. "Could we all fit into it?"

Her eyes were big, and the color especially wonderful today. Jim tried to remember what she'd asked. Her eyes had a way of making him forget things. "It goes back pretty far, we can't stand up in it, but there's room enough if cozy sounds okay to you," he replied when he'd collected himself. "It needs a bit of cleaning out. Maybe we could get it straightened up today—toss the rocks out, anyway—and have it ready in case we need it."

Jamie loved the intense interaction between her friends and believed Jim saw himself crowded in there with Felicia. "You mentioned a screen to hide the cave entrance. We'll leave that to you fellows." She turned to Felicia. "I don't believe I've ever been in a cave. Come on, let's see what we can do with it."

They picked their way over the jumbled rocks, bent down, got on their knees, and readied themselves to enter the cave.

"You think there're bugs or bats in there? I don't think I'd like that. Smugglers would be better than bats—or snakes." Felicia stared wide-eyed at Jamie, a definite look of distaste on her face.

"We'll see, but probably not. Jim didn't mention any from the other day. Would you really prefer the smugglers to bats or snakes?" Jamie laughed, a nervous edge to her voice. She hated crawly things too, and a cave seemed right for such.

Jim tried not to watch as the women knelt down to crawl into the narrow opening, but the temptation was more than he could resist. Fascinated by the rolling motion of feminine behinds, neither man looked away while the women worked their way into the cave. Jamie went in first and Felicia followed. They had no idea of the entertainment they provided, and Jim understood the burning glow in Mick's eyes.

Jamie went farther into the darkness of the cave. Tossing away the scattered rocks, she sat down in a cleared area. "It looks cozy enough, but it could also be a terrible trap with no way out. Let's look back as far as we can. I wish we had a flashlight. Too bad the one in your raft never worked."

In time, her eyes grew accustomed to the dimness of the cave.

"I wonder why there's sand in here, it's not near the ocean. Did someone haul it up here?" Felicia picked a few more rocks away and sat down. "That crawl in here was hard on the knees, but this does seem a good place to hide. Of course, as you say, it could be a trap."

Adjusted to the diminished light of the cave's interior, they saw walls of seamed rock with irregularities jutting out in spots. It wasn't musty—a definite advantage.

"These rocks must have fallen down this way eons ago, creating a small cave," Felicia continued. "It's dark in here, but not unpleasant, a haven, if we ever needed to hide."

"There's not much light, but let's see what else we can find." Jamie turned to crawl farther back. "This wall is the end, but there's a side cave back here. I see a dim light coming from it." She moved out of Felicia's vision.

"I'm right behind you, Jamie. See anything yet?"

"My eyes are adjusting to the dimness. It's much bigger back here, lighter too, and I can stand upright..." Her voice trailed off.

Felicia followed, crawling around the corner of the cave wall. "You're right, it is bigger here. It's a real cave. I never thought I'd get excited over something so pre-historic." She entered the area, got to her feet, and looked around in the dim light. "Isn't that a brighter spot up there?" She pointed upward to an area of dim light that made it possible for them to see the interior of the larger cave. Look, it's almost like a window that lets in light."

Jamie looked up to see a ledge of rock jutting out over the room. "So it does, it might be another entrance or something. Even if it is, we could never get down here from up there. There's no way up there, either. We can tell the guys what we've found, anyway." She turned to peer into the dim areas around the edges. "I wonder what else we might find, Felicia." Moving slowly, hands outstretched, she felt her way. The thought of touching something gross was on her mind, but she kept on, hoping to find something of use. They had so little.

Felicia followed Jamie as she searched the cave interior. "Ouch! What is this?" she exclaimed. "It almost broke my ankle." She reached down to find a rusty looking object, half buried in the sand, and held it out by the splintery wooden handle. "I think it's a shovel."

"Used to be, it's sort of worn out, but it'll be more than we had before. Let's show the guys. They'll want to see this part of the cave, at any rate," Jamie said. "I don't see anything else, and it's gloomy in here. I can't wait to see the sun and get a breath of fresh air. I hope we never have to hide in here for long, I'd hate that."

They headed to the smaller part of the cave, got down, and crawled out into the sunlight. "My poor knees," Felicia exclaimed. "I wonder what this sand is doing to them, besides removing most of the skin."

They didn't see the men when they reached the outside,

but heard the deep sounds of male voices wafting to them from the papaya grove. They heard a few branches breaking, and followed the sounds.

"Son of a damned bitch," Jim yelled. "I knocked off a lot of ripe ones and fell on my knee. It hurts like hell." Bare-legged below the knees, he wore the same walking shorts he'd worn the day they'd sailed on the doomed *Queen Ilikii.* A healthy streak of blood trickled down his leg into his well-worn boat sandals.

Mick left off his own efforts to look at Jim's leg. "Nothing broken, but you have a pretty good gash over the knee. Have a seat on the grass here. Jamie can have a look when they come out of the cave." Hearing the murmur of their voices, he knew they'd finished exploring. He forgot Jim for the moment, waiting to catch a glimpse of Jamie's face. Second nature to him, he always looked for her.

When the women joined them, Felicia gasped at the blood running down Jim's leg and hurried to his side. "Oh, my God. You're bleeding." Looking into his eyes with hands aflutter, she couldn't think what to do. "Oh Jim, are you all right?"

The rusted, worn out shovel, lay forgotten on the rocks.

"How bad is it, Jim?" Jamie looked closer. "It's not too deep, but we need to get to the lagoon and clean it up." She reached for the fraying bottom of her increasingly tattered skirt, tore a generous strip from it, and tenderly wrapped Jim's leg and knee. "That should get us back to camp where we can clean it up and see what needs doing. Let's help him up, Felicia, we can do it together."

"Aw, now, I don't need help, it's not that bad," Jim protested then faltered and weaved off balance when he tried to get to his feet. Looking sheepish, he shrugged. "Damn. Hey, thanks, gals, I guess I did need a little help."

Mick waited to offer assistance but, seeing Jim in capable hands, picked up what papayas he could carry He offered some to Jamie. "Got another patient, girl. You always know what to do, don't you?" The admiration in his voice bespoke his pride in her, and now he could see much more of her long tanned legs. They'd taken on a new shapely splendor these past weeks.

Felicia walked ahead with Jim, holding his arm. "I don't think Felicia is up on nursing as much as I am with all my practice on you, but I don't have much bandage material left in this skirt." She picked up as many papayas as she could carry and with less skirt to carry them in, the effect was pure enjoyment to Mick with the fabric snug against her backside as she strode along.

Dinner would be scanty again and, with the creeping weakness of protein deprivation, Mick knew they needed to catch more fish.

They reached camp, dropped off the papayas, and walked to the lagoon. Jamie unwrapped the dressing on Jim's knee, and Felicia carried water from the lagoon to bathe it. The knee had stopped bleeding, and Jamie bound it up with the newly stained fabric, freshly soaked with their only medicine, salty seawater.

"It's not bad, Jim, thank God. We're lucky it's no worse. Ought to heal rapidly," Jamie said. "So what's for dinner, I'm so hungry, I could eat a shark."

They laughed in relief.

"Let's go fishing, Mick, I'm starving too," Jim said. "We all know that saltwater won't hurt my leg, so let's get at it." He started for the camp and the spears, his gait steady.

"Felicia would you like to tend Jim's leg?" Jamie said. "You can do it. It's not bad, and he'd love it."

Felicia needed more experience with their primeval brand of medicine, and Jamie sought to include her.

"Yes, I'd like to. I need to know these things, and he *would* like it." Serious, her lavender eyes flashed dark with worry about Jim. "Should he be out there fishing with his knee like that? Won't the blood draw sharks?"

"Mick wouldn't let that happen." Jamie chuckled. "At least we won't starve while he heals. Mick can't use his left arm fully, and it's good that Jim can. Maybe he can't climb the breadfruit tree, so how about we get some while they fish? I can climb up there if the guys aren't watching. I don't want Mick standing under a tree while I climb." She couldn't help an escaping giggle at the thought.

"Won't they be surprised if we have some breadfruit to go with the fish?" Felicia eagerly agreed and they left the beach to pick up the netting. The men passed them on their way to the lagoon carrying spears. Mick would keep an eye on Jim while he searched the horizon for those dreaded square sails.

# CHAPTER 18

They reached the great spreading breadfruit tree, and Jamie looked at one of the lower branches. "Here's a good one for starters? I'll climb," she said, gingerly making her way upward. "Keep watch for the fruits and don't let them fall on you."

"Be careful, Jamie, please! I don't know what we'd do if you were hurt," Felicia cautioned, as Jamie climbed about on the wide, thick-leaved branches.

"It's not bad up here, no thorns, and lots of branches. Don't worry, I'm careful." Jamie made her way upward and found four fruits close together. She put them into the netting. "I wonder about this white stuff. It looks like Elmer's Glue." She returned to the ground easily with green globes. "What about these? I don't know about ripeness." Proud of the fact she'd gotten them, she smiled. "What'll the guys say? Let's make a fire and get them started, I'm beyond hungry." Her empty stomach rumbled. "Will I ever know a full belly again?"

Felicia carried two of them. "Who knows? I never feel there's enough to eat. Is it possible we'll starve here, Jamie?" She seldom looked so worried. "I like it that I've lost weight. I always wondered how I'd look thin. But imagine if no one ever comes?" At times, thoughts of rescue were all-consuming, more so than food.

Jamie sought to comfort her. "We're sure to be rescued some time or other. People cannot just disappear, Felicia, but I do wonder what's taking them so long. Look at my skirt, it's half gone now and my undies are shredded. Worse yet, my period is due. What'll we do then? No tampons around here." She laughed. "Now I know why the natives had special houses for women during that time. Can't you just picture it? One more strip off this skirt and my cheeks will be hanging out."

Felicia giggled. "Don't worry so much about it, Jamie, these men have been around and know about things. That is, unless they've been living under a rock somewhere."

The breeze caught her hair as it rippled in the sun. It was a clear day and the smell of the small, bushy frangipani trees pervaded the air about them. Except for constant hunger, they walked in a veritable Garden of Eden.

"You make me feel better about it. I worry about being embarrassed because of the way it is with Mick. Yet if he cares for me the way he makes me believe, he surely knows how it is with us females. But, Felicia, no matter what happens between us, I see nothing but a disaster ahead for me."

Jamie's face was a picture of distress. Felicia hugged her. "Let's not worry till the time comes, Jamie, we have enough to worry about." At camp, they laid the breadfruit down. "Let's get this fire together, and see how the guys are doing. We'll have papaya, bananas, coconuts, and fish, to go with the breadfruit—a real feast!"

Fire soon leaped from the small pile of wood. Waiting for coals to form, they walked down to the lagoon to see the men sitting on the half-buried log, cleaning fish. The sound of their voices suggested an amiable chat. Fair-haired Jim bent to his task, and dark-headed Mick, his wispy beard growing longer, helped. A fair amount of whiskers had grown on their masculine features. Jim, much slimmer these days, remained a big, tall man. Mick, slender, and willowy as whipcord, had honed down to a spare, muscular frame. He'd tied his hair back with the thong, but a few wisps strayed about his long, saturnine features.

The women stood looking at them. "Look at that. What a

pair of hunks." Felicia murmured. "There sit two of the best-looking men a women could ask for, even with the beards." A mischievous giggle escaped her.

"They are, aren't they? I hope those are fish they're cleaning," Jamie replied, as they headed toward the men. "I still think Mick looks wolfish." *But a handsome wolf,* the thought came—it always did.

She fought against it every time she saw him. It was second nature anymore, along with the fading, inner, warning bells.

The men saw the women coming. "Look at them," Jim said softly to Mick. "I've never seen their like. If we must be stranded on some lost, forgotten island, thank God, it's with those two. Mick, you're one lucky bastard. I wish to God things weren't the way they are for you. A man would have a real chance with a woman like Jamie." He liked Mick and wanted things to work out for them.

"Hell, yes, I know that. You know exactly how it is with me where she's concerned. It's hell's fire for me. All I can say is that I'd never hurt her. I'd give up my life for her." The deep, dark color of his eyes affirmed his words.

"I believe you, Mick. I've seen how it is for some time now. I have the same in my corner, but my life's on the up and up. You have a hell of a lot of uphill work ahead of you, and I wish you all the best. God help you," Jim said, turning toward the women as they came up the beach.

"Hey, catch any fish? We're starving!" As they neared, Felicia called out to them. "We've got the fire going."

The four started back to camp with the fish wrapped in seaweed and banana leaves, ready for the coals. Felicia fell in with Jim. "How's the leg? I don't see you limping that much. I'll change the dressing for you, later." Gazing up at Jim, she had a mischievous glint in her eye.

Mick and Jamie walked behind them. "What's got her going now?" he asked. "She high on something?"

"You'll see soon enough," Jamie retorted. "You're moving you're arm quite a bit more. Is the soreness gone?"

*She sounds flippant*, Mick mused, a grin spreading over his long, narrow features. *They've been up to something.*

The fire had burned into a bed of coals when they reached camp, and the women brought out the breadfruit to place into them. They laughed while they shoved the wrapped the large green globes into the coals.

"Hey, how'd you get those?" Jim exclaimed. "Don't tell me you girls went climbing up in that tree. That's my job." Limping slightly, he went on, "You could've been hurt you know. All right, who did it?" His wide grin belied the seriousness of his comments.

"Anyone could get hurt, going up so high," Felicia exclaimed. "Jamie climbed the tree, and I watched from below."

Jamie grinned at Jim. "It wasn't bad, lots of branches to hold on to. I'm so hungry I would've climbed Mount Everest for some breadfruit, or anything else edible. At least tonight, we'll have a big meal, thanks to the fish you fellas caught." She brushed her hands together, removing bits of leaves. "I can't wait."

Mick watched the meal preparation. His appreciation of Jamie grew as he watched her work—a maze of energy, inventiveness, and pure hardiness. He wondered how a woman like that could have been so hurt in her marriage. What an asinine fool her husband was to have missed her fine qualities! He was amazed that Jamie had put up with her husband's cruelty for so long. It didn't seem in character with the woman he'd come to know.

"Jamie, while the breadfruit cooks, why don't we get some bananas and guavas? We'll have a real banquet with the fruit added," Mick offered. He shot her a look from his dark, shadowy eyes.

"It's getting a bit late, don't you think?" she replied.

"We've got about an hour or more before dark, and then there's the moon," he urged. "It's getting bigger every night."

Jim and Felicia were silent, waiting to see if Jamie would go.

"Well, I guess we could gather more food before dark," she murmured, unable to say no to Mick. She turned and followed him into the underbrush like an automaton, her head down, feeling futile about her future.

Jim and Felicia looked at each other as they saw the two heading out into the undergrowth in the slowly gathering darkness. Felicia nestled herself against Jim's sturdy body. "Oh boy!"

"They can't help themselves, Felicia," he said. "He's so gone on her, and it looks like it's reciprocated. I can't see a good outcome for either of them. It's too damned bad. There's something inherently good in Mick. It shows more every day we're on this island. We sure as hell don't know the whole story on that guy."

Mick walked ahead with one of the nets and Jamie followed. She lagged behind. He ignored it. Reluctant at being alone with him, she'd come in spite of it.

As they neared the guava tree, he turned to her. "Should we get some of these now or wait until we pick the bananas?" He came close. "We could pile them here, and get them on the way back." His nearness made her edgy, but he pressed closer.

"Uh...well, let's get a few now then."

She turned away to reach into the tree for fruit. Mick came up against her back, reached around her waist, and pulled her close against his body. He noticed her ever growing slenderness. His arm more than encircled her body.

"Mick, we won't get anything done this way." She dropped the fruits she held and turned to face him as tears began. "We have to stop this thing between us. It can never turn out right."

In the waning daylight, he saw her distress. "I only know this, Jamie. I had to be alone with you for a little while. It's been all day and I've hardly had a word with you. If you'll come out on the beach tonight, I'll hold off, but we have to be together. We haven't had enough time alone." Mick pulled her so tightly against his body she could scarcely catch her breath. He kissed her fully on the mouth, pressing ever deeper and harder.

"Stop, please—Mick, I can't stand it!" Jamie cried, breaking free of him. Tears filled her eyes. She sank down. "You have the advantage over me, and you know it. I don't know what to do anymore."

Mick knelt beside her, tilted her chin up, and looked deeply into her tear-filled eyes. "Oh God, Jamie, dearest girl, I'm sorry if I hurt you, but I can scarcely keep my hands off you and I couldn't help that kiss. Did I hurt you?"

The depth of his feelings lay in that dark, intense, look. Seeing that, she countered, "No, I'm not hurt, just afraid of what's happening. You affect me in some crazy way. I can scarcely breathe. I don't know what it is about you, a kind of magic, I think." She smiled then. "Knowing the kind of man you are, it has to be black magic. Is that what it is?"

The moment lightened, and they laughed together.

"Okay, come on, we'll pick some guavas and leave them to collect later." He held out his hand to help her up and saw her collarbone showing through her over-sized blouse. It gaped open, and he caught a glimpse of milky-white, swelling breast. He gasped for breath. "You're getting thinner, your wonderful bones are showing. You're beautiful, Jamie." He wanted to take hold of her again, but restrained himself.

"I used to be very slim before I married. I've forgotten how good that feels, in fact, hungry or not, I feel wonderfully well these days! I love the way I feel." Suddenly, filled with exuberance, she forgot her worries about Mick. The depression over her failed marriage had passed from her. She rarely thought about it anymore, or the painful ordeal it had been. She realized she was very happy, and it'd been a long time since she'd felt this way.

Turning to Mick, the realization struck her. She knew it was being with him that had wrought this change in her.

"Mick, you know, I've been very happy these days we've been together on this island. Forgive me for being such a changeling, but I've only just realized it." She moved closer. "It's you that's made me feel this way. I know there's no hope for anything lasting between us, but I feel like a normal woman again. I thank God for it—I thank *you* for it."

Jamie pressed against him, put her arms around him, laid her head against his chest, and breathed in his scent. The warmth and comfort of his lean, hard, body was a solid haven at this moment. "Oh, Mick, just holding you feels like heaven to me You're very strong and your strength flows into me in some crazy way."

Her mind told her everything, absolutely everything, about this was wrong. She felt herself leaping headlong into roiling, shark-infested waters, into a relationship with an evil man like Mick! The warning bells tolled disaster—and fell on ears no longer listening.

His arms closed about her, even the left arm. It was painful, though his wound had nearly healed. They stood together for a long moment, holding each other. Mick knew then, she loved him. A tremendous upwelling of tenderness toward her filled his mind. He wanted to tell her about himself, but he could not. *I love her. I would give my life for her.* In silence, he held her, his cheek pressed against her dark curls. His heart was full. This caring and loving feeling, so new to him, had made him hold his wild passion for her in abeyance.

Jamie slowly moved away, smiled shyly, and looked into his dark eyes. "I guess we'd best pick this fruit while we have enough light."

"Yes, let's get to it." Mick's voice, husky with emotion, soothed her as he bent to gather the guavas dropped earlier. "Then we can go for the bananas, eh?"

Jamie laughed. "Eh? Your Canadian is showing, Mick." She reached into the branches for more of the pungent fruit. They were comfortable with each other. She was happy, almost relaxed in his company.

Carefully choosing the nicer guavas, they laid them in a neat pile under the tree and went on to the banana grove, walking side by side, touching shoulders when they could. The undergrowth kept them apart at times, but Mick caught her hand in his at every opportunity, and Jamie felt a soaring happiness.

The banana trees were loaded with fruit. They picked too much and carried it back as best they could. Some of it was green to give them a longer-lasting supply.

At the guava tree, they found their cache of fruit, torn, slashed, and strewn about, ravished by some animal with small cloven hooves. "Mick, look at this! Something's torn up our guavas!"

They looked at the mess on the ground, only a few skins and seeds, spilled about and trampled into the damp earth.

"Those damned pigs were here!" Mick laughed. "Sure, they'd love a nice pile of fruit all picked and ready, the greedy hogs." He looked at Jamie with a wide grin on his lips. "We fixed a nice picnic for them. Maybe we can use guavas for bait, and catch us some pork. I'll check that with Jim."

They picked a few more, took up the bananas, and headed for camp in the growing dark. As they picked their way, Mick turned to Jamie. "Come to the beach tonight, Jamie, won't you? I need to be near you, to talk to you."

"I will—I will, Mick." She felt her color rising as she thought about meeting him under the ever larger and brighter moon. She wondered what would happen tonight. He knew her heart now, but what about his? Did she have enough sense to avoid getting intimately involved with a man like him? Even knowing the danger, she wasn't sure she could keep from being carried away by his power over her. He, stronger than she, had mesmerized her very soul.

In near darkness, they came into camp and lay down their burdens of fruit. Jim and Felicia watched them, observing the friendliness, newly evident in their relationship. Things had changed again. Along with a new amiability, beneath the surface, a new intensity had begun. Jamie's features bore a soft glow that even nighttime couldn't hide as she fussed about, putting down her burden of fruit.

"Hey, now that you're here, I'm putting the fish in to bake," Felicia said as she bent down to place the fish wrapped in leaves into what was left of the coals. "I see a lot of bananas, but why so few guavas?"

Mick put down his clump of green bananas. "These should last a while. We were robbed," he added. "We had a nice pile of guavas set aside and when we got back with the bananas, the pigs had eaten them. Jim, I think we have a way to get us some pork chops. The little suckers have asked for it. They love guavas and, having us lay out a feast makes it even nicer for them."

Elated, Jim grinned. "You think we can trap them? We could dig a pit if we had a shovel."

Felicia shot a look at Jamie. "They don't know what we found in the cave. I dropped the shovel when Jim hurt his leg. We forgot about it, but maybe it would help the guys with their pig hunt."

"Well, it's one more thing they can use. I don't feel sorry for the pigs after what they did to the guavas. We had a nice pile of them. You should have seen the mess they left." Jamie paused a moment, considered, and then laughed. "Well, of course, they are pigs."

"You're all aglow," Felicia said, "and none of it's from firelight. You must have had a marvelous walk, my dear, by the look on your face. What happened out there?"

Her curiosity was plainly evident by her arched brows.

Jamie shook her head. "I'll tell you about it later. Things are clearer for me now."

She fussed about, setting out fresh leaves to eat from and cutting papayas to go with the other things. Felicia noticed Mick sitting off to the edge of camp watching her. Flames from their small campfire reflected like sparks in his dark eyes. She shivered at the mystery of the man. *Jamie's in for one hell of a ride with that one.*

# CHAPTER 19

After a full and satisfying dinner, they tossed the remnants into the fire, spread out the cloths over the soft carpet of leaves, and stretched out to rest.

Mick and Jim talked over their plans to capture a few pork chops.

"Isn't anyone going to ask what we found in the cave today?" Felicia demanded in frustration. "You might be happy to hear of it."

"So tell us, you haven't said a word all day," Jim responded. "I guess you got off track when I tore up my leg."

"We found a big room you can stand up in, and a shovel. I dropped it when you got hurt, Jim, and forgot about it. It's lying near the banana grove where I left it," she added. "You need to see the room we found. Mick, you, too, when you can crawl inside. We could hide there if we had to."

"There's a light coming into it from above, sort of near a ledge," Jamie put in. "It could be another entrance. We wanted you guys to have a look. It could be a great hide-out if we ever needed one. Maybe tomorrow—or soon?"

"We've put things off lately, instead of working on our defense system," Jim said. "There's no wood up on top for a signal fire. We need to get that done as well. Time enough in the morning. It's not as if we had our jobs to commute to, is it? Of course, we may have to go pig hunting." He turned to Felicia. When a patch of moonlight enhanced her striking features, he saw her face shining. A full moon had just emerged over the palm trees and seemed especially bright. It cast a soft luminance over their camp, and Jim's voice took on a new softness, when he said, "Felicia, let's take a walk. I don't believe I've ever seen a better night for it."

He reached for her, and they moved out toward the beach. Their figures were large, though they'd slimmed considerably. They complemented each other. Jim towered over Felicia and bent down to her as they walked away. Something seemed different about them tonight, a new closeness, a languor, in the way they moved together. Jamie sighed, absently wondering if their love for each other had taken a new and more intimate turn.

Mick came to Jamie. "Come, Jamie, let's go to the beach. I don't care where, if we can be together. We'll walk the other direction if meeting those two concerns you." He reached for her with his good arm, and she rose to walk beside him. His arm encircled her gently. Her head rested against his shoulder.

"Just so we don't run into any thieving pigs, I don't care where you take me, Mick." She enjoyed their new closeness, no longer caring that he came from a kind of life she could not imagine. She couldn't think of it anymore. Her feelings for Mick had wrought wonderful, healing changes in her. She felt incredible.

From the beginning, he'd made her feel alive, and it hadn't all been fear of him. She understood that now. It was a man-woman thing. He'd touched her deepest female instincts, and she felt fully like a woman. She was no longer a sad, depressed imitation wife. She might pay a hellish price, but deep inside, the intense feelings she could not hold back from this very masculine man had become a reality. She'd try. *Oh God, I have to try.*

But Mick had a forceful strength about him, and Jamie, drawn deeply into it, no longer had a will of her own.

"Here's the log, and it's deserted. Let's sit a while." Mick led her to it. "I've waited all day for this." He kissed her gently, not pressing his advantage, though he knew he could. He burned inwardly for her and had for weeks. He wanted her, body and soul. He stroked her hair, nuzzling his face into it. "Your hair smells good. It's always shiny and clean and your skin gets into me way down deep. I can't get enough of that either. You have the magic, Jamie. You have no idea what you've done to me. There's something very powerful between us. You know it, don't you?"

"Yes, Mick, something has happened. I finally realized it back on the trail. I knew it a long while before that too, but I couldn't face it. We didn't start out too well if you remember. I thought you wanted to kill me. I remember thinking that day on the schooner, *if looks could kill!"*

Mick stiffened. "What happened on the *Ilikii* couldn't be helped. Things got out of control, at least out of mine. That whole thing was a rotten turn of events. It wasn't supposed to go that way." He finished his words with regret, thinking of the lives lost and the terrible smashing of the lovely schooner.

Frequently haunted by thoughts of the captain, trussed helplessly when his ship sank, Mick regretted the loss of an innocent and good man. The captain had' become entangled in something he should never have known about. He hadn't been aware of the drug trading of his crewmen. It'd gone on for several years in some of the ports they visited, carried out on the sly by a few of his trusted seamen.

Jamie sensed Mick's changing mood at the mention of the shipwreck. She stayed close against him, saying nothing, content with being with him, and the wonderful way he made her feel. But her mind considered his suggestion he had control over things. *What things?*

He pulled her closer, kissed her deeply, again and again, until the familiar weakness crept over her. She returned his kisses with a passion she never knew she possessed. Her only intimacy had been with a man who knew nothing of love. With Mick, everything was completely different. This mysterious shadowy man made everything real. Enveloped in a warm cocoon of love, she tried to tell herself she was foolish to trust him, but was unable to believe it in these moments of madness. The warning bells ringing went unheeded. *Stop now, Jamie, stop while you can.*

"Oh, Mick, I've never had feelings like this. I'm on fire. What are you doing to me?" She clung ever closer, feeling his hands on her bare skin, moving, fondling, caressing. His hands burned against her skin as they moved over her most intimate places and suddenly, she stiffened and drew back from him. "I can't do this, Mick. Please forgive me, we can't. I'm sorry, I can't." Gasping for breath, she tore herself away from his encircling arms.

Crying, she fell onto her knees in the soft yielding sand. Mick reached down to her. "It's all right dearest—wonderful girl. Anything you want is what I want. Please don't take on so, *Jamilla,* my Jamie girl."

He sank down beside her, not touching, just being close. She appreciated that he didn't make her feel she had to run away in fear, even as she knew she couldn't. Her dilemma crushed her.

"I'm sorry, Mick. I'm a terrible coward. I can't go further with you. I want to, oh so much. I know what the future holds for us—nothing. Can you ever forgive me?" She raised her tear stained eyes in the moonlight. "I don't know what to do now."

"We'll just sit here for a while, don't you worry about anything, dear girl. If you need a white dress and a wedding chapel, I'll wait for that, too. Don't you know I'd do anything for you? You're worth it all—everything. I have never cared for a woman before—not like this." His voice, husky and low, comforted her.

He spoke his love to her, gentling her troubled heart. But he'd set a fire inside her soul that would burn until the end of her days. An incendiary fire waiting to burst into devastating flames and she was terrified of its fearsome power.

He put his arm around her very easily, and they sat on the moonlit sandy beach. "I love you, Jamie. No woman has ever heard that from me." He looked into her eyes, willing her to believe him. "I want you in my life. I want children with you. To live another day without you beside me would be the death of my soul."

"I love you too, Mick, I know that now. I'll always love you, no matter what happens to us. I believe you care for me, or you could never say such loving things. You make me feel complete. Nothing like this has ever happened to me. I was married, but I've never known love. I never knew a man could be like you, so loving, so tender." She nestled against him. "It's a wondrous thing, this being in love."

Mick cradled her, kissed her face, and laid his head against hers. "Jamie, when things are straightened out, I want to make my life with you. I can't tell you about myself just now, but in time, I will. Will you think about it?"

Jamie sat quietly in Mick's embrace. *He's talking marriage? Could that be possible? He is a criminal. Is he trying to make me forget we've come so close to making love? Close, I was walking all over it.* "I'll think about it, Mick, I will," she murmured in his ear. *Could it ever be possible? I don't know who or what he is, but I know I love him. God help me, I do.*

"Do you want to go into the lagoon? It's almost high tide, and the water is clear enough to see the sandy bottom, even in the moonlight." Mick got up and offered her his good arm. "You're very beautiful Jamie, you've got a killer figure, and it gets better every day. I've been watching. It's more than beauty—it's the inner woman of you that makes the difference. It makes you more than beautiful." His dark, glowing eyes fixed on her shadowy form gleaming in the moonlight. It made her tremble. "I've seen beautiful before, but not like you, girl."

"I know you watch me. Every time I see you, your eyes are fixed on me. It scared me to death at first. I was relieved you were injured. I could fight you off if I had to." Jamie laughed, telling him that. She felt at ease with him, knowing he wouldn't force her into intimacy.

They walked into the water holding hands and looking at

each other in the moonlight. He had a strong, supple, and fine male body. Jamie hadn't seen many men before, not up close like this. "You truly are a beautiful man, Mick. I'm no expert, but I know beauty when I see it, too. I even thought that on the *Queen Ilikii*, until you froze me with that look. Why'd you do that, Mick?"

"Someday I'll tell you all about it, dearest girl." His voice was firm and Jamie knew not to push him on it. It only added to the mystery of him, making her wonder even more about *who* he was, or *what* he was.

They splashed about in the gentle waters of the lagoon and played, dodging and ducking each other, but with restraint on Mick's part. Jamie slowly relaxed as the intensity of their feelings cooled.

"I guess we'd better get back before they worry about us," Jamie said, looking down the beach. They sat in the sand, watching the high tide lap gently at the pinkish sandy shore. The light of the moon made the lush little island visible in a dreamy way. "I don't think I've ever seen a more beautiful place." She rose from where they sat. "Do you think they'll notice how wrinkled my skirt is?"

"Jamie, I need another buttonhole cut in my jeans, how about it?" Mick smiled at her, knowing she felt edgy about returning to the camp. "Don't bother about things, Jamie. They know how it is with us, and somehow, I doubt they'll be there. In fact, I'd be surprised if they were." He took her arm as they turned toward their camp, and their beds of leaves.

"Mick, tonight was the best night of my life, even the way it turned out. If I never have that little bit again, I could live on the wonder of it, the rest of my life." Jamie leaned close to him as they moved slowly away from the beach. Her face lay against his arm and she took comfort in his warm body scent. "Mick, I'm happy, I hope you are," she whispered against his skin. "I've never been in love before."

"Girl, we're not finished yet. God willing, we'll never

be." He kissed the curly top of her head. "I'm happy too, Jamie."

They found the camp deserted. Jamie looked at Mick. "I wonder where they've got to, they went for a walk and they're not back yet."

"Perhaps we weren't the only ones enjoying the night, Jamie. They're no doubt asleep somewhere—or maybe not." He waggled his eyebrows at her, but she barely saw that in the soft moonlight. "We'd best get some sleep," he added softly. "They'll be in for breakfast, and be starving, just like me. how about you, love hungry?" Mick laughed, and Jamie tossed a handful of leaves at him.

With a deep sense of loss, she lay down to sleep. She'd had to refuse something wonderful tonight. Her sense of survival had won out over the riotous turmoil Mick had aroused in her. Would she be so strong again when she walked out on the beach with him? There'd be another time, and more, unless rescue came.

She suffered fitful sleep for much of the night, with far too much of it spent lying awake, sorting out tumultuous thoughts and feelings over Mick. How many times had she wanted to creep over and lie in his welcoming arms?

*Am I being a fool?*

She fought her feelings until finally, exhausted, she fell into dreamless sleep.

# CHAPTER 20

In early dawn, Jamie rose up, looked for Jim and Felicia, and saw their sleeping spaces empty. She knew they'd entered into a new stage in their relationship and envied the ease between them. Not for her. Mick, revealed to be the lowest of criminals, appeared to be another sort by his present behavior. But was he? She continually tried to sort out the man she'd grown to love so dearly.

Mick was gone. She put dry wood over the few coals left from the evening meal and blew on them until she saw a lick of flames. "We have nothing to cook, but a fire seems good somehow," she said aloud, adding more fuel, thinking how easily the fire burned. They hadn't had rain for several days, and the wood they found burned easily.

Mick returned. The heat rose in her face as she acknowledged his low-voiced, "Good morning."

Trying to sound casual, she returned his greeting, but felt a renewed tension between them. Feeling the loss of last night's closeness, she wondered, *Is it only on my part?* She remembered his wound. "Let me see your wound. It could be torn open after last night." She hated her feeling of shyness. She smiled tentatively, went to him, and removed the dried dressing. "Well, it's in good shape and nearly healed. You must be strong to heal so well."

"I believe it's the nursing care, my love." Mick laughed, he reached for her and caught her arm as she tried to sidestep away from him. He pulled her close for a good long kiss, breaking the tension, and relieving her shyness.

"Wow! What a breakfast, you two!" Jim called out. He and Felicia strolled into camp. "What's for eats? I'd like a generous slab of ham, about four eggs over easy, and a big side of hash browns—don't forget the sourdough toast." His eyes sparkled, seeing Mick and Jamie's embrace.

Felicia smiled and said nothing as she walked with Jim, holding hands.

"We missed you this morning, we were worried." Jamie brought a few bananas to the errant couple. "Here's your ham and eggs over easy, Jim, sorry, no hash browns." She winked at Felicia, and saw the wide grin spreading over her rosy face.

"Jamie, help me gather a few coconuts," Felicia said. She took Jamie by the arm and would have pulled her if she hadn't gone willingly. "So, how're you this morning? It looks like you and Mick have things sorted out. You're absolutely glowing." She kept edging her away from the camp. "I'm sorry to be so nosey, it's none of my business, I know." She couldn't help her infectious giggle. "So tell me."

"Really? It looks to me like you and Jim are together. I'm happy for you. You're lucky you have each other. I want to hear all about it, or at least what you'll tell, Felicia." Jamie took a deep breath. "Yes, I'm in love with Mick. I know it's a disaster. It couldn't be anything else, but I don't care anymore, I can't. I've been dead inside for so long. Now, I'm alive and it feels good." She rattled on, pouring out her feelings, unable to stop. "I feel normal, Felicia. So this is what it feels like to love, and be in love. I was married, but I never felt this way." She looked at Felicia. "There was no love at all in my marriage. Dummy me, I didn't realize it at first. I'll tell you all about it someday, but if I died today, I'd go a happy woman. But, Felicia, I couldn't go all the way with him. I had to stop us. I couldn't do it. I was afraid. I asked his forgiveness, even though I didn't need to." She shook her head, in awe of her experience with Mick, her face suffused with warmth. "Felicia, he's mentioned marriage. Can you believe that? Could it be possible?"

Felicia stared at Jamie, her face, a picture of total happiness and bewilderment. "Oh, Jamie, I don't know. But I love the way he is with you. He must love you. Look how happy you are. It's in your face, and no, I don't know if it's possible for it to work out." She put her arm around Jamie. "How puzzled you must be. For me, Jim and I will be married. We're in love, and we've agreed on it. We'll live in Santa Monica. Jamie, I hope it comes out right for you and Mick. I like him, and so does Jim. It's hard to believe he's a bad sort. But isn't he? Look at the terrible things we've seen him involved in."

Jamie shrugged and shook her head, trying to straighten things in her mind. "Well, let's get a coconut or two, that's a positive thing. Thanks, Felicia, for letting me pour out my woes and joys. It's not something I usually do."

"I know that, Miss Secretive, don't I know it?"

Jamie laughed. "It's hard for me to speak about unhappy things. You're closer to me now than anyone, except my father, and I had a tough time telling him about my marriage. He was a big help and I'll never forget it." She found a coconut, dried and beginning to sprout into the sandy soil. "We need another storm to knock more coconuts off. This one is old and dry, we need the greener ones."

"Maybe Jim could throw rocks up there and get them down. He's very athletic." Felicia dithered about in a glow and couldn't make sense of anything. Jamie loved her for her happiness.

⋐⋗⋐⋗

Jim was full of enthusiasm and in high spirits, reflecting the change his personal life had taken. "Today, let's see if we can catch us some pork chops. If we have a shovel, maybe we could dig a pit and bait it with the guavas since they like them so damned much." He looked at Mick. "How's that with you?"

"Sounds good to me, I'll walk to the banana grove and pick up the shovel. You need to stay off that leg and be thinking what to do once we corner one of those wild little beasties," Mick said with a laugh.

It came from deep within him, and Jamie, thrilled at the fullness of it. Her blood raced, seeing his white teeth against that darkly tanned face. She listened to the discussion. It sounded dangerous, an unrealistic adventure planned by two young boys. "Listen to that, Felicia. They'll probably end up in the pit with the pigs," she whispered, a grin spreading over her face. "We won't be fixing up the cave any time soon. We put everything off lately."

"I hope they don't get hurt with this crazy stunt," Felicia replied. "Have we been here so long, Jamie, we've turned into hunter-gatherer cave men?"

Jamie sensed Felicia wanted to restrain Jim but, seeing his high level of excitement, couldn't dampen it.

Mick approached. "Jamie, would you walk with me to find the shovel? You'll know where to find it. We can bring back a few papayas while we're at it." He stood in front of her, waiting for an answer.

Jamie frowned. *We might never get back with the shovel, or anything else, the way he is.* "Okay, Mick, let's go. We need to hurry if you want to have enough time for your wild pig hunt."

His eyes crinkled at the corners—he'd read her thoughts. "Jim, we won't be long," Mick said. "See if you can fix the ropes from the rafts together, dismantle our shelter, and use anything else we have. We may need to lasso one of the critters."

He nodded to Jamie and they set off up stream. After walking in silence for several minutes, he laughed. "What'd you think we might do on this little excursion? I'm not that bad, girl." He lounged against her side as they walked. Jamie felt content with him beside her, no matter what the purpose. It made her existence complete, doing things with him, talking, or watching his graceful movements. Being with him was enough—almost.

"It's a beautiful day, isn't it, Mick? This is a wonderful paradise island, and we were beyond fortunate to find it." She thought back to those terrible days and frowned. "On the ship, I thought you wanted to kill me, Mick. How little we know what's going to happen before the day is over."

"Jamie, I never had those feelings toward you. Oh, God—never. I've learned to keep my distance from '*regular*' people. It's the life I lead, a life I plan to change when I can. Just for now, things must remain the way they are. You'll have to trust me. That's asking a lot and I hope you can."

She saw regret in his eyes. His jaw bore that familiar firmness. They kept on until they entered the small grove of bananas. Jamie turned away to find the shovel but Mick pulled her tight against him. "Don't look for that shovel just yet." He kissed her over and over.

"Mick, you said we'd get right back." She halfheartedly pulled away, smiling up at him. "I like being with you, but we should get back, don't you think?"

"I suppose we must, but I do love you, girl." He pulled her close and ravished her lips over and over until she lay against his chest, breathless. He laughed with joy, set her free, and steadied her on her feet. "That's it for now. Let's get this stuff, or we'll never get back until tomorrow. The pigs would have to wait."

They found the rusted shovel thrown so hastily onto the rocks.

"Look at this weak, rusted-out excuse for a shovel." Mick held out the rusty shovel. "No wonder it's here. The last people probably threw it away. I hope we can dig with this."

"It beats having no shovel. Come on." She led the way back and stopped by the papayas, looking up at the golden fruit set high in the trees. "Let's get some of those. How do you get them down?"

"I'll knock them off with the shovel." He shoved the rusty blade under a ripe fruit and it fell. "This old thing comes in handy for this, if nothing else." He laughed at his one handed efforts. "Come on, Jamie girl, catch them."

They headed back with the rusty implement in Mick's hand and Jamie's skirt loaded with fruit. He walked behind her until she realized what he was doing. "You sly, disgusting rat! You did that with the bananas, too, didn't you?"

He grinned at her, total mischief glinting from his dark eyes. "Guilty as hell, Jamie, I admit it."

"You know, you really seem devilish with that look on your face. I've always thought you looked like a wolf on the prowl!"

His eyes burned into hers. "I am, girl, I sure as hell am."

His words went searing through her and she was on fire again. She tried to be indignant and found it impossible. Mick wanted her in every imaginable way. She faced the fact that she wanted him just as badly. They walked side by side, each with their own thoughts, and the wondrous thing they shared—loving, and being in love.

The happy pair came into the camp with their treasures, and Jamie carefully laid the papayas on the thick carpet of leaves.

Mick offered the shovel for Jim's inspection. "It's not much, but it's good for picking fruit anyway."

Jim frowned. "Well, any port in a storm, it'll have to do." The shovel looked small in his big hands. "Are you up to this, or do you need to rest a bit? That was a pretty good walk up and back—your face is gray."

"I tire easily yet, but let's have a go at it if you're ready. Any definite ideas how we're doing this?" Mick returned, his face, a dripping mask from the walk. He turned to Jamie. "I'll take the knife. We'll need it if we have any luck."

Jamie handed him the knife. "Please be careful, Mick. I think those wild animals might be dangerous. Remember how skittish they were?" Seeing his pallor, she said. "We'd better eat something. You'll do better with a bit of rest. Those pigs aren't going anywhere."

"Let's cut a couple papayas open," Felicia suggested, "and have them with the other stuff. We'll have pork chops tonight then."

They agreed with her and, since hunger was always with them, it was no problem encouraging them to eat. Jamie saw relief in Mick's eyes at the idea.

They sat under the huge tree. Never far from their minds lurked the constant search for food. Tiring of coconuts, bananas, guavas, papaya, the taste of fresh ocean fish, grilled over a fire or baked in leaves, had been a pleasant surprise. But they longed for something new—the taste of pork.

During the scanty lunch, the remembrance of favorite foods unconsciously crossed Jamie's mind. Sandwiches and pizza, foods familiar at home, brought tantalizing memories.

"Felicia, what would you be eating now if you were in California?" she asked, more to break the silence than curious.

"Well, for lunch, I might have a hoagie brought in, or go out for lunch. We did that a lot," she replied, her face a dreamy gaze of remembering. "How about you Jim, what did you have for lunch on a busy day?" she asked, gazing up at him.

He was taller than everyone, even sitting down. "Most days, we got tangled up in cases and were lucky to have vender stuff. Man, even that sounds good just now," he replied. "One day, Felicia, we'll go out for a real dinner, and we'll think back to right now. Can't you imagine it?"

"This is getting out of hand. I shouldn't have mentioned normal food," Jamie said. Mick's color had improved, but he'd neglected to mention a favorite food—one more mystery about the man. "You look better, Mick. Will you be able to manage?" she asked. "You didn't say what you liked to eat. Will I even know that small thing about you when we get back to civilization?"

"You'll know all there is to know one day, girl—well, almost," Mick said, raising his eyebrows at her. He kept his voice low and confidential. "And yes, I'll manage fine, You gals keep the home fires burning. We'll be back with the pork."

Jamie and Felicia stood together watching the men depart. There was a good chance of injury and it was a worry, but they needed the added food. They could have gone along, but too many humans might scare the wild creatures away. The men stood a better chance without them. Not eager to partake in the slaughter, they knew meat came at a price for the animal. The hunter might pay a high price as well.

"Why don't we find some wood for later and take a swim in the lagoon? We could take our clothes off and go native with the guys gone." Felicia chuckled. "Let's enjoy the rest of the day and not think about that pig hunt. It scares me to death!"

"You bet. Good idea," Jamie replied. "I'll wash my stuff and let it dry while we swim. I've never worn anything for days and days at a time, and what I have is rotting away. If we aren't rescued soon, we'll all be running around naked."

"Let's not worry. Look how beautiful it is. Let's wash our clothes the best we can, and dive in." Felicia, heading for the water, pulled off her blouse, eager to wash her torn and soiled clothes.

She had forgotten the firewood, but it didn't matter. They still had time. Jamie unbuttoned her ragged white blouse and followed. They stripped everything off and, had anyone been watching, they would have seen two large lovely ladies, washing clothes.

They draped their things over handy bushes to dry and went frolicking about in the shallow parts of the lagoon, diving into the deeper pools. The tide was in. They swam and dove beneath the gentle waves, swimming at times with brightly hued fish, unconscious of their nakedness.

"Jamie, do you know how gorgeous you are?" Felicia asked. She saw Jamie as tall and only slightly statuesque these days. Her waist nipped in nicely and her hips, slightly narrow, sloped out into full, rounded buttocks with long straight legs. Her breasts were smallish and fully rounded with a hint of sexy sag. She stood in the shallows of the lagoon, a full-blown goddess, wet hair clinging about her head.

"Thanks, but you should see yourself," Jamie replied.

Felicia, a little shorter, had full creamy breasts, a suggestion of soft rolls about her waist, hips, and to some extent her thighs. Her beautifully proportioned figure, with the physical activities and nutritional deprivation endured daily, had emerged into one of splendor.

Jamie, looking at her, wondered how she'd look, if forced to prolong their stay. She decided Felicia's figure would be mind-blowing, should that happen. Jamie had never minded being large, unless she had feelings about it deep down. She knew Felicia to be happy, satisfied, and content with herself, just as she was.

"We'd better wash this salt water off and get dressed, Felicia, the guys will be coming back soon with our pork chops. We don't want to give them too big a surprise!" Jamie walked out of the water, took a long look out over the booming reef, and headed for the stream. Felicia followed.

"That was wonderful. I love swimming in the buff. I've never done it before, have you?" Felicia asked. She stood beside the little stream, pouring clean fresh water over herself.

"No I haven't, but I find I'm doing a lot of things I've never done before. I can't believe it's me when I see the turn my life has taken. Don't pinch me, I might wake up." Jamie laughed gaily while she rinsed the salt off and headed for the clean clothes, nearly dry where they lay spread over bushes in the dappled sunlight.

With their clothing as clean as no soap allowed, they

dressed. "I can't believe how good it feels to be really clean, clothes, me—everything." Felicia donned her wrinkled shorts and blouse, slightly stiff from drying in the sun. "No dryer sheets to soften this stuff." She laughed as she took up the big-toothed comb and went through her tawny locks. Rays of the sun caught in it, bouncing into liquid firelights.

They got the fire going and went about the belated task of wood gathering, while keeping watch for the men. Jamie felt icy slivers of worry. Could they capture a wild animal without being injured?

# CHAPTER 21

The fire flamed up nicely and the sun had sunk low when they heard the murmur of men's voices. They looked at each other.

"Thank you God, they're coming back. They're both talking so they must be alive and well," Jamie said for them both, her hands wiggling at her side. She waited eagerly to see the result of the hunting expedition.

Jim appeared first. "Well, here you are ladies, pork, maybe not like in the supermarket, but pork nonetheless." His voice boomed out as they strode into camp. "We got a small porker, about thirty pounds by the feel of it."

It had been dressed as well as the little knife allowed. The hide was on, but, as it was getting dark, they brought it in as is.

"This knife isn't big enough for a proper job, we'll have to cut off strips and hold them over the fire." He looked at the girls, and their damp, wrinkled clothes. "What've you gals been up to?"

Felicia giggled. "We had a swim, a shower, and washed our clothes. Oh, Jim, it was wonderful!" She swirled her hair in the dusky light, as she told him about their swim in the lagoon. "We have the fire going. It'll be great to have meat again. Thanks, guys, you were very brave to get this."

"How was it, anyway?" Jamie queried, imagining the death of a wild animal.

"Nothing exciting, we'll tell you about it later," Jim replied. "Would you slice up some of this meat? Mick and I could do with a wash up."

He held out his arms, splattered with dried blood. Mick was cleaner, but they both needed a bath.

Jamie nodded. "Go ahead, and tomorrow we'll wash your clothes for you while you dip in the lagoon. You'll like it, we did. It was wonderful."

She saw Mick's pale face. He'd overdone it. She didn't want to fuss or lessen what he'd done today. His inner strength could overcome most things, she thought, as he went with Jim. She took the small red knife to the carcass and cut jagged strips from the shoulder area, after peeling more of the skin away. "Felicia, could you bring a bucket of seawater, to wash the meat?"

The fire had burned into a large bed of coals. They hung strips of meat on green sticks over them and buried a larger chunk, wrapped in leaves, to roast in the coals. Not sure if it would work, they shrugged and tried it, thinking of succulent roasted pork. Felicia wrapped a couple of breadfruit and put them in as well. As they prepared more fruit, their stomachs growled at the excitement of the forthcoming feast.

Mick and Jim came back refreshed, tired, and wet, but no one mentioned that. They were not about to go unclothed, and it was appreciated.

Jim sniffed the air and walked eagerly around the fire, looking for signs of cooked meat. "So, how's dinner coming? I could eat everything on this island, I'm that hungry."

"Any minute now, Jim," Felicia replied. "I think this strip looks ready. What do you think?"

As she held the strip over the coals, he saw the juices dripping into the fire. The odor of roasting meat and burning fat made his mouth run with saliva in his desperate hunger.

"I think it's done, in fact, I'm sure it is."

Jim's eagerness to taste the hard-won pork evoked giggles from Jamie, but she suppressed her mirth.

"Here, Jim." Felicia served him on a large green leaf.

He burned a couple of fingers pulling at it. The steam rose in a fragrant spiral as he put it to his lips. "Oh, man, this is the best thing I've ever tasted!" He ate the meat with gusto then looked about, wondering if he was the only one eating. "Got one for Mick?"

"Mick's is ready," Jamie announced.

She placed cooked meat on a leaf for Mick and set another to roast. Her face, though ruddy from the heat, bore a flush reflecting far more than cooking and serving meat. Mick saw her flush when a bit of fat dripped down onto the coals, flared and burst into flames.

They cooked and ate joyously. It was not often they had full stomachs. It seemed rather aboriginal cooking meat the men had hunted and killed. Accepted as normal in their circumstance, they relished their new source of nutrition.

"I'm full, and I haven't eaten that much," Felicia announced. "My stomach has shrunk to nothing."

She looked at Jim. He'd finished eating and lay relaxing in the thick mat of leaves.

"That must be why you're shrinking before my very eyes. Felicia, you look great to me, no matter what, but I have to say, with your hair loose and shining in the firelight, you are nothing less than a stunner. And you can roast meat, too!" He chuckled and dodged as Felicia punched him.

Jim had done something today for which his years of higher education had never prepared him. Was it the cave man instinct all men have? *Hum, didn't know I had it in me. Maybe I'll take up hunting when I get home. I wonder what Felicia would think about that.* He already knew his life was tied to hers.

Mick hadn't said much. He ate a good meal, and Jamie knew he had to be tired.

"I'll do up your shoulder, Mick. How's it feeling after the day you've had?"

She tried to sound her usual self, but the mad feelings he'd aroused in her on the beach last evening had burned within her all day long. Her legs felt weak and her hands trembled when she touched him.

"It hurts a bit, with pig wrestling and all. There's a big boar with mean looking tusks. We nearly got him, but maybe it's as well we didn't. I have a feeling he might get us. We'll have to go after them for meat as long as we're here, but we'll have a fight on our hands with that one."

He lay in the thick leaves, relaxing. His color had improved with the bath and food. She sat beside him, her thoughts fixated on the events of the previous night. The heat of it weighed heavily on her mind. The burning intensity Mick had aroused in her had grown exponentially until it raged within her. She longed desperately to lie close against his hard masculine body. Unable to quiet her riotous thoughts, he mind dwelled constantly on them and the wild sensations he'd caused inside her.

Jamie's feelings had drawn her toward intimacy with Mick until she believed she'd die if she never lay with him. She'd faced it, and it burned constantly on her mind. She might be throwing her life away, but that decision was hers to make.

Shaking away her disturbing thoughts, she dug the roasted meat out of the pit using the rusty shovel and looked about for ideas. "What'll we do with this cooked meat? If we leave it out, we may have those pigs here after it."

"How about we hang it up in the tree? It'd be out of harm's way. I'll take it up." Jim rose from his bed of leaves and spread the net. "We can use the netting."

They wrapped the meat in fresh leaves, put it in the netting, and used a bit of rope to secure it. He began his climb "How about just up here?" He indicated a branch about eight feet off the ground and tied the bundle to it. "It might not keep so well, but the pigs won't get it if they nose around. I doubt they would with us so close." He returned to the ground, satisfied the meat was safe.

Darkness grew outside the circle of light from the fire, and it was time to settle for the night. Jamie wondered if

Mick wanted to go out on the beach again and waited. He looked at her, his dark eyes reflecting the firelight. That dark glow set her on fire all over again. She knew it would be painful to stay apart from him during the long hours of the coming night.

"Come with me, Felicia," Jim said softly. "Let's take a stroll before retiring." He reached for her, and, with a dreamy expression over her face, she took his hand. "Good night, you two," he murmured.

This time, Jamie noticed Jim carried one of the tent cloths tucked neatly under his arm. She searched Mick's eyes. Going to him, she nestled close, her head against his shoulder, and looked up at him. "Maybe I should tend your wound again, especially with all the gore you had splattered on you."

His body felt firm where she rested against him and an overwhelming desire she couldn't stop made the skin over her cheeks feel like burning embers. Her heart raced in turmoil.

Restless and nearly wild in her tormented state, Jamie couldn't sit for long. The constant thinking of their scorching encounter of the previous night refused to let her rest. She rose on trembling legs. "Come, Mick, it won't take long."

"I'm coming, girl. I've rested and relaxed watching you around the fire. You'd make do just about anywhere, wouldn't you?" He chuckled softly as he got to his feet. "The moon will come up later tonight. We'll have enough light to do things by. I'd like to hold you again if you won't be afraid of me."

Jamie flushed. "Let's go to our place by the log. I'd better wash your clothes. They're dirty from hunting—they won't get dry by morning, though." Hesitant, she babbled on, not knowing how to stop as she walked with him. *Will he want it all from me tonight? I'll die a thousand deaths if he doesn't!*

"Jamie, you don't need to do laundry for me. That's not

what I want from you. But you can check my shoulder again. It's hurting a bit. Today was a bit rough."

He led her out to the beach. Though darkness lay across the island, they made their way by the phosphorescent glow from the lagoon. The moon came up later each night, and soon there would be full nights of darkness.

In the dim light, she cleaned his dressings and redressed his wound. It had nearly closed and needed little attention these days, but she worried about contamination from hunting. She was so used to his body, her hands instinctively did their work. "There, it's done Mick."

They sat close together on the half-buried log. Her feelings approached riotous heights. She couldn't stop thinking how his burning touches made her feel. It'd smoldered on her mind all day like a banked fire.

Later, the moon cast a soft glow over the lagoon. Mick rose and took her hand. "Jamie, come into the water with me. The tide's in and the water is so clear you can see the bottom in the moonlight." His voice was low, as if whispering a secret. "I want to hold you against me. All day, it was all I thought about." He rose and took off his shirt, and she helped him remove his damp jeans. Jamie laid her skirt on the sand, but kept her shirt and under things on. Together they went into the lagoon. *You crazy fool!* She heard faint warnings from some far off place, but could not listen anymore. A languorous weakness swept softly over her as she followed him into the shimmering lagoon.

Mick held her against him and kissed her deeply. His hands moved over her, seeking out every curve, learning her body's secret, wonderful places. "Oh, girl, you're so lovely, so smooth, your skin's like fine satin."

They clung together, taking in the strength of each other's essence. She melted into his body, lining herself close against his flesh every possible place she found.

She felt the strength leaving her legs as they clung so close. His lips closed over hers, again and again, in deep wanting kisses.

Lost in him now, her clinging passion set him wildly afire. Things had gone too far. Fighting for control, she gave up. His hands moved over her skin, so wet and slick with seawater. Her battle was lost and she knew it. She barely kept to her feet in the warm swirling waters of the lagoon.

He swept his arm under her knees and lifted her up against his body. His lips remained on hers, seeking out the very essence of her soul. She responded frantically as he strode to the sandy beach, holding her close against him.

He knelt down with her and hastily spread her discarded skirt over the soft sand. He laid her gently on the wrinkled fabric and, in the shadows of the moonlight, looked deeply into her eyes. "Darling, it'll be all right, I couldn't stop now. I need you too much. I've wanted you almost from the beginning. I've fought this so long—forgive me, girl."

He laid himself over her body, gently removing her filmy, raggedy under things, along with the torn and ruined blouse.

She uttered no protest and began to assist him. Her acceptance acted like fire in his veins. He kissed her with hard longing kisses, probing the depths of her willing mouth. He sought out her smooth rounded breasts and suckled deeply on them, each one in turn.

The drawing sensation filled her with molten fire, "Oh, Mick! Please, I can't wait any longer for you—oh please!" She reached for his swollen member, frantically guiding him to her.

She thought he tried to be gentle, but neither of them could wait, and they lost themselves in that age-old timeless madness until they laid together gasping for breath. For a time, she didn't know where she was—floating—

"Jamie, girl—*Jamilla*—are you all right?" he whispered, raising himself on an elbow, smiling into her eyes.

She saw the dark glow of his black eyes in the faint light cast by the waning moon. He lay partially over her, reluctant to separate himself from her warm and willing flesh.

"Yes. Oh, yes, Mick. I could cry from the wonder of it! I guess I didn't keep you away for long." Sheepish over her lack of will power, she couldn't stop the smile spreading over her face. "So this is what they talk about. Mick, I never knew!" She pulled him fully onto herself, reveling in the feel and weight of his long body across hers. "I love you," she whispered against his cheek, pressed so close to hers.

"Oh, girl, you're a wonder to me. I've wanted you almost from the first, when I became aware of you, realized what a woman you were. I couldn't help it! Nothing like this has ever happened to me. Even on the raft, something bound us to each other, but I never believed this was possible for me, not in my lifetime." He kissed her face, her eyes and laughed with joy.

He pulled her up, and, together, they went into the water again. He made gentle love to her there in the moon light. They spent the night, waking, sleeping, and loving each other like the lost souls they were, not sure of another day together. Their life hung on a slim thread, yet they clung to each other for the oneness they hoped to know for a lifetime.

Jamie believed disaster waited, but blotted it out of her mind in Mick's loving embrace. She played a deadly game, lying in his arms. And Mick, he'd waited and won the woman he wanted. If disaster lay ahead for them, neither gave thought to it.

# CHAPTER 22

The four lost souls spent their days eking out a scanty livelihood, hunting for wood to burn, and daily grew slimmer with their meager fare. Jamie, though deliriously happy, worried constantly. The ugly specter of starvation loomed over the hope for rescue and the never-ending hunt for food. It became their all-consuming passion. Thoughts of slow death by starvation claimed their minds as they helplessly watched their pitiful food supply diminish.

They set a large pile of wood on the highest outcropping of rocks in hopes a vessel or seaplane might pass near. But the weeks dragged on without as much as the sight of an intercontinental airliner passing overhead. They saw no sails, no cruise ships, nothing. Frequently, hopelessness overtook them, as a deep fear settled into their minds. Were they lost forever, hidden away from the world? Jamie often had the feeling she lived a tragedy in slow motion.

Mick recovered the use of his left arm and did his share in their hunt for food. His love and passion for Jamie increased daily. Obviously involved, they declared their alliance to their island co-inhabitants.

"Like it's a big surprise, you two." Felicia laughed. "Jim and I are planning the big day ourselves, when someone comes to rescue us." Sadness, etched with fear, lay in her troubled eyes.

Jamie didn't voice her despair, nor did the others. They

lived an unreal sort of happiness, idyllic in many ways. Aside from the daily struggle for food, no outside influences marred their days and nights.

"How long have we been here?" Jamie wondered aloud. They'd finished a small breakfast of nearly nothing. "It's been many weeks, or is it months by now?"

"How many times have you had your monthly courses? Felicia whispered. "That's a good way to tell." She giggled. "Or is it?" She frowned and looked at Jamie. They had no safety nets in their present circumstances.

Jamie flushed, trying to remember. The first time it happened, she'd hissed a warning for Mick to stay away for a few days. While picking bananas, he'd approached her, only to hear her order him to stay away.

He'd laughed. "A few days?" Grinning from ear to ear, he told her, "I'm not afraid of that, Jamie. It's a part of you, and I love every part. You might stay out of the deeper parts of the lagoon. Sharks might find you especially attractive right now."

He'd never stayed away from her for one night, for that, or any other reason, but respected her fastidiousness. Not only did she find him mysterious, she thought him amazingly loving and thoughtful.

Hunting far afield these days for food and fuel, Jamie searched for green coconuts. These had become scarce, too. "Mick, you know, it hasn't stormed for a while. When it does, it loosens a lot of coconuts and makes it easy to find them. Jim has knocked off most of them around here. Will we run out of those, too?"

"I doubt we'll ever be without those, but aside from that, we could be in for a *real* blow any day, this time of year," Mick said. "In fact we'd best check out that cave. We may need it for shelter if a typhoon comes our way. Storms like that can sweep over most of a small island like this."

Jamie frowned, her mind filling with new worries. "You make me nervous with your typhoon story. Are you trying to scare me, Mick? Nothing would surprise me anymore."

"It happens often enough in the South Pacific, Jamie." He motioned over his shoulder. "I need to have a word with Jim."

His serious tone left her feeling chilled. Jamie sighed and gazed after his lanky form as it disappeared beneath the trees. She turned to see Felicia gazing dreamlike out over the lagoon.

Suddenly, Jamie stiffened. "Oh, God, it's them! Look out there, Felicia," she cried, pointing out past the reef, over the foaming breakers to the distant horizon. "See, aren't those square-looking sails way off in the distance? It's that Chinese junk, looking for survivors—for us. We have to tell the guys right away!" Heart hammering in terror, she ran toward the camp with Felicia following after.

Mick and Jim stood together preparing to check out the cave. Jamie almost ran into them, her eyes wide with fear. Mick felt his body tighten, seeing her terrified look. "What is it, Jamie, what's wrong?"

Not given to false hysterics, when she saw trouble, he believed her.

"It's them—the smugglers. I saw those horrid square sails. They're far off on the horizon, but God help us, they're out there." She clung to Mick. "What'll we do if they come here?"

Felicia stood there, pale with fright, hands flung out in helplessness as they waited for his answer.

Mick ran to the beach. Returning, he was decisive. "It's likely them. First, put out this fire and erase all trace of our presence. They're still far off, and the tide's out. No one can pass over that reef except at full tide, and that'll give us six or eight hours. Jim, get those life rafts hidden. Girls, look for any bits of clothing, bones, scraps, coconut husks, anything that says we were ever here. Bury any refuse under these big leaves, and scatter them in a natural way. Maybe one of you'd best keep watch from the edge of the trees. They may not get here today, but they *are* in the area. If they're hunting for survivors, someone has been picked up from the *Ilikii*." His eyes filled with panic as he looked at Jamie. His jaw tightened, firming the indentations along his face "Dammit all to hell. Why them, and not some search vessel?"

They set to the task, erasing all signs of habitation. Their friendly little camp literally disappeared as they worked.

"I'll go keep watch," Jamie said, "but later, could we climb the high point of those rocks by the cave to see farther out to sea? We have to know what's happening, Mick, I can't bear not knowing."

Jim looked up into the monkey pod tree. "I'm going up there. The falling leaves and dead limbs have made a mat over some of those branches? I'll put the rafts up there. You'd never see them from down here."

He stepped to the lowest branches and began to climb.

"Be careful Jim," Felicia called, watching his progress.

He reached the heavy mat of old leaves and refuse caught in the wide spreading branches. Still a big man, the tree limbs bent and cracked beneath his weight. "Hey, it's like a big flatbed up here, It'll do to hide just about anything." He came down and got a grip on one of the rafts. Deflated about half by now, they offered little resistance as he dragged the first one upward. Something fell into the leaves and clinked.

Felicia bent to look. "It's the other jar of peanuts. We never got around to eating them. I guess we'll need these now more than ever."

A worried look crossed her beautiful features. Jim returned for the next raft and enclosed Felicia in his arms. "Darling, don't worry so much. We'll get out of this, we will."

He kissed her tenderly and left to place the other raft up in the tree. When he finished, they were not visible from the ground. He stood back surveying his work.

"Good job, Jim, good idea," Mick said grimly. "We may need every trick in the book to avoid the bastards. They won't leave witnesses, not those devils."

He appraised the area carefully. The rising tide would wipe out all footprints on the beach, and the rest were lost in the thick matting of leaves. Satisfied, he went to the beach to look for Jamie, finding her in the shade of the coconut palms bent and leaning gracefully out over the sand and water's edge.

"See any changes, girl?" He embraced her and drew her head against his chest. "Don't worry too much. They may bypass this little island if we're lucky." He wanted to believe it, and in his concern for the women, he prayed for it.

She looked to him for comfort. "It doesn't seem like they're any closer Mick. Maybe they won't come here. If they do, our footprints are all over the beach."

Mick's worries were for the three of them, not for himself. "They can't come ashore until high tide, and that'll wipe our tracks away. There's nothing else on the beach to worry about." They started for the campsite. "I wanted more nights with you on the beach. Damn the slimy bastards."

"Me too, Mick, every time we're out there, I worry it might be the last time." Jamie pressed against him as they walked. "I wonder what will happen next."

Mick admired her courage and regretted the feelings of fear and discouragement she suffered almost daily in this continuing ordeal.

Jim had the camp secured and readied. They picked up all edible fruit, meat, and coconuts, and began the walk inland carrying everything usable from the campsite. Looking back, it looked pristine and unused.

"It looks so deserted. It's like leaving home, isn't it?" Felicia murmured, struggling with a net full of bananas.

Mick carried a net half-full of coconuts, the last they'd found lying on the ground. He looked for telltale tracks left earlier and found that the carpet of leaves hid them well enough. If he saw a footprint, he brushed it out with a branch. "Jamie, we need to check out the trail to the guava tree, in case we left tracks there, but let's wait awhile on that, until we see if the Junk is heading our way. It could take them another day. They may think this small island isn't worth checking out. I'm still holding out for that, and it'd be a lucky break. We didn't see any other islands when we found this one, if you remember."

"I don't remember seeing much that day, Mick—praying for water, dying of thirst, and being scared to death of you." She smiled up at him as they moved slowly to the cave, struggling with their scant household goods.

Jim and Felicia reached the papaya trees and waited there for Mick and Jamie. "Well, now we need to plan what to do, Mick," Jim said. "Jamie, you thought there might be another entrance, up higher?" he asked. "We should have scoped that feature out long before this."

"I think it'd be to the left and higher by twenty or more feet." She stepped around some of the rocks near the entrance to begin climbing.

They stood near the bottom watching as Jamie made her way upward. "Be careful Jamie," Felicia called. "That looks about high enough. Do you see anything that looks like an opening?" Then she giggled. "Jamie, your clothes are flapping in the wind." There hadn't been more than the usual soft trade winds so far today.

Mick wondered about the wind. In fact, it had become unusually windy.

Jamie's tattered skirt could not withstand the challenge of the stronger wind. It sailed upward, revealing every inch of her long tanned legs, and a good bit of ragged, lacy undergarment.

"I don't see the opening yet, "Jamie told them. She poked about in the jagged rocks. "It would be easier from the inside if we could reach up there." The gusty winds caught at her skirt continually, and she tried to gather it close to her holding her ragged clothing against her body. "Darn this wind. Where did it come from, and why haven't we checked this opening before this?"

"I'll go in there," Jim said. "I might be able to think of

something." He turned to enter the cave, kneeling onto hands and knees.

Jamie stood up on the rocks, fighting to keep her skirt somewhere within decency as the increasing winds whipped the frayed cloth madly around her thighs. Mick looked up with a glow of appreciation on his face and chuckled when she caught him watching. He nodded and flashed a wide grin of total appreciation.

Jim crawled into the interior and reached the larger room. "Say, this isn't too bad," he called out. "I'm standing up in here and I see the light up there. What laggards we were, just now seeing this part of the cave." He put his hands to his mouth. "Jamie, can you hear me? Just follow my voice."

"I hear you, Jim," Jamie called. She dug a large rock away, finding a small hole. "Hey, is this it?" She poked her head through the narrow aperture then pulled another rock away, letting a bit more light into the dim interior. "I'm up here, Jim."

"That's it. What are you seeing up there?" he called.

"It's sort of flat, and not very big. A ledge drops off to where you are, but there's no way down there. This hole isn't very big either. I'll mark it and get back down." Jamie set a large odd shaped rock on a nearby flat one and, turning away, carefully made her way down to Mick and Felicia. The wind whipped at her with increasing force. "Do you believe this wind? It almost tore my clothes off." She reported her findings. "It didn't look like anything we could use. Maybe the guys can figure something out." She saw the trees swaying madly. "Where is this wind coming from?" She saw Mick's smile and confided to Felicia, "Smugglers can't stop that man from thinking things."

"I noticed the wind too, but I'm wondering where that Chinese ship is. Jamie, I'm *so* scared."

Felicia looked pale, trembling with fear. Jamie put a comforting arm around her as they waited for Jim to come out of the cave. Mick looked intently at the sky, a frown on his face. He saw a long dark bank of clouds on the horizon, just visible over the high rocky prominence.

"What's Mick looking at?" Jamie said. "I'm scared too, Felicia. It was so peaceful before we saw those damned square sails, now our little world is crashing around us. I want to go on top of that high point. I have to look out, see if they're still coming."

Jim emerged from the cave and Mick joined them.

"We should climb to the top and take a look around," Jamie repeated.

"Yes, we'll feel better knowing where they are," Mick replied. "There's enough time." Looking at the sky with a frown over his features, he added, "We'd best stow our stuff inside the cave. We're in for a blow and it could be a big one."

He picked up the large clump of bananas and headed for the cave.

She remembered Mick telling her it was typhoon season. A cold pang of fear coursed through her at the look of concern on his face. *What was it he said about waves coming over these low-lying islands?* She visualized huge surging waves of water, roaring over them, and shivered.

They put their meager possessions inside the cave and searched about for the trail to the top.

"It's on the right side if I remember," Jim said. He took Felicia by the arm and started walking, leaning against the force of the wind.

Pushing their way around the high outcropping of rock, through the shrubs and plants now so familiar, they found the faint trail. The wind howled around them, branches, sticks, and leaves blew against them. Only the fear of a deadly invasion kept them from climbing for the top.

"Damn this wind." Jim tossed his words into the increasing gale. His clothes rippled and snapped madly from the increasing force of it as he helped Felicia over a rough area. "The cave sounds kind of cozy right now."

Mick stayed close to Jamie while struggling their way to

the top. She noted his increased strength, so different from the first time they'd come up this faded old trail. What a beautiful day it'd been, peaceful, with curiosity and finding food the only things on their minds. They'd all been strangers then.

# CHAPTER 23

Mick moved up near Jim. "I'm worried as hell about this wind. We're in for a really big storm, a typhoon maybe—this is the season for it." He pointed at the sky to the south where a dark mass had formed over the water. "I don't like the looks of that."

Jim nodded in agreement. "Being from Kansas, I'm no stranger to tornados and the like."

They stayed low to the ground, careful to avoid being visible to a watching spyglass from the intruders at sea. The northern sky had scudding clouds and patches of sunlight reflecting off the deeper blue of the ocean depths. With relief, they saw the square sails of the Chinese junk receding into the distance.

"The junk is heading away," Jim said. "Again, we seem to be saved by a storm at sea."

"You're right about that, Jim. If there hadn't been a storm that day on the *Ilikii*, we'd all be dead now." Mick remembered that day all too well. Had the smugglers not run before that storm, he wouldn't have found Jamie's raft, and they'd have all died that day. "They're gone for now, but they'll be back after this thing blows itself out," he yelled into the howling wind, but Jim couldn't hear him.

The wind whipped their faces, hair, and clothes madly as they knelt near the top of the outcropping.

"Look over to this side. See how those big rollers break right on shore? That dark cloud bank means we are in for one hell of a big one!" Mick warned, pointing to the heavy, building storm.

Jamie, relieved to see the departing sails, thought the oncoming storm looked dangerous enough, but the vicious drug smugglers were the stuff of nightmares.

"They have radios, don't they? This must be one monstrous big storm or they wouldn't be running for a port somewhere." Jamie cried into Mick's ear.

"I'm afraid so, girl. This could be a rough one, and we've no way to tell for sure. We'd best get down from here, or get blown off. Come on, Jim. Let's get these ladies off this pile of rocks."

He caught hold of Jamie and led her downward, his protecting arm around her. Jim took Felicia's arm. They picked their way through tangled, up torn roots and flying branches. The ferocity of the wind had increased until they felt it would blow them off the faint trail. Trees whipped madly, bending low from the power of the howling winds. They dodged broken branches, and blowing grass whipped their legs as they struggled toward the safety of the cave.

Felicia buried her head against Jim's side and Jamie heard her cry out several times as flying debris struck her body.

"It's okay, darling, we'll make it," Jim said.

Jamie caught snatches of his voice, urging Felicia, as he sheltered her with his arms.

Mick helped Jamie against the whipping wind. She glanced often at him. He was thrilled that she worried about his welfare as well as her own. She flinched against him as a branch flew past. He glimpsed her pale face. "Girl, are you all right?"

"Yes, but this wind is horrible, Mick. Is this a typhoon?"

"This is the right time of year—could be. I hope to hell it isn't. They're mean, *real* mean." He tried to tell her more, but his words were lost against the force of the approaching storm.

They reached the cave and crawled inside, Felicia, then

Jamie. The men entered as the rains began. Sitting in the shelter of the cave, they shivered at the loud wailing of the wind. The patch of sky they could see through the cave opening, had blackened into midnight shades of charcoal and navy, frequently illuminated from bright flashes of lightning. As they looked out the entrance, the sky cast an eerie light on the trees and rocks. Their ears rang, deafened by the crashing noise. Rain poured in heavy sheets, and, though some blew into the cave, they remained dry enough.

Jamie and Mick sought each other for comfort and security. She rested her head on his chest. Being close to him was as natural as life itself. Jim held Felicia the same way. Without planning or design, they'd gravitated to their mates. With no thoughts of right or wrong, they were where they had to be. Anything else would have been deprivation. They huddled close, humbled by the ferocity of the storm.

"Does anyone realize that if it weren't for those horrible drug smugglers, we'd be sitting out under the big tree, trying to survive this awful storm. It looks like we owe them one, doesn't it?" Felicia observed.

Jamie laughed. "Felicia, if I had a pillow, I'd throw it at you. God bless you, you're so right."

The men laughed during a lightning flash. A thrill shot through Jamie at the sight of Mick's dark eyes crinkling at the corners, lighting his features. She drew even closer into his warmth.

During flashes, they glimpsed trees breaking off or blown flat by the wind. Gusts of stinging rain splashed near the cave entrance. Everything outside their cave whipped wildly, and Jamie heard Felicia cry out.

"Oh God, Jim, will it never stop? I'm afraid of storms."

She held Jim's hands over her ears and lay against his chest.

"This is a bad one," Mick said. "It's likely a typhoon. If so, we can expect high surf and waves that will cover most of the island. If that happens, this cave could be a trap." His voice, edged with dread, told of things he'd seen before.

Frightened, Jamie looked at Felicia. There was no other place to go. "I once said that if I died, I'd go as a happy woman," she said. "That was after I fell in love with you, Mick. I hope that wasn't asking for it."

Mick chuckled and nestled his head in her hair. "If you die today, you'll be held tightly in my arms when you go. Maybe they'll take me up there with you."

They waited. The storm's intensity increased beyond belief.

"I'm from Kansas," Jim said, "and this beats the tornados we've had off the open plains. Of course, I didn't sit out a storm hiding in a cave." His voice could be heard during a lull in the roaring noise outside. The cave, no longer a dark and oppressive den, was, to them, a warm, safe haven.

After an hour, they noticed a rapid sudden cessation of the howling winds.

A cool and rarely fearful man, Mick clenched his jaw. "My God, this *is* a typhoon!" he exclaimed. "We're in the eye of it, right now. It came from the backside of this island. Now we'll get it from the lagoon. Monstrous waves will roll over this entire island when it starts up again!"

"Let's rig a way to protect the entrance," Jim said. "If we block up this hole, a big wave washing up here will recede, won't it?" He looked at Mick. "We might get water in here, but not enough to drown us, how about it? Want to go for it?"

"Good idea. We have about a half hour before we catch hell again," Mick replied.

The men crawled out into quietness and a slight rain. The sky had a strange yellowish cast to it, adding unreality to their surroundings. Working to stave off their perilous situation, they looked about for a rock big enough to fill the entrance. "This one would do, but who could move it?"

Mick laughed. His arm, still weak from the shoulder wound, wasn't strong enough. "We need one to jam against the opening, big enough to block a hell of a lot of water. A wave likely to hit us here would have lost strength against the trees and such before it struck."

They searched about for a likely looking boulder.

They decided on one and, together, tugged and rolled it into close proximity of the cave opening.

"You go in with the ladies," Jim said, "and I'll shove this sucker in as far as it'll go." He gave Mick a look that brooked no refusal.

Mick arched an eyebrow. "And?"

"I'll find a downed tree, and go up to that hole into the cave Jamie found. I'll shove it in up there and crawl in. I'm sure I can find a half way decent tree, long enough to get me down to this level."

Jim was decisive and Mick knew he was right. He crawled back into the cave to face Felicia's questioning eyes. He felt guilty as hell, but with the residual weakness of his left arm, there was no other recourse. Jim's incredible strength was needed to shove the big stone. He hoped Jim would make it back into the cave. If not, Felicia would never stop looking at him with those big purple eyes, making him more of a criminal than they knew him to be. Not one of his finer moments, he regretted it intensely.

Outside, in the eerie stillness, Jim set his feet against the large, angular rock and pushed it into the opening. There was plenty of space around it, but the hole was about three-quarters closed. It appeared to be wedged in tightly enough.

"Looks good, it just might work," Mick called over the open edges of the great stone. "You're one strong son of a gun, Jim, the strongest I've seen."

"See ya in a few," Jim called in return.

He left the cave to find a useable tree and didn't need to go far. Most every living thing lay about, torn up and strewn about, as though some destructive madman had loosed his fury on every bit of vegetation in sight. Looking at the darkening sky above, he also noted heavy gray-black clouds surrounding the island as far as he could see. They truly were inside a ring, in the eye of a dreadful tropical storm, and the respite of that inner ring was fading fast.

Jim chose a fallen tree. It was fairly tall and straight. He didn't know its name or species, nor did it matter. He pulled it free of its fragile hold on the earth and, with several thrusts with his foot, broke off most of the remaining root structure. Tucking it under his arm, he dragged it toward the tower of jumbled rocks and the odd-shaped marker Jamie had left earlier. He wondered why the wind hadn't blown it away with everything else.

Looking at the sky, Jim hurried. The wind increased steadily. The eye of the typhoon had nearly passed over them. He reached the opening and put his head through. Too small. He pulled enough rocks away from it until it looked big enough that he could push the root of the tree through. Being stronger than most men stood him in good stead this day. He shoved the rooted part of the downed tree into the opening with a mighty heave. It made cracking sounds as it went down in, and Jim struggled to squeeze his bulk in after it. He came to rest on a small irregular shelf of rock and found it sturdy enough to support him. Stopping to catch a breather, he heard clapping below.

"Jim, you did it!" Felicia cried.

They all stood on the bottom level, looking up at him. Outside, rain poured down again, the water-filled wind had returned in full fury. The sound of it rumbled like a passing freight train outside the cave.

Jim laughed in relief to be out of the swirling madness outside. "So, where in hell is my tree now?"

When his eyes adjusted to the dimness of the cave's interior, he saw the top of his tree alongside the ledge he rested on and guessed the bottom would be down on the lower level.

Mick laughed, relieved to see Jim in the cave. "That's a sturdy tree. It's a wonder you got it in here. You're one strong son of a gun, man." He hurried over to it. "It's lodged against the wall and the floor down here. I think a tree climber like you can make it down. I'll steady it."

Felicia's attitude had relaxed. Though the storm raged outside again, there would be peace in the cave.

"Here goes." Jim placed his feet tentatively on the smaller upper limbs and worked his way over the edge of the ledge, making it down easily, though he broke off half the branches as he slipped down the lacerated tree.

"Oh—Jim—thank God, you're safe!" Felicia cried. Ignoring bits of bark, roots, and tree branch, she flung herself against him. "You were wonderful." Her voice was filled with pride as she clung to him. "I was so worried you'd be stuck out in that dreadful storm. It's wild out there again."

"What did you see out there Jim?" Jamie asked.

"We are truly in the eye of this thing. It's all around us. We are in the middle of a huge ring of dark, heavy, clouds. Our tornados look like funnels, and, if we're lucky, they stay far away." Jim grimaced. "I've never seen anything like that, ever."

"I have," Mick said. "About two years ago, at sea. Our ship wasn't much bigger than the *Ilikii*, and we nearly lost it before we made a safe harbor. I don't know if this storm equals that one, but it's nasty enough," he said. "I'm glad you got in here, Jim. I think Felicia wanted me dead a short while back." Seeing a slight smile on Felicia's lips, Mike heaved a sigh of relief. "Felicia, I couldn't have done what Jim just did, you must know that?"

"I'm sorry, Mick, I do know it." She looked at him with a wry smile. "But I was afraid of Jim getting lost out there. Now that I've found him, I wouldn't want to lose him."

They crawled back to the entrance and looked over the sides of the rock Jim had wedged into the opening, wanting to see what was happening. It was dark from the storm, but during lightning flashes, they could see things whipping about, debris flying everywhere.

Then they heard booming sounds from the lagoon. "Here it comes," Mick said. "We'll see some monster waves now. I guess we do owe those smugglers a vote of thanks. We'd be lost for sure under that monkey pod tree. No one could withstand waves like those. They can be more than thirty feet high. We'd best hope they've diminished by the time they reach up here."

Jamie, though fearful of the storm, reflected once again on Mick's well-educated speech. Not at all like the greasy-looking sailor she'd seen that fateful day, cursing on the dock before they sailed. *Mick, who are you, anyway?* Lost in thought, she forgot about the raging storm outside.

A whistling, roaring sound came rushing toward the cave.

"Get away from the opening," Mike shouted. "Get into the other part if you can."

Jamie heard him cry, "Oh, God!" as a wall of water, trees, and debris, struck against the cave with a mighty slam. The entire structure trembled.

Water gushed into the cave as if from a dozen firehoses. Everyone ran into the other part and stood up. Water swirled about their knees, but receded, leaving a foot of water or more in the cave to seep away through cracks along the interior, as well as around the big rock Jim had wedged into the opening.

"Now we know how sand got way up here and into this cave," Jim mused. "This must be one typhoon in who knows how many over the centuries. It's a good thing that rock held. We'd be swimming in here if it hadn't."

Jamie felt elated over their success. They'd survived the worst the storm had to offer. Their meager possessions roiled about in the watery mess, but, again, they were survivors.

Several more waves struck their snug little cave, but the force of them lessened with each succeeding one until, at last, it was over, and they realized the storm must have passed from the island. Jim set his feet against the rock, shoved it away, and they went out into the wreckage of the storm-ravaged landscape.

Jim whistled through his teeth as he looked around. "Holy hell! What a mess. I wonder what's left of the place."

*And I wonder what food we have left.* He couldn't voice that concern, but the edge of defeat came creeping in.

Felicia clung to him, staring in disbelief. "It looks like everything's been wiped from the face of the earth. There are only sticks and rocks left. The beautiful trees and flowers are gone! Oh, Jim."

"We'd better see what's left to feed us," Mick said. "For sure, there's fish, but what else?"

In the growing dark, they took stock of the wreckage. Their beautiful, lush island refuge lay in ruins.

Jamie heaved a sigh. "We have the fruit and coconuts we carried up here. It's wet and covered with sand, but we can make do for now, and check things out in the morning. I'm tired from the storm and all. I just want to rest."

Defeated by it all, and wondering how this part of her life would end, she sat on a large rock and let warm, salty tears slide down her cheeks.

# CHAPTER 24

Mick put his hand on her shoulder, pulled her against him, and stroked her hair. "Girl, you're the bravest soul I've ever known, and God knows, I'm worried too."

"Mick, I'm glad for all our nights together. I can stand almost anything, just on the wonder of how it is between us. But couldn't calamity have waited a while longer?" She smiled at that. "I'm so hungry."

They hadn't taken the time to gather papayas into the safety of the cave. Would there be any left after the devastating tidal waves? She didn't want to know about that just now.

They went into the cave to drag out their meager possessions and take stock of what they had left. They still had the tent cloths, the water bottles, the buckets, and the netting with a large bunch of bruised bananas.

"Here are the peanuts, we forgot them, so how about now?" Felicia, delighted with the forgotten treasure, poured some into each outstretched hand. "This reminds me of the first day we came here. Remember, Jamie? We threw the lipstick into the lagoon."

"It wasn't any more use than the flashlight. Lipstick isn't important in our present lifestyle, but these peanuts sure are," Jamie replied. Her hand clutched the precious few round globes, so familiar.

"They go well with bananas, don't they?" Jim laughed,

while he munched the remnants of their last bit of pre-disaster junk food. "I wonder how it happened we never ate these before this. But I'm damned glad we didn't."

"It's dark now," Mick said. "Let's have a night's rest before we see what's ahead of us tomorrow. It's wet in the cave, and its wet out here, but we'll have a little of the moon again." He looked about to find a suitable spot and selected a sand-laden patch of grass. He took one of the tent cloths to spread over it. "Will you stay close to me, tonight?" he asked Jamie. "I don't believe I could stand it if you weren't next to me. I'm tired, too, and I need you."

He took her hand and she followed him to the damp bed he'd prepared.

Jim and Felicia settled together on their own soggy bedding. Soft murmurs came from their direction as they settled themselves. They heard Felicia giggle softly and Jim answer in his deep voice.

Mick lay down and pulled Jamie close against his warm body. They needed the comfort of each other's arms. "Jamie girl, holding you like this, I can survive all the hell old Mother Nature has to offer. You feel so damned good, a healing sort of thing. Rest your head here. To have you sleeping in my arms is—" He broke off, realizing that, nestled close against the warmth of him, she'd had fallen into a deep sleep. "My tired, wonderful girl," he murmured into her hair, his heart filled with the contentment of holding the woman he loved.

∽∾∽

Damp, uncomfortable, and on edge, they managed to get the rest they so desperately needed. Mick's shoulder became increasingly painful because he held her so tight, but he needed that closeness.

Jamie needed it too. When she woke, he whispered things to her that made her ears burn. His passion ran rampant and Jamie lay close enough against him to be vitally aware of it. After hushing him with a warning whisper, she would drift into heavy slumber again. They cherished their intimacy until the sky turned pale with soft hues of dove gray tinged with pale rose.

Jamie turned onto her back and watched the rosy shades tinge the clouded sky. The soft colors changed magically before her eyes and in this way, she forestalled having to look at the devastation around them. Soon enough, they would rise from their damp beds to see what the typhoon had visited upon their island refuge.

Mick lay against her, his arms flung over his head as he slumbered on. The male essence of his body, and the comfort it gave her, seemed right. He was hers and she was his. That mystery never failed to cause a feeling of wonder within her.

Birds wheeled lazily in the early morning sky, bringing a semblance of normalcy to a world she eventually had to face. Remembering the torn landscape, she wondered where the birds had taken refuge. What innate intelligence enabled them to remain alive in a typhoon of such destructive force?

It seemed unfair to Jamie. She thought of events in their lives—starvation, smugglers, and now the typhoon. They'd found a wondrous happiness, only to have it shattered and terrorized by the smugglers searching for them.

*Will we ever know peace or tranquility together?* She turned to look at Mick, stirring beside her. *Am I crazy to think of a normal life with this man? I can't bring myself to face it right now.*

"Morning, Jamie, I loved having you beside me—this night in particular. Together, we can handle anything."

*He must know my thoughts.*

He grimaced in pain when he raised himself up on his right arm. "My shoulder is sore this morning, would you look at it?"

"I'll check it now, Mick. I forgot everything in the storm. I hope it hasn't torn open. You've healed so well."

She moved to his back and pulled his shirt up. "It's red, but hasn't opened, I don't think it will ever open again. Your shirt is horribly dirty." She shuddered. "Oh, Mick, look around. This is a dreadful mess!"

The destruction came fully visible in the early morning light. She heard Jim whistling through his teeth. He was up, looking over the ruined landscape. "We'll have an even tougher time feeding ourselves now," he observed, more to himself than to anyone else in a low voice.

"Ooh, I'm stiff as a board," Felicia moaned. "We didn't have our thick pad of leaves to sleep on." She looked at the devastated papaya grove in dismay. "We still have bananas, maybe some of the coconuts too. I'm so unbelievably hungry." Moving slowly, she worked the stiffness from her body. Her clothing, increasingly loose, was downright baggy these days, and her huge, tattered blouse now draped over small breasts and a flat abdomen. Jamie had done all the alterations Felicia's shorts could tolerate. They draped about her, rather than fit. But not even a storm like the one they'd just survived could dim the luster of her hair.

"Let's eat what we can now, so we don't have to carry it back to the lagoon," Mick suggested when they came together. "I guess we won't need to worry about invaders for a while. That'll give us time to assess the damage to our food supply."

They had the bananas, and Jim found a broken tree stump to open a few coconuts. "It looks like we're back to square one as far as food goes." He offered the coconuts around. Jamie pulled the red knife out of her pocket and poked holes in them for the sweet milk. They ate hardened coconut meat as well. In fact, they ate everything remotely edible.

"I'll need a new buttonhole, Jamie. You haven't had to do that for a while." Mick's wide grin spread over his dark features. "These pants won't stay up much longer if I don't get more alterations, and soon."

She knew it pleased him to see her laugh again. He

dodged the coconut husk she tossed at him. She cut a new buttonhole in Mick's jeans, and a wicked grin spread over his face as she worked. "Hold still, you! How am I supposed to do this if you keep fidgeting?" She lowered her voice as she murmured, "If you don't watch it, I might have an accident, and we wouldn't want that, would we?"

"All right you two, this isn't getting the island checked over." Jim's voice boomed over to them. "Hey, Jamie, I need new buttonholes too, so does Felicia." He held out a very loose waistband for inspection. His disheveled, ragged clothing hung loosely about his tall, gaunt frame. "Look at this, would you?"

They got the alterations needed and set off to survey the damage done by the typhoon. The men walked together. Jamie and Felicia followed. The stream ran fuller and constant. Their water source intact, they followed it downward to the beach, picking their way over denuded rocks and ruined trees. The monstrous tidal waves had left only devastating wreckage behind.

With dismay, they stared at the total destruction. Trees remained, some intact, but most were broken and twisted or uprooted and swept out to sea. They feared for the breadfruit tree. That great shaggy tree supplied their only starchy food.

Approaching what had been their camp, they saw that the monkey pod tree stood. Its great trunk firmly upright, but with many branches broken off, leaves torn away, and the rafts, Jim had so carefully placed up in the branches, missing. The soft beds of leaves were gone, washed away— one more loss. Only sharp bare rocks and debris lay scattered there now.

"After seeing this, I'm afraid to see what's happened to the breadfruit tree," Jamie said. "Of course, the lagoon will be there, but I won't feel comfortable until I see a clear horizon out there." She couldn't help feeling worried and hurried for the shore.

"I'm coming with you," Felicia called.

They walked toward the lagoon, picking their way around torn-up tree roots and sharp rocks, raw and newly exposed.

They came to the beach, only to see much of the pinkish sand moved and changed, and new areas of dark rock visible. The half-buried log was gone, and many of the graceful coconut palms torn away. Coconuts, branches of torn trees, and other debris lay strewn over the sand and in the water. Gentle waves lapped at the water's edge, belying the raging waters that had crashed there only hours ago.

Their island had undergone devastating changes. Sharp rocks lay where lovely flowering trees had flourished. Ugly, compared to the lovely, graceful scenes they remembered.

Jamie sighed. "Oh, Felicia, how destructive the storm must have been to create such havoc. You were right that the smugglers saved our lives. We certainly would never have survived if we weren't in that cave. If they only knew. How strange is that?" Terribly saddened by what they were seeing, she looked out over the reef. It hadn't changed. The surf still boomed over the coral encircling the lagoon. "I don't see any square sails, thank you God, for that."

They searched about for coconuts and took a few back to the half-torn monkey pod tree. The men were examining a large round object with something visibly moving in it.

"Hey, ladies, look here, it's lunch." Jim said as they approached. "It's a sea turtle, and a big son-of-a-gun. It must have been thrown up here by the storm, and landed upside down."

"I've never eaten turtle, Jim, is it good?" Felicia wondered.

"Who cares how it tastes?" Jim replied. "We don't know what we'll have to eat from here on out. This is a beauty, and a lot of meat."

"Actually, they're very tasty," Mick put in. "I love turtle steaks, and it's highly prized with the natives too. They're endangered in many places around the world, and this one is endangered for certain. Jamie, let's have the knife."

"Let's get these things opened first," she said, indicating the coconuts. "Then you guys can do the deed. We'll check out the breadfruit tree while you dress out the turtle. I don't think we want to see that." She went over to Mick. "Here's your knife. It's very small and that's one big turtle."

Wondering, she handed over the little red knife, brushing his hand with her fingertips.

"It'll have to do, won't it? Anything out there?" Mick queried, his dark eyes looking into hers.

"Nothing for now, Mick, The beach has changed so much—it's not the same at all. It's downright ugly and barren, and there're only a few coconut trees left." She swallowed hard. "It could have been worse, I suppose. There's so much destruction." Her voice caught on her tears. "Oh, Mick!"

He comforted her, folding her into his arms and holding her for a few precious moments. "We'll make it out of here, girl. And we can't say we haven't had luck. We've found each other, and that's more luck than I'd ever expected."

His words gave Jamie strength, and she needed it. She turned to go with Felicia. "We'll check the breadfruit tree, Mick."

With regret, she headed into the remains of torn underbrush, washed out roots, wilted flowering trees lying about or caught in the roots of still standing trees. Jamie stared in wonder at the furious power of nature gone mad.

"Could this possibly be any worse, Jamie?" Felicia mourned. As they picked their passage through the wreckage, she stumbled on a half-buried root. "Dammit!"

"It could've been worse," Jamie replied. "For now, we have food with the turtle. Of course, there's always fish. Let's hope that big tree is there."

They neared the area, peering ahead in hope of seeing the ragged tree, still green and filled with those lovely globes of starchy food. However, as they came near, they searched until they found a torn, twisted part of the trunk standing, stripped of most of its branches, and all of its fruit.

Jamie resigned herself to yet another loss. "I guess it was too much to hope for. I wonder how the monkey pod tree survived, and this tree didn't. Maybe these branches were too thick with leaves. Who knows? I don't."

They searched about for fallen breadfruit, found nothing, and none in the tree's few tattered branches.

"It looks like it'll be Atkins for us now, with only meat and coconuts left to eat," Felicia said. "I feel hideously grubby. I need a good shower. Maybe I'll use my favorite shower gel this time, Jamie. Want to borrow it?"

Jamie chuckled. On their way back, they tripped over exposed rocks and walked past piles of wet leaves and broken branches. "At least we're here with good company, right, Felicia? You're happy these days with Jim. It's all too obvious when you're together, and that's constantly."

"Like you and Mick. How strangely it all works out, one day we are worried he's a deadly criminal of the worst sort, the next, who cares? I still say it's better to go for it, than never to know that kind of man. He's so mysterious, so handsome, and he obviously loves you completely." Felicia arched her eyebrows. "How do you feel about it these days?"

"I've no regrets now, maybe I will later. We don't know what will happen to us next in this insanity. I'm glad we've found each other, and I won't worry so far ahead, not anymore. Next, we'll have an earthquake and be trapped under rocks or something, the way things keep happening." Jamie fought the despair in her voice, as her thoughts dwelled on the violence of the past weeks. She shook her head in wonder. *My life is not boring, that's for sure.*

She thought of the long, tedious years of her miserable marriage to Jack Moran. *How did I ever put up with that?* All she'd had back then was food and her caring father. She wondered how he'd dealt with the loss of his only daughter. "I'm not dead, Dad," she murmured to herself, wishing she could let him know. "Oh, Dad, I am so wondrously alive."

"Let's get cleaned up, maybe we'll feel better," Felicia

suggested. She walked close to Jamie and put an arm around her. "My, you're so much smaller, Jamie. Your collarbones are showing. I always thought that looked good on a woman. Mine haven't been visible for years. It looks really good on you, and on me too, I hope."

Jamie blushed, recalling her nights on the beach with Mick, when it was still beautiful. He'd made wonderful, passionate love to her all night long, and her legs went weak just thinking about it. "Mick noticed. He commented on it a while back, when we first came together."

"That good, huh, Jamie?" Felicia laughed, seeing the color rise on Jamie's cheeks. "You go, girl. You've a lot of happiness to catch up on."

# CHAPTER 25

Approaching the camp, they saw a small slip of smoke rising. Jim knelt, blowing on it to encourage the reluctant flames. The dampness from the typhoon had doused the entire island. Finding something dry enough to burn was very difficult. They searched for dry twigs to snap off, dry leaves, anything remotely combustible, to fuel the feeble flames. Desperately hungry, they were nearly drooling at the thought of eating meat. *How disgusting*, Jamie thought. *What are we turning into?*

They finally had a decent fire going, though smoking more than usual. Jamie worried the telltale smoke was visible at sea. "Mick, won't someone see this smoke?" she queried.

"Not if you didn't see any sails out there," he replied. "Don't worry yet. That storm was a bad one. They'll stay in port several days before venturing out again. Possibly, they may not have made it to a safe harbor." He smiled into her eyes to give her comfort and saw her relax.

He tried to make things sound better, Jamie knew, and she appreciated it, even if things weren't.

Relating how they'd found the breadfruit tree, Jamie said, "It may produce again, but it could be years. What a shame. I'd actually developed a taste for them."

"Jamie let's go to the stream and clean up," Felicia called. "They went to see little stream and found an improvement. The stream bed, newly gouged out, had formed a small pond. It was shallow, but deep enough they could submerge in it and enjoy a decent bath. Felicia cried with delight, waded in, and sank down. They had no soap, but the murky, debris laden stream had cleared. "Oh, Jamie, this is wonderful. I can rinse my grubby self clean! Look, it's almost like a hot tub."

They had a happy hour, washing themselves and their clothing.

Mick and Jim heard the happy chatter and sounds of splashing. They wanted to check out what was going on, but weren't sure of the ladies state of dress. They laughingly decided to hold off.

"It's good to hear them laughing, Mick," Jim said. "Lord knows they've been through some tough times."

"You've got that right." Mick frowned. "I'm worried about food. We've probably lost about everything. My God, Jim, it wasn't enough *before* the storm. The smugglers will undoubtedly return to finish their search. Especially, if they've seen our campfire smoke. We're in a hell of a fix, Jim."

Mick could face his fears in Jim's company. He could rely on the man. "Let's not alarm the girls," he said, lowering his voice. "They've suffered so much and been so brave. I'll do whatever it takes to get these women safely out of here. Right now, I don't know what that might be."

"I'm with you, Mick. I'll follow your lead if we come up against it with those junk bastards." Jim's voice held resolve and firmness. "I'm up on the martial arts, and I wouldn't mind a crack at those devils."

"It could be a lot of help, Jim. For now, let's get some of this meat roasting." Mick threaded turtle meat on a slender green limb, and held it over the coals. "We'll have to cook all of this, or see it go bad.

They roasted the meat in the coals as well as on the sticks. When the women came into camp, dripping wet and laughing, wet clothes plastered against newly slimed bodies, they created a picture of total delight. Mick knew they didn't see themselves as they were now. It took a good mirror, and time, to get used to a new image of yourself, be it a good one or bad. Jamie's nearly transparent blouse clung to her, and Mick's breath caught in his throat. How well he remembered his first sight of her unclothed breasts.

He nearly dropped his meat into the fire, until Jim, with a wide smile, nudged him to be careful.

But Jim had his eyes full as well. Felicia had slowly morphed into slender, glorious womanhood and the clinging wet-blouse picture she made stunned them both. Jim's mouth gaped open until Mick punched him. Her hair, wet and drawn back close to her head, outlined the planes of her face. A wondrous beauty, with or without the weight, she was a new Felicia to Jim's adoring eyes. "Darling! You look like a goddess just now, all wet like that!"

"Or a drowned rat," she purred in response. "The stream has a nice pool now. It's wonderful. We had a real bath, sans soap, but fabulous! You guys will have to try it."

The men forgot everything in the mesmerizing presence of feminine splendor.

"That smells so good," she continued. "Look Jamie, turtle meat roasted on a stick." She took a deep breath. Jim's compliment had turned her into delighted mush.

Jim gave her a portion on a scrawny leaf—their usual plates were gone. They had to search long and hard for suitable leaves too. Even that small thing had changed since the storm. Jamie sighed and looked for her portion.

Mick walked over to her. "You look beyond belief, all slicked down like that, girl. I nearly dropped the meat in the fire." He handed her meat on a green stick, his eyes glowing. His look of love and heated words had her burning, inside and out.

Mick watched her. As she sat on the sandy barren ground to eat, her hair, wet and sleek as a seal, revealed more of her face. It had a golden glow. The few freckles scattered over her slim, straight, nose and upper cheeks had faded. Her hair, lustrous and dark, was drying and springing into the halo of curls. Her body had become downright svelte, and he took great pride in her beauty. *And she's mine!*

Always hungry, Jamie ate the roasted meat with gusto, gingerly pulling off hot, succulent bits, and popping them into her mouth. A sheen of fat gleamed from her lips.

"How is it?" he asked.

"Not bad. In fact, it's actually very good, needs salt, but I like it, Mick." She looked up at him, her eyes greener than usual. Her ragged white blouse made her deeply tanned skin appear ever darker. The sheen on her lips looked good, too.

"We need to see if the banana trees made it. I have my doubts. We'll have a harder time feeding ourselves now," Mick said, though he hated to raise her fears about starvation. They'd know it soon enough.

"We're really up against it aren't we?" Jamie replied. "I can take anything, as long as I can be near you." She frowned. "But I can't help but wonder just how bad things will get before we're through with this, the drug smugglers, and God knows what." She finished the meat. "I love that you cooked this over the coals for me."

"Wouldn't a roasted breadfruit go nice with this turtle meat?" Felicia said as she ate her ration with relish. Fat gleamed about her lips and chin, as well.

Jamie laughed. "For sure it would, Felicia. Did you ever imagine you'd miss having breadfruit? I wouldn't have before we went sailing." She shook her head and shrugged, considering what she'd said. "Who knew?"

"Eat up ladies," Jim urged. "We have to use this meat before it spoils. You can't make jerky in this humidity."

"Why don't we put the rest of it in the bailing buckets and put salt water over it?" Mick suggested. "It's worth a shot. What do you say, Jim? It's an idea I've been mulling over. There is far more meat than the four of us can eat in a day or two without getting sick, and we don't need that right now."

"Sure thing, Mick, good idea, what made you think of it?" Jim asked.

"Jamie said it needed salt, and that got me thinking." Mick grinned at her while she finished another bite of meat.

Jamie stood up. "That's all I can eat, Mick. I think my stomach has shrunk, how about you, Felicia?"

"Mine too, Jamie, but for once, I'm not hungry, and that's a wonderful feeling, even if it was all meat," Felicia said. "I'm tired and don't have my soft bed of leaves under a big full-leafed, monkey pod tree."

The huge, dome-shaped tree, wounded and stripped of its fine, feathery leaves, gave little shelter to the castaway souls beneath her. Fecilia sighed, and watched Jim roasting the remainder of the meat.

Jamie found the bailing buckets and headed to the beach. "I'll fill these and we'll put your idea to the test, Mick."

He watched her leave, and immediately felt the loss of her presence. *Bad off as ever, eh, old boy?* he scolded himself.

They prepared the meat to fit in the small buckets. It replaced the salt water, leaving so little it was not likely to keep the meat fresh, but still worth a try.

Jim placed leaves over each container to discourage wandering insects. "We can roast more this evening when we get hungry. For me, I'm a meat eater anyway."

With water bottles and nets, they set out for the guava tree and the banana grove. Mick had little hope they'd find anything left, but his curiosity was strong, and it was important. They needed to know what remained.

The men walked ahead, wondering aloud if the wild pigs had survived. Felicia walked with Jamie and lagged behind. It gave them a chance to discuss things the men didn't need to hear.

"Felicia, did you see the look on Jim's face when you walked into camp all wet like that? His eyes glazed over." Jamie laughed, picturing it. "He's definitely a man in love. It's written all over him. I don't see how you can look as good as you do out here with no makeup, wearing those ragged, dirty clothes. I've always thought true beauty needed to stand a test like that, and believe me, dear girl, you pass."

"Well, thanks for what you said. If we didn't have to worry so much, I'd like hearing it even more. The men think I don't realize the seriousness of the situation, but I do. Even though I'm a woman in love too, I'm *not* that frivolous. I run an art gallery at home, and I do it well." Felicia sighed then frowned. "I've never had to face a situation like this. Thank God, we're here with those two walking ahead. Imagine anything else. I can't." She threw out her hands. "Did we ever think either of us would include Mick in a statement like that?"

Jamie laughed. "You're right. It seems like hell on earth, when everything's so torn up, yet those men make the difference. They make everything right, somehow. I keep wondering how it'll all turn out. I think about it most of the time. I try to figure Mick. He's *not* what he's supposed to be. He's no criminal. I'd stake my life on it, and, in fact, I think I've done just that," she added. "I must trust him. He said I could."

Felicia gave her a hug as they neared the men, standing on a rocky shelf. "I think about Mick, too, Jamie. I pray it goes right for you. Maybe I'm crazy, but I believe it will."

The earth nearby lay gouged and ravaged by the storm.

"I think the papaya tree was about here," Jim said, a frown wrinkling his forehead. "No more of those babies for us." He looked at twisted, torn roots that had been the papaya tree, kicking idly at it with the toe of his worn out deck shoes. "Never cared for them all that much, anyway."

They walked in stunned silence toward the banana grove expecting little better. Food sources seemed to disappear before their eyes, and the ugly specter of starvation loomed before them in a very real way.

Reaching the banana grove, they found only part of the trees torn away.

"There's a barrier against the sea there, a large high area of rocks, much like near the cave," Jim said, pointing toward a high rocky prominence. "Those huge waves were baffled enough to prevent the loss of some banana trees. Actually, the arms of the island probably confined those huge waves from access to some parts of the island."

"Well, that's good news," Mick exclaimed. "We still have a few bananas, eh?"

Hearing the Canadian *eh*, Jamie winked at him, a grin spreading over her face.

"I'll take care of you later, girl!" he whispered and lunged at her, causing a ruddy flush to inflame her cheeks.

"Let's take some back with us," Jim called out from one of the banana trees. "It's been ages since I've had a banana." He chuckled. It helped to have something positive happen and the mood of the four lightened considerably. It only took some small thing these days to bring them a bit of cheer. With nothing positive looming ahead, they had longed for words of comfort or mirth.

"Let's look around this pile of rocks, might find something useful," Mick said. "I wonder why we didn't see it before. We've been here how many times?"

"I think all we saw were bananas. I know I was happy to see them," Felicia said. "I'm delighted to see them now, too."

She tossed her hair in the sunlight. It had dried to a glossy, tawny golden mass. Streaks of dark blonde traced through it. Jim watched the way her hair sparkled in the light and smiled.

"I wonder if the pigs survived," Jamie said, looking about for signs of the guava-thieving porkers. "They won't be stealing guavas anytime soon. I wonder if they like bananas."

Mick climbed the rocky out cropping. "Nothing exciting up here. It's pretty intact hereabouts," he called out from the top, looking out to sea and around the wasted and torn island.

Jamie watched the wind ruffling his hair where he sat on his rocky perch, his dark features lost in thought.

"I wonder what he's thinking about up there," Felicia said gazing up at Mick. "He looks so serious."

"He's worried about getting us off this place, or what will happen if the smugglers come again," Jamie said. "'They will,' he said. We can't stay here much longer with most of our pitiful food supply destroyed. He believes all this will end soon," Looking up at Mick, she felt he carried a burden for them all.

Jim joined them. "I saw a few pig tracks, so some of them have survived. We'll need to figure how to snare one." He nudged Felicia, and pulled her close. "Looks like pork chops will be on our skimpy menu, if we're lucky."

Mick made his way down to them, reaching out to steady himself on the larger rocks. He used his left arm in nearly normal fashion these days.

"See anything up there?" Jim asked when he reached them.

"Nothing out to sea. There's one hell of a lot of devastation all over the island. My God, it's a mess." His somber tone made Jamie believe he was depressed.

"I've seen pig sign," Jim told him. "Maybe we can catch a couple for dinner some night." He shook his head in wonder. "I wonder how they survived, the hardy little buggers."

"Probably hid back in these rocks somewhere," Mick said. "Wild animals are smarter than the domestic sort." He looked toward camp. "We'd best start back."

Jamie came to his side. Seeing Mick troubled caused an unrelenting fear in her. He'd become her rock. If he was fearful, she felt the loss of her own security.

"Something wrong, Mick?" she queried, not sure she wanted to know.

"Nothing new, Jamie. It's just that, soon, we'll be in serious trouble. It's bound to come. You're all innocent bystanders, so to speak, none of you asked to get involved in this mix-up."

She shook her head. "Well, it happened, and something good has come from it. I've found you."

"That worries me more than the rest, if anything or anyone laid a hand on you, Jamie—" His eyes flashed and his jaw clenched tight. "God help me, I couldn't stand that!"

Jim and Felicia came up, interrupting their closeness. A look of alarm flashed over her tanned features, and Jim's eyes held a questioning look.

"Hey, you forgot the bananas," Felicia chided. "What's so important? You're so deep in conversation, something wrong?"

"No, no more problems than we have now." Mick smiled at the seriousness of the people facing him. "I was borrowing trouble, but we can wait on that." He turned to Jamie. "Let's get those bananas before we get into trouble."

When they finished gathering what they could, the four turned toward the camp, walking through the devastated landscape. Jim carried a good-sized clump of bananas. Mick held what he could and walked with Jim. The women followed behind.

"What were you two talking about?" Felicia asked Jamie, her eyes wide with alarm. "Why is he worrying? Don't tell me it's nothing. I saw his face."

"There's nothing new. He's worried about getting us out of here, and how that might happen. I know he's worried about the drug people coming here, and what could happen to the rest of us. He's not worried for himself."

"Oh, that's all," Felicia said, visibly relieved. "I thought he saw something out at sea, and didn't want to tell us. He *is* just borrowing trouble, isn't he?"

Entering camp, Jim checked the turtle meat in the buckets. He came back to them holding out both buckets, empty. "Those rotten, little bastard pigs have been here! Our meat's gone—all of it!" He threw the empty buckets to the ground, his face red with anger. "I'll get those dirty little bastards! Excuse my language, girls, I could've said a helluva lot worse. *Damn them.*"

Jamie, unable to suppress her mirth, burst into wild laughter and was accompanied by Mick and Felicia. The hilarity, though directed at the pigs and at Jim in his bewildered anger, finally affected the angry man. Reluctantly, at first, he finally joined them with a full belly laugh.

"So, what's for supper, huh?" Jim finally gasped,

# CHAPTER 26

As evening came, they partook of bananas and coconuts. Jamie felt they were more relaxed after a good laugh. They'd seen the total devastation, been robbed of their only bit of meat, and had prepared themselves mentally to face whatever hellish thing the next day might bring.

Mick took up one of the tent cloths and beckoned to her. "Jamie, let's go on the beach, find a nice soft bed of sand, and get some rest."

Jamie nodded. They turned toward the beach in the dusk of evening. Jim and Felicia took the other cloth and went their way, each couple seeking a private place as darkness grew.

Jamie followed Mick as he searched for a place to settle for the night. Thoughts of his arms around her, him holding her, saying and doing things to her, set her body on fire and brought a numbing weakness over her. Resistance against him was impossible, had she even contemplated such action. The desperate longing to lay with him on the sand, holding his long, firm, body against hers, knowing again the scent of his skin, hair, and those seeking lips, made her hunger even more for the comfort he had to give.

In her mind, she detailed all that had happened since they had first been alone together, loving, caressing, kissing. She'd never imagined that kind of tenderness from the touch of a man's hands was possible. It seemed weeks, or months, since they'd been together. But any amount of time they were apart seemed interminable in her eager longing for Mick's company and his magical touch.

He walked ahead of her, bent on seeking the place where they would lie together, enjoying each other anew. He selected a bank of deep soft sand and turned to her. "How about here?" he murmured, his voice deep and husky with feeling.

"Yes, Mick, It's fine." She could barely speak as he spread the small area of tent cloth over the sand.

"Jamie, dearest girl, I've waited so long. I thought this day would never end." He folded her in his arms, and she felt the strength nearly regained in his left one. As he held her close, she heard him breathing in the scent of her clean hair and skin. "You smell like heaven, girl. I'll never have enough of you. No matter how long we live, it will never be enough!"

He sought her lips and pressed ever deeper until her lips opened to his searching tongue. She met him all the way in her eagerness.

He laid her on the scanty cloth and then drew away for a moment. "Jamie, you're so sweet and clean. I'll take a dip in the lagoon, before we go further. Hold on a minute." He rose up, removed his clothes, and went into the water. She watched the beginning moon's soft light gleam across his tall, slender body. He dove into the shimmering lagoon, cleansing himself in the warm, tropical waters.

Returning, his skin glistened with seawater. His long form and narrow hips moved gracefully. Like a sleek wildcat, he came to her in the softness of the moon's glow. She saw his love for her in his eyes and her arms opened to welcome him.

"Mick, today was the longest day of my life, worrying something else might happen and we'd never have another night together." She pressed herself against him. "I love you. You know I tried not to, but I couldn't stop it from happening. I am not sorry for anything, and I've given myself into your keeping, for whatever that might mean."

Mick stopped her words, his mouth over hers, going ever deeper with his probing tongue. She met him fully, and more, until she lay gasping against him.

Sitting back he grasped her shoulders and held her in front of him, his dark gaze burning into hers. "Jamie girl, you know I love you. Do you, Jamie—Jamilla?"

"Yes, Mick, I believe you. Not by what you say, but how you are with me. No man could be so loving and tender without love." Her body pressed into his chest, slick with seawater, the scent of him going into her very depths.

Then he took her, driving her to heights yet unknown.

Afterward, he spent the remainder of the night gently and leisurely loving her, quieting her fears, as they shared the wonder and magic of each other.

As dawn approached, he gently woke her. "Jamie darling, last night, in my heart and mind, I made you my wife. For as long as my life will be, it's yours to have and keep. I'll do all in my power to protect you. If you'll have me, when we get to civilization, we'll be married. Would you have me for a husband?"

Jamie heard his gentle declaration. He'd asked before, but not in this passionate way. With tears forming in her eyes, she nodded. "Mick, I *will* have you, oh yes, I will! I'd be proud to be your wife." She rose to her knees before him. "I don't know who you really are, but I know what you are to me. And, Mick, in my lifetime, I could never love any other man."

"That seals it then. I've never been in love before, Jamie, and I'm happy as hell about this. It's because of what you are, girl. I told you once back a while ago that you didn't know yourself. My God, I have never seen your like. You have heart, courage, and toughness. I've seen it and been saved by it. I'd count myself lucky to have children with you when that time comes." He drew her into his arms again and kissed her gently. "Let's have a wash here in the lagoon. I'm sure it'd be a good idea."

They laughed and went together into the clear azure waters of the lagoon. The booming of the breakers out over the reef and the seabirds wheeling about in the pearly-pink-tinged morning sky were part of their world. And there were no square sails.

∽∾∽

The four gathered under the monkey pod tree, making a scanty breakfast of bananas and coconuts—they had nothing else. Jamie knew something was in the wind by the way Jim huffed about the campsite.

"So how about we go pig hunting, Mick?" Jim's big, gaunt frame stood squarely in front of Mick. Still burned by the loss of the turtle meat, his big shoulders were set firm, a frown across his face. "I'm hungry as hell. We all are."

"Sure thing. The horizon's clear out there, and we've got all day. Any ideas?" Mick couldn't keep a grin from his face as he winked at Jamie and Felicia.

"We still have the nets. How about we put them together and rig up a snare. Then we'll lure them into it with bananas? What else do we have?" Jim's attitude was easier, and though still burned at the pigs, he could laugh about their theft of the turtle meat. "We need to lace them together some way. So, Jamie, what was it you said about making rope out of coconut fiber? Could you show us how we do it? We don't have the shovel anymore. I guess we'll have to change our tactics."

"I saw it on the Discovery Channel," Jamie said, now sorry she'd ever mentioned it. "These women in India did it. They made rope for a living. I didn't make any myself, I just saw them do it on TV."

"Hell, if it's that much trouble, can't we use some of these vines? We should be able to find enough, even after the storm." Jim went to search through the torn underbrush. Mick went with him.

The women sat on an exposed root of the Monkey Pod tree watching them.

"What'll happen if they catch another wild pig?" Felicia frowned, looking at Jamie. "They could get hurt, you know. They've been lucky so far, but it's a worry. Those animals looked wicked—remember the one with the ugly yellow tusks? He's out there, and probably meaner than ever after this storm. Jim could get hurt, Mick too." Felicia's thoughts changed with her mood as she turned questioning eyes to Jamie. "Speaking of him, how's it going between you?"

"Oh, I'd have to say pretty well," Jamie answered. "Mick has asked me to marry him when we get back to civilization, and it was a real proposal. How could that be possible? I believe he loves me. I've no doubt of that at all. I'll just have to believe him and wait and see. I love him more than I ever dreamed I could ever love any man." She shrugged. A helpless feeling of wonder spread over her. What would her father think about her relationship with a known criminal? "What chance for a future could we possibly have? But it's all I have to cling to. Tell Jim, when you're alone. Mick can tell him what he wants."

"Wow, Jamie, that's heavy. Somehow, I believe it'll work out. I don't know why, I just know it will." Felicia smiled. "No wonder you aren't thinking of pig hunting! You have far more important things on your mind."

"At least we had another night together, who knows what might happen today." Mellow as mush after her night with Mick, Jamie found it difficult worrying about anything. She sighed and leaned against the huge trunk of the tree. "I'm horribly, damnably hungry. That's what I know."

They saw the men returning with an armload of vines.

"Okay ladies, can you use this to sew us a net?" Jim said, tossing them on the ground. He was laughing, his mood having improved greatly since he and Mick had put the project together.

Aligning the two nets side by side, the women found enough limber vines to bind the pieces together.

Jim wound the vines around the outer edge. "If we reinforce the outside, maybe it will draw into a bag—if we get one of the little suckers in it," he muttered under his breath. "We need a way to draw the little bastards up in it."

Jamie saw Mick grinning widely while they worked with the nets. Jim needed revenge on the porcine predators to ease his wounded psyche.

"Let's rig a snare," Mick said. "We can't be too near, or they'll catch our scent. Being wild, they won't come in if we're too close. A snare will spring up on its own if they trip it."

He had good ideas, and Jim went along with him. They worked up a plan and, after endless discussion, were ready to take a shot at it.

"Do you want to come, or stay here?" Jim asked the women.

"We'll stay right here, but take care—and good luck!" Felicia warned as they left camp and worry shone in the depths of her eyes. "I hope this works out."

"There're two of them, don't worry so much, I'd love some pork again. It's been days since we've had it." Jamie, lost in lassitude, couldn't keep dreamy feelings from her mind. She found no worries for the moment.

Felicia shrugged. "I'd love some too. I worry overmuch at dangerous things like this. I would die if anything happened to Jim now that we're together. What a way to meet the man of your dreams, huh?"

Jamie snorted. "At least we haven't any competition, and it's a good thing Jim's mooning after you. With your looks, you'd have Mick, too. It's lucky he was wounded and needed my nursing care. I think that's what got to him. I do wonder, if we'd met them in a bar in Papeete, would it have turned out the same? We'll never know that, will we?"

They spent the rest of the morning, and the better part of the afternoon, relaxed and talking. Then Jamie sat up and faced Felicia. "You know, we should be fishing. Then if they don't get a pig, we'll have something for supper."

"Do we have any spears? I haven't seen a sign of them since the storm. We'll have to make some again," Felicia said. "We can't make them now, we don't have the knife. The guys have it—" Suddenly, she sat up, her face blanched pale, worry in her eyes. "I wonder what's happening, Jamie? All of a sudden, I'm terribly afraid, and I don't know why. I have to see if they're all right." Panicked, she rose to her feet and started in the direction the men had taken. She didn't wait for Jamie and never looked back.

Believing Felicia based her fear on some inner sense of foreboding, and seeing her agitation, Jamie made haste to follow. *Maybe Felicia is right and the men are in trouble.* "I'm right behind you, what's got in to you?"

"I don't know, but I have a strong feeling something's terribly wrong. I can't rest until we know for sure." Felicia walked at such a rapid clip that Jamie could barely keep pace with her.

Racing through the ruined landscape, they neither saw it or thought of it. Nearly breathless, they hurried in the direction the men had taken until they heard shouting.

"Hold on, Jim, I'll get the nasty little bastard," Mick's deep voice called out. "What the—Hell's bells, Jim, you're hurt! Dammit all to Hell, he sure got you!" He yelled in alarm.

When the girls reached the area, they saw Jim's left arm red with blood flowing from a ragged gash and dripping in thick red gouts off the tips of his fingers. Mick slashed repeatedly at a struggling pig, caught up in the makeshift net.

The blood of life gushed from the pig's neck. "That's him now, Jim, he's done for."

Jamie caught a glimpse of wicked, twisted yellowed tusks. The large boar they'd encountered the first day lay swinging in the makeshift snare. It struggled, then hung limp, swaying lazily in the soiled netting.

Felicia, transfixed with horror, grabbed Jim's arm, coming close, though fearful of the pig. "My God Jim, you're all bloody! Jamie, quick! See if it's bad!"

Mick stepped close to Jim and looked closely. "Damn, he got you a good one. That's not all pig's blood on your arm." He stepped back and nodded at Jamie.

She took a look. Jim had a long ragged tear down the outer aspect of his left forearm, and it looked deep. Blood poured profusely from it, dripping into the sandy soil. She quickly decided. "We need to get this attended to right away. Who knows what filth a pig carries on their tusks?" Without hesitation, she tore a wide strip from her skirt and, folding it, pressed it tightly into the wound.

Felicia tore fabric from the bottom of her walking shorts to tie it in place. "Oh, Jim, I hope that stops the awful bleeding."

"We have to clean it in the lagoon right away. I hope ocean water will be enough, that's a nasty wound, Jim," Jamie cried. "Dear God, what'll happen next?"

Felicia stood next to Jim, tears in her eyes. "I knew something was wrong, I knew it!"

"She did, Jim. It was so strong, there was no stopping her, and we came running to see." Jamie related, while thinking what she could do for Jim's arm. It was a deep slash, and worse, likely filthy from the pigs rooting tusks. Could she clean it out enough to prevent infection?

"Felicia, stay and help Mick with this meat. He can't handle it alone and, after the price these guys have paid in getting it, we can't leave it here." Jamie looked at Mick and Jim. "I must attend to this arm quickly. It'll be dark soon. I need light."

"You're right," Felicia agreed. "I couldn't fix his arm as well as you, and it can't wait." She shuddered as the dead pig swung gently in the netting, blood dripping from a gash in its throat. "Go, Jamie, we'll take care of this business, right, Mick?"

"You girls will do when there's trouble, I'll say that," Mick agreed, approval shining in his black eyes.

Jamie saw his worry over Jim's wound reflected in his face, increasing her own fear for Jim's survival.

She heard Mick's voice as she led Jim back along the trail.

"I can do most of this, Felicia. Just give me a hand."

If she uttered a reply, Jamie didn't catch it.

Jim, obviously in severe pain, followed Jamie, his jaw clenched tight, his face pale. She urged him along as rapidly as he could manage, but she thought he must be in shock, as he stumbled more than once.

Blood seeped through the tight dressing, but Jamie didn't think it was life threatening. She had to get him to the lagoon. If he passed out, she'd never move him. He'd lost considerable size since they'd been here, but his tall gaunt figure still towered over her. Jim would never be small in any case.

"We're nearly there, Jim," she encouraged, "just a little way to go. You'll make it." His face had gone pale and clammy. It wasn't a good sign, and it worried her. "Please, God, help me get him there," she prayed under her breath while she edged him along.

They reached the water's edge, and Jim collapsed heavily on the sand. "Thanks, Jamie. I thought I might not make it. I don't know why I feel so weak." He sighed, blew out his breath, and looked at his arm. "The little sucker slashed at me when I tried to cut his throat. He might be the same one we saw on the trail the first day we saw the pigs. Remember those wicked looking tusks?"

He seemed to gain strength as he talked and Jamie heaved a sigh of relief. His color had improved. "Let's get this cleaned up, Jim," she said. "I think it has stopped bleeding so much." She carefully removed the blood-soaked dressings. Seeing the extent of the gaping, jagged, irregular wound, she gasped. "It's pretty deep." She kept her voice steady, not wanting to frighten him, and tried for a lighter moment. "You'll have a big scar to show you're grandkids someday." *That is, if we are lucky enough to save you.*

# CHAPTER 27

She mumbled her fear and frustration under her breath as she went to the water and washed the strips of cloth. No one had to tell her Jim faced a dreadful battle from here on out.

"I need the bucket, Jim. I have to wash this wound thoroughly."

She ran to the camp to get it and poured several buckets of clean seawater into the jagged flesh. It hurt him severely, but he gritted his teeth and bore it in silence.

"If we don't get this clean, it'll get infected," she said, washing the wound and trying not to get sand in it. "I hope it isn't hurting too much." She worked as quickly as she could. The sun had gone and darkness rapidly approached.

He winced as she pushed the ragged edges together. "It hurts like hell, Jamie, but thanks for taking care of it. It seems you're destined to be our nurse, whether you want to or not. We both know I can die from this, if we can't get ahead of it. I can't say thanks enough."

"I'm going to tear off some small strips and tie the edges together as best I can, sort of like those Steri-Strips doctors use, and then bandage it—not that we have much to work with." She tore small strips from her skirt, soaked them in salt water, and carefully tied them in several places. It had the effect of bringing the edges together. She bound it up with the newly cleansed wide strips she'd torn off earlier, noting they'd already taken on dark stains as the salt water interacted with the blood. "There, Jim, it's the best I could manage with our vast medical supplies. I never knew what happened to the first aid kits that were in our rafts. I used everything on Mick, I guess, and the storm wiped out everything else. I only hope I got it clean enough, but it's hard to see with the light fading."

She was worried, but she'd done what she could. They could only wait to see how things went for him.

"It actually feels pretty good, Jamie. It stings like hell from the salt water, but it feels better. You should become a doctor. You have the healing gift," Jim said. "I'm not just saying that. I mean it. Look how you took care of Mick. He's healed, and no infection. You're a wonder, and we're talking a gunshot wound. Those can be the worst. I can't blame him for falling in love with you, and he has, you know."

"He's asked me to marry him, Jim. Could that ever happen?" Jamie replied, her hands out in a helpless gesture. She felt so bewildered. "What sort of life could a man like that offer a woman?"

"I've said before, Jamie, we don't know all there is to know about that dude," Jim said. " If you love him, trust him to work it out. He's no itinerant seaman. I'd stake my life on it. In fact, I believe we'll all stake our lives on that fact. I have a feeling about it. I work in criminal law, and he doesn't fit the picture of a drug dealer."

Jim appeared to be trying his best to comfort her and, in this discussion, had momentarily forgotten his torn arm. It had to be extremely painful. Jamie felt sure of it, seeing his furrowed brow.

"Let's go back to the camp and get you settled. We'll wait there for Mick and Felicia. I wonder how she's doing? Working with a dead hog wouldn't be her style, would it?" She laughed and so did Jim. "I'm sure she's never had to dress out an animal of any kind." She tried to get a picture of Felicia helping Mick, but it escaped her imagination. She bent to help Jim to his feet. "Can you make it, Jim?" she asked, taking his good arm.

He rose painfully to his feet with Jamie's help. He didn't have the use of his left arm for balance and appeared light-headed. "Damn, I'm not going to be much use to us from now on, as if we weren't facing difficulties enough. I'm really sorry this happened."

She knew Jim was troubled that his anger at the thieving pigs had added to their overwhelming problems.

"Don't worry about it. The main thing is to get your arm healing. I'm afraid you'll have a ragged-looking scar." She urged him along, but not before looking out over the booming reef. "It's all clear out there, for now. At least we haven't that worry, but Mick thinks they'll be back to search this island."

"Thank God, for the all clear, Jamie. I don't know what we'd do if they came now. What the hell can we do?"

Jim shook his head with worry. His helplessness and regret seemed to help him forget the pain of his arm.

She settled him on one of the tent cloths with his back against the towering wreck of the big tree. "Relax while I find firewood. We'll have something to roast tonight, thanks to you. If there are a few coals deep in the fire pit, I can get a fire going before they bring in the meat."

She searched the area for anything combustible, finding bits and pieces of fuel lying about in the dimming light. Night encroached upon the makeshift camp when she heard voices emanating from the direction of the ill-fated pig hunt.

Jamie hurried out to meet them as they struggled toward the camp, dragging the carcass on a fallen tree branch and secured with the bloodied netting. Mick pulled with both his arms, and Felicia did her best to help.

Jamie couldn't suppress a shout. "Hey, you did it!" She went to the tired-looking twosome. "How'd you manage, Felicia? Did you help Mick?"

Mick returned her glance with a wink and a wide grin, as

he nodded. "She was a lot of help, Jamie, a regular pioneer woman." He looked about for Jim. "How's he doing?"

Felicia ran to Jim's side and knelt down. "Oh, darling, are you going to be all right? Is it very bad?' Her beautiful eyes bore tears of worry, barely visible as dusk rapidly fell across their rock strewn campsite. "Is there much pain?" she asked, pointing to the neat dressing Jamie had applied to the injured arm.

He tried to reassure her. "Don't worry, it's rather deep, but Jamie cleaned it out as well as possible. It's fairly comfortable now." His face shone pale with sweat in the dimming light, but his voice sounded steady enough.

"Tell me, Jamie," Mick said in a low voice. The warmth in his eyes told her he was glad to be near her again. "Do we need to worry? A pig has got to be pretty nasty, especially with those ugly yellowed tusks. They root in whatever muck they come to." He stood with his back to that Jim so the man couldn't see his worried face or hear their talk.

"I don't know. It's a nasty wound. The edges are ragged and it's clear to the bone. I cleaned it as well as I could, but I couldn't see too well." She kept her voice low, not wanting to frighten Felicia—or Jim, for that matter. "I worry I didn't get all the muck out, but he said it felt better." She tried to put a brave face on a potentially serious situation. "Mick, it's just one horrid thing after the other. Life is very dangerous, living this way." She pressed her head against his chest, trying to avoid the gore smeared over his clothes.

"Hold on to yourself for now, girl. We have to keep things normal as possible. Felicia might go to pieces if she thinks Jim's in trouble. She's pretty brave, considering her background, but not like you, girl." He held her for a long moment, offering her courage along with a comforting hug, then went to Jim and looked at Jamie's handiwork. "Jamie's got you well in hand, I see, by the nice wrap job. So how does it feel? Can you move your fingers and hand?" He knelt down by Jim and Felicia. "Felicia's one handy girl, she did her part with the meat." He smiled and saw her relax. She needed encouragement just now.

Jim moved his hand and fingers well enough, considering the amount of pain in his arm.

Mick nodded. "Good. You won't lose function. Now we have to get it healed."

"Jim, I'm not sure if I can eat any of that hideous thing," Felicia said with a shudder. "We had to take out the insides and I can tell you, it wasn't pretty."

She wore a look of incredulous distaste on her face, and Jim broke into a wide grin as she told him of dressing out the pig.

Jamie laughed. "Way to go, Felicia."

"How can you laugh?" Felicia broke into a giggle, after a fleeting moment of indignation. Jamie had a way of putting things into perspective.

This broke the sense of disaster for the moment. Mick chuckled. "I see you've found some firewood, Jamie girl, let's cook some of this feisty porker. I'm starving and you must be too." He set about putting together a cheerful, comforting fire. Jamie assured him there were no sails on the horizon. His cigarette lighter had been good for one more flicker, since she'd found no hot coals.

It took them an hour or more to see a few strips of meat sizzling on slender green branches held over the coals. Their ravenous hunger and the smell of roasting pork made them forget the danger and agony they'd endured to capture it.

As the roasting meat neared readiness, they gathered a few leaves for plates.

"How about Jim having the first hunk?" Mick called. "He did the most to get it for us."

He laid it on Jim's leaf plate, and Felicia helped Jim carefully tear off a bit. He tasted it and then, with her help, ate heartily. It left fat on his lips and some down his shirt, but he ate well enough, his painful arm forgotten for the moment.

"Now that's good, damned good. Bastard's a little tough though." Jim ate with gusto, using his right arm for the event. As he sat eating, Felicia sat beside him and also ate, overcoming her disdain of the required processing. Hunger ruled, for her as well as the rest of them.

The camp, nearly silent while they ate the meat and a few bananas, seemed almost cheerful.

"Wouldn't a breadfruit go good just now?" Jamie said, She ducked as someone tossed a coconut husk her way.

They couldn't eat all of the meat and decided to put it up in the tree branches.

"We don't want to feed the pigs again. We can eat more tomorrow, and try to smoke the rest. We haven't tried that yet." Mick looked upward to see where they might lodge the remaining pork. Several solid branches had survived.

"I'll fit it up there." Jamie pointed to a fork a few feet upward. "It'll take two hands to do it, and it's still hard for you to reach up." She grinned. "And I doubt if Felicia wants to touch it again." Mick helped her get it part way up the tree, and she managed the rest. "That should keep it, depending on what other creatures might want a bite." She went to Felicia, beckoning her to go to the small pond for a bath. "I need a bath, and you surely must, after cleaning that pig," she said, still smiling about it.

"Jim's clothes are all bloody. Can't we get him in there and help him wash?" Felicia asked. "He can, if we help him."

"Of course, I didn't realize how bad his clothes were. I just concentrated on his arm." Jamie turned to Mick. "You'll want to bathe, too, eh?"

They helped Jim to his feet, removed his worn deck shoes, and escorted him to the small pool. Jamie supported his arm out of the water, and Felicia and Mick did their best to clean him and his clothes. Embarrassed, Jim tried not to show it.

After that, they sought their beds. Jim and Felicia found a bed out on the soft sand, with a tent cloth under his ravaged arm. His clothes were cleaner, but soggy. They'd gotten used to not having a change of clothes and, for the sake of modesty, went uncomfortably wet rather often.

Mick and Jamie settled away from the other two, but not out of hearing. As they lay together, Mick voiced his fears for Jim's recovery. "That was one nasty animal. Jim's arm could get infected, and we've no antibiotics." He held her close. They didn't feel in the mood for more, and only held each other until they fell into a restless sleep.

Jamie awoke with a start. "I thought I heard Jim moaning," she whispered to Mick. She listened for further sounds, as a dark, foreboding sense of anxiety about Jim's injury came over her. "I don't hear him now, though." Mick's unease about it must have transferred to her. She pressed close to him for comfort. "I'm so worried I didn't clean his wound well enough. If infection gets started, we've nothing to treat it with. Remember, how it was before antibiotics? Imagine what happened to people back then. They died from everything in those days."

"We'll take a good look at it first thing in the morning. We need daylight to reassure ourselves about it," Mick said, his voice soft and low. Holding her gently, he curved his body around hers. She was comforted, her head pillowed on his arm.

"I love you, Jamie."

His whispered words fell softly upon her senses until she fell into fitful, shallow slumber.

# CHAPTER 28

The pealing cries of sea birds circling about awakened Jamie. She rose from their bed of sand to look out over the foaming reef. She saw no sails across the blue distance and went to check on Jim.

He was awake. Felicia sat looking into his eyes and stroking his pale blond hair. Her tense posture and paled features revealed her worry. "Jim, dear, how is your arm?" she asked, her anxiety obvious. "Does the wound hurt much? Anything I can bring you?"

Jim slowly moved to a sitting position, emitting an agonized moan. "It hurts like hell right now. I could use a helluva lot of aspirin and a good slug of Jim Beam, or both." He held the injured arm out, tenderly supporting it with his other arm.

"Let's take a good look at it in the daylight, Jim," Jamie said. "I couldn't see it well enough last evening."

Jim was painful and stiff, sweated profusely, but he got up from the sandy bed on his own. Clinging to a thin shred of independence, he refused their help. They walked him to the water's edge, and Jamie gingerly unwrapped the dried, stained dressing. Crusted blood stuck to the cloth. They opened it to see the ragged wound. The edges had congealed together, and did not look overly reddened.

"Well, so far, so good. I don't see any signs of infection." Jamie's voice revealed the relief she felt. "It's a little red, but considering the damage, it's probably to be expected. We'll watch it very closely and dress it often to keep salt water on it. You need a sling, too."

Felicia washed the dressings while Jamie soaked the wound with seawater, then they wrapped his arm again. The tiny strips had kept the wound edges together.

"I feel a little better now I've seen it," Felicia said. "It's bad, but it looks like it'll heal. Oh, Jim, I hate it that you got hurt. I hope you'll be all right—I *know* you will." She sounded encouraging for his sake, but they both knew he needed antibiotics and the skill of a doctor to properly care for a ragged wound like that.

"I'm thankful for your skills, Jamie, he said. "But I worry this wound is more than anyone can handle without medical supplies, especially lost on some damned island in the South Pacific."

Jamie nodded. "I agree, Jim. God help us. Oh how I agree." She was afraid for him and couldn't hide it.

They prepared breakfast, using the roasted meat from the night before, still edible. Mick stirred the fire into live flames, using the last of the scanty supply of fuel they'd found. Jim rested against the bole of the ravaged monkey pod tree, his face pale, a slick sheen of sweat glistening across his brow. Walking to the big tree from the lagoon had tired him out. His rapidly increasing weakness alarmed Jamie. She faced the horror of knowing his wound was likely a deadly one.

Felicia laid out a few bananas and one remaining coconut. "We'll need more coconuts, Jamie. We're low, even on those." Her voice, laced with fear and tears, relayed the hopelessness she tried to hide. And it wasn't about worry of starvation.

"Let's do that after breakfast. We need to get something in our stomachs first," Jamie said. Sensing Felicia's rising panic, Jamie made her voice as calm as she could. She cut strips of the roasted pork and put them on green sticks to sizzle over the newly formed coals. "Think you could you find more leaves, Felicia?"

Mick watched Jamie working to calm Felicia's rising fear. His pride in her only grew. She seemed to know what to do when things started heading downhill. They made a good breakfast of what they had, mostly meat.

"Here's your ham, Jim," she sang out, as she tried to lighten their grave situation. "but sorry, the eggs and sourdough weren't delivered this morning,"

"Hey, girls, this'll do fine, and it really tastes like back home, too." Jim laughed. "This'd better taste good after the grief that devil gave us." He chewed the meat and commented in disgust. "But it's tough as hell."

Mick ate all he could and urged the others to do the same. "This won't keep much longer, and we can't preserve it." He sighed in relief that Jim's color was better after eating. "I think I'll wander around. Might find something. We didn't see everything the other day." He went to Jamie's side. "Keep an eye on Felicia," he said in low tones. "She's frightened. You did a good job with her this morning. I'm worried as hell that he'll be in big trouble with that arm. He needs a good course of antibiotics, and soon."

"I feel the same, Mick. It's so far so good, right now, but I'm praying under my breath. Find us something more to eat while you're at it. And—I love you, Mick," she whispered, touching his chest with her hands.

"I'll do my best, and I sure love you, dear girl."

Mick gazed into her eyes, and it comforted her to see his desire for her burning there. She forgot everything for a moment as she warmed to his words and his soft, deep, voice. He made her feel that everything would work out. But reality was not so kind. She turned back to her camp duties after watching him walk away.

"How're you doing, Jim?" Jamie knelt beside him. "Is it terribly painful? Sorry, there's nothing for comfort."

"It's not so bad, you know. Feels better each time you change the dressing. Well, so far, anyway." He laughed. "Must be healing powers in that salt water. I live in Kansas, and you're from Colorado. We don't know the ocean that well. I have to say, we're learning a lot the hard way." He laughed again, and Jamie detected the tightness of his rising fear within it.

Felicia's face lit up when he laughed. He was in good spirits, and his color was good. If he fought an inner desperation, he hid it well. Unexpected relief flooded through Jamie, though she couldn't shake her deep-seated foreboding.

"Jamie, let's see if we can find the spears or something, Felicia said, after checking on Jim once more. "We need food, and I'd like more fish. It's great, cooked the way we've been doing."

"You're right," Jamie agreed. "I'd like fish again, too. I'm already tired of pork and Mick hunting pigs alone is out."

They left Jim resting in the shade of the huge, torn canopy of the monkey pod tree and turned away from the direction Mick had taken as they poked carefully through the ruined landscape.

Felicia pointed. "Look, Jamie, a papaya, stuck in this debris. Maybe we'll find more things we can use."

From then on, they poked through every pile of rubbish to find three breadfruits and another papaya. It heartened them to find the few food items, though they realized it was little, compared to what they needed to sustain life on a daily basis.

They returned with their finds, and Jim watched them with a twinkle in his pale blue eyes as he looked over their loot with delight. "You girls are something! Wait until we get home. What a story we'll have to tell. Mick and I have already decided we were beyond lucky, marooned with you two. What're the odds? Two fantastic girls in a million! With those odds we should have been lost in Vegas."

Jamie wondered if he said those things to lessen Felicia's fear.

Jamie reached a hand to Jim. "Let's do the arm again, Jim. It seems to help the healing."

He rose up on his own. Seeing that gave her a faint hope his arm would heal as well as Mick's bullet wound had.

"You're moving better, Jim, but how does it *really* feel?" Felicia asked him as they walked to the beach.

"It's damned painful, but maybe a bit less," he replied. Walking close to Felicia, he put his good arm around her, and gave her a good squeeze. "You're slender these days, dear, and growing thinner with each passing day."

She giggled. "You know, I like being slim. It's a first for me. Even without a mirror, I know I look a lot better in so many ways. But I wish I could get a good look at myself. What overweight person hasn't dreamed of being slim, if only to see how they'd look? That is, if the specter of starvation didn't seem like a downhill slide into hunger and death."

Jim squeezed her tight against him. "Aw, come on, darling." But he couldn't think of anything more to say on the subject.

They were frightened over his arm and the dreaded junk's reappearance, not to mention finding enough to eat, but Jamie was relieved to see Jim's spirit reviving. "Watch it, you two! You have to take care that arm isn't over used." In delight, she heard Felicia laughing again.

Jamie thought the wound edges were more inflamed, with a hint of purulence in one especially torn spot. She soaked it in seawater longer than before, and redressed it. The cloths were a bloodstained mess, but it was all they had. His wound was dressed with wet saline. She thought that was the best anyone could do.

Felicia's shorts looked more like a wrap skirt these days as she tore off enough to make Jim a sling. Relieved to have it supported, he stood straighter and caught sight of more tanned leg as well.

"There you go, Jim. We'll dress it again before dark."

Jamie didn't ask him how his arm felt, being afraid of the answer. She was fully aware that the increased redness and pale green exudate in the wound meant bad news, but couldn't bring herself to speak of it. Jim would have increased pain if it got any worse, and she actually wondered why he didn't have deeper pain even now. She wished Mick would get back. She'd prefer to confide her worries to him rather than Felicia.

Mick returned with more bananas and a faded wad of print clothing. "I walked all over that end of the island and didn't see anything for food. I went around the backside of the island, and found this cloth hung up on the rocks." He held it out for inspection. "I wondered if any of you might recognize it."

Jamie and Felicia looked it over. It was a very large print skirt.

"I don't remember seeing it on anyone," Jamie commented, fingering the cloth.

Felicia didn't either, but Jim cleared his throat. "I saw that on the woman called Jane. You remember the lesbian couple, Felicia?"

"Were they, Jim? How'd you figure that out? Because of the way her friend dressed?" Felicia frowned. "Why would you remember what she wore?"

"I'm trained that way, my dear. I told you about my work," Jim said with a mischievous wink of one pale blue eye.

"I guess she wasn't one of the survivors then," Jamie said. "The poor thing. What a terrible way to die, lost in that raging storm and all alone, or I suppose, she was—we'll never really know, will we?"

"I'm sorry about that. It's too bad," Mick said as he sat down next to Jim and shot him a friendly grin. "How goes it, old man?"

"Not bad. They redid this mess," Jim said, indicating his wounded arm. "It looks about the same. Doesn't hurt any worse, thank God."

Mick looked at Jamie. "So what've you two been up to?"

"Oh, we found a few things, had more luck than you, by the looks of it," Jamie chirped.

Mick, knowing her, caught her deep worry about Jim's arm. "Let's go check the lagoon for sails. Come with me, girl." He was insistent, and Jamie followed, eager to see him alone.

Felicia settled near Jim, and Jamie heard her say, "I'll watch over you, dearest, while they're gone."

Mick led Jamie to the beach and turned to take her into his arms. "What's going on, girl?" he said, looking down to her. "I see the fear in your eyes."

"It's the wound, Mick. I see beginning signs of infection. It was redder, more swollen, and I saw a bit of pus, at least I think it was." Tears formed in her eyes when she related this to Mick. "It wasn't there before, but maybe it's just the healing process, I don't know." She tried not to sob aloud, but she was tired, and worn out, from trying to hide her fear from Jim and Felicia.

"I'll look at it with you when you change it again. I have some experience with these things." A smile played about his lips, letting her know another infinitesimal bit of knowledge about himself. He foresaw Jim's deadly peril if a fulminating infection set in. Without the benefit of modern medicine, he had no reasonable chance to survive.

"You do? You never told me you had medical knowledge. All the time I took care of your wounds, you never said a thing!" She wanted to be furious with him but satisfied herself with a slight punch to his chest.

"Hey, cut it out!" He laughed. "You did a fine job. I wasn't much good at first, if you remember. I'm no doctor or anything close. I just know a bit about medical things. I've been around a lot of bad scenes. I had to learn." He calmed her, but he felt tied in knots about Jim's arm, the same as she did.

This little dust-up benefited and relieved her. He bent and kissed her lips until she relaxed and settled in his arms, and he gave thought to wandering off with her. He wanted that, more now than ever, but they couldn't at present. *How slender she's become!* His fingers played across the emerging spines down her narrow back. *My, God, but she's beautiful!*

He gazed at the slender face before him, oval, tanned, and slightly freckled, and loved the look of her. Those legs, so long and beautifully tanned, with most of the skirt missing from her medical work, revealed their full, lovely length, reaching down from slim, fully rounded hips. He never tired of that view.

Mick nuzzled her hair. "I debated whether to bring that dress back. I wanted to tell you, but I hated to add to your worries." He frowned, considering the fate of the woman who'd worn it. "It probably doesn't matter, at any rate. Whoever wore that is surely lost."

Smiling sadly, she turned in his arms. "Let's head back, Mick. The way I'm feeling right now, we'd never get back, but certain lovely things must wait."

They walked back to Jim and Felicia. Her inner spirit, refreshed by their time alone together, had brightened Jamie. It pleased Mick. He knew they had to get away for a bit—for them both.

"It's selfish, but I need time with you," Jamie said. "I want you, Mick." Her voice had deepened with need.

"It's not selfish, dear girl. Who has a better right than you for a bit of downtime." Mick smiled into her upturned face, and held her close against his body for another moment, before returning to the others.

They fixed more of the meat and had a banana or two. With Jim settled, they went about making new fishing spears to supplant their protein supply. They'd never found the earlier ones and decided they never would. Jim wanted to try fishing. Mick talked him out of it and found no difficultly in discouraging him.

Mick shaped several spears, enough for everyone. He beckoned Jamie, and they went to the lagoon to try their luck. The tide was far out, but they found several fish caught in tide pools. Mick looked at Jamie. The breeze coming off the lagoon held her thin and ragged blouse against her slender figure. "Girl, you should see yourself. It warms my heart and everything else with it." He grinned, with total appreciation at the sight of her, sun-browned, tall, and lovely and moved toward her as she backed away. "You're so beautiful, Jamie!"

"Mick, we need to catch fish for dinner. I've had enough pork for a while. We must be serious about it."

He wondered if she still saw visions of a stalking wolf when he came near her. She'd often thought of him that way and told him so.

"Wait until tonight, we'll get serious, girl." He laughed, filled with joy at being with her. They momentarily forgot their troubles and reveled in the feeling.

"You're impossible!" Jamie splashed a handful of water at him and turned to run for safety, but the water held her legs.

Mick, quick as lightning, caught her around the waist, buried his face in her neck, making her scream in protest.

"Stop it Mick! We're acting like two kids that haven't a care in the world," Jamie protested breathlessly, her face glowing.

"I know. It feels damned good, doesn't it, darling, wonderful girl?"

Her mood deflated quickly. "Jim and Felicia will feel left out, now that he's hurt. But it was fun, Mick. I'm glad you can play. It's a wonderful trait." Jamie remembered Moran's dour outlook on everything. "I love you all the more for it."

"The tides on its way in, so we should have a better selection." Mick grinned and his white teeth flashed against his darkly tanned face, a sight she never tired of seeing. He turned to hunt for something to spear. Jamie followed him.

After catching a few fish to fill out the supper menu, they built the fire up for dinner. Finding fuel had become a bit easier as the refuse around them had dried enough.

"Let's check your wound before dark, Jim, need help?" Mick asked.

"I'm doing fine, Mick, feels better all the time," Jim grunted, struggling to his feet. "I'm sick of lying around so much. I'd like to fish again. You're doing all the work, makes me feel like a piker." He chuckled as he said it, but his face paled from pain of getting up. The effort had cost him.

They went to the water's edge and undressed the wound. Mick stood close by to get a look at the ugly, reddened site. Jamie tried to be casual. "Let's get this cleaned up and pour lots of salt water over it."

She found the wound more flushed, and the entire arm warmer. Mucus with a greenish cast appeared in parts of it. Jamie raised her eyes to meet Mick's. She read his answer, and a chill moved through her. They hid their worries from Jim. Not sure what to expect if deadly infection raged through his body, it could be nothing good. Jamie felt sick inside at lack of modern medicine.

"How's the pain Jim, better, or worse?" she asked.

"Listen, you two, I know what you're seeing. I've been around these things." Jim kept his voice low. "I don't want Felicia to know. It aches deep in the wound and hurts like hell. It's bad and I know it. Don't coddle me. I'm no baby. I worry about Felicia," he continued. "She's never had to face things like most people. She's a gentle, happy girl. It'll devastate her to know I'm facing death with this. I'm asking you to keep it from her as long as possible, if you will." The tears in Jim's eyes spoke volumes. He looked out to the water's edge where Felicia wrung out his dressings. "We've found something wonderful, and I love her more than my life."

Jamie fought the tears that wanted to flow. "We'll give it all we've got, Jim."

Mick nodded. "We'd best apply heat to that arm. It'll help. We need hot salt water to pack the arm with, but how?"

A good question. "We'll manage with the few things we have," Jamie said. "The Indians used hot rocks to heat soup and things. Why can't we do that? We have the buckets."

Mick, worried as much as she, grasped onto her suggestion. "We'll try it. Anything's better than nothing."

"What's wrong?" Felicia came up with the wet dressings and sensed the tension. "It's worse, isn't it?" She firmed her stance and faced them. "I know you think I'll faint or go hysterical, but I'm no delicate baby. I want to know what has everyone so worried." She looked down where Jim sat on the sand. "It *is* worse, Jim, isn't it?" Her tone demanded an honest answer.

"Well, it's more inflamed, so they're going to apply heat to it. That can do a lot of good." He remained calm. "You'll be busy now, with all this fuss," he added. "My mother mentioned hot-packing wounds as a girl. It draws the infection out. They had no antibiotics when she was young." He tried to boost Felicia's confidence, but she fully realized the severity of the wound and the deadly consequences.

Jamie waited to see her reaction.

Felicia put her hand on his forehead. "Jim, I had a feeling. Your eyes were too bright, like you had a fever. Well, if you do, it's not much for now." She sounded relieved as she murmured, "thank you, God."

Jim laughed. "It's not fever. It's you, Felicia, that's what you do to me whenever I see you."

She giggled in response.

Mick looked at Jamie, relief shining in his eyes. "Well, let's get this show on the road. The sooner we start, the better."

Jamie wrapped Jim's arm and they headed to the campsite in the growing darkness.

They fed the fire up. Jamie found smooth round rocks and placed them in the coals. "These will get the water hot. It'll be dirty, but the arm is covered." She turned to Felicia, "Any more cloth around those shorts? We need more than we have now and my skirt is a mini already."

"I'll cut off all I can, and more after that," Felicia answered, as she took the knife and severed all the spare fabric left on her shorts. "It's good they were walking shorts—and I'm so much smaller now, there's more to cut off." She giggled at that.

Jamie filled the two buckets with seawater, and put hot rocks into them using green branches to move them from the fire. It heated the water, though made it filthy with ash and soot. "This cloth is hot. Here goes, Jim." She wrung out the cloth, burning her hands, and laid it over Jim's wound.

"The heat feels good. It could work. I guess we'll see in a day or two," Jim said, sounding encouraged.

It cheered them. Felicia placed leaf-wrapped fish into the coals, while Mick kept the rocks heated. Jim had a fine sheen of sweat over his face. The climate was warm enough without added heat. He lay on a leaf-padded bed while they worked over him.

They managed a few bites of food, and after an hour or two, they halted for the night. Jim sweat profusely during his treatment, and they decided it might be enough. They'd begin again when daylight came.

"It feels pretty good right now," he said, glad of the respite from the heat.

Felicia settled herself next to Jim. She'd scrounged a good bit of leaves and such for a little comfort of her own. Reluctant to leave Jim's side, she snuggled close for the night.

Mick and Jamie went out on the beach. There was no moon. A lovely phosphorescent glow emanated from the waters as they walked. The slim shred of hope that the heat treatments might help eased their worries for a while.

"Oh Mick." Jamie nestled into his arms, tired from the work on Jim's arm.

He held her, nuzzling her hair, neck, and down over her lovely breasts. "Girl, I can't help it!" he cried.

He grasped her in his arms and took her fiercely, as if loving her would make all their troubles go away. And she responded fully, her fatigue causing her to reach heights of feeling that were almost painful.

*೬ೂ೬ೂ*

In the early morning, Jamie hurried to Jim, hoping the hot soaks had proven effective. He lay awake. Felicia was curled at his side, her respirations deep and even.

"How is it, Jim?" she whispered to avoid disturbing Felicia, whose features bore deep traces of fatigue. Jamie thought he looked flushed. Was it just his fair complexion? She laid a hand tenderly over his forehead, checking for fever.

"It hurts like hell, Jamie, but it doesn't feel like infection so much as just plain old pain. It's a ragged bitch of a wound you know."

"Let's go to the water and take a look. I hope we did some good last night. We'll do it several times a day, if it helps. In fact, if it isn't, there's nothing else to do." Jamie kept her voice at a whisper, but Felicia's eyes were open.

"Don't you two try hiding things from me." She rose up from her bed. Her eyes were snapping and especially purple this morning. "I know Jim's arm is infected, and I want to do all I can to help." She groaned while she worked to loosen her stiff limbs. "When I get home, I'm going into the bedroom and kiss my wonderful mattress! I can't believe how hard this rocky ground is, and that's comparing it to the leaves and sticks we had before that storm."

"Felicia, I see you have strengths we never imagined," Jamie replied. "And I agree about the bedding. Makes sand look like fluffy cotton, eh?" She winked at Mick as she used his Canadian bit of speech. He grinned back, and she treasured it.

Mick had the fire stirred into life and enlisted Felicia's help in the constant search for wood. "We'll have to hunt for more fuel from now on to keep heat on Jim's arm, as well as to cook food," he told her. "There's plenty of wreckage strewn about.

"Oh, Mick, will Jim be all right? And don't lie to me,

please!" Felicia cried. They were out of earshot of Jim and Jamie. Her eyes brimmed with tears.

"I don't know, Felicia. We'll try our best. That's all we *can* do. We might have hit on something using heat. We'll keep working on that, so we'd best get the fuel."

He encouraged her, as much as he dared, and felt like a phony. They searched far, gathered wood, and took it back to the camp where Jamie led Jim from the lagoon, his arm covered with fresh, wet seawater dressings.

"So, how'd it look this morning?" Mick asked, for Felicia, as well as himself.

"About the same, a little greenish drainage and red edges, but it didn't look worse. Maybe the heat treatments are helping," Jamie said, edging her voice with a note of hope. "Let's keep up the good work, guys."

Mick got the fire going. "Let's find something for breakfast and get these rocks in the fire."

The last of the pork had soured, but roasting over the coals made it passable, and they ate it.

"That's the last of you, you nasty SOB" Jim said with a hollow laugh as his shoulders slumped. "We did for you, and I hope to hell, you haven't done for me."

They applied the heat to Jim's arm until he begged off. "Hey, all right, you trying to cook me?" He chuckled, but his face was ruddy and covered with a slick sheen of sweat. "I'm ready for a siesta."

He rose painfully and headed to the beach. Felicia followed, bringing the tent cloth to lie on. They found a ragged palm tree arching out toward the lagoon. He lay down in the speckled shade of it to let the cool ocean breezes fan him.

Mick, seeing Jim settled for a while, turned to Jamie. "Let's explore and look for food. Our need is greater by the day. We're in danger of real starvation if we don't find something."

Felicia returned from the stream with a water bucket for Jim.

"I did worry about Felicia," Mick said. "But I'm thinking she's not the fragile girl we feared. You can tell her whatever you want to about this."

"I hope you'll find something more to eat while you're exploring," Felicia said. She sounded cheerful, but Mick thought it was for Jim's benefit.

Mick and Jamie took netting, the other bucket, and left the beach where Felicia and Jim rested. The sun was high in a cloud-dotted sky, and the soft tropical breeze ruffled Jim's hair as he relaxed in the shade with Felicia. A last look out over the restless, foaming reef revealed no sails. Clouds were scattered about the sky, displaying a dappled pattern over sea and land. Sea birds wheeled, darted, and dove, and things seemed right with the world, at the moment.

"I'm hungry again," Jamie mourned. "There's almost nothing to eat but fish anymore, with everything so torn and wasted. I hope we *do* find something."

"I'm afraid not, girl. It'll get worse than this if we are not rescued soon, and that's not even talking about Jim's arm. I don't know what good it will do for us to hunt. Will we find anything? Probably not, but we can have some time alone, and that *does* matter—it matters a hell of a lot, Jamie." He took her into his arms. "This is my medicine."

He held her for long moments, his head on hers. Finally they parted and went on. They found a few bananas in that area.

"Not many of these left," Jamie said with a frown. "Half of what had been a stable food supply was lost, and this remaining grove has to satisfy four appetites with so many less trees. I wish we could go to a restaurant and order. It sounds wonderful—if only."

"Let's check the back side of the island," Mick suggested. He wanted to get her thoughts off starvation. They walked around the outcropping of rocks going toward the windward side. "Watch your step—it gets rocky from here on."

Stiff winds whipped their clothes. They saw huge rocks, thrown up in a jumble by a volcanic action, and a few bent and twisted trees. Mick and Jamie went hand in hand, picking their way, watching wild hungry waves that had rolled across thousands of miles to crash against this broken shore. The breezes cooled them, the sun was high, and clouds occasionally covered the sun. A wild, magnificent vista lay below them.

"This is about where I found that skirt thrown up on the rocks," Mick said.

They stopped a moment and made their way carefully to avoid another casualty.

"Wow! It's wild over here, isn't it?" She held onto Mick against the stiff breeze. "It's good we didn't find this side that day," she said, shuddering at the thought.

"We've had a lot of luck, all in all, girl."

He bent to kiss her lips. She eagerly returned it. He decided it was fortunate they were standing in huge jumbled rocks, or they'd rapidly forget why they climbed over these jagged black chunks of basalt, the igneous result of ancient volcanic eruptions.

"Let's check down by the water. I think we're close to the area." He grinned at her, knowing what fomented on both overstressed minds.

"What are we looking for around here, Mick?" Jamie asked. She clung to the huge chunky boulders, steadying herself against the stronger winds on this shore.

"I wanted to see if there was a body to go with that dress, I'm sure there won't be, but I need to make sure." He edged his way around huge jagged stones. "I mostly want to spend time alone with you. I like what you say, how you do things, and the way you think. You continually amaze me." He looked at her with total appreciation. "It's no wonder I love you, girl."

Finding nothing of interest, they turned to go back. Jamie took care, as she made her way, and Mick watched her long legs reaching carefully for each step, fascinated by her movements. She was graceful as a gazelle.

"Mick, do you remember seeing the two really big, fat

ladies?" she asked. "They were having the time of their lives with the native guide, Niko. He flirted terribly with them, and they enjoyed him so much. I wonder what happened to them. He kept trying to get them into a raft, and they were so terrified, they screamed continually. I saw one of them get off. I wonder if she made it."

"We can't change what happened. It was a bad deal, all the way 'round," he replied. He regretted the loss of innocent lives and wondered if he might have prevented it. "No, to answer your question, I don't remember seeing those ladies. Niko would have had fun with them. He was an outrageous flirt on those trips."

They turned away from the wild scene on the backside of the island. That side hadn't changed at all from the typhoon, but their side, with all the beautiful trees and food, had suffered devastating changes. When they reached the sheltered area near the banana trees, Mick turned to Jamie, and together they sought a shady area to rest. He wanted her and she wanted him. On a small patch of grass beneath a banana tree, he began to caress her. He kissed her deeply until she gasped for breath. "Has it been so long, Jamie girl? It seems a lifetime since we were together."

She pulled away. "Mick, it's been a lifetime, since last night. I need you too. This is the only sane thing left in our lives. I know I'm bereft of my senses, but it's what you've done to me."

He reached for her, and she met him fully.

❦❦❦

They brought more bananas when they returned. Jim and Felicia still rested on the beach, and Jamie took them some of the fruit. Jamie knelt down to look at Jim. His face looked flushed. Was it the sun? She felt the icy shivers of defeat and fear sweeping through her, leaving pain and doubt in its wake.

"So, how's our patient?"

"I'm doing fine, Jamie, but I'd like you to look at it again, if you're ready." Jim rose slowly from the sand, a groan escaping his lips. The arm had become more painful. Would it look worse when she saw the wound again?

Jamie unwrapped the dressing, removing as much as she dared. The redness had increased, as well as the purulent drainage, and a foul odor was present. "It is worse, Jim, definitely more inflamed. It has an unusual odor. Of course, it could just be the healing process. I don't know too much about things like this." She turned to Mick, deferring to his expertise regarding the status of Jim's wound. "Mick, what do you think?"

"It's worse and I don't like to say it. We'd best apply more heat—that's all we have, Jamie." He put his hand on Jim's shoulder. "It's going to be a tough fight, old man, but we'll give it our best shot."

The increasing infection in his wounded arm placed Jim's life on the line. Seeing Mick's helpless frustration at their lack of medical supplies tore at Jim and broke Jamie's heart.

Felicia stood quietly listening to the conversation about Jim's situation. "I'm not letting you get away from me, Jim, now we've found each other." Her jaw was set tight and her magnificent eyes flashed fire. She appeared to be a valiant woman, ready to fight any battle to save her man. Jamie saw Jim take heart, just hearing her.

"If anything gets me through this, it'll be this brave woman." He hugged Felicia with his good arm. Tears waited behind Jamie's lashes, ready to flow, but she fought them. Heartened by Felicia's fighting spirit, Jamie took a new grip on optimism. She already knew the power of love.

She poured salt water over Jim's wounded arm, noting that the edges were still together. She'd expressed her nagging doubt to Mick, wondering if she might have left debris in the depths of his ragged, filthy wound. Digging it open now, would be punishment beyond imagining and was not an option. She wrapped the arm with the terribly stained saline-soaked rags and prepared to give Jim more heat treatments.

They kicked the fire into flames and set about heating water. Leaving that in feminine hands, Mick went out to the lagoon to catch fish for dinner. Upset at the increased infection of Jim's arm, he knew the man's fate lay in a higher power than theirs. He liked and respected these people. The world sorely needed more citizens like them. He wanted desperately to help, but found no real answers. Aside from the hot packs and catching fish, they had nothing.

This modern age had wonders galore, but right now they were nearly a century away from the mercies of modern medicine. A brilliantly hued fish went gliding by. Mick stabbed frantically and missed, and cursed in anger at his utter helplessness.

# CHAPTER 30

At the camp, Jamie heated water with hot, sooty rocks and Jim lay on the bed of leaves and debris that Felicia had made. They kept heat to the wound. During a lull in their activities, Jamie got the print skirt and held it out.

"Felicia, let's use this." She held the material out for inspection. "What'd be wrong with that? She won't ever need it, and we do." Felicia nodded, and Jamie tore off a large piece. "Jim, you won't mind if we use a skirt worn by one of those ladies, will you?"

"How do we know what they were?" Felicia asked. "Did anyone say that?"

"No one had to. Everyone on the boat thought it, and so did you. Deny it if you like, but I saw you ladies observing those two." Jim laughed. "I remember being glad to see that you ladies had an eye for the male gender. In fact, I was downright relieved. I'd planned to ask Felicia for a date before all hell broke loose."

"Oh, Jim, you were?" Felicia exclaimed. "I'd hoped you would. Jamie and I talked about that on the cruise. I had big plans for a night on the town with you, Mr. Big. Funny the way things turn out." She quieted, returning to reality. "Jim, how come you're just now telling me you wanted a date? And I do feel badly about the woman being lost. I wonder what happened to her."

"It couldn't have been good, that's for sure," Jamie put

in. She wrung out another cloth for Jim's arm. "Does this make it feel better, Jim?"

"I really think it does, girls, although I feel like a boiled lobster about now." Jim laughed about it. If he feared the severity of his infection, Jamie thought he kept it well under control. "I wonder how Mick's doing with his fishing. You gals could go help him, if you're done cooking me."

The women left him and started toward the beach. They stopped when they were out of Jim's hearing. Felicia held back tears while she confessed her desperate fear. "I'm so afraid for Jim, I'd like to scream and cry my eyes out!"

"Me too, Felicia, but it wouldn't help him, and it won't help Mick, either," Jamie said. "Look at him out there, stabbing blindly at fish, taking his feelings out on the poor creatures. I'll bet he hasn't caught a one."

Felicia couldn't suppress a giggle at seeing Mick. "He must feel as scared and helpless as we do, by the looks of that."

"If we want anything to eat, we'd better give him a hand." A giggle escaped Jamie. "Men have their ways, don't they?"

She called to Mick. He made another angry stab at a shadowy fish beneath the outgoing tide then looked up to them with a half grin on his face and came out of the water toward them. "I'm not doing so hot out here," he admitted.

He was wet, with his loose jeans plastered against slim, wiry hips. His body, burnished to deep bronze, and slick with sea water, made Jamie's heart swell with pride in his fine masculinity.

"We came to lend a hand, Mick," Felicia said. A poorly suppressed smile lurked about her lovely face. "Looks like you need a break. We'll fish for a while. Jim's tired of us cooking his arm and told us to come help you."

Mick handed his spear to Felicia and, winking at Jamie, went to Jim. Jamie snorted, taking up the other spear Mick had left on the sand. "Maybe we'll have better luck, if he hasn't scared them off with his antics."

They went about their fishing with a different attitude and, with a bit of luck, caught several flat, colorful fish. They felt no regret at destroying the beautiful creatures, as they had in the beginning, and by now, they'd become proficient at spearing fish. *How long have we been here anyway*? Jamie often wondered.

Mick sat down next to Jim, who lay half-asleep under the torn monkey pod tree, looking more flushed than he had a few hours ago. Was it heat treatments?

Jim stirred, sensing Mick's presence. He grinned, his eyes bright with pain and fever. "Hey, Mick, catch any fish?"

"No luck for me. The girls are out there doing my job. I guess my heart wasn't in it." Mick placed his hand over Jim's forehead. The heat radiated from it. "You've got a fever, man. How's the arm?" He hated to hear the answer.

"It hurts like holy hell, Mick. It looks bad for me, and I know it. I don't think I ever appreciated the healing power of antibiotics, but I do now. I need them, and damned soon."

"When did this start? You didn't have it this morning. It's nearly dark now, you been like this all day?"

Jim shook his head to clear his thoughts. "It's been coming on since noon, I don't know for sure. My thinking gets fuzzy at times."

"God in Heaven!" Mick murmured to himself. "We've got to get him out of here, if not, we'll lose this guy!"

Turning away from Jim, Mick crossed himself and raised his eyes upward then went to the small stream and dipped one of the cloths the women were using and placed it on Jim's forehead to cool his burning skin. Mick stirred the fire to life and added more wood. He heard their careless chatter as they came back with fish and dreaded the moment they saw Jim's feverish condition. They'd hoped the hot soaks might have reduced the infection.

Felicia took one look at Jim and dropped the fish she was carrying. She rushed to his side, placed her hand on his forehead, and felt his burning skin. Jamie saw by her stricken face, she held back a scream. "Jim, honey, it's Felicia, how're you doing?" she asked softly, holding her voice steady.

He smiled at her with bright, fevered, eyes. "Oh, I'm doing fine, darling, just a little warm, that's all."

Jamie touched his burning forehead then looked at Mick, worry mounting with frustration. "You are a bit feverish, Jim, when did this start?"

"He said it started in the afternoon. We've got to cool him as much as possible if we can and continue the heat to his arm, as well. It's all we've got to fight this." Mick, deadly cool with determination, feared losing this new friend.

"We have this added material and may as well make use of it," Jamie said, tearing the rest of the tattered skirt into pieces. Shivering, she wondered if the torn areas were the result of a shark. "We'll use one to cool him, and the other one to heat the arm." She set up the stones to heat. Felicia went to the lagoon for seawater.

They cooked the fish, and ate them with a banana each. Jim barely ate, which caused additional worry. They worked far into the night, cooling him from the stream, and applying heat to the arm.

Finally, they took turns, so they could rest. Mick took the first watch. "You girls take a break, get a few winks of sleep. We need everything we've got if we're going to pull him through."

Jamie and Felicia protested, but Mick sent them away. They made beds nearby on skimpy mats of refuse and leaves and fell into deep, restless sleep.

Hearing the fatigue in their heavy respirations, Mick felt pity, mixed with admiration, and love, for both valiant women, struggling against odds that would make a seasoned soldier wince. He kept on with his ministrations to Jim.

The sun was barely lighting the tropical skies above them, when he heard Jim murmur, "Hey, Mick, you're one hell of a nurse, you know that?"

Mick noted that Jim's eyes were clearer. He also felt cooler, and Mick's heart lifted with a modicum of hope, seeing that Jim's fever was down. He still had a fever, but his head was clear and that gave reason for optimism.

The women awakened and came fearfully to Jim's side. Jamie raised questioning eyes to Mick. "How is he this morning? I'm sorry I slept so long."

"Take a look for yourselves. He's better for now," Mick replied. The fatigue in his voice tempered his surge of happiness at Jim's improved state. "We'll need to keep up with the heat, but he needs a break from that too. If you ladies will take over, I'm for a short nap myself."

"Thank you, Mick—thanks!" Felicia said, her voice filled with emotion. She knelt beside Jim and felt his forehead. "Jim dear, you're cooler, thank God."

Jamie smiled in pride at Mick. His dark features were pale and drawn with fatigue. "You've worked a miracle, you dark-eyed devil. I wouldn't have believed he'd ever come out of a fever like that." She came close and gave him a warm embrace, snuggling her head against his chest.

"Dark-eyed devil, huh? Careful, girl, I'm not that tired. In fact…" His voice trailed off as she pushed him away to find his bed on the beach in some shady spot.

"Another scanty breakfast!" she cried. Desperate for food, Jamie knew they had to hunt for something, anything to eat, and firewood as well.

Weakness and occasional dizziness crept into their bodies relaying the message. They needed more protein. Without discussion, it would be fish and whatever they found caught in piles of refuse. For Mick, alone, hunting pigs was not an option, nor did he suggest it. He knew the storm of opposition he'd face. The battle to save Jim's life became all they thought about. Unless starvation drove them to it, pig hunting would not be a factor. Jim ate little. Was it because he knew they had almost nothing, or was he too sick to eat?

"We need to scrounge up more breadfruit. If we found some the last time, there might be more if we hunt hard enough," Felicia said. "Jim isn't getting enough calories to help him heal."

Jamie watched for signs of hysteria on Felicia's part, but in this crisis over Jim, she'd proven to be of sterner stuff than her frivolous ways indicated. Jamie decided to forgo further worries regarding Felicia. They needed her additional strength more than ever. She squatted beside him. He looked improved this morning. *His eyes are clear. At least that's something.* "You're right, Felicia. We can leave him alone for a little while. Jim, you'll be all right while we're gone?"

"Go ahead, ladies, you won't find anything under this tree worth eating. I'm no hothouse flower you have to constantly tend, and Mick'll be back soon. I suspect he's a light sleeper."

Jim sounded better. *Could the heat packs be working?*

They left him a full water bucket and set off in search of anything edible. "We're a fine mess aren't we, scrounging for food. It's like dumpster diving," Felicia said, trying to laugh. She hadn't washed her hair since Jim was injured and it had lost some of its luster. Still, she flipped it in the sunlight as was her habit.

"Maybe so, Felicia," Jamie replied as she headed out. "I don't give the tiniest little damn about that anymore. If we find a couple of breadfruit, I'll happily take them out of a dumpster. I agree Jim needs a full meal under his belt. I'll feel better about him, myself. Let's do our best anyway."

They went farther afield and found a couple of breadfruit caught in a pile of sodden leaves and grass left by the storm. They were overjoyed with this small contribution for dinner, and picking it out of garbage no longer crossed their minds.

They searched a while longer until Felicia, anxious about

Jim, insisted they turn back. A clear day, the sun beat down, burning into their exposed bodies. With so many trees missing, the heat soon became unbearable. They returned to Jim with reddened faces and sweltering bodies, carrying their pitiable bit of food.

"Let's jump in that little bathtub Mother Nature made for us in the storm, that is, if Jim's okay," Jamie said, wiping sweat off her face, neck, and body. Her clothes were sopping as well.

"You've got it!" Felicia agreed. She looked hot, her cheeks flushed and rosy.

They each carried a breadfruit with no thought it might be rotted. Their poor dietary standards went unnoticed. Everything looked edible these days.

They found Jim asleep when they returned, and Mick nowhere in sight. They headed for a quick dip in the pool and ran to it peeling off their clothes. With utter joy, they threw themselves into the clear warm waters.

"Oh, this is heaven!" Felicia cried out in delight, scrubbing her hair in the cooling waters. They submerged completely in this new pool.

"I'm with you. It couldn't feel any better than this, grubby as I was. The lagoon isn't as much help keeping clean, being so salty." Jamie ducked her head under for the tenth time. We'll need to get busy on Jim though, soon as he's awake."

They rinsed their clothes and wore them wet when they left the little pool.

Mick, awake now, worked at applying warm soaks to Jim's arm. He'd heard the women splashing about and chatting. For this small, precious moment, things were right with the world.

He looked up to watch them come, hair dripping, clothes plastered to their newly streamlined bodies, and relaxed smiles on their shining faces. He enjoyed the picture both women made.

Their beautiful features, enhanced by wet hair plastered

against their heads, were the absolute image of classic beauty.

"My God, what a pair," he murmured.

He'd said it low, but Jim heard and nodded agreement. His eyes caught the sight, and his admiration was evident by the smile that creased his emaciated face.

Mick was relieved to see the women able to relax a bit. "I see you took time for a shower. I think I will too, Jim's pretty good for now." He felt better about things. "Jim, how about you? Do you want a wash up yourself?"

"Damned right, I'm for that, Mick," Jim replied. He was eager at the thought of cool water washing away his pain and fever. "I sure would if you'll help me. These girls have been cooking me for so long, I feel damned crusty right now."

"We'd better take a look at that arm first. It hasn't been changed since last night," Jamie said. "Come on, let's go out to the lagoon and put fresh seawater on it. We need to clean it again. Maybe with all our work, we'll beat this infection yet."

Mick noticed how easily her enthusiasm caught hold of them, lifting their spirits.

They watched Jim, groaning in pain, rise slowly to his feet, stiff and unsteady from lying down all night. Mick walked with him out from camp to some handy bushes. Jamie giggled at the groan of relief from that direction.

At the lagoon, she opened the dressings, crusty with old drainage. With a soaking of seawater, they came off. Jamie felt a shock seeing the wound had increased in swelling, inflamed edges, and yellow green mucus. The odor was less, but present. "It looks like hell, Jim. It's a wonder you have less pain than yesterday."

"I see how it looks. I need a tremendous course of antibiotics right now, Jamie. I needed them a long while ago and I know it." Jim's whispered voice betrayed his despair. "But I do think the heat has drawn some of the garbage out of it. I'd like to continue it. I might just pull through. With the nursing care I've had, how could I help but make it?" He gave a weak laugh and Jamie heard the tinny sounds of bravado again.

Felicia, listening to their comments, looked at the wound. "You'll make it, there's no doubt in my mind." Her violet eyes flashed, and her newly rinsed hair gleamed with glossy hi-lights while it dried. "I can't lose you, Jim, I won't! After all we've been through together, I couldn't bear to lose you now. I just couldn't!"

Jamie poured seawater over the wound while Felicia did her best to clean the dressings in the lagoon. They were a disgraceful mess and grew worse as each day passed. She redid the small strips holding the wound edges together, due to the increased swelling. The wound held together, but she couldn't take the chance of it opening up. They redressed Jim's arm, and went back to continue their desperate fight against his burgeoning, deadly infection.

# CHAPTER 31

While they tended Jim's wound, Mick waited to bathe.

"Hey, man, I still want my turn at that pool," Jim said. "I've sweat enough for ten people!"

"I'll take Jim for his bath," Mick said. "He'll do better without female prying eyes anyway." With his mouth in a devilish grin, he winked at Jamie and led Jim away.

Both ladies knew the men bathed in the buff.

"I wish I could wash Jim's clothes, but we'd better stay away. Who knows what we'd run into?" Felicia giggled, and Jamie delighted in hearing it.

The hopeless fight they faced, trying to save Jim, filled Jamie with sick terror. After seeing his arm this morning, and the foul drainage, she wondered why he was cool at all. *Were we looking at stuff drawn out by the heat? The heat does that.* A tinge of hope crept into her worried mind as they stirred the fire into life, heating the stones again.

Jamie heard the men shouting and splashing about in the pool. Enjoying their antics, Felicia managed a small giggle. Most women likened men to small boys, though they could be fierce as lions when they needed to be. Jamie knew their softer side because of Mick, yet he was of the toughest honed steel. Her father was a gentle man. She wondered if he had toughness too. She'd never had to see that side of him.

Her father must believe her dead. She hurt inside, when

thinking of his pain. After her mother died, his desperate sorrow had nearly killed him. She'd been in junior high then. She whispered the words she wished he could hear. "Dad, I'm alive, if you only knew. I'm more alive than I've ever been." She said it softly while her thoughts turned to Mick. Anymore, she wasn't sure of much, except that she loved him with all her heart and soul.

Roused from her reverie by the men's return, she turned to watch them enter the camp.

Jim was jovial, having enjoyed the refreshing bath and been cooled by it. "I guess you'll start cooking me again." He laughed with eyes too bright, and that meant returning fever. She had a sick feeling that, from here on out, things could only get worse. Felicia straightened and fluffed the debris beneath Jim's bed, hoping to make it comfortable. They settled him on the mat and began again.

"You smell nice, Jim," Felicia said, smiling at him.

Mick looked at Jamie with telling eyes. He'd kept the injured arm out of the water, but it was soaked with seawater anyway. Jim settled to allow them to work their magic. Wanting desperately to save him, Jamie worked continually, keeping heat to the wound. His increasingly fevered eyes followed her movements.

Felicia beckoned to Mick and walked away from Jim. "Mick we tried everything to help him, but it's frustrating, the poor medical care we're able to provide."

"I know, Felicia," he replied. "We need fish for dinner and I'm going for it while you gals tend this guy." He turned away and Jamie went after him.

Out of Felicia's hearing Jamie nearly sobbed. "He's heating up again, and it'll be so bad this time. Mick, I feel so helpless. Can we do enough?"

"I don't know, girl." He took her in his arms. "This would be all I'd need, all I'd *ever* need." He nuzzled her hair and down her neck. "I'd better catch a few fish to go with your breadfruit. I hope Jim will eat, he needs food more than ever." Mick kissed her again. "I hate to leave you. You need my arms around you, and I need yours. I never tire of the comfort I find in you."

"I want that, too," Jamie said. "We were lucky to find anything to eat. I don't know where to look next. Mick, we're running out of food."

"But not out of fish. We may have a steady diet of it soon." His laugh sounded hollow. "I may need to go pig hunting again."

"Over my dead body," Jamie exclaimed.

"Never in my lifetime, girl, not that lovely, wonderfully alive body of yours." He went out to fish, but didn't look out over the reef as he usually did. His thoughts were of holding Jamie, and wondering when they would be alone again.

Jamie returned to work over Jim with Felicia. His face now flushed a fiery red and his forehead fairly burning. Felicia saw it with alarm. "Do you think it was the bath? Maybe he shouldn't have gone in the cool water."

"No, Felicia, you saw that wound. It's a wonder he's stayed cool as long as he has. We'll have a bad time of it from now on. We have to keep on with this for a while longer and let him rest. Keep cool cloths on his forehead and let's get all his clothes off that we decently can. Mick can help with that when he gets back." She wished he'd hurry.

They used one bucket for cool water and one for hot, and worked over Jim. He slept off and on until Jamie began to wonder if he was even conscious. Then, he began to rave. "Mom, why can't I have more cookies? I'm so awful hungry, Mom."

His fever had brought delusions. The sick look on Felicia's face, accompanied the renewed fear in her eyes. Jim began thrashing, throwing his dressings off, and kicking his legs about in the rocks and debris.

Felicia wanted to scream in agony. "Jamie! What'll we do?"

"Go and get Mick. We need him now!" Jamie felt an ice

cold fear. She'd never seen anyone this ill. "Hurry, Felicia."

Felicia ran to the beach for Mick. He'd speared a fish and it splashed wildly about as it fought for its life. She waded out to him. "Mick, please come quick, it's Jim. He's out of his head! He's fighting us. We don't know what to do. Help us," she pleaded, though she didn't need to.

He turned with the fish and plowed through the shallow water, running toward camp with Felicia close behind. In their fear and haste, neither of them looked out over the booming reef.

"Oh, hell's fire!" Mick cried. "He's burning with fever and its worse this time." He held Jim down until he quieted. "Let's keep doing our best. There's nothing else we can do now, except pray. Maybe God'll take our side in this. We have to keep trying."

Jamie witnessed the distress written on Mick's face and heard it in his words. A part of their strength in fighting Jim's illness lay in Mick's strength. He had no answers for them other than his stubborn willingness to try. But Jamie knew nothing they did would be enough, and she tried to face it. But his words sparked another question. *Would a drug dealing criminal be calling on God for help?*

Mick's voice broke into her thoughts. "Jamie, could you get some fresh sea water? This stuff is nearly gone and dirty as hell."

She realized he'd seen her frightened face and wanted her away from the desperate struggle to save Jim's life. She caught her breath for a moment, hoping the quiet azure waters of the lagoon would sooth her troubled heart.

She hurried with the bucket, glad to leave that hellish scene behind. Jim's fair complexion flamed red, he babbled nonsense, and it tore her apart to see it. Reaching the water's edge, she looked out over the reef, as was her habit.

*Oh, God help us!* Her heart froze in her chest. She saw square sails coming steadily onward toward the foaming waters breaking over the coral reef. She ran back to Mick, the bucket forgotten in her hands.

"Mick—t—they're coming—it's the junk. They're really coming. There's no saving storm for us this time, and they're nearly to the reef."

"I'll take a look. Wait here." He ran toward the beach and looked, careful not to be visible. The square rigged ship stood just outside the reef, keeping a good distance from the jagged coral. He also noticed, with a grateful heart, the receding tide. "Thank you, God, for that, anyway," he breathed. The devils couldn't get a boat over the reef for hours, not until high tide came again.

As it was already late in the day, he guessed they'd wait until daylight. This gave his group several hours to secure themselves in their hiding place and erase all evidence of the camp. It was fatal for Jim, but so were the deadly drug-trading pirates. The choices had narrowed to certain death for Jim.

There could be no heat treatments while the men from the junk searched the island to destroy witnesses. They'd mercilessly wipe out anyone who could testify in a court of law. A sick man like Jim would be lucky to warrant a merciful bullet.

Mick walked back. The women looked at him. They read the truth in his pale, drawn face and knew what they faced. It had been discussed, but Jim hadn't been in deadly peril then. There could be no treatment to save his life while hiding in a cave.

"What do we do, Mick?" Jamie asked quietly, face pale, her deep gray-green eyes alert, ready to do his bidding.

"We'll move Jim up to the cave, and I'm hoping like hell we can get him to walk. He's hallucinating. We'll have a problem if he fights us. He's too big to carry. What a hell of a time for them to come now."

He took charge gently, letting them know what they had to do. Seeing the terror in Felicia's face, he believed she needed action and purpose to keep her from melting into a quivering mass. "We have time. They can't land for nearly twelve hours. The tide is going out. The reef will keep them outside the lagoon. My guess is they'll wait for daylight and high tide. Put out the fire. Felicia, could you do that? Sorry about Jim's arm, but it has to be done. Jamie, pick up everything you can find that might give us away. Put any food, including this fish and the breadfruit into the nets. When everything is ready we'll see if we can move Jim—we must do it!"

Felicia hurried to throw water on the fire. It raised clouds of steam and smoke. "Oh, Mick, look at it. They can't help but see that."

"Felicia, they've seen our smoke for quite a while. We've been working up a lot of fire lately, so they've seen it anyway." He calmed her as best he could. "What they don't know is *who's* on this island. That's our best hope. We can't allow them to discover you ladies. That's my concern, and it'd be Jim's, too."

"If we have as much time as you say, Mick, let's concentrate on getting Jim up to the cave and worry about this stuff later." Jamie had everything gathered as well as possible in the fading light. Evening advanced quickly and they had no moonlight. That would come later. The moon came fuller each night again, and they could use it to gather the remaining things.

"Good idea, girl. Felicia and I'll get him moving. Maybe you could bring the water things, the food, and a bit of his bedding." Mick went to Jim and bent down to him. "Come on, old man, we've got to get a move on. Come on, Jim." He tugged on Jim's good arm and Felicia coaxed him in her gentle voice.

"Jim dear, come on, get up so we can go for a walk. Come on now." She used her most encouraging, wheedling tones, disguising the desperation in her voice.

"Hey, whatcha waking me for, Mom?" Jim responded, his words muffled and confused.

He tried to rise from the bed and, finally, with Mick and Felicia urging and pulling, they got him to his feet. They started upstream with Jim weaving unsteadily between them and he appeared to gain strength as he moved. Felicia urged and complimented him on how well he walked. Jamie gathered his mat, much of the leaves for padding, and rolled it into a bedroll. She then put the fish and breadfruit in the water buckets. Felicia and Mick had the job of walking Jim.

They made slow, torturous progress upstream. Jim, sweating profusely, babbled on, discussing the best ways to proceed with an impending court case they were trying in the morning. It was slow going, and they struggled to keep him from lying down to rest several times. Mick allowed no time for pity, or rest. Felicia appeared near tears with worry over Jim, but kept going.

"I know it's hard, but you're doing a great job with him. It's just a little farther." Mick encouraged them both, but Jamie believed he worried more for Felicia in this situation.

She had to be devastated seeing Jim forced to walk. There'd been little hope for recovery *with* the heat treatments, and now they had nothing. Would he live long enough for the smugglers to leave the island? They each held back the fear they could not voice.

The pitifully small chance for Jim's survival had evaporated with the loss of the heat treatments. They tried to sound hopeful for Felicia, but had none themselves.

They neared the cave entrance as darkness fell. "Can we wait until the moon gets up before we get him in the cave?" Jamie asked. "It comes up later each night, and we have enough time."

"Good idea, Jamie, we need a breather anyway," Mick agreed.

They helped Jim lay down on the mat. He appeared to sleep immediately, and seemed cooler to Mick when he felt his forehead. Even that tiny bit of good news caused a frantic spurt of hope in Jamie's eyes. She was so ready to grasp at straws in her desperation.

Felicia sat close to Jim and held his hand. "It sounds like he's sleeping normally right now, just listen to him," she said softly, daring to hope.

Jamie bent down to listen to Jim's deep even breathing. "It does sound normal and he's less feverish, too. Maybe it's cooler up here, being a bit higher."

"I'll make a fire and we can cook what food we have," Mick said. "Whatever happens tomorrow, I doubt we'll be making fires."

"Good, I'm so famished," Jamie said as she scrounged about for twigs and any burnable refuse—it was more plentiful here where it hadn't been already gathered. The moon peeped over the ragged landscape and lent a bit of light as she searched.

Mick made a ring of stones and set a fire. "This lighter still works. I find that hard to believe, but I'm mighty glad of it." He held it in the palm of his hand, the shiny black cover giving off a dull gleam in the moonlight.

He followed Jamie in her search for additional wood. He came close to her and slid his arm around her. "I've been wondering how we'll get Jim in that cave," he said softly. "He's almost too big for the opening on a good day, and the way he is now—" He shrugged his broad shoulders and shook his head. "We've got to get him in there and out of sight."

"I've been thinking about that too. If we lay him on the mat, can't we pull him in head first?" she suggested. "If you and I go inside, we can do it together. Felicia can help from the outside. What do you think?"

"Girl, that sounds about right. You always have a good idea, you beautiful thing." *What a survivor!* Mick felt heartened by her constant willingness to try. "We've got to get him in there. Those devils would kill him in a minute. As for you and Felicia—I can't think about that." His face tightened at those hideous thoughts. "We have to get all of you in there, and disguise the entrance from the outside."

At his words, cold chills shook Jamie. *He wasn't coming into the cave!* "Mick, what about you? You can't stay outside the cave, they'll kill you. Oh please, don't do it," she pleaded, clutching him and pinioning his arms to his side.

As her face became visible in the emerging moonlight, he saw the terror in her eyes. "Think about it, girl. I know them and they know someone's here. I have a chance. None of you, not one, have a prayer with those men. They are pure evil." He held her out from him. "Jamie, it's our *only* chance."

His jaw, set in the now familiar pattern and lit by the softness of the beginning moon glow, was unmistakable. She could not change him. "Mick, I see you're right. It's just that I don't think I'd want to live without you in my life. I've been so happy. It's hard to face losing what we've had. How can I do that, Mick?" She clung to him, her eyes full of tears.

"Jamie, after we eat, we'll go together and pick up the rest of the things from the camp. There *is* something else we need to settle. We have *that* much time. We'll go after we get Jim and Felicia settled."

His voice was decisive and she had to go along with him. She'd never been able to press him or change him. What else did he have to tell her? *He's going to tell me goodbye, I know that much.* Her heart sank into despair as she wrestled with thoughts of losing him forever.

# CHAPTER 32

They cooked the last breadfruits and the lone fish. It was a scanty meal and would be the last for a time. After eating, they set about getting Jim into the cave. He had eaten fairly well and seemed nearly lucid, but when he called Felicia "Mom," they knew he continued in the throes of fever. It took hard work encouraging him to get up and move around the sharp rocks jumbled near the cave entrance.

"Honey, we want you to lay down on this blanket now," Felicia crooned.

Near to tears, she fought them bravely, as she worked with Jim to gain his cooperation, comforting and cajoling his fevered mind.

Mick and Jamie went into the cave to pull the large, gaunt frame through the small opening. Jim lay on the tent cloth and Felicia kept his arms in, safe from the sharp edges, as he slid through the narrow opening.

"Well, girl, another one of your good ideas has proven fruitful," Mick complimented her, but Jamie scarcely heard it.

With a frozen, sinking heart, she awaited his "*talk.*" It couldn't be anything she wanted to hear.

They settled Jim far back in the cave on his mattress of debris and Felicia settled next to him. Mick told her they were going for the rest of the things.

"Take care, watch your step," she said. "And please hurry back. Jim's asleep now but I don't know what he'll do next."

Jamie heard the defeat in her pleading voice and knew unseen tears lay in her eyes.

Mick helped Jamie out into the moonlit night, and they slowly picked their way to the campsite. Wondering what Mick would say to her, knowing it had to be goodbye, froze her mind. She believed it would be forever if he faced the drug people. They'd shot him once so what would they do this time? Even if it proved final, she could do nothing to change things. He'd chosen the only possible way and his bravery and sacrifice overwhelmed her.

Slowly, almost leisurely, they made their way. Her tension grew until she felt nearly out of her mind, dreading the loss of him.

He stopped, turned to her in the soft glowing moonlight, and looked into her face, outlined with silvery shadows. "Jamie—*Jamilla,* my dearest love. Tomorrow will be a hellish day for all of us. You must be the bravest yet. You cannot make a sound or let Jim babble. He must be quiet if they come near the cave. One sound from him and all our planning will be for naught. Keep watch and listen by the opening. I will shove a big rock against it and toss some broken stuff around the door to make it look like natural debris. If they don't hear anything, they may believe I'm alone here."

He held her shoulders between his two strong hands. She had the fleeting thought that he had fully healed. There was no weakness in his left arm now. He held her in a grip of steel.

"What was it you wanted to tell me, Mick?"

She knew he had more to say. She looked into his long, saturnine features, clearly visible in the moonlight, and saw a quizzical look on his face, a half smile.

"Girl, I love you as I've never loved any woman. Remember I told you I made you my wife that one morning? Do you recall that?"

"How could I forget it, Mick? You've made me over-the-moon happy, though I've never been able to imagine how marriage between us could happen. It was only a dream, wasn't it?" She wanted to cry her heart out.

"If things go right, these people will take me away with them. You might think the worst of me, and I can't help that, but I must know you love me—trust me. Can I know that, Jamie?" His hands held her in a vice-like grip and, by the light of the moon, he looked deeply into her eyes. "Say something, girl! Tell me you're not sorry about *us*. Tell me that. I couldn't go on in this world if you didn't love me or want me," he added. "If you believe the worst of me, I can handle that, but I can't hear the other."

"Mick, there'll never be a day of my life that I won't love you. I gave myself into your keeping long ago. But now, it's nearly certain you'll be killed by those men. They tried to kill you once before."

She let go and sobbed quietly as he folded her closely against him, his chin on her hair, breathing in the scent of her.

"I've a chance, girl. For you three, there'd be none. You know that." He held her close in their mutual distress. After long moments, he said, "Let's get the rest of the stuff. I want you safely stowed away in that cave before they get too near."

"Mick, I'm so afraid. Will we live through tomorrow? I guess I'd die happy. I've said that before." She became pensive in his arms. "I do trust you. Everything you've done since we've been here makes me believe in you. I wish my father knew about you. He'd like you, he really would, Mick."

"Let's not borrow more trouble than we've got already." He had a lilt in his voice that made Jamie forget everything.

They collected the few things left at the camp. Before reaching the cave, he caught her close and they made love. It could be the last time they'd ever be together and her feelings faced the ragged edge of pain. It was intense and bittersweet between them as he whispered his love and hope for the future. "My wonderful darling, someday I'm going to tell our son about tonight." He chuckled softly. "When he's older of course."

"What?" Jamie gasped at his strange declaration, his crazy bit of wishful thinking. "What are you saying, Mick?"

A strange, crowing little laugh escaped him as he helped her to her feet. "Don't mind me, I'm just daydreaming."

They hurried back to the cave, carrying the few things left behind at their camp beneath the mangled monkey pod tree. Jamie was puzzled by his words. He was not someone given to such frivolities.

At the last moment, before they reached the cave, he caught her to him. "Jamie girl, I've said this before, but it *will* come right for us. It *will*, dearest girl." His soft words forced her to believe in him.

She sank against him and wound her arms tightly around him, taking in the masculine scent of him. She wanted to hold this man and stay in his arms forever, knowing she never could. She raised her eyes to gaze deeply into those glowing eyes, darker in the waning moonlight. Seeking to etch the look of him into her heart forever as she faced the wrenching reality—she'd never see Mick again.

It was lightening into morning by the time Mick had them hidden in the cave and sealed inside with several large rocks shoved in front of the cave entrance. After he'd bid Felicia and Jim goodbye, and kissed Jamie's lips for as long as he dared, he left them. He threw debris over the rocks, blocking the entrance, until he thought it looked like storm tossed refuse. With one more whispered goodbye through the cracks, he turned to face the heartless drug people.

They must have landed by this time to search the island and Jamie, nearly paralyzed at losing Mick, watched him walk toward the lagoon to meet and intercept the devils who searched to destroy them. Through a crack between the debris and rock, she saw him square his shoulders in readiness. He willingly faced death from them to keep her and the others safe in their hiding place.

Felicia crouched beside her, peeking out as well. Jim lay sleeping in the coolness of the cave. "Oh, Jamie, he's so brave," she whispered. "I wonder what he'll do when he meets them, and he will. I know he will." Hiding the dread in her voice, she put a comforting arm around Jamie, hoping to ease her breaking heart. "We'll lose both our men on this dreadful island, the way things look for us now."

"He expects to meet them, he told me that. He hopes to get them to leave the island as soon as possible. We won't be safe until that happens." She couldn't take her eyes off Mick's departing figure. "How's Jim?" she asked, glancing quickly at the vague outline lying asleep on the sandy floor. "He's quiet now." In her worry, a quick glance had to suffice. She couldn't stop watching Mick.

"I don't know, Jamie, he's so feverish. He's asleep right now. Actually, I wonder if he might be unconscious. It's for the best I guess. I'd hate for him to yell for cookies if the smugglers were close." Felicia gazed lovingly at the large, gaunt form stretched out in the dimness of early morning light.

Barely enough daylight seeped through the blocked entrance to make him out in the dim interior.

Their attention snapped back to Mick when Jamie heard yelling and jabbering from the direction he had taken. She could no longer see what was happening, but they both knew he'd met the drug traders. "Felicia, they're here, on the island." She waited, with excruciating anxiety, to hear gunshots. Not hearing that, she whispered to Felicia, "I wish I knew what was happening out there. I've got to know."

It grew lighter as the sun made its way leisurely into the heavens, uncaring of the fearful events taking place below. Jamie didn't heed the torn and twisted landscape or the wheeling birds in the morning sky, all that was familiar. She gazed frantically out of the cracks around the huge stones Mick had shoved firmly into the entrance. "Felicia, I can't see what's happening."

"I don't know what to say." Felicia held out her hands to

Jamie in bewilderment. "We haven't heard any shots, so they haven't killed him yet."

"Well, they must have other things, like knives. I can't stand it, locked in here." Jamie crawled back into the cave and toward the other room. "I'm going out there—I have to see what's happening."

"Jamie, what are you doing? Mick said to stay here until they left the island. You can't get out that way." Fear and desperation rose in Felicia's whispered voice.

"Oh yes, I can. I'm climbing up that tree. You know, the one Jim shoved in during the typhoon. I can see everything from the top. I'll be careful, Felicia, I promise. I don't want those monsters finding us. Don't worry."

Reaching the bigger room, Jamie stood up. Felicia followed. The light, poor and dim in the early morning, revealed the drying tree with most of the branches broken off by Jim's descent the day of the storm. Jamie went to it and tested the remaining branches. "I think this will work just fine. It may be the only way out anyway. I'm not sure we can move those big rocks Mick put in front of the opening."

"Please be careful, Jamie. If they spot you, it's death for all of us," Felicia warned.

Jim moaned and she hurried back to sooth his fevered murmurings. He dared not babble or call out now.

"I'll keep low," Jamie promised. "Don't worry. I just have to see what they're doing to Mick. I love him so much, Felicia, I have to know." She began her climb, easily making her way to the top, and eased out the hole. Jim had enlarged it considerably the day he'd squeezed his bulk through coming in from the typhoon.

Jamie welcomed the fresh air as she wriggled out of the cave. She kept low and behind rocks. Peeping cautiously over the sharp edges, she found the group of men she'd heard. "They're speaking Chinese or something. I can't make out a word of it," she whispered, fixing her eyes on the group.

They'd stopped about halfway up from the lagoon, haggling over what to do. She made out Mick's tall form among the smaller stature of the oriental men. Trying to make out what they were saying, she only heard snatches of conversation. Most of what they said sounded Chinese, until she heard Mick's voice.

"You come late to thees island. Jees' I starve here, long time. How come you seenk my sheep, you bastards?" He sounded almost jovial, standing tall among them, waving his arms about.

Jamie saw a Chinese man put his arm around Mick like a long-lost friend. Did he know this man? She couldn't stop the feeling he played a game. *Or has he played a game with the three of us? What's going on? Who is this man, anyway?*

She watched the gathering for hours, it seemed, occasionally shifting her cramped legs, staying low. Traitor or not, she remembered Mick's words of warning. They might not kill him, but they'd kill Jim and worse for her and Felicia. She knew Felicia waited anxiously for her return. She was about to go into the cave again, when she saw the party of men heading to the boats they'd beached on the sand.

"Oh, thank you God, they're leaving," she said in hushed tones.

She'd never draw an easy breath until the last of that evil lot left the island. The tide must be going out and they needed to hurry, or stay on the island for another tidal change, another twelve hours of hell on earth.

She breathed a sigh of relief seeing two small motorized boats heading for the break in the circle of coral that enclosed the lagoon. The taller form of Mick sat amongst the smugglers as the boats made their way out through the break in the foaming reef. After what seemed a lifetime, the men from the junk reached their vessel. She watched their tiny forms climb a rope ladder to board it. Shortly thereafter, the chunky ship turned away and, as it grew smaller on the horizon, she knew they were safe at last.

Puzzled at what she'd seen, she remembered Mick's assurances to her. But seeing him so jovial and comfortable with those deadly men set her mind and heart into turmoil. Had she played the fool with a criminal? Unable to formulate an adequate answer, she turned to the duties at hand. Jim's life was in their feminine hands from now on. Dared they hope to do enough to save him?

Left alone, they must survive on their own and help Jim. His infection had reached the point of impending death. How much could they do? She stuck her head into the opening. "They're gone, Felicia—off the island, and out of sight. Let's open that entrance and let in some fresh air."

"Thanks, Jamie. Oh God," Felicia cried.

Jim began babbling again, and her soft voice soothed him.

The danger from the smugglers had gone, and Jamie felt certain they'd never bother to return. She gingerly picked her way down the jagged rocks, careful not to present a picture to anyone using a telescope from the open sea. She wouldn't feel safe from observation until she got to the devastated trees outside the cave. She went to the entrance and pulled the debris away, puzzling how they might dislodge the huge boulder Mick had shoved in place to cover the opening.

Felicia peeped out from the edges to see through the cracks. "Jamie, what happened to Mick? What'd you see?"

Jamie pulled smaller rocks away and tried, but couldn't budge the big one. "I'll tell you and you won't believe it, but I've got to open the cave door so we can move in and out. It's got to be stuffy in there." She struggled mightily with the huge boulder. "Can you push from your side and help? Maybe we can move this thing out of the way."

Felicia got against the boulder and shoved. They were unable to move it, though they rocked it a little.

"I'll get something to pry it away—hold on." Jamie searched the area for something to use and spied something black and shiny. She picked it up. "Why it's Mick's lighter," she said. "He remembered to leave it with us before he went to meet the drug people." It was like a message, somehow, saying, *I haven't forgotten you.* The warmth of remembering passed through her body at his thoughtfulness.

She found a sturdy bit of tree trunk and took it back to the cave entrance. "Okay, let's try again, Felicia."

With the power of the rugged pry bar, they finally moved the huge rock enough for Felicia to squeeze out into the sunlight. "Oh, Jamie, thanks, I was getting claustrophobic in there. I wish we could get Jim out but I know we can't. It's actually cooler inside so it's better for him in there." She choked back a sob. "He is so sick! He can't last much longer the way he is. We'll soon lose him and I can't bear it." Distressed and in tears, Felicia finally asked about Mick.

"He met them about half way up here. I heard him talking the same way he did on the docks the morning we sailed. He sounded so ignorant, Felicia. What game does he play?" Jamie shook her head. "One of them threw his arms around Mick like a long lost friend. I don't know what to think about him anymore." She held out the lighter. "But look at this, he left it for us to find, like a message that he's taking care of us while he's gone." Lost in confusion, Jamie shook her head. "We knew what he was in the beginning, but then he seemed different. I fell totally and completely in love with him, and I love him still. But what do I really know about him? Nothing—he has told me nothing at all, except that he's French-Canadian. In telling me a little about himself, in reality, he never gave me a clue about himself, and hasn't since we came to this island." She shrugged in futility.

"He's well educated and playing some kind of role. That's what Jim thinks. He mentioned it several times."

"Mick asked me to trust him and I'm trying," Jamie said. "Trust or not, I love him, and I'm not sorry for anything. Right or wrong, he made me feel normal and right again, no more that beaten down ninny I once was." She sighed. "Thinking back, I wonder how that happened. I guess I've made a complete one-eighty. I'm not the same Jamie I was, Felicia."

Felicia shook her head. "It's too much for me. I wish we had Jim to talk to, he knows things. He liked Mick a lot. I do know that. I wish I could do more for him, Jamie. He's so desperately ill. I'm losing him and I know it!" She re-entered the cave to check on him and Jamie followed.

# CHAPTER 33

He's very feverish," Jamie said. "I'll get cool water, and we'll bath him. We need to remove his clothes. I'll get seawater for his arm as soon as possible."

The two set about trying to save Jim with all the strength they had. The bad guys were gone and would never return to a devastated, useless little island.

Together, they undressed Jim and applied cool cloths to his entire body in their efforts to drop his fever. They undressed his arm, and even in the dimness of the cave, saw it was a putrid, inflamed, and dying mess.

"Jamie, it looks dreadful," Felicia said. "How long can a man live with an infection like this? We need to eat, too. Could you find us something? My stomach's been empty for so long." Felicia's voice betrayed fear, but she'd proven to be made of sterner stuff than they'd ever believed.

Jim raved in his delirium. "He must love his mother very much, calling for her so often," Jamie said. He lay silent at the moment, and they hoped he slept. They knew he couldn't last much longer. "His strength makes the difference, Felicia. Had he not been so strong, he wouldn't have made it this far."

Terrified, the two worked desperately to save him, and had nothing but seawater and forlorn hope. Felicia never went far from Jim's side. It fell to Jamie to search for food and bring seawater for his arm.

A day later, she had speared a couple of fish and, nearing

the cave with her catch, shrank away in fear as a large shadow flitted over the island above her. She looked up in disbelief to see a helicopter *whup-whup-whupping* heavily overhead. She knew a desperate moment of fear until she saw *US NA*VY emblazoned on the descending machinery.

Jamie ran into the open, waving frantically at the helicopter. She screamed for Felicia, but her words were lost in the roaring sounds of the big bird. Felicia had heard it, emerged from the cave, and looked up in utter disbelief.

Jamie ran to her, the fish she'd caught were dropped and forgotten. "Oh, Felicia, they've come for us. We're saved at last!"

Felicia burst into tears as they stared in wonder at the rescuing machine as it settled slowly to the desolate, littered ground. "Oh, thank God. I hope they're in time to save Jim. He's dying, Jamie, I know he is."

Together they waited. Two men jumped off, before the helicopter hit the ground, and ran to them, crouching down to avoid the whirling propeller blades overhead. The men stared at them as though they were apparitions.

"Hello, ladies," the first one said. He nodded first to one and then the other. "We heard you needed a little help here." He held out his hand in friendly greeting as he eyed them, trying to size up what he was seeing. The officer with him doffed his cap and introduced himself.

"I'm Captain Roger Timmons. I'm a doctor. We heard you might have need of medical assistance." Tall and dark haired, his searching blue eyes, rapidly took in the scene before him. Medical bag in hand, he searched for someone who needed him. He indicated a young sandy-haired man who joined them. "This is Bones, my assistant. He's a medic, and a good one."

They finally found their tongues and, at once, cried, "Oh, yes, thank heavens you've come. Please come and get Jim. He's so terribly ill. He's dying."

Felicia dissolved into tears again as she tried to take them to the cave. Her relief at rescue was a hazy dream, rendering her nearly helpless. Jamie led them to the cave and, after moving the big rock farther out of their way, they crawled in to Jim.

The rest of the crew gathered in the jumbled rocks near the entrance ready to help. Jamie heard the doctor say from the interior. "Bones, let's get this guy out of here. He's in a bad way."

They called for a stretcher and the men outside passed one into the dim interior. In short order, they pulled, tugged, and brought Jim's big frame out of the narrow opening.

"My God, he's a big dude," someone exclaimed.

The women in their scanty ragged clothing went unnoticed during the struggle to bring Jim out of the cave. They carried him to level ground and carefully set him down.

In the open air, Dr. Timmons looked at the swollen arm wrapped in the filthy dressings. "Can someone tell me what's happened here?"

Jamie stepped up and told him about the pig hunt and how the injury occurred from a filthy tusk. She didn't see or care that the rest of the crew covertly gazed at the sight of her legs. The frayed and torn skirt now hardly covered the essentials. The edges of her frayed undergarment were visible but she did not care. Her only concern was for Jim.

The medic, Bones, his eyes squinting, looked at the raggedly dressed women before him. "Does this man have any allergies?"

"We don't know. We had no medicines to give him," Jamie replied. "We never checked his pockets. He had on shorts." She went into the cave to retrieve Jim's ragged shorts, torn filthy shirt, and handed them to the medic's aide who rummaged through the pockets.

Dr. Timmons cut away the filthy-looking dressings and assessed the swollen arm. "God Almighty—what an infected mess! Let's get this man to our sick bay ASAP. We need to hurry!" He quickly cleansed the nasty wound with what Jamie thought was Iodine, rewrapped the arm in clean gauze, and ordered everyone aboard. Numerous willing hands assisted Jamie and Felicia. They had no possessions. Jamie had the lighter and the trusty red knife in her pocket—all she had left of Mick.

The suddenness with which everything had changed on their island was lost in the flurry of getting them aboard. The swiftness of their departure set their minds in a whirl of desperate hope for Jim's survival.

The giant rotors whirled above them and, seated in a craft strange and new to her, Jamie glanced down to see the ravaged little island grow smaller in the misty distance of the vast ocean. The helicopter's mighty engine took them rapidly upward into the tropical sky. She watched that blessed bit of life-saving land where so much had happened fall away to disappear in the mists of the far horizon.

That blessed island had changed forever the meaning and course of all their lives. Jamie felt salty tears flow down her cheeks. She tried to take in the immediate feeling of relief and rescue, but her tears were for the loss of Mick.

"I'll have to live on memories now. I once said I could, and now it's become a reality," she whispered softly. "I wonder if I can."

Felicia sat looking at the unconscious Jim. His stretcher lay on the floor of the helicopter. A medical card in his battered wallet said he had no allergies, and they had quickly given him several shots and started fluids infusing into his good arm. She didn't know what they'd given him, but prayed fervently it could save him. Noticing Jamie's tears she reached out and patted her. "Don't worry, Jamie, he said it'd come right. Try to remember that?" She handed Jamie a wisp of tissue from a box beside her seat. "Look, a Kleenex! When's the last time you saw one of these? Imagine, even this small thing is a wonder to me now."

The crew, endlessly curious to glean any detail from the tattered survivors about their experiences, found ingenious ways to elicit information. It served to distract them both from their worries over Jim and, certainly, the fate of Mick.

Being in a modern conveyance and Jim receiving medical care was a magical dream, an answer to fervent prayers for them both. Jamie felt she was in the midst of an unrealistic dream and didn't feel like saying much.

Sorrows were lightened in snatches of conversation with the helicopter crew, but it was very noisy, and impossible to satisfy many questions. The crew offered Hershey bars around and Felicia managed a small giggle as she accepted one.

Holding them, they both stared in surprise at something, at once familiar, yet strange and wonderful. Jamie could only look at it. "I haven't tasted anything like this for so long. It's like heaven. Thank you."

Felicia ate the candy in dainty nibbles, relishing every morsel, savoring the taste of something long denied. Worry over Jim dampened thoughts of food to a very great degree.

Jamie, slowly enjoying the taste of the candy, noticed the covert observation of their state of dress. Their ragged and scanty attire was of great interest to the crew. It had become obvious to her, and not a little embarrassing. "We've been wearing the same clothing since the shipwreck and using the bottom of my skirt for dressings," she told them, in her defense. "We're wearing our best."

She laughed about it, along with some of the crew, but held her head high. Jamie found no offense in the admiring glances from these wonderful saviors. Felicia, too busy watching Jim, never noticed.

Jamie was sure they'd get some answers now. How long had they been lost on the island, what island, and where? Why did they come for them? This thought had roiled in her mind as soon as she'd seen the huge helicopter whirring overhead. "It must have been Mick!" she whispered to Felicia. "He sent this helicopter, but how?" Her heart soared at the thought. *It had to be a good sign.*

It was cool on the helicopter, due to the altitude. Bones pulled out a light blanket to cover Jim. The medic said his temperature was over 104 degrees. They tended him gently and Felicia clung tightly to his hand, whispered to him, and frequently leaned down to kiss his burning face.

As they began the decent, Jamie caught a glimpse of a huge gray military ship growing ever larger, sitting on the ocean swells like a city unto itself. "Felicia, look at that! It makes my heart swell with pride to see something so beautiful."

"I hope they can save Jim," Felicia cried out at the sight below. "Oh, Jamie, thank God, they came when they did. It's beautiful. So big and gray. I wonder what it's called?"

"She's a cruiser, ma'am, the *Fort Hamilton*, out of Tokyo. We're just out on maneuvers, and we came right out as soon as we got word. Sure hope your man will make it." He'd been the first man to reach them on the island. Concern was evident on his sun-browned face, and his pale blue eyes were nearly like Jim's.

"Thanks, it's a lovely ship," Felicia answered, "and we're beyond grateful for you're saving us." She cast her tear-filled eyes down at Jim. "I pray for him. He's got to make it."

He hadn't raved, and Jamie worried he was too sick, even for that.

The medic, Bones, kept gazing into Felicia's eyes, mesmerized by the lavender shade. *I'll bet he's never seen anything like those orbs*, Jamie thought.

"We'll have him on systemic antibiotics as soon as we get him to sick bay. So far, it's just shots. Doc Timmons will take a closer look at him then. They're waiting for him down there, right now. It'll only be a few more minutes," Bones, told Felicia. "He'll make it. He's a strong one. Hang on to that. You can call home when you get off here. Maybe not until they debrief you, though."

"Debrief? They're going to debrief us? Why is that?" Jamie asked. She'd often wondered what the outside world had heard about a sailing schooner lost at sea. Earlier, the man had said. *'As soon as we got word.'* Jamie's heart soared. No one but Mick could have sent the helicopter. She clung to that hope.

"I can't rightly say about the debriefing ma'am," Bones replied, "but it's been big news, you know, losing a boat-load of tourists at sea."

"It has?" they exclaimed in unison.

Further comments and questions were on hold as the crew went through the mechanics of touching down. Instantly, men in drab-hued scrubs whisked Jim away on a stretcher. When Felicia tried to follow, Dr. Timmons put out a hand. "We'll take care of the gentleman. You two will want a shower and some clothes." He smiled. "You might like a meal when you're ready. And later on, the captain will speak with you." He handed them over to a group of female personnel, eagerly waiting to guide them to their new quarters and make them welcome.

A slim, perky redhead stepped up. "I'm Seaman First Class, Susan Albright. I'll show you the way, and we're dying to know everything that's happened to you two! There are forty-five female personnel aboard, so among us we'll find you something to put on. Tell me, what sizes do you ladies wear?"

Jamie and Felicia stopped in the companionway and looked at each other, then at the female sailors.

"We haven't a clue." Jamie laughed, feeling a bit uncertain. "We were attending an obesity convention in Tahiti when this happened." She looked down her long, slim, tanned legs, and held out her blouse—baggy, torn, and filthy. A wide grin spread over her face as this wonderful moment blotted out their tangled, terrifying past few months. "I'm dying to find out, though."

Worried about Jim, though she was, Felicia giggled. "I wore a two-X before we went for a day sail on the *Queen Ilikii*. Now I don't know." She held out her shredded blouse and her filthy cut-up shorts, which spoke volumes. She looked at the sailors, a quizzical smile across her lips.

The female sailors gathered around them in excitement. "Hey, guys, what've we got for these lovely ladies of the islands?"

They didn't know who said it, but offers poured in from all quarters as they headed for their first showers in…how long? Jamie wondered constantly how long they'd been lost.

The female seamen provided them with shampoo, conditioner, scented soap, and thick Navy issue towels. They entered the showers in delight and scrubbed themselves properly. It had been a long, long, time.

"Now I know what real luxury is. It's a wonderful shower with all the necessities." Jamie laughed, but prayed, thanking God for their rescue. "Please watch over Mick and Jim," she asked.

After luxuriating in the showers, they found a plentiful array of clothing awaiting, generously offered, and gratefully received. "These are civilian issue. We wear them when we're on shore or off duty," a uniformed young woman informed them.

Jamie held out a short skirt of heavy tan sateen fabric. "Will this fit? It's a size eight." She put it on and zipped it up. "It does. Even a little loose. Can you believe this?" she asked, in awe of the size. She chose a white short-sleeve T-shirt that complemented the skirt and her deeply tanned complexion. Looking through several pair of footwear, she tried on beige sandals and found a fit, then tried to look in the small, inadequate mirror on the wall.

"Jamie, you look wonderful, so civilized," Felicia told her. She giggled while slipping into a skirt of deep blue gabardine and found a lemon color top to go with it. "Hey, this is a ten. My body hasn't seen this size since the sixth grade. I've never been slender in my entire life, but I love the way I look." She pirouetted in front of the insufficient mirror. "Is this really me?" She dug into the pile of footwear and found a pair of raffia style sandals that fit. "Oh, Jamie, this is wonderful, and I'm dying to eat, but I must see Jim, first. Will they let us?" Her joy over the shower and the new size was heavily tempered with worry over Jim.

"We'll have to see. We can ask. My hair has grown so much, it takes longer to dry, but with all these civilized potions, it feels wonderful." Jamie dried her hair and it sprang into unruly curls. "Let's see about Jim and then hunt for some food. I'm even hungrier after that candy bar. I wonder what they serve on a huge ship like this. I've forgotten how things taste, and my stomach aches and grumbles to find out."

Felicia had her gleaming hair in hand. When they stepped out of the shower area, the female seamen set up a roar of approval at the changes they saw.

"We don't know who to thank for the clothes, but they're wonderful," Jamie told them.

"These are a far cry from a two-X and I love them," Felicia exclaimed and twirled around to show them, her glossy hair catching the light. "We'd like to see Jim before we eat. Can we?"

As wonderful were showers and normal clothing, she feared for his life. He was deathly ill and she easily forgot the smaller clothing in her concern.

"I believe so. We'll take you to sick bay first, and then to the mess. You must be starving after where you've been. Then, the captain requires an interview with you."

This informant, slightly older, was very trim and correct in her uniform. Jamie noted a no-nonsense persona in her attitude.

She introduced herself. "I'm Ensign Hannah Menke. I'll escort you." She led them down a metal stairway and through long metal corridors until they came to the ship's sick bay. Jamie reached the conclusion that everything was metal aboard this ship. Hannah led them through double doors and, after introductions, turned them over to the medical staff.

They entered a small room where Jim lay on a bed clad in hospital garb. He rested on fresh clean sheets with two bottles of fluid running into his veins. The male nurse attending him said his fever was coming down slowly, and he'd been awake for a few minutes. He looked to be asleep.

"Jim, Jim dear, are you awake?" Felicia whispered. "Please say something, darling."

His eyes fluttered. He turned his head toward them and tried to focus. "Hey, Mom, is that you?" His words slurred, but he managed a weak smile as his pale blue eyes focused on Felicia. "Hi, how're you doin? Where're we? This isn't the island, is it? What happened?" Then his eyes faded, his head lolled back, and he dozed off.

They'd bathed and shaved him. His hair remained lengthy, but he was clean and in capable hands.

"Rest now, darling, the navy came just in time, Jim dear. They're taking care of your arm. They've saved us, Jim. We'll be all right now. You rest, my darling. Oh, Jim, you're going to be all right." Felicia couldn't stop the flow of tears. "Oh, Jamie, he's still so sick!" But realizing the possibility that she wouldn't lose him, she whispered a prayer of thanks. "I love him so."

Jamie stood close, an arm around her. "I know he's going to make it and keep that mess of an arm, too. I'm happy for you."

She led Felicia away. Jim had sunk into a deep healing sleep.

# CHAPTER 34

I believe we're supposed to have something to eat," Jamie said to the nurse.

"Yes, ma'am, they're waiting to escort you."

Jamie noticed his look of approval as he took them to the door. In the companionway, members of the female crew waited. To them, escorting her and Felicia to an outlay of food, when they hadn't eaten a normal meal in months, was no doubt an exciting event.

In the mess, the two faced an overwhelming array.

"Real food, Jamie, our first in months." Felicia took a metal tray. "It's so much—where do I start?"

"Better go easy, Felicia. Our stomachs aren't used to much. I know mine isn't. It might be the motion of this ship, but I'm feeling a little queasy. Maybe it's the smell of this food." Jamie chose a few things. A bun and butter, it looked *so* wonderful. Pickled beets, a piece of fried chicken and a plop of mashed potatoes completed her tray. "I'll eat this and see how it goes." She frowned. "We're going to be 'debriefed' after we eat. Wonder what that's about."

She sat down to eat, taking small bites, tasting everything as if it was the first she'd ever tried them. Thoughts of whether or not Mick lived never left her mind, and her heart ached with worry. *Where have they taken him? Is he safe? Was he one of them?*

The crew kept them company, wanting to know everything. Enjoying their first real meal for such a long time, they wondered what the debriefing meant. Jamie ate only a little. Her stomach had shrunk to nothing, it seemed. "I feel like I've had a stomach stapling," she commented.

"Well, I feel the same. I haven't finished my tray and can't eat another bite. That's a *big* change for me. I'm hanging on to that. I like being this size. I can't believe how different I look." She frowned at Jamie. "You're pale, feeling okay?"

"Yes, but I can't eat anymore. If I do, I'll upchuck all over the place. Wouldn't that be just my luck, after all we've been through, to get sick now?" With a weak smile, she pushed back and held out her tray, not knowing where to put it.

Willing hands took care of the details. They were then, escorted down more long metal corridors to the captain. Jamie asked about calling home. Felicia needed to call her mother as well. The sailors said that would be after the debriefing. They were ushered into the captain's office.

A tall, slender dark-haired man in his fifties addressed them. "I'm Captain Alan Jamison, and this is Commander Harlan J. Wilkes, my executive officer." He indicated the man standing next to him, medium height, thin, sandy haired, and younger. "We're very pleased to meet you ladies."

He bade them to sit in comfortable, padded chairs and offered them anything they wanted to drink, including alcohol. They took a refreshment and a seat.

"You've been through a terrible ordeal," the captain continued. "Naturally, we've known about your case for weeks, but no one knew if there were survivors until about three weeks ago. A few people were picked up on a distant island by a fishing boat. From them, the authorities in Tahiti began to get a glimmer of what happened to the *Queen Ilikii*. Extensive searches were conducted after that, but apparently not in the right area."

His eyes were a warm brown and his face tanned and clean cut. Trim and fit, his warm persona put them at ease.

Commander Wilkes had a twinkle in his dark blue eyes. The men began the debriefing, curiosity evident in their features.

But Jamie held firm, sipping on a seltzer. "How did you know to come for us, sir?"

The captain knew by her tone, this would be the first question answered. "Our orders came through the Department of Justice and on through the Department of the Navy. More than that, we don't know. We had the correct coordinates to your location. Once we had word, we got right on it, and in the nick of time for the gentleman, we're told." His eyes and voice were full of sympathy for their suffering. "I've orders to interrogate you ladies as to the happenings aboard the sailing schooner, the *Queen Ilikii*. I'd like you both to tell us as nearly as you can, what took place that day, and since then as well."

Jamie could wait no longer. "First, Captain Jamison, how long were we lost and where *were* we, that no one looked in all that time? Honestly, it was as if we had dropped off the face of the earth—forgotten by everyone."

The captain seemed to understand their need to know and nodded. "You were lost on January fourteenth, and this is April twenty-seventh. You've been lost to us for more than three months. The island we recovered you from is called Teraroa. That island was devastated completely about twenty years ago by a severe typhoon, one of the worst storms ever recorded in the South Pacific. Being one of the low islands, it's oft times washed clean of vegetation in these typhoons." He paused and sipped his own drink. "For all intents and purposes, it was written off the maps as a wasted atoll with nothing left alive on it." He shook his head in wonder that the sea-lanes had not brought a ship near enough to see the recovery and new growth. "I understand you recently suffered through another typhoon on that same island. I'd personally like to know how you did that as well." His look of respect for them made Jamie relax.

That's a long time!" Felicia exclaimed. "No wonder

we've gotten so thin!" She looked lovingly at the newly slim, sun-browned limbs extending from beneath her blue skirt with renewed wonder, seeing legs so new to her they might have belonged to someone else. She couldn't help a small giggle. "You must have heard we were attending a convention for *big* people when this happened."

Jamie almost forgot where she was, wondering how Mick had gotten word out to find them. She didn't mention what she thought, believing it could implicate Mick further. She got herself in hand and nodded at the captain. "We'll tell you what we can."

From then on, they gave the details as they remembered them.

Jamie hated to speak of Mick. She found it painful in the extreme to describe his part in the destruction of the *Queen Ilikii*. She emphasized his helpfulness during their sojourn on the island, hoping that input would somehow help his case when he was arrested. And she believed he would be.

The authorities would consider Mick's friendliness with the drug smugglers in a very dim view. She'd never been sure what to make of that herself. Other thoughts rolled over in her mind. *Mick did send them—I know it.*

Jamie could not tell by the commander's facial expressions what his thoughts about their commentary might be. An aide sat quietly taking notes. Her primary worries were of seeing Mick hauled away in chains, to spend long years behind bars in some dank and musty cell. That is, if he was found and taken in arrest. Possibly, he hadn't survived the voyage with those evil men.

They met with the captain and commander for more than two hours. She had the feeling he found some of their exploits difficult to take in. They told about the pig hunts, Jim's injury, and how desperately they'd worked to treat it. The ship's officers raised their eyebrows.

Neither of the women felt the need to delve into intimacies, alliances, or sand shampoos. The female sailors would find greater interest in those details.

Jamie thought of the promised phone call to her father. She'd been lost for so long, he must believe her dead. "When can we call home, sir?" she asked, when the questioning died down. Unable to wait any longer, she was adamant. "They said we could, after we finished with this debriefing. I can't think of anything else we could possibly say, other than repeat how grateful we were to see your helicopter today."

Felicia quickly agreed with Jamie. "I'd like to call home too, but not until I see Jim again. I have to know he's going to make it." Her firm tone was unmistakable, as were the brimming tears in her great violet eyes.

"I guess we've kept you ladies long enough," the captain replied. "You must be exhausted after what you've been through. We've arranged sleeping quarters for you and, with your consent, I'd like our ship's doctor to give you both a good checkup. We'll do that in the morning, however."

Both men rose and extended hands to them. "Thank you both," Captain Jamison said. You've filled in more than a few areas we were missing. You ladies have quite a story to tell. There has been a great deal of publicity about this incident. You might want to prepare yourselves for that when you reach Tahiti."

"Tahiti! We're going back there? Why, for heaven's sake?" Felicia exclaimed. "When can we go home?"

"The Tahitian authorities require your presence as witnesses," Commander Wilkes answered. "The acts of piracy were committed in their waters and against one of their ships. Their courts will handle the entire affair," he added. "We were in this area when we got word, and you *are* American citizens, which of course makes it our affair. We needed information as well." He rose from his chair. "It's been our pleasure to help you and provide any necessities or assistance you might need." He led them to the door and called an orderly.

Felicia and Jamie were quickly guided to sick bay. Jim

lay asleep. He was very pale. The male nurse on duty said Jim had awakened for a short time and was very confused, but not to worry. "He has an extremely serious infection. We'll have a tough fight saving that arm. Give him another day or two to come out of his fever." He patted Felicia's shoulder. "We're keeping him as comfortable as possible and watching him closely. If he has family, they'll want to know he's safe aboard our ship. You ladies are pretty big news all around the world. Are you aware of that?"

Jamie read his thoughts. Two beautiful women and he wouldn't mind being marooned on an island with either one of them. Being appreciated and thought beautiful gave her a heady feeling. A surge of power and strength swept over her, and it felt wonderful! Should a man's appreciation mean so much to a woman? It had meant a lot coming from Mick, that was for certain.

Felicia stood over Jim's bed watching him sleep. An occasional moan escaped his lips. "Oh, Jim, you have to make it, you have to," she whispered. Her voice, soft and intense, caused a reaction from him. He stirred, eyes fluttered open, and his legs thrashed weakly on the clean bedding.

"But, Felicia, darling, we *have* to go hunting! We're out of meat again. Don't worry, Mick and I—we'll be careful." He babbled on about the nets and bait. Felicia, near to tears, stood at his bedside shaking. Jamie took her hand.

The nurse, observed the dark lines of fatigue beneath their eyes. "Don't worry, he'll make it—he's strong as an ox, and his temp is coming down a bit." He grinned as he said it. "I'll watch him. You two have a few calls to make. I'll check Jim's stuff, maybe find a phone number for you, if you'd like to call his people. You both look like you could use some shuteye."

He reached into a small cupboard near Jim's bed and fished out the ragged, stained shorts they'd brought in with him. He pulled out Jim's wallet and thumbed through it.

"How strange," Felicia murmured. "I've never seen Jim's wallet in all the time we've been together."

Jamie laughed. "We never went shopping to need it, did we?"

The nurse showed them an ID card with a home address and someone to call in an emergency. "I guess this'll do. It says Bernice Healy and gives an address in Kansas City—a long way from home." He scribbled the number on a slip of paper.

Felicia took the bit of paper from the nurse. "I'd like to call this person. Would that be all right?" she asked. She turned to Jamie, the paper shaking in her hand. "I pray it's Jim's mother and not his wife. He said he wasn't married."

The nurse took them to the door and an orderly took them to the communication center. She was a new female seaman and they both wondered if she was one of the those who had donated clothing. They weren't sure they would ever know who had been so generous.

"I'm Jennie Sondheim, Seaman Second Class. So, how did you like the captain? He's an okay guy. We all like him. We don't get on the wrong side of him, though. He runs a tight ship, that's for sure." She chatted away as she ushered them to a long line of phones. "Okay, go to it, the directions are on the wall by the phones. You can call anywhere on these." She settled nearby to offer assistance if needed.

Jamie picked up the telephone. She hadn't seen one for so long, it felt strange in her hands, but she followed the detailed instructions and finally heard it ringing on the other end. It rang several times until she heard someone pick up.

"Hello," she heard a sleepy voice say into the phone.

"Dad? It's me."

"Jamie?"

"Yes, Dad, It's Jamie. I'm all right. They picked us up today. Dad—can you hear me?"

"Jamie, honey, is it really you? Oh, thank God! I never believed I'd lost you forever. I *wouldn't* believe it. Are you all right, can you tell me?"

She thought his voice sounded shaky, but it became stronger after he'd listened to her voice, heard her words, and knew she truly lived. She talked a long while, reassuring him she was well. "Please come to Papeete. We'll be there in a few more days."

"Of course. I'll be there as soon as I can get a flight."

"Great, Dad, I can't wait to see you," Jamie cried out with joy.

Successfully reaching her mother, Felicia alternately laughed and cried into the phone. "Oh, Mother, I have so much to tell you. We'll be taken to Tahiti. Will you come there, please?"

When she'd completed the conversation with her mother, and Jamie had finished her call, Felicia nervously, with trembling hands, set about calling the number from Jim's wallet.

Jamie knew what set her on edge. "Just call her, Felicia, she'll want to know Jim's alive, and how he is. I'll stay beside you."

She watched Felicia's trembling hands dial the numbers. They didn't know what time it was in Kansas City, but with news like this, time zones wouldn't matter.

"Hello, Mrs. Healy," Felicia said. "I'm calling to tell you that Jim has been found." She looked at Jamie with a little smile. "She's crying, it sounds like she's his mother." Then Felicia said into the phone. "Yes, Mrs. Healy, we were lost with him. He's going to be all right. They just found us today and we're on a big navy ship." Then, after listening for a short time, she responded, "He was injured and is very ill, but the doctor says he'll recover. He'll call you in a couple of days, or as soon as he's able." She spoke for a few more moments and then said goodbye. "It's his mom. She said he was a strong boy and she knew he'd recover just fine. She cried a lot, knowing he'd been found, and that he's okay."

Jamie noted the relief in Felicia's voice.

Seaman Jennie saw they were finished. "I'm to take you ladies to your quarters. You look absolutely bushed, if I may say it." She led them to a room and said good night.

They saw actual beds with real sheets and a soft sleeping

garment placed on each one. The female contingent had thought of everything.

"Oh, Felicia, I don't remember knowing such fatigue. I can't wait to hit these sheets. What a day, *phew*, one I'll never forget!" Jamie flung off the borrowed clothes, put on the thin nightie, washed her face, and fell into bed. She wallowed in luxury for a few moments, wondering what the doctors would find tomorrow. She said prayers for Mick and Jim and fell into the sleep of worn-out, deep exhaustion, safe from harm.

Felicia followed her example, praying for Jim, and wondering what kind of mother-in-law she'd have. She fell asleep with the gentle movements of the huge ship that held them in safety.

# CHAPTER 35

"Hey, island ladies, rise and shine."

They awoke to the friendly voice of Seaman Susan Albright.

Her bright face peeked around the door as she called to them. "Breakfast time." She came into the room and snapped on the lights.

Jamie, half asleep, noted they were not on the island.

"What's happening?" Felicia rose from her bed, shaking her tousled head and blinking at the light. "I remember it all now, it's like a wonderful dream. Wake up Jamie, breakfast." She got up, smiled at Susan, and ran her fingers through her shining hair. "We're safe on your wonderful ship, Susan, and Jim's going to live! Thank you all so much." She grabbed a towel and headed for the shower.

Jamie moved to the edge of the bed and sat up. "I feel like I've been run over by a truck." She shook her head, tossing her unruly curls about. She needed a haircut. She yawned, said a sleepy good morning to Susan, and groped for her clothes.

"After breakfast our doctor will check you ladies over," Susan said, lounging against a desk. "You've been through a rough ordeal, and he'd like to make sure you're okay."

Jamie asked her to have a seat on the bed while they got ready.

Felicia came out of the shower with a towel wrapped around her hair. A cloud of steam followed. "Whew! That was good. I guess it'll take me a while to get used to luxuries like shower gel and shampoo." She laughed gaily and flipped her hair about. "Look how far this towel wraps around me, Jamie. I can't believe it."

Jamie nodded and headed into the shower, feeling an unusual sensation of light-headedness. Her face felt cold. Neither Susan nor Felicia noticed her difficulty. Jamie passed off the dizziness as residual from their arduous three-month ordeal.

When they were ready, Seaman Susan took them to the mess. Felicia took bacon, scrambled eggs, toast, marmalade, fruit, and coffee.

Jamie took toast, fruit, and coffee. "I don't feel like eating much yet. It all looks wonderful, but I'll wait until later."

She took a seat with Felicia. Several sailors eating in the mess cast them looks of overt interest. Jamie realized they' were objects of curiosity. All eyes were pinned on them, their darkly tanned skin, new-sized clothes, what they ate—everything. She mentioned it to Susan. "What are they looking at? Are we that interesting?" She felt conspicuous with the added attention. In their short time aboard this ship, they attracted undue attention wherever they went. She remembered the appraising eyes of Jim's nurse—him too.

"You don't know what an international furor there's been over your shipwreck. Now you're found and we've had a part in it. I think you'll be famous for a while. Our guys can't help feeling the excitement of your being on our ship," Susan explained, but they had difficulty taking it in. "Another item of interest will be the fact you were at a convention for overweight people, and look at you now! That alone is *big* news. Besides, there are also the fantastic stories you have to tell about pirates, typhoons, criminals and all, "she added. "Some people might want a book out of a story like that. We're respectful of your feelings here, but I can't imagine what you'll face in Tahiti," she finished with a concerned look on her face.

"We have to testify in Tahiti," Jamie said. "That should be interesting enough for everyone, but I can't imagine it just now." Her thoughts were of Mick. She felt like a traitor if she spoke of him. Nothing she could say would make Mick look like an honest man, in spite of his fine behavior on the island. Gathering her thoughts, she shook her head in dismay. "We don't know who else survived. Your Captain Jamison said there were other survivors, found only recently. We know of some who couldn't have lived." *Would they call Mick a murderer? See his hand in the drug trade?*

"I wonder what good our testimony is, unless it helps put those junk people behind bars." Felicia put a hand on Jamie's shoulder. "I saw that pained look cross your face, Jamie. I wish it could be some other way. You worry our testimony will convict Mick. So do I, I liked him. We definitely owe our lives to him."

Breakfast finished, Susan said the doctor was ready to see them. She led them to the medical area near sick bay.

Felicia requested to see Jim first. Her tone was urgent and firm. "I have to see him, Susan. We're engaged to be married. We fell in love on the island." She giggled, remembering their better days on the little island, and all her wonderful nights with Jim.

They entered the small room, where he lay on fresh clean linens. He was stirring. They saw bedding move as they approached his bed. He looked up at them with reddened eyes, the pale blue had been ravished by fever, but they saw recognition in his gaze. He smiled weakly, a wide grin spreading over his pale face. Felicia wanted to cry with relief—some days he hadn't known them.

"Hey, you gals, it's great to see you!" His voice boomed a little in spite of his weakened condition.

Felicia threw herself as near into his arms as she dared. He hugged her with his good one and buried his face in her glossy hair.

"Jim, you're really awake, and you sound good. How do you feel? How's the arm?" Felicia, a bundle of anxious questions, gazed lovingly into his eyes. "I talked to your mom last night!"

"I know you did, Felicia, I just talked to her myself. I told her about you. She was overjoyed to hear from me, and she thanks you for calling her. She knows about *us* now. We are still on, aren't we? Hey, I'm doing great. My arm's an awful mess, but the doc said I'd get to keep it." He nodded at Jamie. "Remember, you said I'd have an awful scar to show my grandkids. The doc agrees with you, some souvenir, huh?" He turned back to Felicia and stared at her,as if he couldn't get enough of her beautiful face.

The seaman interrupted them. "The doctor's waiting, one at a time."

"I'll go first, Felicia, stay with Jim," Jamie said. "You can go when he's done with me." She left with Susan, happy for Felicia, desolate for herself.

Dr. Timmons gave her a very thorough exam. When asked about her last menses, she tried to remember, but was hazy. "I can't be sure, Doctor," she answered. "I am sure of one thing. It's no fun when you have no supplies or change of clothes, a nightmare, really. Now we know why the native women stayed in special huts during that time. We are especially attractive to sharks during that time as well." She chuckled, remembering the day Mick had cautioned her about it.

The doctor's eyes twinkled at her comments. His manner and questioning were gentle. "It makes sense. You're saying you had it *one* time during your stay on the island," he asked. "Hum, I believe I'd better check you out on that, too, if you don't mind. Have you felt fairly normal these past several weeks?"

He got a female orderly to assist him with the exam and, when he finished, asked her to step into his office to hear his summary of findings.

Jamie dressed, entered the doctor' office, and sat down.

From his seat behind his desk, he frowned, his fingers tented in front of him. "My dear, I suspect that you are pregnant." His brow furrowed with confusion when he asked, "Is that a possibility? We only took one gentleman off the island, and he seems to belong to the other lady."

"Yes sir, it's possible, *very* possible. Jim wasn't the only man on that island. There was another man. He left with the drug traders before your people came for us. It's a long story, and I guess, in looking back, not such a good one. I don't know what's happened to him, sir. I don't even know if he's alive."

Jamie, learning she carried Mick's child, felt as though she was someone else as she explained about him to the doctor. She couldn't imagine being pregnant and didn't know what to think about it. She would talk it over with Felicia and her father too, when they met in Tahiti.

She left the doctor's office in a daze. Seaman Susan, seeing her unsteady gait and pale features, asked, "Are you all right?"

Jamie couldn't form an answer as the young seaman escorted her carefully to Jim and Felicia.

"Your turn, Felicia" Jamie said as she approached Jim's bedside.

After Felicia left with Susan, Jamie looked at Jim. "I don't know how to say this, but…ah…the doctor feels certain that I'm pregnant." She gave a half laugh, holding her hands out in a helpless gesture, a woeful expression on her face. "I can't believe it, Jim. It looks like I'll always have a part of Mick with me, anyway."

He looked at her, his eyes fixed on the uncertain mien of the young woman before him. "You're what? Oh, Jamie, if Mick only knew, he'd be the happiest guy on earth. Felicia will be over the moon about it when you tell her. I guess it's a lot to take in, especially things the way they are." He reached for her hand, a smile playing about his lips. "We'll be there for you, Jamie, don't worry about it. It'll work out. I've always felt it would somehow. I can't wait to see a kid of Mick's. I'll bet he'll have those same long features. Can't you picture it?"

Jamie felt an urge to swat him, but held back because his joy at the news was more than obvious.

"Why are you so happy about it? This child won't even have a dad. I don't know where Mick is or if I'll ever see him again, especially after that last day when he went off with those junk people, all buddy-buddy." Her eyes filled with tears and Jim changed the subject.

"Jamie, Felicia told me everything she could about that day. I have no memory of anything during that time. Not going to the cave, the Chinese junk returning, any of it. You girls are the bravest souls on earth. I've said that before, but it'll always be a wonder to me. Mick and I talked about it many times, and agreed we were the luckiest bastards ever, to be marooned on an island with you two." He squeezed her hand. "He loved you completely Jamie, and I hope he didn't lose his life keeping those devils away from us. Tell me about it, maybe Felicia left something out."

He was so clear this morning. Jamie breathed a prayer of thanks. She felt weak, found a chair, and told him about those harrowing days. How they tried to save his life, the hot soaks and hiding from the smugglers. "Felicia stayed inside the cave, to keep you quiet. I was going crazy because I couldn't see what happened to Mick. I climbed up your tree in the big room and squeezed out to watch. He kept them away from the cave. They only got half way toward it." She edged closer. "When he met them, he sounded ignorant, using that dreadful broken speech again, like he did the day we sailed." She lowered her voice. "What do you make of that? I saw him laughing when he met them. He walked away with them as if they were long-lost buddies. One of them even had an arm over his shoulder, and it was a struggle for the guy. Mick was so much taller."

"I've always wondered about Mick," Jim said. "An idea about him has hung in the back of my mind for a long time."

"An idea like what?" Jamie asked. Receiving only a grunt in reply, she went on with her story. "After they left the island, we spent the time working over you and hunting food." She finished by telling him how it felt to see the helicopter. She even remembered dropping the two fish she'd caught. "Mick sent them, who else? They told us they had all the right coordinates to find us, Jim. It came from the Department of Justice. Figure that, if you can."

A thoughtful look came over his face, and he slowly nodded His pale blue eyes seemed darker. "I'm sure it did. No one else could have. It deepens the mystery of the man."

Felicia came out after a long time, a look of wonderment on her face. "I don't know where to begin." She suppressed a giggle, but it escaped as she flushed rosy red. "Jim dear, did we ever talk about having children?" Her hands fluttered about as she looked at him, a strange smile spreading over her glowing features.

"Come on, Felicia, out with it. What's going on?" Jim's agitation increased. But after his chat with Jamie, his mind rapidly caught the idea.

"Jim—Jim, darling—we're pregnant! I can't believe it, can you?" She held her hand over her mouth to stifle an escaping giggle.

"Yes, my dear, I can." Jim had begun to face his new role in life.

Jamie hugged her. "You can rest assured, I believe it. Felicia, you're not the only one. Guess what the doc told me?" She uttered a nervous little giggle, flushed pink herself, and broke into a halting little laugh. "Oh, Felicia, I don't know what to do now."

Felicia stared at the helpless look of wonder on her face. "Jamie, not you too? Oh, this is wonderful! We'll raise our little island children together. I wish Mick knew. He'd be so proud, happy, too—he would, you know." She gave Jamie a hug in her own joy and for her friend's news as well.

"Hey, don't forget about old dad over here," Jim said. He had a grin on his face bright enough to light up a stadium.

Felicia bent over and kissed him soundly. "I'm happy,

Jim, and I'm glad you are too." She twirled about the small room, swinging her shimmering hair as she moved.

Jamie, happy for their joy, wondered how Mick would handle this turn of events. She wished she could tell him, and be with him as they'd been on the island. *Where is he now, and what has happened to him?* She was constantly troubled about Mick's fate among the desperate men who'd taken him from their island, and he never left her thoughts. She needed him now and he was gone.

ℰᗢℰᗢ

Dr. Timmons sat in his office contemplating the events that had just taken place. His thoughts were on Jim. "Both those ladies are pregnant! If there wasn't another man on that island, that son-of a-gun must be one hell of a stud. He's batting a thousand!" He uttered a chuckle as he mulled over the facts in his thoughts. "I believe the captain will be interested in my findings."

# CHAPTER 36

Ten days aboard the huge cruiser brought the needed rest, a gradual return to reality, and the wonders of life so readily available in the real world. After mess and seeing Jim, Jamie physically dragged Felicia from Jim's bedside, and a smiling Susan escorted them about the cruiser's wide deck. They worked their way around huge guns and mysterious things painted the same drab color.

Walking the expansive deck, looking out over the blue vastness of the ocean where so many terrible, yet wonderful things had happened, Jamie pondered constantly on her situation. She had another being to consider and faced impending motherhood, on her own. She'd have her father, but not Mick. He was lost to her. Would she ever see those black eyes and that long, wolfish face again?

"The ocean looks different from up here, and we don't have to watch for square sails anymore." She pointed out to sea. "Look how high we are—the water is about a mile down." The sight gave her momentary dizziness, or was it that?

Felicia, lost in her own world of concerns, frowned and shook her head, to clear it. "They said we were to go to Tahiti. Do you think Jim will go with us, or be transferred to a hospital in Tahiti? I wonder what sort of medicine they practice. I wonder about our talking to the authorities, Jamie. Do they speak French or English? The whole idea worries me to death. What do you think?"

Jamie just shook her head.

They required a guide lest they get lost on the cruiser, or have an accident, and Susan walked with them. The female sailors were fascinated by the stories the women told and Jamie didn't mind their curiosity. The female sailors didn't want to miss further details regarding their life on the island. They'd heard about washing their hair in sand, spearing fish, and hunting for food. They kept an ear tuned for additional information on things unbelievable, fascinating, and fearful.

"How do we get to Tahiti from this ship?" Jamie asked Susan, curious. "It's too big for the little harbor we saw."

"Probably by helicopter. We're getting closer to the Society Island Group, and the captain or the commander will decide. We'll near the area in another day or two. They'll likely do the transfer when we're close enough, depending on your gentleman's condition, and arrangements in Tahiti."

"Thanks, Susan," Jamie said. "You've been wonderful. We'll put our lives back together, and your treatment of us on this ship has given us a great start."

Susan laughed. "You three have made this by far the most exciting detail any of us has had since being in of the navy."

"Felicia, don't worry," Jamie said. "Jim's going to live. He'll be cared for, and he's well on his way to recovery. For me, I'm wondering how my father will take the news of my pregnancy. How can I tell him? I'm more mixed up by the minute. I'm happy I'll have Mick's baby. I'll love that man until the day I die, and if I see his face in our child, I'll be happy for that."

"If your dad knew Mick, he'd like him," Felicia said. "Didn't you say he wanted to be a grandfather? You *are glad,* aren't you? You *are!* You loved him that much and more. Jim and I always saw it between you. He used to say you couldn't help yourselves, and he meant both of you."

Jamie giggled. "I am happy, of course."

Felicia joined her in laughter.

Except for her deep fears regarding Mick's fate, Jamie was happy. Not knowing if Mick lived tore her heart in two. She also knew if she didn't find him again, she'd never be a whole person. Deeply satisfying to her was the knowledge he'd found a way to send help. Jim had readily agreed with her about that.

She enjoyed the way the sea air flowed through her hair. The safety they felt on the big ship took her mind off her worries. She gazed out over the sea, feeling a new contentment, and wondered if being pregnant made her that way.

"It's nice to take it easy, not hunt for food, or worry about drug-smugglers," she commented to Felicia. "Now we're found, will they try anything against us in Papeete? Those guys have eyes and ears out everywhere in the Pacific."

"Oh, Jamie, you don't think that will happen, do you? Are you saying we won't be safe in Tahiti either?" Felicia frowned, her eyes narrowed. "We'll need police protection as soon as we land, if that's the case. We'll have to see about that." With a frustrated sigh, she clicked her tongue.

"Well let's not worry yet," Jamie said. "It's a habit from our time on the island. We're in civilization now. We shouldn't have to worry about them again." She was emphatic, hoping to calm Felicia's worries. "I'm sorry I brought it up. We've had enough exciting news!"

They hadn't shared their news with Susan. Shocking and new, they only spoke of it between themselves and Jim. But Jamie knew they hadn't made a secret of their impending parenthood. It was known in sick bay after hearing Jim's excitement over it. She laughed. "Felicia, if news travels as fast on shipboard as it does elsewhere, I'll bet everyone on this cruiser knows we are pregnant."

Winding down emotionally, they continued their leisurely stroll, blissfully unaware of any gossip. The doctor had forewarned them they might experience a deep period of depression, perhaps an illness of sorts, as they mentally recovered from their long period of fear and deprivation. "It frequently happens after sustained periods of stress. You may become very ill for a time. A mitigating factor might be the happier times you've had on the island. I can't be sure, but you need to know of the possibility."

Jamie considered they might be in danger in Tahiti, and the edge of fear remained within her. She shivered, knowing they'd never breathe a free breath until they were on a plane heading home.

"I wish I hadn't said that about Tahiti," she apologized. "It puts a damper on everything, and we don't know that for certain, do we?" Felicia taking on even a slight hint of worry made her sorry for the remark. Jamie planned to make sure they'd be secure wherever the police placed them. She had a child to consider entered the equation. "Our things were left in our hotel rooms the day we sailed. Won't it be a kick trying to wear that stuff?" Jamie said with a laugh.

Felicia forgot about impending troubles, picturing them trying on their former huge clothing. Tired of walking the decks, they went to see Jim. The fresh salt air felt wonderful, but they tired easily.

Felicia tossed her head and her honey gold-streaked hair gleamed in the sun. "Is this fatigue part of that let-down the doc was talking about? We have no need to worry right now and I plan to enjoy it."

Glancing around at the deck, Jamie believed that move was noticed by more than one hundred seamen, male and female.

Every sailor, who was near, constantly cast discrete glances at them. Big news all over the world, they couldn't grasp the scope of something like that. Being rescued and safe continued to hold them in comfortable unreality.

The naval personnel remained at a distance unless they could render some service. They extended the hand of friendship where they could without invading their privacy, as Jamie and Felicia had recently been rescued from a harrowing ordeal.

The ladies appreciated their consideration and wondered if the captain had ordered it.

Jim sat in a chair when they entered sick bay. Pale and weak, he managed a wide smile at sight of them. "Hey, you two, what's going on out there?" His left arm remained heavily bandaged and held securely in a thick, padded sling around his neck and shoulder.

Felicia went to him. "Jim, how's the arm today? When we leave for Tahiti, will you go with us?" she asked. Her eyes fixed on his, a hint of worry on her face.

"The doc said I'd go with you," he answered. "They'll take us by in a helicopter in a few days." He looked into Felicia's eyes. "I missed you so much, from wherever I was. From now on I'll take care of you and God willing, we'll never spend another day apart. I love you, Felicia." His pale blue eyes deepened in color as he spoke his deeply held love and longing.

Seeing tears in Felicia's eyes as Jim spoke to her, Jamie stayed back. Her heart ached for the sight of Mick, while she rejoiced for the love her friends shared. Things were *right* for them. They could begin their future together without a hitch.

But for her and Mick? Jamie thought about him day and night. "God protect you, my darling," she murmured, softly as a prayer.

Felicia stood behind Jim, hanging over his shoulder. Her hair hung over their faces as a glossy curtain. She smothered his cheeks and face with kisses. Her face had flushed rosy pink. "I'm so happy, I'd marry you this minute if I could."

"If you mean that, Felicia, it can be arranged," Jim said. "Want to?"

"Oh, Jim, Could we do that? Get married?" Flustered and excited, she tried to grasp his words. "What are you saying, Jim?" She knelt beside him hanging onto his good right hand and looking into his china blue eyes.

Jamie listened. His fever was gone. He must know what he was saying.

"The captain will marry us, he can do that. All ships have that capability. If you'll say yes to me right now, I'll arrange it."

"Yes, oh, yes, Jim, I'd be the proudest woman on earth to marry you," she answered emphatically, stars shone from her eyes as she looked at Jamie. "I'm going to marry Jim. I'm so happy. He's getting well, and we're going to be married!" She grew thoughtful as she faced Jamie. "I'd like you to stand beside me, Jamie, and I wish to God Mick could stand up with Jim. He'll do that for Mick, when that day comes for you, and it will, Jamie, I know it." Her happiness clouded over for a brief moment, thinking of Mick, but her effervescent nature would not be denied for long.

"Of course, Felicia, I'd be proud to be your maid of honor. I'd love it!" Saying that, Jamie drew Felicia into her arms and hugged her. "I'm beyond happy for you." Truly happy for them, she uttered a silent prayer for Mick's welfare, silently praying, *will it happen for us?*

The personnel in sick bay volunteered to get things moving. "We'll notify the captain. He'll need to know and likely attend the services. We have a chaplain on board who'd do a better job of getting you two hitched." The male nurse turned to a female nurse. "Alert the ladies aboard. See what finery we can improvise for the nuptials. The chaplain can handle the paperwork. We'll get this done right."

From then on, they found themselves swept along in a mad whirl of events. The chaplain came to sick bay to interview the increasingly nervous couple. He stuck out a hand to Jim, nodded to Felicia and Jamie, and introduced himself. "I'm Chaplain John Clement. I'm protestant, but that will not matter on board this ship. If needed, you may repeat your vows again at a place of your choosing, but this marriage will be legal and binding. I know of your rescue and some of what you've suffered. But at this moment, I need to know that there are no impediments to a marriage between the two of you. Otherwise, we'll proceed when things are ready." The slim, slightly balding man sat down with the couple and had a chat, wanting them to be sure of this important step. "I believe marriage to be a lifelong commitment and wish to impress this upon you both." He spoke with them until he'd satisfied himself as to their competence to enter the married state and then took his leave.

Jamie longed for Mick to share the happy event. He'd happily stand up with Jim, if Jim could stand. Her heart ached for him.

After that interview, the female sailors whisked Jamie and Felicia off to their quarters and deluged them with clothing suitable for the impromptu nuptials.

Felicia was glowing with happiness. "He took me at my word that I'd marry him *right now!* Do you believe this, Jamie? Imagine me being married. I've never come close to it before today. Of course, I'd already said I would on the island."

Someone bought out a filmy, pale, creamy pink-tinged dress. The blonde young woman handed it to Felicia. "I think this might fit you. I only wore it once and I had a wonderful time in it. It's a good luck dress."

"Oh, are you sure? It's beautiful. I'd be proud to wear it. You guys are so wonderful. We'll never forget the US Navy." She held it out, looking at it. "Don't forget, I was a two-X not so long ago and here I'm being married in a gorgeous filmy dress so small." She twirled around with the dress before heading for the shower.

A shy young woman handed Jamie a gossamer-sheer chiffon dress, in a pale smoky-blue shade. It complemented her tanned skin and her gray-green eyes. Wishing Mick could be here for this wedding, she clung even closer to his last words. '*It'll come right for us in the end, Jamie, you'll see.*'

Believing in that helped lighten her heart and take joy in the wedding of her two best friends. *I've only known them for what three months or so? Yet I know them better than anyone in my life, even my father.*

Captain Jamison decided they should have a sunset wedding and sent out word to make the necessary provisions. This provided more time to prepare and they used it to good advantage. The entire personnel of the cruiser, *Fort Hamilton*, were on alert for the nuptials and preparations went wild. Not one of the crew remembered such an event happening on a military ship. Jamie joined in, though her heart ached for Mick until she thought it might tear apart.

# CHAPTER 37

The sun edged lower until the huge glowing orb hovered above the western reaches of the trackless Pacific Ocean. The bride, accompanied by nearly the entire female complement, was ushered out the door.

Felicia was increasingly nervous as the hour approached. "Oh my Lord, Jamie, I'm being married. I never thought it would happen. Then I saw Jim and all those things happened to us, getting shot out of the water…" She babbled on until she reached the main deck.

There, in disbelief and wonder, she saw hundreds of sailors dressed in their whites, standing at attention along the sides. Down the center, the ship's officers formed a long double line. Looking down through it was Jim, pale as a ghost, dressed in regular clothes, and standing on his own. The medics from the rescue helicopter stood with him, Dr. Roger Timmons on one side, and Bones on the other. They may have been at Jim's side to hold him up, but no matter, they stood with him as he made ready to take a wife.

Felicia gasped. "Jamie, there he is, standing by himself! Just look at all these people. They've come to our wedding."

As she stood there, Jamie saw the look on many lonely sailors far from home. Felicia presented a breathtaking picture, her head held high and poised for her wedding walk down to Jim.

Her dress, filmy and sheer, complemented her figure,

and some of the female crew had worked a few pale flowers into her hair.

The ship's impromptu band started the wedding march and Jamie, as maid of honor, stepped slowly down between the double lines of officers. A stately, slender vision in the pale, blue-tinged silky dress, she walked down the impromptu aisle. The ocean breezes caught the delicate fabric against her, outlining her trim, darkly-tanned figure. She heard a few muffled gasps as she made her way slowly toward the waiting bridegroom. Reaching Jim, she gave him a wide grin as she stepped aside to stand next to Dr. Timmons. She caught the look of admiration on his face before she turned to see Captain Jamison step up and take the bride's arm.

Felicia gasped with delight that Captain Jamison would give her away and felt the honor deeply. With her lovely head held high, she walked slowly down the aisle with the captain to meet Jim and become his bride. Her borrowed dress suited her and floated about her with grace. Soft winds held it against her as she walked, white sandals were on her feet, and several pale pink anthuriums created an exotic tropical bouquet.

With flashing violet eyes and glowing tawny hair, she presented a picture of feminine splendor that enthralled every man on the cruiser. Jamie read their thoughts. They, to a man, thought Jim was one lucky dude. Imagine it, marooned on a lonely island with something like that, and not one lovely, but two!

Jim stood nicely dressed in casual beige civilian wear, appearing pale and weak. He met his bride standing on his feet. His medical groomsmen remained close at his side while Jim held Felicia's hand in his good one. At the appropriate time, he placed a donated ring of sparkling blue stones on her finger. They never knew who gave it, but it completed the ceremony. Jim had guessed well, because the hastily found ring fit her finger as if made for her.

After the ceremony, the entire contingent roundly congratulated the new couple, getting in numerous congratulatory kisses, until the bride begged off.

The former reticence of the crew disappeared with the festivities. For most on board, separated from home and families, this was a touch of home, and they took full advantage of it. They feted the new couple with a wild and boisterous celebration. The mess did their best on refreshments, and the festivities lasted far into the night with endless partying.

Weak and shaky, the bridegroom sank back into a wheelchair. He was returned to sick bay shortly after the nuptials, before he passed out on the floor.

Felicia bid him goodbye for the night as they wheeled him away. Jim endured severe razing and cat-calls about his honeymoon night, alone in sick bay. He laughed at the good-natured comments, but his face was pale and beads of sweat had formed across his brow.

Felicia started to follow, but Jamie held her back. "You're not leaving me alone in this crowd. Jim will be asleep before they put him to bed. It may not be the best honeymoon in the world, but I believe it was the best wedding I've ever been to. How many girls get walked down the aisle by a ship's captain?" She gasped in wonder at the treatment they'd received aboard this naval vessel. "Felicia, I'm so happy for you. If only Mick had been the best man, it would have been complete."

Jamie tried to believe Mick's promise, but the continual deep mystery of him was something she'd never been able to sort out. Tired of thinking about it, she joined in the celebration and put it out of her mind.

Roger Timmons, the doctor, claimed her for a dance. "You were a vision walking down that aisle, Jamie." He held her close and she felt the warmth and appreciation he directed toward her. He was a fine dancer, and she soon realized his interest was more than medical. It surprised her.

The crew feted the two island refugees and nearly danced them off their feet. More than a few men boldly offered to stand in for Jim on this unusual wedding night. Felicia merely laughed, politely refusing their generous offers. She took their proposals as part of the fun, but it helped her realize how greatly enhanced her feminine appeal had become. The slenderness gained during her trials on the island had added dimensions to her self-image she hadn't yet given thought to.

As the night wore on, Felicia found Jamie. "I'm so tired, and my feet are killing me!" She nearly begged." "It's wonderful, and I'm beyond happy, but right now, I could sleep for a week."

"But Felicia, what a wedding! Won't your mother be surprised when she finds out about this? She *is* coming to Tahiti, isn't she? I hope someone took pictures. I'd love to see how we looked in these beautiful dresses. You know, we don't look the same anymore. I guess we'll have to get used to that, too. I won't find it hard, will you?"

Jamie rattled on, thinking how she'd look in a few more months, and giggled. "We'd better enjoy this slimness while we can, it won't last much longer."

Felicia, still high on the night's revelry, had tell-tale lines of fatigue etched beneath her lavender-hued eyes. "I guess not. I haven't had morning sickness yet. Aren't we supposed to have that? I don't believe I've ever felt so good in my entire life."

Jamie, with Felicia beside her, sought out some of the female crew who had done so much to make this wedding memorable and spoke to one of them. "If it's not impolite, we'd like to find those great little beds you folks have set aside for us."

"I don't think either of us could fully express our appreciation for all you've done to make my wedding so memorable," Felicia added. "You've been so wonderful, it's incredible." With a frown on her face, she told them, "We leave by helicopter tomorrow to Papeete." She fought the tears that sprang into her eyes. "We'll miss you. You've done so much to help us return to reality and—civilization."

She squeezed Susan's hand in a show of appreciation.

"That was the best wedding I've ever seen," Jamie said. "You ladies worked a miracle, all of you."

After many, many thanks, they walked haltingly down to their quarters and Jamie slumped onto the bed with a heavy sigh. "Wow! What a night." Deep in thought, she undressed, and slipped into the filmy nightie.

Felicia, in a glow of happiness, readied herself for the night. "I guess they wouldn't want me down in sick bay at this time of night. I wonder how Jim is. He's my husband now." She tried on the words, so new. "I'm Mrs. James Healy, now. Felicia Healy, hum…how does that sound anyway, Jamie? Jamie?" She looked over to see the sleeping figure of her friend sprawled onto the bed, breathing heavily in exhausted sleep. Felicia yawned and dropped onto her own bed, still in a glow, trying to believe the suddenness with which her marriage had taken place.

Tomorrow, they would be taken by helicopter to Papeete. She and Jamie had concerns about safety after reaching there, but Felicia was tired and much too happy tonight to give it further thought. She turned off the light and settled into the clean bedding. That was still a wonder to her, too.

*Tomorrow we return to civilization. What will happen to us there?*

∽∾∽

A cheerful call roused Jamie from an exhausted sleep. "Hey, island ladies, rise and shine! They're readying the helicopter as we speak." Red-headed Susan Albright, looking her perky best, roused them with a chirpy good morning.

She snapped on the light. Jamie raised her head and blinked. "Wow, what a wedding! I thought they'd dance us off our feet. It was so much fun. You sailors really know how to party." She sat up and shook the sleep from her eyes. "I knew this nice, safe ship was too good to last. We have to go back to Papeete to testify about what happened to us and that poor little schooner." Her voice, husky with sleep, held a tinge of reluctance.

"Will that be so tough?" Susan asked. "Somehow, being sent to Tahiti doesn't sound all that bad to me."

Curiosity, so evident in her eyes, told Jamie she could not possibly know of the tight little knots of icy fear crawling through her gut. The smuggler's vengeance lay ahead for them in Tahiti.

"We have to testify against those drug smugglers. They could come after us. They don't want witnesses," Jamie explained. "We're asking for police protection."

Listening from her bed, Felicia rose up on her elbow. "Oh, Jamie, let's not worry about that until we have to. After all, they *will* have to protect us, won't they? We can't testify if we're dead." She sat up on the edge of her narrow bed. "Frankly, I'm sick and tired of worrying about those smugglers anyway. I'll be glad to get on that plane to Los Angeles, I can tell you that." Her eyes brightened. "I forgot I got married last night, what a honeymoon night! I guess we'll get to that later." She laughed, tossing her head in wonderment. "It was so sudden. That Jim sure knows how to get things moving, what a guy!"

"Well you two had better get it together if you want breakfast before you leave. I want to read the book you gals will write about your adventures, and I'd love to keep in touch, if you'd care to. In fact, everyone would like to share in some of your wild adventures. We haven't heard nearly enough." Grinning, she stepped out and closed the door.

"We'd better get moving, Mrs. Healy." Jamie headed for the shower.

"Oh, you!" Felicia flushed at hearing her new title as she followed Jamie into the shower. "After the scare tactics you just put me through, I'm awake enough. You don't suppose we'll have to run scared again? Really, Jamie, haven't we suffered enough?"

When they came out and dressed, she shook out her hair and began to comb it with a borrowed big-toothed comb. Then she noticed Jamie's puzzled frown "What has you so deep in thought, Jamie?"

"Just wondering about Mick. How could he have gotten help for us from the pirate's ship? It had to be him."

"I'm sure you're right. Hopefully, we'll know all the answers one day. You remember how often Jim said we didn't know everything about Mick. You've got to hold onto that Jamie. It may be hard to believe, in the face of everything, but even on the island, he was two people. You know that much about your man of mystery. The educated man we came to know and the ignorant sailor. Those guys must have bought his act—they didn't kill him."

"Oh, Felicia, you give me hope, and I need it. I believe what you say. I've thought about it until my head's about to split wide open! He said to trust him. Everything will come out all right. He said he loved me, and wanted children with me—I guess we got that part right," she ended with a laugh. "We'd better get a move on or we won't get any breakfast. It sounds good this morning, how about you?" Jamie asked. "Let's wear the same clothes they gave us at first. After all, they're very presentable, especially to someone who wore the same rags for more than three months."

They stepped out of the little room to be escorted them to the mess. The curiosity of the sailors hadn't decreased at all.

The mess was mostly deserted by this time, and they had fewer questions to answer while they ate.

Jamie took scrambled eggs, and toast to start with. Her stomach was touchy in the morning, but now she knew why. Smiling to herself, she wished Mick could share even this small thing with her. "This looks good, or does it?" She ate the toast, but not the eggs. "My stomach isn't used to so much, not yet anyway."

"It's not the food, you know what it is." Felicia stifled a giggle as she looked at Jamie's skimpy plate. Her plate wasn't carrying much either. "I'm still okay with food—so far."

Jamie flipped a crumb her way. "Your turn will come one day soon."

They finished the meal and were led out to the upper deck. Roger Timmons stood beside Jim sitting in a wheel chair, arm neatly bandaged and in a sling. Jamie noticed how the ocean breezes ruffled his fair hair. He sported a new haircut to go along with the daily shave. His color was decent today, his eyes clear and light blue. His deeply tanned face had lightened with his illness, but he remained bronzed enough that his eyes shone like pale blue china from their darker surroundings.

Felicia ran to him. "Jim dear, you look wonderful today. Was the wedding awfully hard on you? You have nice clothes, too. They've been very kind to us on this ship," she babbled on as she lightly touched his heavily dressed left arm.

"You bet they have, my darling wife, and I'm doing fine. I believe marriage agrees with me." He smiled into her eyes as he used the new marital words. He laughed, winked at Jamie, and announced loudly to all present, "This glorious creature is my wife, and I'm a damned lucky son-of-a-gun!" He laughed in his nearly recovered, booming voice. "How's it going this morning, ladies?"

"Oh Jim, you are stronger! You were barely standing at the wedding. I worried, but you made it, standing on your own. I was so proud of you." Felicia leaned down and kissed him. Her glossy hair hung over them as a curtain, shielding their kiss from prying eyes. "You get to come with us to Tahiti, dear, isn't that wonderful? We weren't so sure they'd let you come. Are you strong enough for that?"

"Sure, I'm on antibiotic pills now, and they've arranged for a doctor once we get settled at a hotel. You'll be with *me* now, how about that? You know we all need new clothes. Nothing of my old stuff will fit me, at least not what I wore when we went for a peaceful day sail on the lovely *Queen Ilikii*." He looked at the two women before him, seeing the way they'd changed, and how beautiful they were. "You both look wonderful, and the new clothes don't hurt either. But I confess I rather liked you both in rags like on the island." He ducked as Felicia pretended to hit at him.

Jamie stifled a grin. "Felicia, I feel terrible about wearing these clothes off here, but I guess we can't go naked. I think they burned our other things. It'd be tough getting off the helicopter in that scruffy old stuff. How can we *ever* repay those who lent us these things?" She went over to Susan. "who can we pay for these clothes?"

"Don't even think about it," Susan chirped happily. "We were glad to pitch in and won't miss a few items. We did make out names and addresses though. We hope to hear from you gals when you're settled somewhere." With a wide grin, she handed Jamie a small plastic bag containing rolls of undeveloped film and slips of paper with hastily written addresses. "Last, but not least, here are some shots of the wedding. They're only snapshots, but we knew you'd want them. It was the absolute best wedding, and we were excited to be a part of it."

Jamie took the film, but didn't see the package Susan furtively added to the helicopter.

# CHAPTER 38

With tears in her eyes, Jamie stared at the film. "You beat anything we've ever seen. I can't say it enough. I've formed the greatest respect for our navy. Men and women, you've got it all. We'll never forget your kindness—not ever. Thanks again." She fought tears, realizing she was still not all there emotionally. She moved to Jim and Felicia, holding out the bag. "Look, they took pictures of the wedding and said to enjoy the clothes, and to wear them with all good wishes."

"Thanks, you guys—oh!" Felicia was speechless as she faced the female sailors before her. She fluttered her hands and her eyes shone brightly in the morning air. "Thank you all. You were wonderful to us. We'll never forget you!"

The *whupp-whupping* of the helicopter began. The pilot motioned them to get on board. Doctor Timmons got on with them, yelling over the sound of the whirling blades as he helped Jim to a seat. "Well, you old married man, you look better for this ride than on the last one." He placed a seat belt across Jim and one for Felicia.

Many willing hands helped the ladies in, and Jamie thought someone did more than enough, as she'd felt a masculine hand casually move against her breast. All faces were innocent when she looked at them, a wary glint in her eyes.

They waved goodbye. The machine lifted off the deck, and they watched in fascination as the huge gray ship grew smaller. "Now, we begin another part of our adventure in the South Pacific," she murmured.

No one heard her over the noise as the great machine carried them aloft. Her knuckles grew white, she clutched onto her seat, and it was not fear of flying. "How far are we from Tahiti?" she asked Roger. He sat beside her and Felicia sat with Jim.

"Only about fifty miles, this is as close as we plan to get, an easy jaunt for this bird."

She caught the reply, along with his look of overt interest, and obvious regard. Warmth radiated from his eyes, and Jamie decided if it were not for her love of Mick, she would definitely want to reciprocate what she saw there. How nice to see that look in a man's eyes. It'd been a long time since that had happened—until she'd met that French Canadian. *Thank you, you black-eyed devil!*

Feeling a warm glow inside just thinking about it, she smiled warmly at Timmons. "Thanks for all you've done. We'll never be able to thank you enough."

"I'd like to do more," he said, gazing deeply into her eyes. "I know you've been through a lot these past few months. If you ever need me, I'd love to be there for you in any way I could. My hitch is up in three months. I could be available."

Tears sprang to her eyes at his offer. "I don't know what to say, Roger. But there is someone. He was on the island with us and we're deeply involved. He's the father of the child I carry. You're aware of that, of course, and it makes me appreciate your offer all the more." Tears glistened, stung and prickled, as she told him a little of Mick. "He said it would come right when this was over. I'm clinging to that."

"He's a lucky man and I wish all the best for you." He took her hand in his and squeezed it gently with his strong firm one. "Women like you don't come along every day, I'm sorry as hell I missed you."

She watched the ocean far below, sitting there with Roger. *He'll be a great guy for some lucky girl, and he's handsome too.* Her thoughts played with the idea, but her life lay in Mick's hands from now on, for whatever that might mean. Still confused about him, her attention fixed on Felicia and Jim, sitting close, heads together. They touched frequently and talked over the thrumming noise of the helicopter. How lucky they were, with nothing to cast shadows over their happiness. *Oh, Mick, are you all right? I need you now, more than you'll ever know.*

Many shades of green clothed the tropical island emerging in the distance. It sat as a great green jewel in the darker blue sea. Pale, luminous, emerald waters lay in the coral-ringed lagoons around it. Numerous rugged peaks rose high above the ocean. Clouds floated from them in lingering misty shreds, as if caught on the dense green foliage growing wildly over the rugged peaks while trying to drift away on the constant trade winds.

"How beautiful it is from here!" She nudged Roger. "Look, there're two islands joined together. We never explored at all before we went on that little sailing trip."

What lay ahead for them on the beautiful island below? Their lives had taken a different course since they'd suffered the terrible things caused by the smugglers.

Her very being had been altered forever. She'd found an unbelievably wonderful love with a man who, though ever a mystery to her, had changed her. Because of Mick, she'd found strength, resourcefulness, and the ability to cling to the forlorn hope of his promise. Almost afraid to believe in him, she nevertheless clung desperately to his promise of a future together.

Felicia and Jim, seeing the lovely view ahead, craned their necks, trying to get a better look. She wiggled in her seat and pointed. "Oh, Jim, look how beautiful!"

"We'll be there soon, darling. It'll be great to be back in civilization, although I think there're a lot of things we'll miss about our lost bit of earth in the Pacific—something we'll never have again."

Jamie knew instinctively he'd miss the camaraderie the four of them had forged during their days on the island. Waiting now for normal life to begin, she knew it would never be the same. She now had far more confidence, had handled situations, and handled them well. No longer, the beleaguered ex-wife of Jack Moran, she wondered why she'd let that happen? Perhaps the gentle upbringing by her father had shielded her from the harshness of reality. She'd been too young to challenge a controller like Jack.

"Here we go!" the pilot called out and headed to a small X marked on the ground. Two small cars sat on the side. The helicopter settled gently on the ground, the giant rotors whipping, but slowing. "Hold on until we give the all clear. We'll help you ladies off, then the patient."

When the door opened, Roger leaped out and Jamie felt his firm grip on her as he assisted her to depart the craft. She took the look of regret on his face as a compliment. He gave Felicia a hand down. When they stood on terra firma, he bent inside the helicopter, found the small bundle, and handed it to Jamie. "The female personnel asked me to give you this. They said you might want souvenirs."

Accepting it, she wondered what it contained. They had no baggage.

Roger reached into the vibrating craft and unbuckled Jim. "How's it going, Jim, ready for civilization?"

Stiffly and carefully, Jim worked his way out of the helicopter, with Roger's firm hands steadying him.

"You bet we are," Jim replied, pale and shaking. "If I could imagine some way to properly thank you, I would. You're the damned best!" He shook hands firmly with Roger. Jamie saw tears forming, despite his best efforts to hold them back.

Roger beckoned to the men beside the cars. Two uniformed men came forward. They shook hands after the introductions and received papers from Roger.

They took Jim by the good arm toward one of the little cars. Jamie noticed that Jim was sweating profusely. Was it the heat, weakness, or apprehension? The men of the *Fort Hamilton* re-entered their helicopter, the doors shut, and they took off. The survivors all watched them go.

"Do you think he's overdoing?" Felicia whispered to Jamie, worry expressed in her lavender-hued eyes.

"Probably, but I'm glad to have him to speak for us now. He's in law enforcement," Jamie answered. "That might be a good thing if there's anything for us to worry about." She held out the bundle. "What do you suppose this is? Roger handed it to me, said it was from the female sailors."

"I'm sure I couldn't guess. I hope we haven't anything to worry about being in Tahiti. As you say, we have Jim with us. I felt so lost while he was sick. Our lives are entwined already. I don't like being without him. I still can't believe this happened. I'm married---" Felicia rambled on, lost in her thoughts.

With the trades blowing their hair, and ruffling the borrowed clothes against their slim bodies, the two policemen spent more time looking at them than attending to Jim. Jamie noticed that with a smile, reveling in her return to slenderness. She enjoyed their male approval. It was normal. Felicia noticed the male appraisal as well, but most of her attention was on Jim.

"*Bon jour, madame, et mademoiselle,*" one of the officers said, approaching the women. He shifted to English. "Welcome to Tahiti, we will escort you to *le hotel, pour favor.*"

"I am Officer Etienne Jobert," the taller and older of the two said. "And this is Officer Charles Du Soir. We are to provide security for you while you are here in Tahiti. There is nothing for you to fear, but we have our orders. If you would be so kind as to allow us, we will escort you now."

With a wink, and more than a glance of appreciation, he curtly indicated the other tiny car sitting to the side of the small and obscure, landing site. Squeezed into the miniscule car, Jamie and Felicia nearly filled the back seat.

Felicia giggled, with her hand over her mouth. "Jamie, I feel fat again."

The man named Charles rode in front with a driver. Jim rode in the other small car with Etienne. The car, an ancient thing, started readily and moved out of the secluded area into what Jamie was sure had to be island traffic. They saw everything with new eyes, like the refugees they were, unable to stop staring at the rush of humankind bustling about their daily activities.

"It's all so different, isn't it?" Jamie murmured beneath her breath.

Open-air vehicles hauled people about. Food venders, here and there, peddled quick lunches. And masses of flowers grew wherever they found a bit of soil. The lurching ride and the smell of traffic fumes soon took a toll on Jamie's queasy stomach. She leaned over to her open window in preparation, should it get worse.

"What's the matter, Jamie?" Felicia asked with concern. Then she remembered, and she couldn't stop her look of amusement. "Oh, oh, we'll get to the hotel soon. Try to hang on."

The fresh air was helpful, and Jamie hung on. They soon wheeled to a stop in the back of a large and very grand hotel.

"Where are we staying?" Jamie asked.

"Your hotel, *mademoiselle*, Le South Sea Islander. We must get you in without attracting notice," Charles explained. "You're famous, and it's better."

"Why, are we in danger?" Jamie asked. Her face felt clammy with nausea and now a tinge of fear. She'd already borrowed this trouble and feared it to be true.

"Precautions, *mademoiselle,* just precautions. If you wish to leave your rooms, you must notify us. We will escort you anywhere you wish. There will be someone close by at all times." Charles was very serious about his orders.

Jim disembarked from his tiny auto, appearing tired and faint. "Don't worry, we won't be here long," he said. "They said we could leave after they take our testimony, and the trial. I believe there's something more, but they haven't said what."

Not wanting to hoist such a big man, the driver hurried to find the manager. He appeared immediately, and seeing Jim's condition, called for a wheel chair. Very soon, a small, dark native man hastily approached Jim with a wheelchair, and Jim gratefully sank his bulk into it. "Whew," he said as he mopped his dripping brow.

Felicia fussed about him. "Jim dear, you need to get some rest. I'm glad he's found that chair, you needed one."

He was pale and sweating. It was warm in Tahiti, but Jim had tired considerably from the flight and the move to the hotel. It took little to tire him after his fight for life, and Felicia's lioness instinct had kicked in.

"Honey, you'll do in a pinch," Jim said. His smile was weak as they trundled the deserted halls and up an elevator. He and Felicia were together. Jamie was alone.

"Sir, my father is coming here to meet me," she informed the officer as he showed her to her room. "How will he find me?" She felt a new desperation. Their fear and trials were not over. "And the nightmare continues," she cried and slumped down in the nearest chair, tears coursing down her cheeks. "How many times have I made that statement?"

Like most men, a woman's tears spurred him into action. "We will find your father, *mademoiselle*. What is his name, please?"

"His name is John Shipley. He may have arrived and is looking for me. Could you please find out?"

*"Oui, mademoiselle,* it will be done." Etienne looked in her large gray-green eyes. In appreciation, he breathed softly, *"Oui."* He bowed slightly and left her.

With the ring of the phone, feelings of familiarity began to take hold. It was Felicia. "Oh Jamie, this is the best room! Is yours like ours? I'll knock on the adjoining door— open it from your side," she added. "It has refrigeration!"

Jamie opened the door. Felicia strutted about the room,

and Jim lay sprawled across a king-sized bed. "I'm glad you're next door, Felicia," she said. "We've been together for so long, it seems strange to be alone." She cast an anxious glance at Jim's huge, gaunt frame. "How's Jim? It's only been a few days since he was at death's door."

"He went to sleep as soon as we got him on the bed, poor guy. He's better, but he tires easily. Maybe he'll get enough rest, settled in one place. Did you notice how flirty those French police were?" Felicia looked at herself in the large full length mirror near the bathroom. "Jamie, I can't believe this is me. Honestly, this new *me* will take some getting used to. I love it and I think Jim does too. He'd never say that weight made a difference, but who knows?"

They heard Jim moaning on the bed, and Jamie spoke softly. "You do look wonderful, Felicia, but I doubt Jim ever got past your fantastic eyes. He never saw your weight in the first place." She turned. "We can talk later. I'm going to rest for a while myself. Maybe they'll find my dad soon. We've so much to talk about."

She returned to her own quarters and, looking around, saw a beautiful room. Her luggage from before they'd sailed on the *Queen Ilikii* had been deposited there., She didn't care what was in them. *No, everything would be pre-Mick*. Without opening a thing, she fell onto the bed. "How different it all is," she murmured and drifted off to sleep wondering about Mick. *Will I ever see him again?*

Jamie awakened with a sudden start at the knocking on her door. The chill of alarm raced through her body, as she rose from her bed, trying to remember where she was. Looking about the room, she remembered enough to pull her thoughts together, and rush to the door hoping against hope—

"Who is it?" she called.

"Jamie, honey, it's me. It's your dad."

She flung open her door and saw her father standing there, blinking back tears. Her eyes took him in, that familiar face and loving eyes. She threw herself into his arms.

"Dad, oh Dad!" she sobbed, and he held her until her storm of tears from her terrible trials passed. Sniffing and blotting her eyes, she smiled lovingly up at his tall, solid figure. "Hi, D—Dad," she said haltingly. "I've so much to tell you. I don't know where to begin." She led him to the adjoining door and knocked softly, so as not to wake Jim if he were sleeping. "But first you must meet my friends. They were with me on the island."

The door opened and Felicia's tanned face and lavender eyes took in the man standing there with Jamie. "You must be Jamie's father!" she cried, seeing the tall, ruggedly handsome older man. She led them into the room. "We have so terribly much to tell! Come in and meet Jim."

Jim sat on the bed, propped up on several pillows, grinning from ear to ear.

"Jim dear, this is Jamie's father. He's come all the way from Denver to be with her."

The men extended hands and shook in greeting.

With introductions taken care of, they slowly began to tell Shipley some of the things that had happened to them. Jamie realized the telling was a healing thing, and he allowed them to inundate him with details, until he raised his hands.

"Can we go out for a meal someplace?" Shipley asked. "All this is too much to take in. Good Lord, it'll take days to tell, and I'm starving."

"We're hungry too, right, Felicia?" Jim looked at Jamie's father. "Would you mind if we ordered room service? I'm recovering from a hellish infection in my arm here, and am still weak as water." He indicated his heavily wrapped arm then carefully added, "They've requested that we stay undercover until we testify in the courts here. We've guards keeping watch over us."

"Well, what the hell's going on here? They're keeping you kids prisoner?"

They saw, with the tiniest bit of humor, that John Shipley was completely ticked off at the idea that these worn out, emaciated survivors of a shipwreck and death threats were being held prisoner, instead of the criminals that caused it all. The color rose on his neck and face.

"My God! Baby, you're in danger even here? I'd like to get my hands on those filthy bastards!" Visibly shaken, he tried to understand. he couldn't believe his daughter was not safe, even though rescued and brought back to Tahiti. He had the same gray-green eyes as his daughter and springy brown hair, laced with strands of silver. "Jamie, There's something else," he observed. "You've lost so much weight, I hardly knew you. There's more, a lot more. What is it, my daughter?" He looked at her then enfolded her in his arms. "You look wonderful, Jamie. Something good must have happened on that island."

Forgetting the smugglers, she looked at her slim legs. "We're *all* much thinner and look different—oh Dad, what we went though." She gulped. "Trying to find enough to eat wasn't my idea of a weight loss plan. We never knew if we'd have *anything* to eat. At first it was a few coconuts. Nothing came easy. We hunted all over the island, carried everything to the camp, and tried to make edible meals if we didn't get rained out. Jim climbed trees for breadfruit and threw rocks to knock off coconuts. Mick was too sick and hurt to help, but he knew about living in these islands." Jamie had opened the door regarding Mick. It was inevitable. Her father had to know.

"Mick? Who is he and where is he?"

"You'll know it all, Dad. It'll take time and I hardly know how to begin." Tears lurked close. Talking about Mick was emotionally taxing. She smoothed her father's hair lovingly and feasted her eyes on him. They'd always been close and the worry he'd endured while they were lost hurt her. Noting the new deeper lines in his face, she believed her recent travail to be the cause.

It fell silent in the room. Shipley watched his daughter. Her story was important, and he'd have to wait for her to tell it. The closeness and camaraderie displayed between his daughter and these new friends enabled him to understand, in part, the horrors they'd endured. In time he would know it all.

He was satisfied that her previous sorrows with Moran lay forgotten. This Jamie seemed renewed and far stronger. But he saw something else, a deep troubled longing that didn't fit with the lightheartedness she displayed. She would tell him when she was ready, and he accepted that.

"Your daughter is the bravest person any of us have ever met," Jim said. "There's time enough to sort things out. And, sir, it needs telling in full detail."

"Dad, it's just that the smugglers tried to kill us several times," Jamie said, avoiding the mention of Mick, "and they don't give up easily. We've lived in fear so long, we'll never feel really safe until we're headed for California. I know I won't!"

# CHAPTER 39

"Oh, Mr. Shipley, don't worry," Felicia said. "The guards are keeping watch, and we can go out if they come with us. Maybe we could go for a drive tomorrow if Jim is stronger. He has to see a doctor soon, too." Felicia turned her eyes on Shipley and Jamie smiled to see those violet depths working their charm on him.

"Hey! Let's give room service a try," Jim suggested, trying to lighten the mood. "I'm for a civilized meal. It's been too long since my stomach said hello to a great meal. I couldn't eat much out on the ship." He looked ready for a square meal to fill out his massive frame, gaunt from their long sojourn on the island. He reached into the drawer for a menu and found it. "Felicia, check out some of these things, but hey, what'll we do? There's no breadfruit on this menu." He broke into a hearty laugh.

They enjoyed deciding what to order, exclaiming over food items to a ridiculous degree. Only someone deprived as they'd been would get that excited over basic, trivial things.

The food came, lots of it, and with excess merriment they dug in. Shipley realized, with amazement, that they were excited over cutlery, salt and pepper, and butter. Tears sprang to his eyes as he joined in their merriment, trying to envision their deprivation on the island.

They ate as much as their shrunken stomachs would allow. Shipley realized that Jamie ate very sparingly and her face had a slight pallor, unusual for her. "Jamie, what is it? You're so pale all of a sudden."

As he spoke, Jamie clapped a hand over her mouth and headed into the bathroom. From where he sat, the sounds of retching were clear. He paced the room, unable to hide his concern.

Jamie came out of the bathroom with a sheepish grin over her face. "Dad, let's go back to my room. We need to talk."

Felicia hugged her, and let her go. The door between the rooms closed, and Jim sighed. "Well, he needs to know about this, and she needs to tell him about Mick. I'm waiting for the day this is all straightened out. I *still* believe what he said. It'll come right in the end." With his good arm, he grabbed Felicia. "Come here, you luscious thing!"

❧❧❧

"What's going on here, Jamie?" her father asked. "I love you very much. You can tell me anything. You know that." He hugged his daughter, waiting for her to begin.

"Dad, I don't know where to start…I'll start at the beginning." Jamie sat him down and, over the next hour or so, told him everything about Mick. She told him about their life together on the island. "I love him, Dad, and we're going to have a child. If I never lay my eyes on him again, I'll love him still," she ended, looking into her father's eyes. Her expression was a mix of wonderment, longing, and determination.

"Well, there are a few surprises left for this old bird, yet. You amaze me, honey. I never realized how strong you were. Don't worry about the child., I'll love it the same as you. I'll be the father for him or her, if this Mick doesn't show, but somehow, if he is anything like you describe, I believe he will."

Jamie smiled, knowing her father was already thinking

about his first grandchild. Meeting the father was second-ary.

"Dad, that's what Jim says. He has always believed in Mick and thought the world of him. When you talk with him, you'll both agree on it." The air of mystery between herself and her father had cleared. The color had returned to her cheeks. She felt relaxed and sleepy now her discussion with her father was over. She did not want to separate from him, even for a nap. "Do you want to go back and see Jim and Felicia?"

"Yes, if he's not asleep, or otherwise involved. I believe these are newlyweds we're talking about." He laughed. "We'll need to do some shopping for you. The only clothes you have won't fit anymore. You won't need maternity things yet for a while. Can we arrange with these guards for a shopping trip first thing tomorrow?"

"You know, we don't look the same as before the sailing thing. How would anyone recognize us anyway?" Jamie, elated at the idea of shopping, couldn't wait for an outing. She went to the adjoining door and knocked softly.

The door squeaked open a bit, and Felicia came into their room. "Well, how did it go?" she asked, casting violet eyes on Jamie's father.

"It went just fine. I'm very glad you were with her on that island. What a story you have to tell!" Shipley then answered her unspoken question about the child. "Yes, I'm glad about the forthcoming child as well. I always wanted to be a grandfather, and now I will. I believe your Jim. This Mick will bring things together, I'm convinced, and I ha-ven't met the man."

"I'm so glad to hear that. You and Jim must talk, but he's asleep now. He always liked Mick. We really knew nothing about the man, and we never found out anything either. Jim said there was something going on, a man of mystery, but I have to say, a devilishly handsome one." Fe-licia chatted gaily, and Jamie saw her father become totally enchanted with her light-hearted ways.

They spent the remainder of the day reminiscing, resting, and getting reacquainted with themselves, until Jamie tired of all the talk. She walked to the large windows and drew the drapery away. Glowing with the aura of electricity, the tropical city of Papeete lay spread out below. It had grown into dusk. Lights twinkled from eatery signs, streetlights, glaring red tail lights of cruising autos, and flashing business advertising. "Look at all the lights out there." She pushed the sliding door open, and a cacophony of sound wafted up to them. "Listen to that, Dad. That's something *we* haven't heard in a while."

She pulled Felicia over to the open door. They stepped onto the lanai and looked over the railing. They stood on the third and highest floor. She remembered that in Tahiti, no buildings were built higher than a palm tree. Looking out to sea, she found herself looking for the square-rigged, stubby vessel that had taken Mick away.

"Jamie, are you still looking for that Chinese ship?" Felicia looked at her in disbelief. "You don't expect to see it here in Papeete after dark?

"I guess it's just a habit with me, one I'd like to get rid of. I'm so paranoid." Jamie laughed at herself, but if she saw it anchored out there, Mick might be somewhere in Papeete.

They took in the scented air of Tahiti, noticing it mixed heavily with the odor of food, exhaust fumes, and familiar smells from the harbor.

John Shipley joined them on the small lanai, took a seat on one of the cane chairs. He leaned back with his hands behind his head, and looked at the two beautiful young women. "So what are we seeing out here?"

"Just looking at civilization, Dad, but it doesn't smell nice like our island did. We had a lot of flowers and no gas fumes."

"She's out here, looking for that Chinese junk, Mr. Shipley. It's a habit with her," Felicia teased, as the glow of the city lights gleamed in her hair.

They heard Jim stir. Felicia ran to his bedside and Jamie turned to her father. "If I saw that stubby little ship, it would mean Mick's here somewhere. The police would have arrested the crew for drug smuggling and murder. They deserve it Dad, they were the most vicious-looking men I've ever seen." She leaned over the railing, to look outward. "I don't know how that would affect Mick, not good I'm afraid." But their lanai did not face the harbor and her efforts were fruitless.

Felicia came out to join them. "Jim's awake and getting restless. He says he's bored just lying around. It must mean he's getting better." She laughed. "I'm married now. I wonder what I should do. There're no coconuts to pick, no breadfruit to cook, and we can't go down and spear fish. I guess that leaves one thing—we need to go shopping for new clothes! I guess that'll have to wait until tomorrow. I don't have my credit cards anymore. How can I buy things?"

Jim appeared in the doorway of the lanai. "Hey, my wonderful wife." Laughing, he'd heard Felicia's comments about shopping. "I'm an old married man now and my beautiful wife wants to go shopping. Darling, I have a couple of credit cards. They were in my wallet." Winking at Felicia, he walked slowly to a seat by John Shipley. He held his heavily bandaged arm carefully and gingerly seated himself. "How's it going?"

Shipley liked the look of Jim and felt a surge of warmth knowing his daughter had found friends like these. "I appreciate the care you took of my daughter while you were lost on that Island. I'm forever in your debt for that." He wanted to ask about Mick, and hoped Jim sensed it.

"Your daughter took more care of us than we did of her. She's amazing. Mick and I said that many times over." Jim wanted to talk to Jamie's father. The women retreated into Jim and Felicia's room. Jim leaned toward the older man. "You'll want to know about Mick. I don't think there's much that Jamie hasn't told you."

"She loves him, and she's trying to believe he'll reappear magically in her life somehow, even when things look completely averse to that happening. I'd like to get your fix on this. At least you've had time to know this man."

"He's inherently good. I know bad men. I'm a criminal prosecutor in Kansas. I've seen my share of rotten bastards," Jim went on. "The man is playing a role as an itinerate sailor for some ungodly reason, but when he was with us, his speech indicated a highly educated man. He never revealed a thing about himself, though."

"A real man of mystery, eh?"

"He's that, for sure, but you should know one thing," Jim continued. "I've never seen a man more in love. They were caught up in it together—neither of them could help what happened. Felicia and I saw it every day we were there. He watched her constantly and looked like a lost pup when she left camp. I swear I've never seen anything like it. He used every excuse in the book to get her alone. She was afraid of him, yet drawn to him at the same time. They finally got together, and I don't think she'll regret it," he finished. "I hope not."

"Thanks, Jim, Jamie told me what you'd say, but I wanted your opinion. I guess we'll have to wait it out. Here's another one who waits for it to come out right, especially for her and their child. She's been through so dammed much."

Shipley shook Jim's hand and rose to take his leave for the night. "I need some sleep. I'll say good night to those two beauties in there. How'd you manage to get stuck on an island with two like that, anyway? You lucky son of a gun!"

Jim laughed in response, reveling in his own good fortune, while Shipley took his leave.

"Jamie, I'll see you in the morning." He left them and stepped into the hall. "You can call me if you need, here's my room number." He handed her a slip of paper and closed the door.

"Oh, Jamie, I like your dad. You know he's a hunk," Felicia said with a giggle.

"My dad's a hunk?" Jamie repeated. She hadn't seen him that way, but looking through Felicia's eyes, she could see her father was indeed a fine-looking man. "I guess he is, now that you mention it. I never thought of him that way."

"My mother should be here soon, I wonder what she'll think of him. She hasn't looked at a man since my father left us years ago. She doesn't trust men anymore." Felicia went out on the lanai to sit with Jim.

Jamie decided to open her old luggage. She dragged the case to her bed and hoisted it up. Reluctant to open it, she fought unwelcome memories of Moran. Shrugging the feeling away, she unzipped it. Hotel personnel, no doubt had packed the clothes when they'd gone missing, stowing it, should they be found. Her things were stuffed in and wrinkled. "What a mess! I really don't care, everything is too big now. I'll give it to the nearest thrift store."

She stopped talking to herself and stepped out on the lanai. "Felicia, have you looked in your luggage yet?" She laughed. "It's stuffed in and wrinkled. It won't fit."

"No, I forgot about it. It'll remind me of before I met Jim." She sat close to him in the darkness. "Maybe some of the shoes will fit. Could my feet be smaller?"

"Mine are. These sandals from the sailor girls are a size smaller than usual." Jamie shook her head, still becoming acquainted with her new self. "I'm giving my stuff to whatever charity they have here. It's part of another life."

Jim and Felicia came off the lanai with the dreamy look they used to get on the island. They took their leave. "Good night, Jamie, tomorrow will be time enough time to sort this stuff out."

# CHAPTER 40

Jim's visit to the doctor, as arranged by the Tahitian authorities, was set for this morning. Felicia awakened Jamie with a gentle knock on the door.

"I'm calling Dad, he can accompany us," Jamie said. "Afterward, maybe we can go buy a few things. Here we are, wearing the same things for days and days again. I'm so hungry, I wonder if I can get something down this morning."

"Jim can order room service while we finish dressing." Felicia looked slightly pale and Jamie thought she detected faint tracings of purple beneath her eyes. "How are you today, then?" she queried.

"Why are you asking?" Felicia squinted, suspicion in her eyes. "Not yet, Jamie," She laughed. "I'm just wonderful. It's all so strange, isn't it? We're supposedly safe in civilization, yet we have to be on guard. I'm sick of this whole thing." She sighed. "I'll be glad when we are on that plane to California."

Then she laughed, "With an escort, we can get out of these rooms for a while, see something of this place, and do some shopping." She frowned. "After all, isn't this the most exotic spot on earth? Maybe they'll let us do some 'touristing,' too."

Jamie called her father, and Felicia went in to speak with Jim. A soft knock sounded at her door. Shipley entered, groomed and ready for the day. He wore a loose white cotton shirt, tan lightly woven slacks, and looked rested. He gave her a warm hug. "Good morning, Jamie, sleep okay?"

"Yeah, Dad, I'm fine, but hungry. Jim's ordering now, so we'll eat here. He goes to the doctor this morning. We hope they'll let us out of here for a while. We're ready to do a bit of shopping. We haven't anything to fit us."

"You look wonderful, Jamie. I can't get over the change in you. It's not just the weight loss, it must be this Mick. I'd like to meet the man, and hope to hell, for your sake, he's all you say he is."

"I don't even know *what* he is, Dad. He said many times to trust him, but he stayed totally secretive about his affairs, and the things he does. All we know of him is what we've seen, and that was terribly criminal." She felt the sting of beginning tears. "On the island, he was completely different. Believing him takes faith that's hard to come by, at least for me, with my past. But Dad, I love him more than my life, so where does that leave me?"

"Jamie, dear girl, I don't know, but he's made you happy in some way I don't understand. I'm glad for that."

"Hey in there, come and get it! Breakfast's here." They heard Jim's voice booming out from the adjoining room and scurried over to join in another round of eating and reveling in real food.

The dark-eyed waiter left a large cart laden with gleaming metal covers. "I'm sorry we don't have any cash on us," Jim said." I'll put your tip on the bill, okay with you?"

The man nodded his acceptance, and turned to slip quietly away.

Shipley stepped up and shoved a few bills in the waiter's outstretched hand. "How's that, young man?"

The slender waiter smiled, nodded, and left the room, but not before he took in the rest of the occupants with his black sloe-eyes.

Jim grinned at Jamie's father and nodded. "Thanks, man, that was nice of you. I've got to visit an ATM when we go out. It's hell being out of ready cash."

"No problem. What's for eats on this over loaded cart anyway?" Shipley walked over, lifted some of the lids, and chuckled. "You ordered for half of Tahiti, son. This'll put some meat on your bones."

Jamie had caught the appraising glance from the waiter and felt chills crawling down her spine. Fearful thoughts filled her mind but, not wanting to lessen the joy of a real breakfast, she kept her own counsel. *Here, too? Could it be true? They have eyes everywhere?*

Her face felt clammy, but these days it was usual each morning. She approached the cart cautiously to see what looked good. She felt a ravenous hunger and hoped she could keep something down. She was thin enough.

They loaded their plates with bacon, eggs, fried taro, toasted rolls, and many kinds of fruits. Felicia seemed more cautious than usual. Jamie had an idea that impending motherhood had finally caught up with her. Jim and her father were shoveling their food in, and the women's dainty appetites went unnoticed.

When Felicia hastily put her plate down and rushed into the bathroom with her hand over her mouth, Jim halted his meal, with a look of surprise, "Hey, what the hell?" he called after her, but he only heard the sounds of retching.

"Don't worry about it, Jim," Jamie said, "it only lasts for a couple of months—hopefully less." She couldn't stop the grin coming over her face at his amazement and went to help Felicia. This was women's business. The men stayed away in their uselessness and wonder at the condition of the female gender.

Shipley, grinning widely, extended a hand to congratulate Jim on his impending fatherhood. "So that's the way of it. I vaguely remember something like that when Jamie was on the way. Congratulations, son, it was the best thing that ever happened to me, but figuring these things out with women can be tough at times. They're a constant wonder, if I remember correctly."

"They're that, all right. I'm here to tell you. I'm still getting used to all that's happened to me. Is this a package deal?" Jim laughed and called out to his wife. "Felicia darling, are you all right?"

She came out with Jamie holding her arm. "Hi honey, I'm fine." She looked pale, but giggled. "I'll be keeping this slim figure a while longer, Jim."

Their present guard, Emile, said they could walk out on the street when they were ready. "There will be many who watch over you in addition to me. They watch all the streets for trouble. Do not fear for your safety."

Jim had to see the doctor in two hours, and Emile acted as their guide. He said they could have a tour around the island later, if they liked. "How about a bit of shopping then," Jamie suggested. She glanced at her father. "Dad, I'm afraid I lost my purse, all my credit cards—everything—when the ship went down."

"No problem, honey. Nothing would make me happier than putting new clothes on that lovely slim figure."

Having decided to buy clothing for now and see more of the island later, if Jim was up to it, they went out of the hotel. Everywhere, there were masses of scented flowers, blooming in well-tended areas. On the teeming streets of Papeete, the muggy air was filled with the scent of flowers mixed with the multiple odors of a tropical city. A busy scene, vehicles, bicycles, and people bustled about. They caught scent of cooking foods which might have been pleasant but, to Jamie, it was not.

They entered several stores. In one, Felicia held up filmy French under things. "Jamie, did you ever see anything this nice? And I can wear them—at least for a while. I can put everything on Jim's credit card. How about that? It'll take getting used to. I've always been very independent about money. He won't mind, it'll be me, settling into the marriage thing."

"You two'll do just fine." Jamie sighed. "Any situation like that requires an adjustment, just be glad Jim's with you to make it. I wish Mick were here helping me pick out underwear, and he'd love doing that, if I know him. That man loved everything about women, and definitely this woman."

They shopped happily, holding up the wonders available in some of the finer French-influenced shops. The men stayed in the background, watching in amazement as the ladies chose one filmy thing after the other. Emile interrupted to whisk Jim off to the doctor for an hour's visit.

Returning later to continue with the shopping adventure, Jamie thought Jim was uncomfortable around lingerie, but he helped a bit with a few other choices. He and Shipley stood back watching them pick clothes, shoes, handbags, and, to them, a bewildering assortment of feminine requirements.

"Man, do you believe all this stuff?" Jim laughed in amazement at his new wife. He'd entered into a new world, that of the husband. He felt a warm glow at the knowledge he would spend his life with this glorious creature. She had completely captured his heart. He was deeply happy with Felicia. He watched Jamie, joining in the merriment, enjoying the company of her father and her friends. But the sadness in her eyes betrayed her quiet longing.

Fatigue set in, especially for Jim, and they returned to the hotel. After a good rest, and taking stock of their new finery, Jamie sighed. "Dad, they said we might go for a drive, maybe a tour around the island, if Jim feels up to it."

After a light lunch, which the Jamie and Felicia managed without adverse symptoms, they had a deep discussion filled with curiosity about the Island of Tahiti. During the planning, a soft knock sounded on Jim and Felicia's door. Felicia answered it, a questioning expression over her features.

"Yes? Mother, oh, God, you're here at last!" She threw her arms around the older version of herself standing in the doorway. "Oh, it's so good to see you. There were so many times I wasn't sure I would *ever* lay eyes on you again. It was awful Mother. We were starving on this lost little island. Jim was there, Jamie, and Mick, too." She finally stopped her excited ramblings and tugged at her mother's arm. "Come, meet my friends. They saved my life and were with me." Seeing Jim, she said, "Mother, here's Jim. Remember, I told you about him." She brought her mother to her husband.

Rising from the bed, he got unsteadily to his lofty height to meet his new mother-in-law.

"We were married on the cruiser that saved us," she continued. "Do you remember we talked about him, when I called you that day? You have a son-in-law." Flustered, she babbled on. Finally realizing she couldn't tell her mother everything that had happened to them in three and a half months, her excitement wound down.

"Felicia, I hardly knew you!" Her mother stared in amazement at her newly slender, daughter. "It must have been a dreadful ordeal, oh, my poor child." She looked up at Jim, towering above her, and extended a hand to him. "Hello, Jim, thank you for taking care of my girl, and if she loves you, so do I."

Tears of joy glistened in her wide, gently faded, lavender shaded eyes. She appeared slightly rounded, but not more than most women of her generation. Her hair had the same ropy, tawny, thick texture as her daughter, but she kept it short in a style becoming to her.

Jamie and her father stayed back, waiting, while Felicia and her mother got themselves in hand. Jim grinned widely at the two of them. He had a smaller dressing, freshly wrapped, on his left arm. It remained in a sling, or he'd have folded both of them in his arms.

When the furor died down, Felicia turned to Jamie and drew her forth to meet her parent. "Mother, this is Jamie, we met the day before all this happened. She was a rock for all of us. Jamie, meet my mother, Adelia Benton."

"Just call me, Dee, and I'm very pleased to meet you, Jamie. Thank you for helping my daughter." She gave Jamie a gentle hug. "There are too many things for me to catch up on, and I need to catch my breath too. It was a long flight, over eight hours. I think it must be jet lag, I don't believe I've ever had that before."

"Come meet my father, Mrs. Benton, he came here to be with me." Jamie drew the older woman to John Shipley. "Dad, this is Dee, Felicia's mother."

Shipley took her proffered hand. "Pleased to meet you, ma'am, you have a fine, lovely daughter." He looked into her eyes, seeing the same mesmerizing shades of lavender, only slightly faded with the years. "I'm very pleased to know you," he added softly and held her hand too long, but neither of them noticed.

Jamie stared in astonishment at her father. She turned to Jim and Felicia with a sly smile and tentatively raised eyebrows.

Felicia knew Jamie's thoughts. The attraction taking hold between their elders held an aura of magic. The intensity between them shone in their faces.

Felicia hated to break the moment. "We were planning to take a circular tour of the island. Would you want to come with us, Mother? I'm sure there's room. We've been cooped up here and need something to keep us occupied. Besides, since we're here, we should see everything we can. After all, this *is* Tahiti."

"Cooped up? What *are* you saying child, are you ill?" Dee exclaimed.

"We'll tell you everything as we go. None of it's believable anyway, and besides we have the police guarding us. We don't need to worry about the smugglers for now." Felicia, casual with her words, had just caused her mother to turn pale with shock at such unbelievable information.

"What's going on here—*smugglers?* Why would they place a guard over you?" Dee's anxiety, bordering on hysteria, made Felicia regret her tale of criminals and crime.

John Shipley spoke up, seeking to calm Dee's fears. He took her hand again. "It's the damned pirates, or whatever the hell they call themselves. The police are protecting these kids from them until they testify, and we get the hell off this island. It may be a beautiful, exotic place, but not under *these* conditions." He put a hand on Dee's shoulder. "Don't you worry about it, ma'am, the officers seem competent enough. It should be over with soon, of course, depending on how they manage their judicial processes here."

"Oh, dear, I do have jet lag, but I couldn't sleep now. I guess I'd like to go on your tour if there's room." Dee said, looking discretely at Shipley.

Felicia knew her mother's distrust of men. But Mr. Shipley, aside from being a fine distinguished-looking man, was already part of the relationship.

"A ride around this place wouldn't hurt," Dee said. "I don't want to be separated from my daughter so soon after finding her again."

Jim stepped out to let Emile know about the new passenger. Felicia smiled secretly at Jamie. She'd stirred up a hornets' nest of worry without thought of how information of this sort might be taken by people who hadn't recently been through the hell of being shot at, marooned on an island, and lost to the world.

A giggle escaped Jamie, watching the protective air her father had assumed over Felicia's mother. "Well, you did it that time, Felicia. People can never grasp what we went through. I wonder if we aren't getting used to being threatened and shot at. From now on, we'll have to watch how we tell about it."

Jim lounged in the doorway. He wore new togs found on the shopping excursion, and though they hung loosely, they suited his big frame. "Emile is ready for us, let's go. I'm sick of this room. I'm an outdoor guy nowadays."

Jamie noticed Felicia's mother covertly watching Jim. The happiness he'd brought her daughter, after she'd despaired of her ever marrying, delighted her. No one mentioned Felicia's condition. It wouldn't be a secret long, not after the nausea of this morning.

Outside of the hotel sat a ramshackle truck-like affair, too large, but reserved for this group alone. The sign on the side said *Le Truck*. They climbed in to sit on rather rudely padded seats. Windowless, it was open air all around. There were two additional guards. They recognized Charles, the guard from the heliport.

He winked at Jamie when he caught sight of her. With a rumble, the vehicle started and lurched forward, heading out into the main street traffic. The driver was used to driving in Papeete, and they jostled about whenever he swerved to avoid pedestrians, dogs, pigs, or bicycles.

Dee sat next to John Shipley and he didn't seem to mind when she jounced unexpectedly against his side. The weather seemed warm and muggy, but the welcoming breeze of the moving truck cooled them. Jamie and Felicia watched their elders surreptitiously as much or more than the scenery.

"Look, Jim. It's called Avenue Du Charles De Gaulle, after the famous war general. I read about him in history class." Felicia pointed excitedly at things. "Look how French all the names of stores and restaurants are."

The breeze blew her hair in a swirl about her face, and strands played about Jim's lips. He smiled as he inhaled some of the expensive French perfume she'd purchased with his credit card.

Most of the houses were smallish and flimsy looking. The larger structures had red tiled roofs and their construction style made them look like they were set in a French town with tree-lined streets. Sidewalk cafes completed the picture. Only the heat and humidity reminded them where they were, that and many local people dressed in colorful native wrap.

It shocked them when a beautiful woman smiled, and they saw few, if any teeth.

They left the congested main street, to rock slowly along, passing woven-walled huts on poles, pigs and chickens, and many gardens growing in lush green patches outside native homes.

"They're very poor, most of them, aren't they?" Dee uttered. "I feel sorry for the natives under French rule. I wonder if they're happy, living that way."

The air felt cooler out along the edges of the lush island of Tahiti. They worked their way around the island on a narrow macadam road that clung near the beaches or crashing surf. On the other side of the island they moved past high and very jagged peaks covered with verdant green, tropical growth. Occasional wide, deep valleys were visible with huts and crops growing in profusion everywhere. Traversing along the side of the tallest mountain, their driver-guide offered occasional bits of information. Jamie took it in with great interest, but her eyes frequently sought the expanses of the wide blue Pacific, where she sought the familiar form of the square-sailed junk.

# CHAPTER 41

The high peak up there, we call, *Orohema*. Is cooler up there, but we don't climb up, so rough going, those mountains." The native driver chattered away as he deftly dodged a pig rooting at refuse in the road. Knowing this was a special group, he made the attempt to point out the sights of interest. The eastern curve circling the island passed the entrance to lovely waterfalls, and a leper colony site. They could see far out to sea, unless obscured by dense tropical growth. Lush, magnificent flowers grew wildly everywhere. Their fragrance scented the air they breathed.

Jim shook his head at seeing Jamie, by force of habit, gazing out over the deep-blue shades of ocean, watching for signs of the junk. Mick would be here somewhere if she saw that vessel. He thought about Mick constantly himself, aside from the distraction of his new wife.

They saw a breadfruit tree. "Jamie! Guess what that is?" Felicia called out. She clung to Jim's good arm as they jounced along. "I guess those days are over, huh? But I'd still like to try one with butter, and salt and pepper."

Felicia's mother listened in wonder to what she heard. "My poor child, I have never known her to be excited about a tree," she said to Shipley. "What has she endured to make these changes?" She looked up at him. "My thoughts have run wild with wondering." She sat very close to the man, and didn't move. "Are you having the same bewildering thoughts about our children?"

He nodded. "I'm quite sure we'll never know everything."

They rounded the backside of the island where a smaller island attached. It made Tahiti an hourglass in shape. Suddenly, Jamie cried out, clutching her father's arm, "Oh, God! There it is! That Chinese junk that has terrorized us for so long!"

Jamie tapped Charles on the shoulder. "If those pirates are captured, where are they?"

*"Oui, mademoiselle,* they are captured, but maybe not all of them. That is why we must guard you until we are completed the case," he answered eagerly, happy to pay attention to the beautiful girl.

"Where are they being held?" she queried, fearing the answer.

"*In le prison, mademoiselle*, until we finish this case."

"You say some of them are at large, and a danger to us?"

He shrugged. "*Oui,* some of them, maybe, we are not sure. We look everywhere for them. *Le French Foreign Legionnaires* help with that."

"Thank you, sir." Jamie, no longer a tourist, felt her face tighten with anxiety. She no longer saw the passing scenery. With icy dread for Mick, she buried her face in her father's chest and cried bitter tears.

His strong arms held her, but he was puzzled. "What the hell just happened?" He patted her. "There, there, daughter, what's wrong? What have you seen?" He looked to Jim for answers. "What in the hell's going on?"

Jim moved close to Shipley and told him what he thought, adding, "We can't be sure about anything, not yet."

Dee listened with a look of disbelief at their discussion of murder and drugs, and her head lifted at hearing of a criminal named Mick, the man whose very name brought bitter tears to Shipley's daughter.

Jamie dried her tears and sat in stunned silence. *How can*

*I see him? I have to find out if he's in custody, and if they'd let me see him?* She didn't know the rules about such things in Tahiti.

She took comfort from her father's presence, but she'd ask Jim when they could speak alone.

Jim sat on the crude seats of *Le Truck*, bouncing joylessly over the paved, narrow road, pondering the same as Jamie. He, as well as Jamie, no longer saw the lovely tropical scenes they passed. Recovering from his recent fight for life, he tired rapidly. Seeing the junk this close was a shock. He wasn't sure what it meant.

"Stop!" Jamie cried out. "Charles, please stop the driver. I must see that ship anchored out there! It terrorized us so long. I have to stand here and *look* at it."

He spoke rapidly in French to the driver. Shortly they ground to a shaking halt.

Jamie, as well as the others, stood on a small promontory overlooking the small cove. The bulky little ship, bobbed gently on the undulating Pacific swells. An uplifting breeze from the ocean cooled the watchers. Sea birds drifted and darted on the updrafts, but those lovely sights could not calm Jamie's aching heart.

The Tahitian Territorial flag flapped lazily over the junk. That alone made a difference in her appearance. No longer was the chunky ship controlled by dark, vicious sneering men, who sold life-destroying drugs, enslaving unwary fools. Only a short time ago, those same men had come seeking Jamie and her friend's deaths as well.

"Not so scary now, huh, Jamie?" Jim remarked, sweating with fatigue.

"I had to take a good long look at that nightmare of a ship. It has haunted my dreams and struck fear into me, even here on this island. I can't stop looking for it every time I'm near the ocean." She looked at Jim. "Mick has to be here. Is there any way they'd let me see him? You're in the law, would you see if it's possible?"

"Sure thing, Jamie, I'll see to when we get back. I knew

what you were thinking—me too. We hoped he'd make it off that ship alive, even if it means he's in custody." He hugged her with his good arm and kissed the top of her head. "I know you're terribly torn apart by this, but now we have a clue, don't we?"

A lump tightened in John Shipley's throat at the sight of the loving relationship among the three young people.

Dee stood beside him, trying to envision the dreadful things that had befallen her daughter. "My God, John," she exclaimed.

He folded her hand in his, but had no answer for her, only a nod of understanding.

After a time, Jamie sighed and returned to the sturdy *Le Truck*. "Well, that's it. I don't know what to do now, Dad. Mick has to be here somewhere, if he lives. Jim will help. He's an attorney in Kansas. That ought to pull some weight."

"We'll get on it soon as we get back. But, Jamie, it might not be good for you to see him like that," Shipley said. Jim nodded.

"Dad, I need to see him if he lives. I don't care a whit what his circumstances might be. I'll die if I can't see his face and talk with him once more. They might send him off to prison for years. I *have* to see him!" She still clung to his promise, and her head swam with confusion.

The tour, dampened after seeing the junk, wound to an end. They returned to their rooms. Jim, pale and sweating with fatigue, collapsed on his bed after inquiring if they'd be allowed to see Mick. Emile said he would see. They were witnesses against the very same man. Jamie waited in agony for his answer.

Emile returned an hour later. "*Non, monsieur*, it is not possible. It is not allowed." He shrugged as only the French know how, with an expression of bewilderment on his face. "May I ask why you wish to see this man?"

"He was with us on the island. He saved our lives by his actions. We wish to thank him." Jim did not want to enlighten Emile further on the subject of Mick. The mystery of him hung heavily in Jim's mind, as well as Jamie's, and was no nearer a solution. They didn't want to cause him danger by calling undue attention to him.

Jamie's heart throbbed with joy knowing Mick still lived, but now she felt the pain of his situation. It could not go well. He was close, on this very island, and she couldn't see him. To look into those glowing black eyes and hear his reassuring words once again would be heaven. Heartsick and frustrated, she threw herself onto her bed to stare blankly at the ceiling.

Shipley looked helplessly at Jim. The pain of his daughter's suffering lined his solid, strong features, and darkened his eyes. "When in hell is this trial supposed to take place?" He wanted his daughter out of this place that had hurt her so much. He entertained thoughts of placing her on a plane, and leaving it all behind. "Hasn't she born enough misery in this God forsaken part of the world? Jamie, what if we could just get out of here? Would you do that?"

She sat up. "No, Dad, I'll never leave this place until I know what has happened to Mick. There are too many unanswered things about him. He doesn't know about our child."

She had a determined look her father had never seen. His daughter had changed, matured. A different, stronger young woman stood before him—almost someone he no longer knew.

He patted her head, and hugged her. "I hate seeing you suffer, child, but I can't fault your strength in the matter. I've never seen you this way, Jamie. You've grown up. It's a good thing, I suppose, but we'll have to get acquainted all over again."

Jim ordered room service, but before it came, John said to Dee. "Would you have dinner with me? We aren't incarcerated like our children. I'd like to see a bit of this place. I'll get you in early, I know you're tired with all this, and jet lag too."

With a nod, and shy smile, she rose from her chair. "Yes, I will, John, if you don't mind eating with someone a bit travel worn." She smiled at her daughter, Jamie, and her new son-in-law, and left on Shipley's arm.

"Well! How about that?" Felicia finally found her tongue after a stunned silence. "Jamie, my mother doesn't trust men at all. Maybe she'll get over it with a hunk like you're your father."

Felicia giggled, looking at Jamie and Jim after their elders left. The budding relationship between their parents lightened everything for the three of them, and they did well with their dinner when it arrived.

Jamie said goodnight and shut the door between the rooms. Unable to sleep, she spent an hour or two looking out over the city lights of Papeete with heavy heart. "Mick, where are you tonight?" she whispered in the darkness. "I need you. I have so much to tell you. I wait in agony for things to come right, like you said. It's getting more difficult to believe—Mick, I love you. I always will."

Jamie, restless as a tigress, because she knew Mick had to be close by, tossed and turned until she finally found the sleep she sought. Though she rarely dreamed, she had wild, intensely vivid, visions of lying in the moonlight out on the sandy beach, holding Mick in her arms. She felt the strength of him, caught his exciting masculine scent, and felt the wonderful sensation of her skin pressing close against his hard smooth body—so wonderful, so real...

With a start, she came awake to feel a strong hand pressed against her lips. Bucking wildly against the heavy weight across her body, terror coursed through her, until she heard the soft whisper. "Hush, Jamie, it's me. Don't be afraid, dearest girl, it's Mick. I'm right here, my darling."

He uttered a soft chuckle as he watched her come awake in the reflected glow of the city lights below. She struggled awake enough to look into his eyes and grasp recognition of him.

Finally, with a dawning realization, astonishment and

disbelief, she struggled to speak. "Oh, my God! Mick, can it really be you?"

Now fully and completely awake, she worked to assure herself he was not a figment of her imagination. The fleeting thought that he should be wearing the gaudy stripes of a prisoner passed through her mind, but he was dressed in black as far as she could tell. A thin knit black shirt, and dark pants. His long, slender feet were bare. She recognized his elongated saturnine features in the glow of lights cast in from the lanai. He wore the wispy moustache and his hair looked the same, bound up in a thong. His hair looked clean.

"It's me, *Jamilla*—Jamie. I had to see you, and know things are right with you. Are you well, my darling girl? Tell me." He laid his long body half laid over her. A long, muscular leg imprisoned her further.

"Mick, how on earth—"

He stopped her with a long kiss.

"Mick, how'd you get here?' she asked when he broke for a breath. "We saw that junk anchored on the back of this island. I hoped you were alive and here somewhere. We asked if we could see you and they said no. Did you escape?"

Excited and elated, she struggled to get the words out. Her heart pounded with happiness as her questions poured out. He lay against her, holding her so tight she could scarcely catch her breath. His hands moved slowly, sensuously, over her, seeking, touching, and tasting, as if he reassured himself she was real.

"Don't worry about anything just now. I can't explain this to you. I'm here. I love you, dearest heart. I need to know you're well."

"Yes, I am, but there's something I must tell you Mick. I don't know where to begin. I was so tortured not knowing about you, or if you still lived. How could you do this to me? I've died a little every day with not knowing."

"I know, Jamie, and I can't enlighten you as you deserve. You'll have to forgive me, and if you still can, trust and believe in me. You have something to tell me. What is it, my dearest, darling, Jamie? Just tell me."

She saw his face smiling in the scant bit of light from the lanai. "Mick, we're going to have a child. I found out about it on the ship that saved us." She gasped. "You did that, you sent them and saved Jim's life, didn't you?"

She forgot about the child, remembering the day the saving helicopter arrived. She'd never forget hearing the giant machine *whupp-whuppping* above her that day, with the life-saving medics. She even remembered the forgotten fish she'd dropped at her first sight of the big machine descending down to them.

Mick, lying on his side, looked into her face with his large, black, shining eyes. "Would you repeat that first part, and, yes, I sent the medics. The child, tell me about our child, Jamie."

"They gave us physicals on the cruiser, and both of us were pregnant. Jim and Felicia had a wonderful wedding right on the ship, a few days after, or as soon as he could stand up. Oh, Mick, he was nearly dead when they came for us. They told us they had all the right coordinates. We knew you'd sent them, no one else could have. We blessed you over and over that day."

"So tell me about our child. I know about the rescue, and thank God it was in time—I wasn't sure it would be." He uttered a sigh of relief. "Tell me about you. How are you doing with this? I'm afraid I've never had this particular experience to deal with, so how does it go with you?"

"I've wished you were with me over and over. I'm so alone in this. My father is here, and he welcomes a grand-child. He'll love our child as much as I will, and will be the father figure too if we don't have you, but he's not you, Mick. He's just not you! I need you so much."

"You're well then?" His lazy smile spread over his long features as he grasped her ever tighter in his arms. "You're not sorry for this? Tell me, girl, tell me."

"No, Mick. I knew I'd have something of you to cherish, if I never saw you again, or things didn't come right, as you said so often. Yes, I'm well, except for sometimes in the mornings."

She laughed at that, feeling content, warm, and whole, being in his arms. But, instinctively, she knew he would not stay long with her. Her heart soared to the heights, deliriously happy to have him, if only for a few precious hours. She grasped him ever more tightly, hoping to make these stolen moments last.

"My darling girl, before we parted on the island, I was sure you were carrying my child. I was happy and proud as hell, but with so much on your mind that day, I couldn't add to it. I've missed you day and night for so long. I've lived for this moment when we'd be together again, at least for a little while." He kissed her deeply while removing her flimsy gown. He ran his hands over her smooth skin then stopped to question her. "You're even smaller than I remember. Are you eating enough?"

"Yes, Mick, it's the way of things for now. Later on I'm sure I won't be so small. How could you know about this child if I didn't?" Joyously, she helped him remove his things. "How did you know? Is that why you said you'd tell your son about that day, then told me you were daydreaming? It's heaven to hold you. I never thought this would happen ever again," she murmured as they blended their bodies together in the heat and closeness of their love. His kisses took her breath away and his hands burned on her skin, until she stopped him. "Mick, how could you know about it?"

"I watch everything about people and something as fascinating as female issues wouldn't escape me. You were so busy just trying to survive, and doctoring everyone, you couldn't keep score, but I did."

"Sometimes you scare me, Mick. Will I ever really know you?"

"Girl, I love you so. You *are* the wife of my heart, and

my life. Darling, our day will come, I've told you this before, and I say so again." They clung closely and desperately together, loving each other in wild abandon as the world
outside wound its way into early dawn.

Jamie slept against his chest, breathing the familiar scent
she'd grown to hold so wonderfully in her mind. With Mick
so close, she was complete, all of her fears relaxed, and finally let herself go into deep, heavy slumber.

# CHAPTER 42

"Jamie, are you awake, Jim's ordered breakfast."
Jamie awakened to the sound of knocking on the door and Felicia's voice. The dial on the bedside clock said eight-thirty. Suddenly alert, she remembered it all and looked about for Mick. He'd gone from her bed. She knew again the empty feeling of his absence. "I'll be over after I catch a quick shower," she called through the closed door.

She sat up, wondering if it all had been a dream. It had not. Mick's scent lingered on her skin, in her senses, and she knew so well the familiar ache of a body well used in the acts of passion.

Smiling a dreamy smile at the memories of last night, she headed into the shower. *How can I tell them? Dare I?* Mick hadn't said, but she knew instinctively, to be careful with news about his visit. She could tell Jim. He'd know what to do and would want to know about his friend.

When she entered the next room, breakfast was ready. She was hungry, but could not concentrate on eating, or stop the dreamy expression across her face.

Jim looked quizzically into her eyes. "Okay, what's going on, what's happened? Come on, out with it."

Felicia took notice, reached out, caught Jamie's hand, and pulled her closer. "Jamie, what is it? You're scaring us."

"If I tell you, will you swear not to let on?" she begged them. "You have to." When they nodded, she continued.

"Mick came to me last night. I fell asleep before he left, but he knew about our baby, and he wasn't dressed in prison clothes." She paced before them, a smile she couldn't hide on her face. "I'm more confused than ever, but oh, it was beyond wonderful to see him again. I wonder who that man is and what'll happen next."

"Jamie, you saw Mick?" Felicia cried. Her excitement was obvious, but Jim had little to say, his brow furled.

"That gives us something to think about. That son-of-a-gun has some dark secrets. Something is definitely going on there." He grinned and shrugged. "Will we ever really know the man?"

"We haven't testified so far, Jim," Jamie said. "Will this ever be over?"

"I don't know what's keeping them. We've been cooped up like *we're* the guilty parties. No one has taken our testimony, or however they do things in Tahiti. It's about time *something* happens, that's for damn sure!"

Aside from his excitement about Mick's appearance, Jim's impatience and three shades of anger and frustration this morning over the delays tickled Jamie.

"Jamie, here's some toast, and this fruit is very nice, but I couldn't manage the eggs." Felicia looked slightly pale, but held her own. "I'd better stop now, or be sick again. I haven't had a chance to tell my mother yet, either." She managed a small giggle with a sly conspiratorial look. "Speaking of Mother, I wonder how the night went. They looked nice together, didn't you think?"

Jamie, distracted by thoughts of her wondrous night with Mick, worked at pulling herself together. "I wonder if it's a good idea to tell Dad about Mick's visit. He might not understand a thing like last night. How could he, when I don't myself?" A little chuckle escaped her. "We surely can't tell the police. That wouldn't help Mick at all, would it?"

"Well, of course *we* understand how it is with you and Mick, but why burden your father with useless worry. There's enough to go around as it is," Jim replied.

With a knock on the door, Felicia's mother appeared looking refreshed from a night's rest. "Good morning—oh, you're eating in the room again." A frown crossed her fine features. "You poor dears, how long must this continue?"

Jim offered her a plate. "Until the trials are over, and they haven't taken testimony yet. I expected it to be over and done by now."

"Thanks, Jim, I'm rather hungry this morning."

"Well, Mother, tell us, where did you two go last night? Was it fun?" Felicia was overly curious, knowing her mother's adverse feelings toward men.

"We found a little French restaurant, *Le Amelia*, I believe it was. It was very nice." She proffered no more information. Her mother was not talking.

Shipley came to Jamie's door and the five of them shared the generous breakfast. Felicia's face took on an unmistakable pallor. With a muffled sound, she cried, "Oh God," clamped a hand over her mouth, and scrambled for the bathroom.

Her mother rushed to her at the sound of retching, and the secret was out. Amused smiles all around disarmed her. She embraced her daughter and tall son-in-law. Tears of joy lay in her eyes. "Felicia, I feared this day would never come, and now I'm to be blessed with a grandchild and a new son-in-law. It's a lot to take in, along with you being rescued. I couldn't believe you were lost forever. It's wonderful. I'm happy about it. God bless the two of you."

Jamie knew her father wouldn't tell her anything about his evening with Dee, but it helped keep her from wondering and thinking constantly of Mick

With a smart rap on the door, Etienne appeared. "*Le Inspecting Magistrate* is returned to Tahiti, and wishes to meet with the three of you. He will expect you this morning at ten o'clock, in his office." He gazed about the room, seeing the new faces. "We will of course, escort you."

"Etienne, this is my father, John Shipley, and this is Felicia's mother, Adelia Benton. They came to be with us."

Jamie managed the introductions, but with the trial so near, her face felt moist. She feared for Mick.

Etienne bowed a bit and gallantly kissed Dee's hand. *"Oui, madame, enchante."* He shook hands with Shipley. *Monsieur, enchante."* He clicked his heels. With a slight bow and a sly smile, he winked at Jamie.

"May we be present at this inquiry?" Shipley asked. " It would mean much to us, we've waited so long for answers."

The man nodded. *"Certainement, monsieur."*

Later, the five were ushered into a slightly musty wood paneled office. It was located in a large, red tile-roofed public building, surrounded with ornate iron fencing, amid lush tropical landscaping. The man behind the desk stood and proffered his hand as he received introductions to them.

He sat back in his lofty chair, not unlike a throne, and surveyed them—Americans all. "I am *Monsieur Henri Du Montaigne*," he replied, "the Inspecting magistrate for this sector of the Society Islands." After handshakes, they took seats. "I must express my condolences regarding the tragic occurrences at sea. We are delighted at your rescue and welcome the opportunity to convict these felons."

Cold chills raced down Jamie's spine at the man's words. Of course, he meant Mick as well as the others. Her face tightened at the magistrate's words. Her heart ached with pain at what must come. Mick had proven to be a good man while on the island. But what or who was he really, aside from a shadowy man of mystery?

"Please, I beg forgiveness at the delay," the magistrate continued. "However, I was summoned to *Riatea* on urgent matters. It could not be helped. You have been comfortable with your quarters, *non?*"

He wore dark rimmed spectacles and tended to look over them as he spoke. Portly of build, and dressed in a fine lightweight dark suit, his hair was dark, kept short and neat. His sideburns were neatly trimmed. Overall, he slightly resembled an owl. That he wielded a certain amount of power over their lives was a given—it exuded from his very pores.

He rattled a sheaf of papers in his hands. The delay was agonizing to Jamie. She'd waited and worried so long about Mick's fate. Now she would literally be forced to give damning evidence against him.

Finally, the magistrate called in a secretary and another man, introduced as Monsieur Louie Garnier. "He is the examining magistrate, and will assist me in the taking of information. So let us begin." He beckoned to Jim. "Sir, if you will, tell us exactly what took place on that fateful day. It is true you are in much the same profession as we?" he asked, his black, owl-like eyes curious.

"Yes, sir, I am a prosecuting attorney in my home state of Kansas." Jim went on to recount details of the day the *Queen Ilikii* met her fate. The men scribbled notes, as well as the secretary, who sat at his tiny machine ticking at the buttons. He used a recorder that stood on a metal stand. Jamie idly wondered whether he was taking it down in French or English? The inspectors frequently interrupted with questions geared to hone the details to their satisfaction.

Describing the exchange between the *Queen Ilikii* and the junk, wrung Jamie's heart. Jim, Felicia, and her own reluctant self detailed Mick's involvement in the drug exchange prior to the sinking of the schooner. During the long, agonizing period of the interview, she could not escape the feeling that Jim's testimony carried more weight than that of the female interviewees.

Finally, each of them completed their own testimony, covering the same ground as Jim, but from their individual points of view.

"Tell me more about the man, one Michael Sands," the inspecting magistrate asked later on in the questioning. His eyes narrowed. It was during Jamie's interview, that he posed this question.

Finding it too painful to say anything detrimental regarding Mick, she gave a positive picture of him. "After we arrived on the island, he helped find food, and kept the smugglers from capturing us." She looked into the owl-like eyes and told of Mick's bravery. "At no time were we fearful of him during our time on the island. In fact, he was different from the man he seemed to be on the *Queen Ilikii*." She drew a deep breath and continued. "We believe he notified our navy to rescue us and saved Jim's life."

After long, endless hours of detailed questioning, Jamie asked, "Sir, were there others rescued from the *Ilikii*?"

"*Oui,* there were others, only a few—so very few." He shook his head sadly. "Many lives were lost, as well as the schooner. She was a fine ship, that one. Like a woman, so slender, so lovely." His dark eyes bore into Jamie and Felicia's. Jamie was sure he'd seen Felicia tossing her hair without thinking.

"May we know who the other survivors were?" Jim asked.

Jamie felt his frustration at receiving little real cooperation.

"*Non, monsieur*, all will come out at the trial." The closed look on the magistrate's features told them they'd have to wait for that day, whenever it might be. The man called Garnier indicated the interviews were completed. They were to leave and he summoned Etienne.

They walked out into late afternoon heat. Jamie the breathed flower-scented air. It was wonderful after the long, tense, hours in the magistrate's stuffy chambers.

"Well, I'd never have believed people could sink a ship out from under you in this day and age. It's unbelievable!" Dee found her voice after listening to the harrowing details affecting her child. "Felicia, you must have been so frightened!"

"I was, but with Jim beside me, it wasn't so bad. A lot of it was wonderful, Mother, an experience I'll never forget, but wouldn't want to repeat. We never had a full meal, except for a few times." She clung to Jim's arm. "Who knows? I might never have gotten to know this guy. You made it wonderful for me, Jim," she added with a laugh.

"No snacking—a few peanuts, and some mushy Ding Dongs."

Shipley took his daughter's arm. "Jamie, I'm astounded you went through that and lived. Your mother, God rest her soul, would be as proud of you as I am."

His protecting arm around her, made her want to cry, not for herself—for Mick. "Oh, Dad, I hope what we had to say in there won't hurt Mick's case too much. How could I ever tell this child my testimony sent his father to a skuzzy tropical prison? I don't even have a picture of him."

She remembered the bag of undeveloped film the female sailors had thrust into her hands as they left the cruiser. She grabbed Felicia's hand. "Where are rolls of film they gave us on the cruiser? I can't wait to see the pictures."

"I left them at the hotel desk for developing when we got here, or the next day. They should be ready, depending on how they do it here."

They settled in their rooms, and ordered room service. Upon request, a clerk brought the pictures to them. He cast an inquisitive eye around the room, and appeared to be of oriental decent. Jamie felt a chill when he looked into her eyes. He quickly cast his eyes away, and that quick movement filled her with dread.

*Now this one is looking at us!* She remembered the other dark-eyed waiter who had brought up a food cart. He'd had the same inquisitive look about him. *I must be overly sensitive about dark-eyed men. But how can I forget, these people have eyes everywhere?*

"Jim, did you look at that waiter?" she asked. " He looked at me. It made me think he was one of *them*. They have eyes and ears everywhere. Isn't that what Mick said?"

"I saw him giving this room the once over." A frown came over his face. "We've given our testimony, so what does it matter now? It's too late for them to stop us from talking. Let's not worry about it. I'll mention it to the guard."

"Here you are walking down the aisle in that filmy blue

dress, Jamie. You looked absolutely glorious!" Felicia laid the photos out on the bed. "These are great!" She giggled. "Look, Jim, there's you, pale and weak, standing there waiting."

"Look at you, Felicia," Jamie said. "Those sailor gals did a great job taking these pictures. I never knew they did that. I have to say, no one would ever recognize us, we look so different. Why we can't go out on our own?"

They spent time pouring over the pictures. Underscoring to Dee and Shipley even more, the adventure they'd survived. Dee looked at her daughter in the filmy, pale, pink wedding dress and shook her head, going from one snapshot to the next. "Felicia, you're so tanned and gorgeous in this picture, I can't believe the drastic change in you. What a wedding! I'm sorry I missed it."

"Dear girl, you look like a tanned goddess in these shots," Jamie's father whispered to her, "No wonder Mick fell in love with you."

"Dad, he saw me fat and in rags, but he still fell in love. I didn't look like this on the island, maybe toward the last I was thin, but by then, my clothes hung in filthy ragged shreds. I'd torn most of my skirt off to make dressings for all the wounds. The helicopter guys really gave us the once over. We were a terrible sight."

"Yes, I can just imagine the picture you two presented. Sure they were looking. You girls provided the US Navy with a few thrills during your stay on the cruiser, and the thrill of a lifetime, rescuing beautiful damsels off a deserted island."

Jim laughed at Shipley's comments. "You should have heard the razing I got on our wedding night. I barely made it, weak as hell, and nearly passing out."

"There were a few who offered to stand in for you, Jim." Felicia giggled and gave him a wifely peck on the cheek. "I turned them down, of course. They nearly danced us off our feet instead. We'll never forget their kindness, the beautiful clothes, and that wonderful, wonderful wedding."

Shipley, seeing everything was quiet in the room, asked Dee if she would like to walk about and see more of Papeete. She assented, and he took her arm as they left. Jamie looked at Felicia. Both women wore smiles across their faces. Jim shook his head at their female machinations.

Jamie needed to rest. She took a few photos to her room. Her mind swirled with worry over the damaging things she'd said to the magistrates. Her words would send Mick to prison. It haunted her. *But how did he escape to visit me?*

# CHAPTER 43

S he finally noticed the bundle that Roger had handed her as they left the naval helicopter. "I forgot about it. What could be in here?"

She pulled off the string binding. It was the clothes they'd been wearing from the island. The ragged contents, washed and neatly folded, made Jamie sob with gratitude for the girls on the ship.

*Whether we'd ever want to see this pile of worn rags again or not, they gave us the option.* Jim's ragged shorts and shirt were there, too. She stepped to the dividing door between the rooms and gently knocked.

The three friends held the ragged clothing, remembering things all over again. "Wait until mother sees these," Felicia said. "She'll cry. She will when she sees how we must have looked. Look, Jamie, at all the places you cut new button-holes." She chuckled, the warmth of her friendship with Jamie coursed through her, as she remembered the better times they'd had on the lost little island. They had closer ties than family, and always would.

After reliving in memories some of their island days, Jim stepped out to talk with the guard, Charles Du Soar. "What about the dark-eyed clerk, and the waiter who brings our food—are they with your outfit?"

"*Oui, monsieur,* no one comes to your rooms, but those in our service. You have no need for worrying about that." His voice exuded confidence.

Jim informed the women. "We'd like to have a night out," he then asked the guard. "We're in this exotic city and wish to see something of the night life. We've given our testimony, why not?" His voice testy, he added, "We're fed up with incarceration."

Charles smiled at Jim and shrugged. *"Certainement, monsieur,* it will be well. There will be two of us with you. You will not see us."

☙☙☙

The women fussed about, putting on their new finery. Jamie tried on the softly printed silk French creation she'd never have imagined buying in Denver. Felicia wore a silky draped white dress that made her look like a goddess. Dee came in wearing a softy gathered green dress that brought a flush to Shipley's face.

The soft glow in his eyes amazed his daughter, and she winked at Felicia.

They walked out of the hotel into the busy nightlife of Papeete. Jim walked with Felicia, John with Dee and Jamie. They enjoyed a fine French meal. The price was a shocker, but the men never batted an eye. It was good to be out and about.

Later, they wandered into a small beachcomber hotel and Tahitian dancing, a review on stage. The dancers energetically wriggled their swinging hibiscus-bark skirts and tropical print parus.

"Tahitian dancing is exotic, erotic, and energetic." Jamie laughed. "They tell a story. I've no idea what about. I read that in the brochure, oh, so long ago."

Jim laughed too. "I could hazard a pretty good guess after watching them. Felicia, think you could learn that dance?" He nudged her shoulder.

"It might get this baby all stirred up." She giggled, her eyes fixed on the wild gyrations of the darkly hued men and women of Tahiti. "I'd like to see you up there, Jim. I've an idea you'd be good at it."

The young women took fruit-laced drinks, while the others were free to imbibe as they desired. Jim and Shipley had an icy Island Lager, while Dee enjoyed a fruity concoction she'd guessed at from a French menu.

Dark eyes watched them wherever they meandered. They refused to be troubled. Their safety lay in the hands of their guards. Were they that efficient? The group all looked at each other, gave a French-style shrug, and totally enjoyed themselves.

Jamie's underlying sadness about Mick dampened her joy, but the wild Tahitian nightlife and the wonder of her father's relationship with Dee, overshadowed her concerns. She knew all about falling in love, and he'd been alone for so long.

"Jamie, what do you think is happening there?" Felicia whispered.

"She's the first woman he's looked at in years. I love them together. They go so well." Jamie grinned secretly to her friend. "We'd best leave them alone. We'll embarrass them if we comment on it."

"Maybe we'll be real sisters. I'd love that after what we've been through together. You're as close to me as a real sister, and they'd be double grandparents. Is that part of the attraction?"

"No, Felicia, he was taken in by your eyes, and when he saw those same eyes on your mother, he was a goner." Jamie watched them dancing. "I'd be happy to see them together. Look, he's holding her a little tight. Her dress is riding up."

Jim pulled Felicia out on the slick wooden floor. "You next, Jamie girl, I'll have this first dance with my beautiful wife."

Big and graceful, he folded Felicia in his arms and, careful of his bandaged one, they whirled away. She saw the wooden floor give slightly as he glided past in big shining shoes. He proved to be a fine, skillful dancer, and Felicia appeared to be in heaven as they moved. Her eyes were closed, her head lay against his chest, and his head bent down to her as they swept along.

Jamie, knowing Mick's dancing skills would match the cat-like grace she'd seen in him so often, ached to be held in his arms. Would he come to her again?

"Oh, Jamie, I'd have married him sooner had I known he could dance like that." Felicia laughed with joy when Jim returned her.

He took Jamie out onto the broad smooth dance floor. "You miss Mick terribly. I'll see when the trial will be held. We need this business over with so we can get on with our lives—whatever that means for you. This waiting is for the birds. I don't know French law, but we'll find out soon."

He held her close and she took comfort from his friendly, sheltering arms. Tears sprang unbidden to her eyes at his friendly words.

Jim took a turn with Dee, and Jamie danced in her father's arms. "Gee, Dad, I didn't know you were such a great dancer." He glanced frequently at Dee as they moved about. "You get on well with Felicia's mother. She's nice, and I like her."

"We do get on well. She isn't too sure about me, but our families tie together, and we seem to be in each other's company. It's not like meeting a total unknown. I do like her, Jamie. She's a fine woman, and a hell of a looker to boot."

"Dad, I saw the way you were taken in by Felicia's lavender eyes, and with Dee having them too, you couldn't miss taking that second look. She's a lot like Felicia. She might seem frivolous, but we found out differently when Jim was deathly ill from that pig's tusk."

After a night of eating, dancing, watching local natives, French sailors, and tourists, their feet were tired as they left for the hotel. The trades constantly sent soft winds flowing over the night sky. A few stragglers made raucous noise on the streets, singing in French and weaving about on their way to the next bar.

Tired, they said their goodnights. Jamie prayed Mick would come to her again, but he didn't. She fell asleep with empty arms that ached to hold him.

⊘⊘⊘

The date was set. They longed for home, but this was one of the largest court actions ever known in French Polynesia, and their attendance was required.

Other witnesses remained unknown to them, and they frequently wondered who might have survived that day, how they'd survived, or what their story would be. Marveling at their own luck, they shivered at thoughts of what might have been.

"I wonder if Niko was able to get those big ladies off in a raft," Jim commented. "They were so hysterical, he had a tough time of it. He was a strong, robust man, and got one off, but did he get the other one into a flimsy raft in that awful storm?"

"He really had them going with his flirty ways." Jamie laughed. "I wonder if the sailors who stole the raft away from the passengers survived. Would I remember any of them in court nicely dressed and pointing a finger at the smugglers?

"Jim wants me to see a doctor about this pregnancy," Felicia murmured. "I feel like a million, except in the mornings, like you. I suppose one should see a doctor, would you want to do that?"

Jamie was adamant. "No, I'll wait until we get to the States. I feel well enough. I want Mick to go with me." She flung out her hands. "Look at me—still holding out hope things will work out like he promised. I told my dad about Mick's visit. He didn't say much. He's as mixed up as I am about him."

Jamie frowned, unable to make sense of the shadowy, mysterious man she loved. She needed normalcy in her life with a child in the picture.

Felicia sensed Jamie's confusion. "That's what Jim does when Mick is mentioned. He says nothing. He keeps his thoughts about Mick to himself."

Jamie sighed. "I'll live close to my father for the baby's sake." She loved him, and there was Dee now. "Those two seem closer than ever with the long days of waiting. Dad would have a real chance for real happiness with your mother, Felicia. I hope for that. They're so good together."

Felicia shrugged. "I hope for that too Jamie, and you're right, they are!" She took her leave, returning to Jim. His vitality had returned with good food and a healing arm.

❧❧❧

"Hey, let's go to that waterfall out on the circular road and take a swim," Jim said, several days later. "If we stay here long enough, we'll see this entire place."

They moved about freely after the police determined they were no longer in danger. They had taken more suspects in for questioning, and, as a consequence, lightened their protective surveillance. Not knowing where John and Dee had gone, the others caught a *Le Truck*, riding with other islanders and tourists out on the narrow macadam road that curved around Tahiti Nui. The smaller portion was Tahiti Iti.

They passed the old Leper Colony. That disease so deadly and hideously disfiguring for long centuries, no longer fit that description due to antibiotics. The building stood empty, a testament of what used to be. Over a high suspension bridge, they looked down on the Papenoo River, and came to the drop off for Tefa'aurumai Waterfalls. They walked the distance, enjoying the cooling trade winds flowing off the ocean's surface, a reminder of their island days.

They spent pleasant hours sloshing about in cool waters below magnificent splashing waterfalls. "This water is so clear, it looks drinkable, but here in civilization, I'd be afraid." Jim laughed at the difference. Thinking of the pure, good-tasting water they'd been blessed with on the island.

୧ଓୣୄ

The fateful day came. Jamie—along with Jim and Felicia, John and Dee—filed into a large, rather airy courtroom. Her stomach, tied in tight knots, caused her a fair amount of discomfort. She'd see Mick today—in chains.

The large room, paneled with dark wood, contained three high judiciary benches. She wondered if Tahitian law used three judges to hear evidence. The center one was higher than either of the two on the sides. Did the judge in the center have more bearing on decisions than the other two?

Large ceiling fans rotated slowly above, making soft whooshing sounds as they moved the tropical air. People moved into the room. Jamie looked for prisoners, where they would sit, and saw none at present. Looking for other survivors, she nudged Jim. "Isn't that Corrine over there? She wouldn't know about us finding her friend's dress. I wonder if we should tell her."

Corrine gasped in surprise. She saw them, but made no move. Had she been cautioned, as they'd been, against speaking to other witnesses? They noted two young people beside her, a girl and a boy. They looked to be in their teens. Unconsciously, Jamie noticed a resemblance between them and Corrine. She realized the woman appeared considerably smaller and wondered what rigors she'd suffered before her rescue. She also wondered how she recognized them in their new slim bodies.

"Sure, if it isn't her. Man! I wonder what this trial will bring out. We'd best wait until it's over to decide about telling her what we found," Jim murmured low. Felicia leaned close against him to catch his words. "I've been waiting for this trial because they use a different system from ours in the States," he continued. "I'm interested in their procedure. They use the Napoleonic code, I know that, but little else."

"Corrine looks so sad, she knows by now they'll never find her friend. We know it for sure—poor thing," Felicia whispered.

She looked glorious today, with her hair pulled high on her head, her long graceful neck bare, and tanned skin gleaming. She hadn't replaced any of her weight, partially due to morning sickness, but also a desire to keep her new look as long as possible. Jamie noticed Jim's appreciation had remained constant. His attention gravitated to her if they were anywhere near each other. She sighed. Her own attention had always fled to Mick.

People filled the courtroom. They tried to identify some of the sailors they'd seen working on the *Ilikii*, but found it impossible. Everyone looked different, certainly Corrine did, yet somehow, they readily recognized her. They spotted Niko—he'd survived.

They looked for the very heavy women and finally spied a woman they thought could be one of them. She'd lost considerable weight, as they had. Jamie wondered what her story would be. Shipley and Dee sat together on the other side of Jamie. She needed her father next to her during this dreaded trial.

With the bang of a gavel, everyone stood up. Three judges wearing thin, fine dark fabric suits filed in. The words called out during this moment were in French, no doubt the equivalent of "All rise."

Everyone took their seats, and they named the judges. Le Honorables' Georges M. Lesceaux, Henri Du Bardien, et Marcelle Guilloux. They heard a quiet harrumph from one of them as he cleared his throat. The severe expressions on their faces bode poorly for the condemned.

"I wish I'd studied my high school French a little better,"

Jim murmured. "I don't believe these judges will allow a lot of nonsense in their courtroom."

Jamie nodded in agreement. She believed the entire proceedings were going to be in French. *It might as well be Russian. Now we'll never know what's going on.*

A side door opened. They heard the clinking of chains as the accused were escorted into the courtroom. Under close armed guard, they were handcuffed and shuffled the shortened steps allowed by the chains on their ankles. The first few were mixtures of Chinese, Korean, and Filipino. Among them, shuffling in short steps, Jamie saw Mick. Tears filled her eyes seeing him thus. Where now was the tall, fine-mannered man she'd known on the island? Prodded to an enclosed area, behind a short partition, they sat on rows of benches, guarded by four armed men in uniform.

Jamie didn't know with what armed force they were, nor, in her abject misery, did it matter. She tried not to stare at Mick, fought to prevent it, but cast her eyes his way whenever she dared. She feared calling undue attention to her attachment to him. Her father held one hand tightly, and Jim took the other.

They heard a loud sob from Corrine's direction, and the effort to stifle it. The center judge shot a severe look in that direction. The sounds muffled then ceased.

The Public *Prosecteur*, M. Du Lac, stood and announced in French the nature of the proceedings. The same words were repeated in English for the benefit of those requiring it. Jamie sighed when he detailed descriptions of the charges brought against the crew of the Chinese junk, giving the names of each, in turn. At the listing of their names, some of the dark-eyed prisoners cast ugly, baleful stares at Jim, Jamie, and Felicia. They also shot threatening looks out to others in the crowded courtroom as well.

In addition to naming the Orientals one by one, he named the man seen on the dock arguing with Mick, Monsieur Armand Specter. Monsieur Michael Sands and five others, identified as sailors from the *Queen Ilikii*, followed.

With the mention of the ill-fated schooner, they heard the muffled sob again. Looking in that direction, Jamie saw the younger people with Corrine comforting her.

Apparently, Corrine had had some incriminating and scathing things to say about Mick, and most all of the other sailors involved.

In turn, the inspecting magistrate, Monsieur Henri Du Montaigne, gave his evidence, involving each of the condemned, except the smuggling crew. They were accused as a group. *Is that legal?* Jamie wondered. The examining magistrate, Monsieur Louis Garnier gave much the same evidence in turn. He ticked off the information, detailing the criminal deeds done by the condemned men sitting crowded together on the poorly padded benches.

From then on, they listened to the long droning questioning of each witness by the Public *Prosecteur* M. Due Lac, before the three judges.

When it was Corrine's turn to testify, she pointed a finger at the smugglers in general, and Mick in particular, wailing her deadly accusations in their faces. "Your honor, they opened fire on our sailboat and smashed it to smithereens," she sobbed. "They laughed in our faces while they did it! They wanted us to die that day, and they killed my daughter!"

Her sobbing testimony completed, she required assistance to make it back to her seat. One of the court officials took her arm gently and aided her. Felicia wore a bemused frown across her lips, thinking how wrong they'd been about the women's relationship.

The accused were represented by their lawyers, but the defense they presented was lackluster, at best, with half-hearted attempts to refute certain points as brought out in testimony. That they would be found guilty as charged seemed likely.

Niko testified and then Clara. They now knew the woman was indeed Clara. Jim and Felicia testified late in the day. Jamie felt ill as the day ended. Mick sat erect on his bench, not looking at her more than a surreptitious glance. She made eye contact several times, but he looked away. She couldn't get an idea of what he thought or how he felt. Each glimpse of him filled her with thrills as she took in his rangy form, while ice shredded her veins in her fear for him.

# CHAPTER 44

The trial lasted nearly one week, and each day was agony beyond belief for Jamie. Her happiness slipped away daily as the testimonies continued. Her day came. When she testified near the end of the fourth day, it was heart wrenching. She could barely speak at times, trying to shield Mick from further harm as she conveniently forgot much about his actions during the short few hours they'd sailed.

No mention was made of his presence on the island, for some reason it was not brought out. She puzzled over that, but guessed it didn't matter to the court, just the criminality of the prisoners.

Mick looked straight ahead, steadfastly avoiding eye contact with her. This caused intense pain, though she believed he meant to suppress knowledge of their intimate relationship. In furtive glances, she noticed he appeared pale and gaunt. He needed to be in the sun and diving into the waves as he once did during those wonderful, glorious days they'd played together in the lagoon.

Lost in a daze of agony, Jamie lost track of the proceedings. Desolate at the way the trial had gone against the criminals, she tried to take her mind away to the lazy, wonderful days, when they were able to live the love they'd found in each other. Tears slid down her cheeks and she found no way to stop them.

The proceedings lasted for, what seemed to her numbed

mind, hours upon hours until that last day. Sonorous sounding words jumbled in her mind, bringing to an end, all hope of a life with Mick. The prisoners filed out under direction of their guards, and they all stood as the black-clad judges left the courtroom.

As Jamie and the others left the courtroom, they saw the young people with Corrine nearly carry her away. It wasn't the time to talk to her, not yet. They hadn't received information as to that. What would they say, when at last they had the required permission to speak with other witnesses? What was there to say?

Jamie stood in shock when Jim told her they returned tomorrow for the sentencing. "It's not over? Poor Mick, he'll sit on those hard benches another day."

"Jamie, get hold of yourself. You sound like you're floating off in space or something." Felicia tried comforting Jamie, but nothing got through to her friend. In fact, she and Jim grew increasingly concerned at her spacey mien.

Shipley put an arm around Jamie and held her close, wishing he knew how to ease her pain. "I know it was tough on you, honey, seeing him that way. He's a fine looking man. I understand your feelings for him, but try to remember what he said. If he said he could work things out, maybe he knows a way."

He put her to bed as soon as they reached their rooms and sought a modicum of hope for his forlorn daughter. "It's not over till it's over, child."

Jamie had nothing to say and refused to eat when they ordered room service. In her mind, she kept going over the things Mick had promised. He'd been so sure of the future. Anger arose within her. She tried to find reason in what had happened in that courtroom versus what she'd been told to believe. *Again, a man is torturing my very soul, and this time I walked into it with my eyes wide open.* "He will always love me, he said it to me over and over. I believed him because of the way he was with me. I told him I could live on the love between us for the rest of my life. Can I do that, like I said? Or am I still the weak and cowardly thing I was with Moran?" she cried, fighting a battle for life and stability, thinking of her impending motherhood. Her own welfare, no longer her primary concern, gave way to thoughts of her child to be.

Jamie stood up. Shaking off her weakness and indecision, she made the firm resolve to survive the events in that courtroom tomorrow. To live for Mick's child, if not with him, became her mission. He'd shown her what love was. If payment for his crimes had to be long years of imprisonment, she would love him still and count her loneliness as payment for knowing and indulging in that love. She'd wait for the day they could be together—it was all she had left.

She opened the door to Jim and Felicia's room and walked in. "What are we doing? What's for eats?" She managed a weak grin to answer the questioning look on the faces of her father, Dee, and her friends. "What?"

"Are you all right, dear?" Dee came to her with a comforting hand on her arm. "You've been through so much."

"Yes, after this long miserable week, I put into perspective all that happened in that dismal courtroom. I told Mick long ago that I could live on the love we had together for the rest of my life." Jamie faced them with new resolve. "I can't go back on him now when everything looks so bleak. I'll wait however many years it takes. At the very least, I'll have his child to love." Though she felt despair and the deepest kind of sorrow, she'd also found a renewed strength and fought to keep it.

Her friends saw the determined Jamie they'd known on the island. "But oh, God, he looked so pale sitting there." She couldn't stop a few hot tears forming.

"Would you be able to eat a few bites?" her father asked.

Amused, Jamie realized he had fallen back onto the feeling that if you can't help things, you can at least eat something. It was all he had to offer. "I'll try, Dad. Eating is still an adventure after hunting for every mouthful for so long." She took a plate and half-heartedly selected a few things.

Her stomach remained queasy with the emotional issues she faced.

"I was shocked seeing that pale ghost of Mick," Jim said. "What the hell's happening here? Are French jails that bad?"

He said no more, but his mind nearly spun out of control. *There is a hell of a lot more here than meets the eye, or he couldn't have come to see Jamie that night.* He'd formed opinions about Mick before this and kept his own counsel. It would do no good to voice them now.

ೞೞೞ

The morning brought renewed apprehension. This was the day of sentencing. As a group, the five entered the courtroom, their tension high. They found seats. Corrine and the youngsters with her were already seated.

Large ceiling fans circulated lazily, cooling the courtroom, soon packed with spectators and newshounds. Those whose lives had been turned into chaos—the day the *Queen Ilikii* had been blasted and sunk down into those deep, dark ocean depths—sat waiting for justice to be meted out. The news people waited like circling sharks for their chance at the survivors. Anything they could eke out of them would be worldwide news.

For Jamie, the world was about to stop, yet things about her went merrily on as if nothing out of the ordinary had happened. People in the courtroom laughed and chatted without worry. Newspaper reporters waited to tear at them. It was the story of the year, and they'd spent weeks waiting, like wolves with saliva dripping. They hadn't been allowed speak with witnesses. When this was over, what then?

Jamie's heart leaped at the sound of the gavel. With the French version of all rise, it began again. The black suited judges filed in, then the prisoners. Walking with shortened steps and clinking chains, they filed in to sit in their enclosed and heavily guarded area. The sight of her beloved, sitting pale and straight in his striped prison garb, tore her heart to shreds. She kept a straight face and dry eyes, trying desperately not to look directly at Mick. It proved to be a struggle, for she ached to see his love for her shining from his eyes once more. *Please God, just once more!* She wanted to see him again before they took him away to spend long, lonely years locked away in a dank tropical prison. Inside, she felt torn and raw from her struggle.

They began as always in French, until they switched to English for the benefit of the concerned Americans. The judge, named Georges Lesceaue, spoke. "We will pronounce the sentences for the following condemned in the matter of the crew of the Chinese sailing vessel. They are guilty of murder and piracy on the high seas, as well as buying, selling, and providing illegal substances in the environs of French Polynesia for more than three years. For these—" He read the long roster of their names, one by one. "—the sentence will be not less than thirty years, or more than fifty years in Le prison de Marseilles at Rangaroa."

Those men, now sentenced, were prodded to rise. They shuffled from the courtroom, heads hanging low, eyes downcast. A few managed to cast venomous looks at those witnesses against them.

"You evil bastards!" came the anguished cry from the spectators. "You killed my daughter! You sank our little ship with your canon and killed my daughter! I hope you rot to death in that prison!" Corrine brandished a tightly knotted fist in the air, and the young people with her pulled her back to her seat to comfort her. She collapsed into a storm of weeping while one of the judges banged the gavel. The prisoners continued their shuffling gait from the courtroom.

"*Ordre in le court!* We will have order!" He looked with sympathy at Corrine, however, he would maintain decorum in his courtroom. "Order, madam," he repeated in a softer tone. "Monsieur Armand Specter, you are found guilty of buying, selling, and distribution of dangerous, illegal substances. You are sentenced to not less than twenty years, or more than thirty years, in *le prison,* De Gaulle, en Tahiti."

They ushered him out, wearing his same tan, thin, and increasingly wrinkled suit, to begin his fate. They heard the faint clinking of chains as he cleared the courtroom. He did not look about, but they heard distant sounds of sobbing somewhere in the courtroom. Jamie surmised that even this low creature had someone who loved him and would mourn for him. Could she apply that same logic toward Mick?

Then sentences were pronounced upon the sailors of the *Queen Ilikii,* and they too, were sent to prison on the Island of Tahiti.

With ice tearing through her veins, Jamie heard the judge say, "Monsieur, Michael Sands, citizen of Canada, you are found guilty of trading, selling, and transporting illegal substances, in and around French Polynesia for the past two years. We have taken into consideration the fact that you rendered assistance for some of the survivors. You are hereby sentenced to not less than fifteen, or more than twenty, years in prison, the sentence to be carried out at le prison, De Gaulle, en Tahiti." He banged his gavel sharply.

They waited while Mick walked from the courtroom between two guards with his chains lightly clinking. His head lowered, he did not make eye contact with anyone. Her heart sinking to the depths of despair, Jamie watched her beloved Mick disappear from her life.

She did not hear the final dismissal of the proceedings, only the roaring in her head. Reeling in agony at the length of Mick's sentence, she cried inwardly. *Our child will be a teenager before he sees his father!* Pain-filled thoughts tore through her troubled mind.

Roused from her deepest misery, she heard Felicia saying, "Jamie, this is Corrine. She wanted to talk to us, but was cautioned not to speak with other survivors as we were. It's over now, and we're free to talk."

Jamie pulled her thoughts from the depths of her pain. "I'm sorry about your daughter. That was a dreadful day, and we never knew who else made it off the schooner and lived. The ocean was so wild right then." She thought of the skirt Mick had found, and wondered if they should tell her about it. Jamie knew she'd want to know everything. "Corrine, we have small bit of information you may want to hear."

"Yes, please, if you know anything, it would mean so much to us. These are her children." She introduced them, James and Michelle, while she waited to hear what Jamie had to say.

"We found a skirt washed up on our island. Jim recognized it as the one your daughter wore that day. We were sorry to have found it. At that time, we didn't know if anyone else had survived." She hesitated. "We used the skirt for placing heat ono Jim's arm." She indicated his bound arm held in the sling. "We had so little to work with. I hope it was all right."

"You found her skirt? Tell me where you were. It won't change things, but somehow, just knowing that tiny bit ties up a loose end."

They talked for a bit, exchanged addresses, and promised to correspond with other details remembered.

The conversation with Corrine helped dispel Jamie's shock over Mick's severe sentence, if only for a little while. She felt a tug on her arm.

"Hello, my name is Clara. My friend and I were on the *Ilikii* that day, and, with Niko's help, I made it onto a raft, but my friend was lost. I never saw her again." There were tears in her eyes as she told her story. "I see how thin you've all become. It happened to me, too. A fishing boat picked me up. I was out of my head for weeks before they knew who I was or what happened. They notified the Tahitian authorities and I've been waiting here for everything to be over. I just want to go home." The note of sad finality in her voice said it all. She waved a timorous goodbye and turned to leave. A deep sadness clung about her.

Jamie understood the harrowing experience that Clara

had survived, as well the loss of a friend.

They said goodbye and then walked into a snarl of noisy reporters, fending them off with "No comment," and made it to their hotel with heavy hearts. Jamie walked with dragging steps. Every step took her farther from Mick, and she fought the depression and disillusionment that had taken hold of her very soul.

The final outcome was more devastating than she had imagined. Certain Mick could never make things right, she would go on alone for the baby's sake. And the emptiness without the man she'd grown to love---. Could she live with that? Her words, she could live on the memory of their love, had come home to roost.

❧❦❧

The trial over, going home became the major thing invading and holding their thoughts. The tickets that brought them to Tahiti were reissued. Jim and Felicia wanted to be together, and Jamie's father decided to visit Santa Monica before departing for Denver. Jamie was happy with that, having no desire to see Denver again with its disastrous memories. With a child coming, she wanted to stay near Jim and Felicia. Their closeness had become a lifetime bond.

No one in the world could relate to her, the loss of Mick and the new child, as well as these newfound friends. Jim would be a wonderful uncle. He'd had a high regard for his island friend, and believed him in the face of dreadful odds. He'd repeated more than once. "I'd love to see a child of Mick's. I'll bet he'll have that same long, face. I'd like to be handy for that event."

"How do you know it's a boy, Jim? It's just wishful thinking by you men. You all think you have to have a son, but it's daughters who turn your hearts to mush," Felicia chided him.

Blissfully happy, she tried to tone it down for Jamie's sake, but her own joy seeped from every pore.

Dee said little, but extended an invitation to Shipley to visit Santa Monica as her guest. More than attracted to him, as well as his beautiful, sad-hearted daughter, she welcomed them to her home. She lived several miles from Felicia, but within the same general area. She'd reached the point with Shipley that she could not bear to have him leave her so soon. The trials of losing and finding their children again had created a very strong bond between them.

Aside from Mick's child growing within her, the relationship between her father and Dee lifted Jamie's heart. She felt a deep joy seeing the two of them together. Comfortable with each other, they laughed often, their heads touching.

Packing was simple for Jamie. She discarded all the *big* clothing and packed her few new clothes, as well as the clean tattered rags the female sailors had so kindly saved for them. She handled fondly the clothes with crudely cut buttonholes, and ragged print skirt that had made so many bandages. She had part of the wedding pictures, and they planned to have them copied so everyone could have the same.

Her heart was heavy and her movements sluggish. Leaving Tahiti meant leaving the place that held Mick in that dark prison. She'd asked to see him, and they refused. New prisoners were not allowed visitors for thirty days. She' would return to Tahiti to see him, and would do that before she grew too heavy with his child.

Tears escaped, coursing down her cheeks as she gathered her few belongings. *I suffered miserably before for nothing. With Mick, the pain I have now is worth it all. The feelings he aroused in me made me a complete, full-hearted woman. I know what love is, and I'll love him to my dying day.*

# CHAPTER 45

D ad, I'm glad to go to the States, but you know where my heart is. It'll be a long time before they'll let Mick out of prison. I'll come to visit him when they'll let me, but nothing will ever be the same again." Jamie had said it before, but verbalizing it, eased the deep, searing pain suffered from the loss of him.

Shipley didn't know how to help her, and Jim didn't offer much in the way of advice. He remained close-mouthed, more than Shipley would have expected. While he worried about his daughter's fragile state, he failed to take notice of Jim's air of nonchalance about it.

They needed two of the small French cabs to transport themselves and their luggage to the airport. Fa'aa International was only a short distance from their hotel, and they rode in silence, each of the survivors thinking of their glorious days spent on an idyllic island, forgetting the dark times, only remembering pink sands, a clear lagoon, and the wondrous love each had found there. Time and distance worked to cloud their memories of starvation and disastrous events.

Standing in the check-in line for luggage and seating assignments, they completed the process without incident—until it came to Jamie's ticket.

"Excuse me, *mademoiselle*, but thees ticket for you is changed. You are in first class. I will change thees for you, one moment, *sil vows pleas*." The woman behind the counter punched the buttons on her computer, leaving Jamie in helpless confusion.

"B—But I did not ask for this c—change, m—miss," Jamie stammered.

"I am sorry if thees is not convenient, *mademoiselle,* but thees is the only seat available for you now." The dark-eyed ticket agent shrugged her French-Tahitian shoulders and handed Jamie the ticket, telling her the gate and time to board. She turned to help the next in line, and Jamie realized she'd just become invisible to the airline agent.

Jamie turned to her father with a look of bewilderment. "Now look what's happened, Dad." He'd overheard the exchange with the ticket agent. "Now we can't sit together," she continued. "I guess you'll just have to sit with Dee. That'll make it a pleasant flight for you both, won't it?" She grinned at her father, knowing he'd be happy with that arrangement. "You'll enjoy the flight. Go for it, Dad."

She only wanted to curl up in the narrow seats and sleep her pain away. For her, this was an improvement in arrangements.

They moved to the boarding area. Jim and Felicia, close together, murmured to each other. Her father stayed close to Dee. Utter desolation settled ever deeper into Jamie's heavy heart.

Boarding, Jamie went on alone and waved to the others as she entered the jet way, patting the plane before boarding. That bit of symbolism ensured a good flight. She found her row and settled herself into the large, soft leather window seat. She found first class seats much wider. It would be easier to curl up in after take-off.

They offered a choice of beverages immediately, and she decided on a juice, waving away a snack. She settled into her own personal cocoon to hide away from everything for this long flight away from the man she loved. She requested a pillow and one of the little blankets to use later. It was an eight-hour flight, and she wanted to sleep it away.

A large plane, it required more than forty-five minutes to

complete the boarding process. No one noticed the small black car pulling up near the jet-way to discharge a tall figure. The man climbed the outer stair, entered the plane, and made his way toward the forward compartment.

Jamie felt someone move into the seat next to her, discerned a slight jostling and heard the click of the seatbelt. She felt no desire to converse with anyone and did not turn or acknowledge the new passenger. In her misery, she faced the window with eyes closed, as if sleeping. It was a man by the sound of his breathing and his weight as he settled into his seat.

She wished he'd relax and stop rustling his newspapers. She heard his soft "*Merci*" in thanks for his refreshment. Something in the sound of his voice jarred a feeling that touched deep memories. Her skin prickled on the nape of her neck.

She caught the aroma of male-scented aftershave, unknown to her, but nonetheless pleasant. The faint scent of his person sent alarm bells tinkling far off and set her heart trembling in her chest. *No, please, no more of this. I will not have these crazy feelings again. It's over for me. I can't think of it anymore. I won't see his face again for so long—like forever. Oh God.*

The jiggling movement of the plane, beginning its slow movement out on the runway, interrupted her wild thoughts. A stewardess instructed the passengers in over the water safety. First in French, then English, and after that, what she thought was Japanese. Soon the thrusting Mercedes Benz engines roared to the fullness of their power and the plane swept up into the tropical skies over Tahiti. Hot tears of pain slid freely down her cheeks. She'd left, abandoning and deserting the love of her life, to serve alone long, miserable years in a dank Tahitian prison.

As the huge plane ascended rapidly away from all the wonderful and dreadful things that had happened to her, Jamie's hopeless tears burned her eyes. Startled, she felt a strong, warm hand firmly grasp hers. Alarmed and feeling angry, she turned in her seat and opened her eyes. Disbelief shook her to the core as she looked up into very dark, liquid brown eyes, so wonderfully familiar.

She nearly fainted and thought her heart would never start again, trying to believe what she saw before her. "What—Oh, God—Who—Is that you, Mick? Can it really be you?" She looked at the hand holding hers then back at his face. He wore a small, finely trimmed moustache, with his hair in a trim, short style. Gone were the long strands that had so often played about those long saturnine features. She stared into his face, speechless, looking at him in disbelief. "Are you real? Is it really you, Mick—How?" Large tears formed again in her eyes, tears of happiness—but then anger rose within her, at the cruel deception he'd played on her tortured soul.

"Yes, it's me, Jamie girl, and this time it's forever." He kept his voice very low, as if to warn her. "We'll never be separated again, not ever again. I swear it on my life." He smiled into her eyes and wiped her tears away. "God, I love you, girl. I'm sorry for the way things had to be, and, when we're alone, I'll tell you everything, or as much as I can." He kissed her lips, trying not to be too overt in the open area of the plane. He wanted to hold her and worked to restrain himself. *How pale she looks. Is she ill, or is it shock?*

"Mick, what's happening? How could you let me go through that hellish trial? How could you *do* that?" Her voice rose slightly in her agitation. "You never looked at me, not even once did you ever glance my way. I thought I'd die every day during that agonizing time. Did it have to *be* that way?"

Anger burned in her eyes as she accused him of unbelievable cruelty, of emotional torture.

"It had to be that way. I'll explain it to you, but *not* in public. I'm doing my job. We do things you don't want to know about. It's necessary. We work all over the world. I'm French speaking, and they needed me in this area of the Pacific." He kept his voice low, for her hearing only, needing her to understand the seriousness of what he had to say.

"Jim had an idea about you, I see that now, but he couldn't say anything either. You were both so conspiratorial. I can't believe you're really here. Oh, Mick, I was prepared to raise our child alone and try to visit you whenever I could. How sad is that?" She punched his arm ever so lightly, her passionate anger rapidly turning to delight. She feared her touch, however light, would set him on fire. "This is an eight-hour flight, Mick. I wonder if I can wait so long." She managed a sly giggle in her new found happiness. "I waited for you all those other nights, but you never came. Why only once? I wanted you desperately. I worried myself half to death, not knowing where you were or if you would spend the rest of your life locked away in some horrible prison. I needed you, Mick."

"I had to see you, to know you were all right, you and our child to be. Have you seen a doctor about this? You're so pale."

"No, I feel wonderful, except for worrying over you. I wanted *you* with me, Mick, for the first visit. My father would have come, but now he won't need to."

"Will you marry me when we get to the States?" His eyes bore into hers, smiling in his joy. Sure of her answer, he pulled out his Canadian passport. He opened it. "Could you marry a guy with a name like this?"

"Michel Solnier? You're not Michael Sands, either?" She stared at him in wonder. "Will I ever know the real Mick, or isn't it, Mick? You're such a man of mystery. I wonder if you haven't a trunk full of these passports hidden away." She shook her head. "How do you pronounce that anyway?"

He taught her how to say his name. "You can call me Mick, I always loved the way you said my name." He sneaked a kiss. "And you are my darling, dearest Jamilla, my Jamie girl."

He held onto her hands and they stayed as close as possible, without causing undue notice.

Jamie knew she must wait for privacy before Mick would tell her more about himself. She still harbored doubts about him, but didn't care. In her rising excitement, she wanted to tell Jim and Felicia, and her father, but wondered if they had to wait for privacy on that, as well. "Mick, I'd like you to meet my father. Jim, Felicia, and her mother are on this plane too. Can we manage that?"

"I'll take care of that. We'll get Jim. Do you know where he's sitting?" He beckoned to the nearest flight attendant. "Miss, we'd like to have a word with one of your passengers. Jim Healy, a big blond man in about..." He turned to Jamie. "What seat, darling?"

He grinned with joy at the normalcy of their situation. Jamie told him what she thought were the seat, and row. He passed the information to the dark-haired young flight attendant, who boldly made intimate eye contact with him.

Jamie frowned. "Humm, I guess I'll have new worries over you now, with the way women are looking at you. Did you see how that stewardess looked at you?"

"Jamie, never worry about me. I've had women, if I wanted, but only fell in love once. You'd know all about that, darling. I can't wait to start our life together."

He felt a firm punch on his shoulder and looked up to see those familiar pale blue eyes shining from a tanned face. The greeting was subdued. Jim heeded the warning he saw in Mick's eyes.

"So, you old son-of-a-gun, leaving the glorious Society Islands, are you?" Jim took his hand and they shook firmly, with more meaning than Jamie ever thought a simple handshake could deliver. She saw the glimmer of tears in Jim's eyes. He brushed them away and sat in the empty seat across from Mick. "I'd like to say thanks, old man, though it would never handle what I want to express. I damned glad to see you again, under *these* circumstances."

"Jim, would you consent to stand up for me? I believe we have a wedding in the works here." Mick reached over and kissed a beaming Jamie. "Say, you *did* say you'd have me? I mean this time. You said yes when I asked you one other time, if you remember."

A slight blush crossed her face. "I'd have to say yes to that, Mick."

"That's settled. We'll get this going when we hit LA. God, it's good to see you, Jim! How's the wife? Jamie told me about your shipboard nuptials. She's got pictures, but they must be packed away somewhere." He was babbling a little, but a terrible long term strain had lifted from him, as well as the others. He worked now to adjust himself to civilian life.

Jim wanted to know the details, but held his questions. "Where will you be staying in Los Angeles, have you given thought to that?"

"I'll see what my intended says. How about it, Jamie, will you stay with me? I've made arrangements." He looked into her shining eyes. "I doubt I could manage alone, not anymore—not ever." He used his wheedling tone and knew by her small giggle, she was beyond happy to hear it again.

"I'll stay with you, Mick, and we'll all come. We need to talk about everything. There's so much I don't know. I need to know as much about you, or as much as you'll tell. Dad doesn't know about this yet either, but there's been enough commotion on this plane for now. You can pass the word Jim, if you will."

Jamie snuggled against Mick's arm after Jim left them. He said nothing, but his black eyes were bright with joy.

# CHAPTER 46

Getting out of the airport became another form of madness. Reporters had caught scent of their arrival, perhaps from information leaked by flight personnel. Their shipboard disaster and subsequent recovery were big news, as they'd quickly learned in Tahiti. They were fair game for every reporter in the area, and they were numerous and extremely aggressive.

Mick cleared customs first. He left them to order a hotel limousine. When it arrived to gather them at the curbside, the tall, dark-haired, dark-eyed man sitting in the long sleek auto as it pulled alongside the curb was not visible. The driver shooed the reporters away so they could enter and ride in privacy. They enjoyed luxuriously leather upholstered seats behind dark, glazed windows, as the big auto pulled away.

They left the airport, heading to privacy and security from casual eyes and voracious reporters. Pulling under a lavish portico, they were helped out by a brightly costumed doorman.

With foresight, Mick had pre-arranged accommodations and, taking the elevator to a posh suite on the highest floor, they met together in his accommodations.

The introductions given when they'd met together at the airport had been polite and subdued, but now it was safe to talk, and they began.

"Tell us Mick. What *were* you, and what were you working on out there?" Jim said. "I had my ideas all along, but I'd sure like to know."

"I work undercover for Narcotics Bureau International. I've been in the field for nearly ten years, here and there. But since my life has taken a turn for the better, I've requested transfer to the San Francisco Office as an interpreter of information and an instructor for new recruits." He looked over at Jamie, sitting beside her father as they listened to Mick's story. "Would you consider living there, dearest girl? You might like that city? It's not so far from Jim and Felicia."

"Oh, Mick, it wouldn't matter where, but I'd like that fine." She frowned at him. "In all that time, you never gave us a hint about yourself. Why, Mick? Why did we have to suffer so horribly, and be afraid of you?" Her face reflected the pain not knowing had caused. "Why did we have to see you hauled away in chains? Where were you all that time?"

"Darling, it was hard on me too, but we are bound to deepest secrecy. There is more about my work that you'll never know. If you can accept me as I am, I'll be a civilian from now on, and your devoted and loving husband. I had to play it that way in the courtroom." He paused. "There's this thing. It's called *retribution.* I couldn't let any of that touch you, Jamie, not ever, or the rest of you. Another thing, I watched you as much as possible while you were tooling all over Tahiti. I had to be sure you were safe. We'll never get all of them." His eyes bore into hers, his face sad as he explained his life as much as possible to the woman he wanted for his wife. "Remember, Jamie, they have ears everywhere, and I couldn't place you in jeopardy, not my wife and child. It was the hardest thing I've ever had to do, staying away from you." He smiled at the people before him. "There'll be no more of that."

Jim shook his head in amazement. "Wow! I had a feeling it was something along those lines. I've never heard of your outfit. But I'm glad as hell to know it's turned out right for you two, after all the times you said it would. I believed you, but I had a hard time figuring out what in the hell was going on. None of us thought you were an itinerant sailor drifting about in the South Seas, Mick, you son of a gun." He went to Mick and shook his hand. "How about this guy, Jamie?"

Shipley followed suit, grasping Mick's hand with both of his and patting him on the back. "Mick, I'm pleased to know you. My daughter thinks you hung the moon, and I can't fault her judgment on that. I hope you put away plenty of those drug-dealing bastards during your time in the field."

"I've puzzled over something for the longest time, Mick," Jim said. "Maybe you'd know. We were out there using sail power for the fun of sailing that way, using old-fashioned wind power, but why in the hell in this modern age, were those drug-running bastards using sail power? I couldn't figure that one."

"They used it to prevent sonar detection for one thing, and it worked pretty well for the most part. Aside from that, most of them were excellent sailors, and liked to use sails whenever they could. It saved diesel fuel in the bargain. In the long run, it didn't save them, but another guy and I had a hand in that."

Jamie interjected with a question. "So who was the Chinese guy that was so friendly, and tried to put his arm around you like a long-lost friend when you met them on the island that day?"

"Him? That's Jack Lim, he works with us, too. You never heard me say that, remember. He's coming for a visit later, after the first of the year, wants to see the baby." Mick laughed, happy to explain, then grew serious. "How could you see that, Jamie? You were supposed to stay in the cave where I left you. What were you up to, then?"

Felicia was quick to answer that question. "She couldn't stand not knowing what was happening to you. She crawled up Jim's broken tree and squeezed out that hole. She stayed down low and watched the whole thing from up there."

She happily filled in all the details, not seeing the shocked glance Dee shot Shipley at hearing another detail of the harrowing events their children had suffered.

"Later, when the helicopter came," Felicia continued, "we figured out it must have been you that sent them. No one else in the world could have known where we were in that forgotten part of the Pacific. Oh, Mick, I'll never forget seeing that huge bird coming down! Jim was nearly dead by then. We thought he couldn't make it. You saved his life." Huge tears formed in her lavender eyes as she looked at Mick.

Jim went to her, taking her in his arms.

"I worried they wouldn't reach you in time. Thank God they did." Mick turned to Jamie, shaking his head in wonder at this fine, strong woman in his life. "Girl, what am I going to do about you?"

Felicia laughed. "Jamie, you're going to *marry* this glamorous guy, just like in the movies." She gave Mick a hug. "It's more than good to see you again and we can't wait to see that baby of yours either. Jim says it's a boy, and he'll look just like you." She tossed her shining hair. "Jim, it's time we went home, and let these people get some rest. I haven't seen my house for so long. I mean, *our house*, Jim." She went to Jamie. "See what you'd have missed if you'd been afraid to take a chance on a handsome devil named Mick," she whispered. "I can't wait for your wedding— we'll get right on it." She hugged Jamie good night. "I'm so happy for you both."

They got up to leave, and Dee went to Mick. "Thank you for taking care of my daughter out on that terrible island. I think we'll see a lot of you and Jamie from now on, and I'm glad for that. Welcome to California." She gave him a warm embrace.

"Your daughter's the brave one. She fought like a tigress for Jim's life. He's lucky to find a woman like her." Mick smiled at Dee, then turned inquiring eyes on Jamie. She hadn't commented on the information he'd given about his work. He wondered what her thoughts were. *Maybe she won't want to marry a spook like me, now that she knows the truth of what I am.* Shards of doubt stabbed through him like liquid ice. He held his concerns while the rest of their party took their leave.

The sky had darkened long since, and the masses of city lights sent a glow far into the night sky. If there was a moon, it'd be hard to find it in this huge, sprawling city's crowded night sky. Jamie gazed out the window so high above the teeming, sprawling city. The same moon had shone on them so many other nights during their sojourn on the lost island.

With the rest of their party gone, Mick went to her. She sat quietly on the bed, her face reflecting a muddle of questioning thoughts. "Mick, is it all over? Are we to know peace at last, and have a life together, like ordinary people?"

"Girl, you'll never be *ordinary people*, nor will I. We've known too much and seen too much. But I believe we can make a good life together. I love the person you are, the brave, caring girl I fell in love with. I wouldn't want to live at all, if you wouldn't have me. I've been a loner all my life until now." He reached for her. "Tell me, girl, will you still be my woman, my loving wife, now that you know what I am?" He grasped onto her shoulders the same way he had when they last spoke together on the island. He pulled her off the bed and held her before him. His eyes bore deeply into hers. "Please *Jamilla*, Jamie—say something."

Jamie, seeing the tight line of doubt edging Mick's jaw, sagged against his long frame. "Oh, Mick, God help me, I'd want to die if I couldn't have you. Don't you know that? I'm horrified at the things you've had to do, but you tried to save people from being addicted by what those men sold or traded. I know, by now, you'll always be a mystery man, but I'll be a happy woman spending the rest of my life trying to find out what makes you tick. Felicia said I'd be sorry if I missed knowing a man like you. She was right about that, Mick—my wonderful, shadow man. You've made me whole again and, for that alone, I could never leave you, my dearest soulmate, and I love it that we'll have a little Mick with us in time."

He moved against her and took her slowly into his arms. "You've always been an all-together girl, Jamie. You only needed a little adversity to bring it out. Remember, I said you didn't know yourself. It wasn't long before I saw what kind of woman you were, and I thank God for you."

She went into his arms and into his very soul that unhurried night. His lips claimed hers over and over again with the narcotic spell she remembered so well. Leisurely they went to the bed and cemented their life together. He thought he heard her murmuring softly, "Oh, Mick, I can't believe this is really happening." With a small giggle he heard her ask, "No square sails?"

# EPILOGUE

In the back yard of the large Spanish style home in Santa Monica, the smell of fragrant wood smoke drifted, bringing with it the promise of food. The guys sat together. Mick grabbed his five-year-old son racing for a ball. "Here, Jimmy, say hello to your uncle."

The slender dark-haired boy with his longish face and dark eyes smiled. "Hi, Uncle Jim," he said, before running away and punching a soccer ball with a boy of the same age.

"My turn, Jimmy," Micky yelled in close pursuit. "You said I could."

Jim punched Mick in the arm, laughing. "I swear, Mick, that boy looks more like you every day. He looks just like I knew he would. He's got that long, wolfish-looking face of yours."

Jamie rose gracefully from her chair. She'd kept her fine figure through these past few years. A single strand of gray streaked through her hair, but her gray-green- eyes were clear. Jim saw a happy woman as she reached for a small child. "Come on, little Dee, let's go find Auntie Feesha." She set the toddler on the grass, and they went hand in hand into the house.

"She's still a looker, Mick, How's everything?"

Mick laughed. "Job's boring as hell, but the home life makes up for it."

He'd put on a few pounds around the middle but retained

much of the lean hungry look Jim remembered from their days on the island. For both men, the warmth in their eyes had never faded.

"You're looking damned good yourself, Jim." Mick said. He and Jim were closer than brothers. "These yearly get-togethers are important for us and always a highlight." He laughed. "Those girls love any excuse for getting together and going over old times. I'm happy we fell into this routine. It's special in a dozen ways. So, how's police work in Santa Monica?"

Jim's brow furrowed. "No matter how many drug bastards we send up, there're a dozen more to take their place."

"It's not so different for us. They're like cockroaches," Mick replied.

Felicia and Jamie sat at a shaded table. Two chubby little girls chased a small black puppy around the flowerbeds.

Felicia caught her daughter as she darted past. "Here, Jamie Lynn, give this to little Dee, would you, sweetheart?" She handed a soft baby doll to the little girl, who dashed off, holding the doll in outstretched hands, calling to her friend. Felicia settled back into her chair, and sighed. "Did you ever think we'd be so domesticated? Not in my wildest imagination. Jamie, I'm a happy woman with Jim and the kids, and here's you, looking so wonderful." She laughed and without the slightest thought, tossed her glowing mass of hair over a shoulder. A motion never lost on her husband.

Felicia had gained some weight, but made a conscious effort to provide her family, and herself, with healthy choices, except for the occasional splurge, which she and Jim both totally indulged.

Jamie flushed and flung out her hands in happy helplessness. "There'll be another little Solnier in about seven more months. I haven't told Mick, but I imagine he knows and is waiting for me to tell him. I'll never get ahead of that man. I still wonder if he hasn't a box of aliases and passports stashed away."

"Oh, Jamie, that's wonderful news—isn't it?" Felicia

laughed. "Not me, we've decided to hold it at two. I put in time at the Art Center, two days a week. I'd like to keep that up. My mother watches them on those days."

From the side of the house, John and Dee Shipley strolled into the area, their arms laden with packages. "Hi Dad, and Dee," Jamie rose to greet them. Shipley hugged his daughter, shook hands around, and headed for his grandchildren, a wide smile over his face.

Dee laughed. "I swear, if that man isn't crazy about these babies. He can't get enough of them."

She caught at little Jamie, who rushed into her arms, crying "Mam, Mam."

In all the confusion of family greetings, Jamie knew her husband's dark eyes seldom left her. She never tired of his attentions, contented, knowing his love burned strongly as ever. He made her life whole, and she'd done that for him. She often thought, *If I never live another day, I would die a happy woman with what we've had together*. The thinking brought tears near the surface.

Shipley held little Dee as he laughed. "Well, what are we having for eats?"

They all knew the menu for *this* day. Over in a corner screened away by tall, swaying, royal palms, they had a pit ready with hot coals. Jim wrapped several large green globes in banana leaves, readying them for baking. Mick wrapped chunks of pork. The fish would go in later.

"Does this take you back, or what?" Mick clapped Jim on the shoulder. "My life began on that island, Jim."

"I know what you mean, friend." He gazed toward Felicia, sitting in the shade with Jamie. "I'd have to say these get-togethers bring it back, you black-eyed son-of-a-gun. Where'd you get these breadfruits anyway?"

Mick laughed, secretive as ever. "I have a few connections. I had them flown in."

Jamie came to them. "We're having more than water for our drinks, okay with you two?"

"As long as there's a cold beer on ice, and a soda or two,

it is," Jim told her. "I love that we do this every year, but those kids will want something besides water, too. After all they weren't lost out there."

Later, after they'd eaten, looked at pictures of the ship-board wedding, and were relaxing, Felicia held out their worn rags. "Look at these. Were we ever this big? Jamie, we should burn these old things, but they do conjure up some wonderful memories, don't they?"

"I'd have to say they do. Look at the ragged buttonholes. You guys made me do all the cutting, remember." Jamie tried to look accusing, and failed.

Mick looked at his wife, a contented grin over his long-ish face. "Well, it all came right in the end."

Shipley hugged his wife, still mesmerized by the color of her eyes. "For everyone—look at all these grand kids."

Jamie looked again at her mysterious husband. He knew her secret, and she couldn't stop the flush coloring her face as she nestled into his arms.

"Those two are just as caught up in each other as they were on the island. They still can't help themselves," Jim whispered to Felicia as he held her close in the cool of the evening.

The End

# About the Author

Ramona Forrest is a retired RN. She keeps busy writing novels—and traveling whenever possible. Forrest has resided in the back country of Arizona, assisted in round-ups, worked in Saudi Arabia, and has had the pleasure of traveling extensively. She now resides in Phoenix and spends much time gardening, writing, and entertaining friends and family.